Butterflies

Lily Hayden

Melissa.
Good luck in your
new job.
Hope you enjoy Butterflies
Best Wishes
Lily
x

ISBN: 9781980946311

Butterflies by Lily Hayden is published by independent publishers Hayden Woods Creative.

For rights, books, news and contact details, follow us on Facebook, Twitter, Instagram and LinkedIn at Hayden Woods Creative.

We're excited to bring you news of upcoming titles and look forward to meeting you online! Your feedback and reviews mean everything to us. Thank you for reading!

Acknowledgements

Firstly, a huge thank you to all those that supported me on my crazy journey to write my first book.

To my favourite ex-colleagues, Rachel, thank you for helping me to work up the nerve to make this my day job and Sam, thank you for being the original butterfly! Loyalty and heart is everything.

Becky, Jodie, Liv, Sam & Tyler- my day-one ladies who support everything that I do. It honestly means the world.

Dave & Josie, my ride-or-die besties, thank you for being amazing.

My number one bestie, Mark. I'd have written hundreds of books by now if it weren't for you, but I wouldn't have had as many laughs!

My Mum, Dad & Nanny Moy for inspiring my love of all things books!

Mike, for believing in me.

And last-but-never-least, Ethan, Grace, Lila and Max, my reason for everything. I couldn't love you anymore.

Love, Lily x x

Chapter 1

I felt the rage building up inside me. All my senses were heightened so the overriding sensation was the hot blood pumping through my veins. My shoulders tensed as the fury pumped through my arms causing my hands to involuntarily flex open and shut into fists. I felt my jaw set hard and my eyes narrow. I was very aware that I looked like a caricature of myself. The tension built up and I knew that I had just seconds to defuse this before I completely blew and made things a hundred times worse.

I took a deep breath filling my lungs. I slowly exhaled over a longer period. My shoulders started to relax, and I repeated the process; trying to focus on my diaphragm expanding and letting the breath go. I repeated this several times. The fury I felt slowly started to evaporate until the rage was a controllable simmer. Crisis averted. I moved slowly to the fridge, took out the chilled Chablis and poured a generous glass. I gulped at the cold liquid and closed my eyes to savour the after taste. I drained the glass and poured another to sip in a ladylike manner. I was now ready to face the matter at hand.

There was no earth shattering event that had triggered this reaction. This was the norm for me; a 35-year-old banker and mother of four, raging silently in my kitchen at 6pm on a Tuesday over nothing.

I rolled up the sleeves of my dark grey fitted shirt and pushed the pile of breakfast and dinner dishes one by one into the dishwasher. I counted four dinner plates which meant one of my little darlings has left theirs in their bedroom. Probably Esther. Or maybe George. The eldest two were the worst for cleaning up after themselves. I put this down to them existing when they were the centre of our world in comparison to the younger two who were born into a family where time was already scarce. As I stalked back down the stairs carrying the lost plate and cutlery, I remembered a funny tweet I had seen earlier that said something about how going into your teenager's room was like taking a trip to Ikea: pop in for a browse and come out with 10 glasses and 6 plates. My mouth turned up into a smile at this thought. That made me happy- if I could find things like that amusing then I hadn't completely lost my grip on life just yet. Maybe I was just hormonal. I glanced at the calendar wondering when my period was due. There was no fear of another pregnancy as I clung to my contraceptive pills like a woman in a life raft. I wondered if other people's hormones got worse with age.

Maybe nobody bothers to tell you, I pondered to myself, simultaneously sipping my wine and snapping open a bag of nachos as I couldn't be arsed to make myself dinner.

Dishes done, I padded around the house tidying with Hermione, my faithful Spaniel, tripping under my feet every few yards. Ron, her brother, ignored me from his basket as always; much preferring the company of my husband, Steve. As I tidied and assembled bags for the morning, I oversaw with one eye the two homework projects that had landed in my lap moments after I walked through the door.

Yes, they had to be in tomorrow. Yes, we told you about these weeks ago. Yes, of course we have an endless supply of craft glue and paper to make this shit. I fed Hermione a few scraps from George's plate that I'd located next to his bed/ pit. Just as I started to feel I had this circus under control, a high-pitched wail of "Mummmmmmmm" filled the house. Hermione looked up at me with sad, knowing eyes. I rolled my eyes at her as we shared a moment of mutual contempt for our cohabitees. The thud of not-so-tiny feet came racing at unnecessary speed down the stairs. Eleven-year-old George was in hot pursuit of seven-year-old Leo, who was still shouting. George had resorted to his failsafe technique of shouting even louder. My ongoing study of the behaviour of these animals had led me to conclude that this was to prevent any accusations being heard, which was not a bad tactic. Maybe I would try this at meetings in work in future.

I automatically stretched out my arms to my sobbing younger son and raised a hand to silence George. This seems like an effective command, but it is not. It doesn't work with fearless reprobates. As I listened to Leo's accusations through the incensed protests of the innocent George, my phone pinged to alert me of a message. I had had enough of playing referee and listening calmly, so I screamed like a banshee at George to get to bed and checked my phone as I soothed my darling Leo.

"Leaving the office late. Going straight to the gym. If you need anything from the shop, text me." Steve had written.

No kisses. Fuck you, Steve, I silently replied in my head. I hit the home button and left the selfish prick on "read". Leo, now comforted by the fact his brother was in trouble, wandered off and was instantly replaced by 5-year-old Matilda clutching a crumpled piece of paper and proclaiming she needed to wear a Victorian costume to school tomorrow.

I picked my phone back up from where I'd tossed it amongst the debris of lunch bags, water bottles and permission forms and hit reply on Steve's message. My fingers typed out "wine" and pressed send before I took another exaggerated mindful breath and gathered the glue and the safety pins ready to tackle the next project.

Several hours passed and I was sat on the plush grey sofa; still in my tights and shirt. My tights now had an attractive coat of dog fur adhered to them and my shirt was creased and speckled in nacho crumbs. There was something trashy playing on the TV and my wine bottle was emptier than my soul. Hermione sat loyally at my feet and we tried to drown out the sound of various YouTubers blaring from bedrooms above us. Esther hadn't been seen for hours but I could predict that she still had a face full of makeup on and was busy snapchatting her "Streaks". George would be watching something wildly age inappropriate on the iPad whereas sweet Leo, who was clearly born into the wrong family due to his lovely nature, would be reading a book. Matilda should have been asleep by now, as a normal five-year-old, but the girl was born nocturnal and was currently in my bed watching videos of people opening Kinder Eggs. I felt the usual overwhelming guilt for lying on my sofa, half-drunk, when I should have been reading to my offspring, policing screen time and enforcing a bedtime. On a positive, the house had been tidied, lunches were ready for the morning, a Victorian costume had been created out of thin air and a cardboard replica of the Taj Mahal and the Solar System were on the table by the front door ready to go in the morning.

My silenced phone lit up with a notification. It was a Snapchat from Steve. It was an explicit image of him from the gym changing room. Gross. Accompanied by a line of text that said, "Miss you" as if that made the picture any more romantic. However, I was drunk and horny, so I replied with a "splash" emoji. Out of curiosity, I clicked on Steve's name on the app and checked his score, which showed how many pictures he had sent and received. I often played this game; checking ten minutes later as an indication of who he was "talking" to and how serious it was getting.

While I waited, I scrolled through my missed call list and returned the call to my lovely but needy best friend. Andy answered after the first ring.

"Hiya babe" He greeted me, before launching into a long-winded description of his day at work. I "oohed" and "oh no-ed" in all the right places and eventually he wound down his summary and asked about my day.

"Same old," I replied. "Are we still on for Friday?"

“Ah, well, the thing is,” Andy started, his tone defensive. “I’ve got a thing on that I forgot I said I’d go to…”.

This translated as Andy had a date.

“Right?” I waited for him to continue, annoyed but not surprised as he was always letting me down if he had a better offer.

“I’m so sorry!” He sensed the irritation in my tone. “I can try to get out of there as early as possible and meet you later?”

“It’s fine, babe.” I reassured him.

To be honest, the thought of having to make an effort to look nice wasn’t high on my agenda of things to waste my precious time on. We chatted for a few more minutes before we hung up.

I wasn’t even upset that Andy had cancelled on me, I told myself. My life was just a Groundhog Day of school runs, work and arguments with my husband. I loved Andy but sometimes having to listen to his amazing life was equally exhausting. I was genuinely happy for his successes but the only part of my life he envied at all was the fact I wasn’t single. Some days I fantasised about being single. Ok, most days. I was slightly rankled that I was the obvious disposable choice though. I shook this thought away before I risked slipping back into my rage or, worse, self-pity. Fifteen minutes had passed by now and I checked Steve’s ‘snap score’. It had gone up by 10 points. Wow! Someone clearly enjoyed his picture. I unbutton my shirt, adjust my cleavage and fire off a picture of my own to Luke-from-work. My immediate notifications gave me the validation that I craved, and I went back to watching the TV feeling smug and attractive. At the back of mind, I was vaguely aware of a sensation that may or may not have been shame but I pushed it away and let the mind- numbing reality TV contestants distract me. As the credits on the show rolled, I realised that it was almost 10.30pm. I jumped to my feet; snapping off the lights, ushering the dogs to their beds and chastising my children for still being awake. My threats of confiscation worked and they all snuggled up to sleep begrudgingly, even allowing me to kiss them goodnight. My heart swelled with love for these precious beings as I finished my nightly checks, and I slipped into my own bed feeling contentment and relief that I had survived another day. My head had barely touched my pillow when I heard the front door open and Steve arrive home. After what felt like an eternity of him banging around downstairs followed by a noisy shower, even though I had photographic evidence that he had already showered at the gym, Steve slipped into bed naked and still damp. He slid an arm around me and pressed up against my back.

"Babe?" He enquired, kissing my bare shoulder.

I went against all my feminist principles and arched my back in response. We had quick, impersonal sex and I came first, which pleased my petty nature. I slid away quickly, making it clear that I was finished. I went into the en-suite and got back into bed wearing a pair of unflattering granny pants.

"Babe, I need to finish." Steve moaned, frustrated.

I felt like laughing but instead I rolled over and kissed him gently.

"I'm too tired." I mumbled, in a sleepy voice.

Steve pressed my body to his strong chest and kissed me again in the hollow of my throat. Despite my contempt for him, I felt myself responding and let out a tiny moan. That was all the encouragement Steve needed and he ripped away my vile underwear and pulled me up on top of him. I rode him hard and fast until we were both dripping in sweat and finally Steve came deep inside me. For a moment, I felt a connection with my husband and I wondered, for the millionth time, if there was anything I could do to make this marriage work again.

I lay in my bed, enjoying the post-orgasmic feeling, with these thoughts running through my mind. Steve popped his headphones into his iPad and sat up to watch something sports-related. The sound blared through his headphones and the light flickered in the darkness of our room, disturbing me even through my closed eyes.

My irritation returned to me instantly and I held it close to me like a comfort blanket as I fell asleep with all the reasons that I hated my husband rolling through my mind.

Chapter 2

The barking of a dog shattered my coma-like sleep. Steve snored obliviously next to me and I prised one eye open to check the time. It wasn't even 5am yet so I elbowed my husband sharply in the ribs and hissed his name until he responded.

"It's Ron," I growled. "You get him."

Steve groaned but slipped out of bed and went down to let the dogs out.

I closed my eyes again, but it was no use, I was awake.

I followed Steve down to the kitchen and flipped the switch to brew some fresh coffee. We sat and breakfasted together in companionable silence.

"How was your meeting yesterday?" I broke the silence, remembering that I hadn't asked him about the first board meeting with the new bosses since the merger at his company.

"Not too bad," Steve replied. "One of the junior execs working on the transition is Charlotte Barrington-Carr that I used to work with at Forrester's, so that's a positive."

"That's cool," I yawned into my coffee, not recalling a Charlotte from the time when I was a young, ambitious analyst at the same company as Steve. "Do you fancy taking the dogs out before work? Save me a job?"

I always got up twenty minutes earlier than Steve despite him leaving the house before me so that I could drag the pooches around the streets before the kids got up. I was hoping that my athletic, passionate bedroom antics last night had put Steve in a generous mood.

"I'll take them, babe," He offered draining his coffee and getting up. "I'll be late again tonight."

For a change. I rolled my eyes when his back was turned.

Steve worked in the City in Finance, whereas since having George I'd left that world to work in a high street bank where I was an Assistant Manager. The branch was only 20 minutes away from our home and the hours were so much easier with the children. Steve's career, which had started on par with mine, had gone from strength to strength which was great news for our hefty mortgage payments on the four-bedroom terrace with a garden in our London suburb, but was a point of envy for me. I had had Esther straight out of Uni; being pregnant for my last few exams. Steve and I had both been ambitious, young analysts for the same corporate machine fresh out of education, and we'd moved in with my mother and step-father to help us cope with parenthood and the financial pressures. On a really honest day, I could just about bear to admit to myself that they pretty much raised Esther up until I got pregnant with George two years later. We had both worked long hours and, while I had dashed home the moment I could leave the office to my infant daughter, Steve had distanced himself from me; staying out and joining friends on weekends away.

Steve cited this as being down to the lack of privacy of living with my parents. We struggled to make our living arrangements work and broke up briefly due to my constant exhaustion from trying to do it all and the subsequent feeling that I was failing at both my career and being a mother. I fell pregnant with George during one of our rocky patches and my now exhausted parents gifted us a large sum of money which enabled us to buy our own home. They then packed up their own belongings and bought a property overseas; opting out of doting grandparenthood and into six months a year of retirement in the sun. Not that I blamed them, and I would be forever grateful for the otherwise impossible bunk up on to the property ladder. My hormones during my pregnancy with George were unbearable and I struggled under the guilt of leaving Esther with childminders and nurseries for up to 11 hours a day, which were the hours we needed to commit to just keep our heads above water in the greasy corporate world we were trying to succeed in.

I had a full-on meltdown in the office one day. Esther was two and a half and her nursery were putting on a nativity play. I had tried to wrangle time off work to see her, dressed as an angel singing Christmas carols, but my boss had insisted I was required to attend a critical meeting on her behalf. I was currently in the early stages of pregnancy, struggling with morning sickness and the stress of buying our first home. Moments before the meeting, one of my colleagues, Nadia, had made a passing comment on how my boss wasn't able to attend as she had booked to have her hair done before her own daughter's Christmas carol concert that evening. I burst into furious tears and, in a fit of pure rage, I had hurled the tray of canapes (it was a working lunch meeting) at the glass meeting room walls. I took sick leave for the duration of my pregnancy and settled on a less stressful role in a high street bank after a few months off with my new baby son.

After having Leo, a few years later, I had cut my maternity leave to a super-short period in return for a role as Assistant manager in the branch I worked at. The hours were manageable and while the salary was a lot less, the staff I worked with were more down-to-earth and fun. This thought led me to think of lovely Luke, the mortgage advisor that worked at a neighbouring branch. I had forgotten to open his snapchat last night. We worked closely with the other local branch as we covered each other during peak times and my branch were meant to be meeting up with Luke's later for someone's birthday drinks. I glanced at the calendar to establish whether this would be possible. The kids' schools all ran various after school activities which was great for working parents, however this gave me enough time to haul my arse onto the train and not enough time to actually make plans with other humans or squeeze in an hour at the gym to keep me in enough shape to stop Steve leaving me for one of his sexy, svelte colleagues. Although to be fair, the thought of the maintenance he'd have to pay me and the horror of him having to stay in with four children in a one-bedroom bachelor pad every other weekend would be enough of an incentive for him to stay married to me no matter what I looked like.

In the time I'd been sipping my coffee and day dreaming, Steve had been out and back with the dogs.

"I'm going to jump in the shower, babe." He said, bending to kiss my head as he passed.

As soon as I knew he was safely in the shower, I clicked open the message from Luke. I fired back a flirty reply. My mum was back in the country at the moment. I would phone her on the off chance that she'd pop over and watch the kids. I could either join my colleagues for drinks or head to the gym.

"Muuuummmmm!" The familiar whine broke my peaceful morning. Esther woke up ridiculously early for a 13-year-old, in order to discreetly contour her face into a real-life Instagram-filtered Kardashian look-a-like and meticulously straighten her natural curls.

"Morning, darling!" I called up, starting to pack the bags. "What's the matter?"

"I can't find my headphones!" She called back. "I can't catch public transport without headphones!"

I headed up the stairs, mentally fixing on my super-hero cape to avert a morning breakdown.

Barely an hour and a half later, my unruly tribe were up, fed, dressed and ready to go. Esther had left; obviously too cool to travel anywhere with her mother and siblings. George, now in his final year of primary school, lagged behind while Leo, proudly carrying a lopsided Taj Mahal, and Matilda dressed in her homemade Victorian costume, chatted happily to me as we walked the short distance to the school's Breakfast club. I signed them in and, with kisses from my youngest and a dirty look from George, headed off to catch my train to work.

Andy called me, predictable as ever at 8am sharp, as he was rolling up to work knowing that I would have dropped the kids off and could now be all ears.

"Morning, babes!" I breezed cheerily as I grabbed a takeaway coffee for the short journey.

Andy launched into a ten-minute monologue of everything that had happened in his life since I had spoken with him the previous evening, which was a lot more than you'd think when you're a cosmetic surgeon by day, aspiring comic by night, property developer by weekend and all-round-super-social-butterfly every minute of every God damn day.

"So," Andy summarised his monologue. "Basically, I need you to come with me tonight."

"It's Wednesday," I whined at him, sounding alarmingly like Esther. "I need to go to the gym. I'm fucking repulsive right now!"

The couple next to me exchanged disapproving glances, and conscious that I was a grown woman wearing the uniform of my employer, I flushed and lowered my tone.

"I'll phone my mum and see if she'll babysit." I knew there was no point arguing with Andy. He knew exactly what buttons to press to manipulate and emotionally blackmail me into being his one-woman support squad after all these years of friendship.

"I've already asked her!" Andy declared triumphantly.

"That is so intrusive!" I hissed. "She's my mother!"

"Su madre es mi madre," Andy parroted back at me. "Anyway, I've got to dash! Lives to save! See you at 8- I'll send you the details!"

I sipped on my coffee and fumed silently for the rest of the journey. He did not have lives to save. He was a bloody cosmetic surgeon. I'd been looking forward to an hour in the gym and this meant I would have used my babysitting card and wouldn't be able to pull any favours from my mum for at least a month. They were heading back overseas to their villa at the end of June, so I'd be lucky to get one more night out during their time in the UK. Steve had a golf weekend scheduled this week, so I was resigned to a weekend of double football runs and catching up on housework.

Andy was such a monopoliser of my time. I'd been hoping to fit in seeing my friend Jen for dinner or drinks but the chances of getting a babysitter were slim to none. I remembered, with glee, that Andy had cancelled on me this coming Friday and I already had my neighbour's daughter booked to babysit. I wondered if Jen would be free at this short notice and decided to text her on the off chance.

"Morning, doll!" Lois, my favourite colleague, was waiting outside the bank for Roger to open up. Lois looked perky and immaculate as always.

"Morning!" I plastered on my professional smile. "How are you? You're early?"

"Great," Lois beamed. "I managed to fit in an early morning swim and gym. Dave's working away. I'm at such a loose end without him."

"Wow, you're good," I replied. "When is he home?"

Roger opened up and let us in; grunting a 'Morning' in our direction.

"Not until Saturday," Lois replied, both of us not bothering to speak to Roger knowing how miserable he was in the morning. "He's got an early flight back, so I'll pick him up from the airport. I've booked us a table at Lucio's in the evening."

"Ooh lovely." I said on auto-pilot. Lois blabbered on about darling Dave for the time it took me to log into my PC and check my calendar for the day.

"Oh, for fuck's sake!" I interrupted Lois without thinking as I saw Roger had cancelled my appointments this morning to schedule a meeting with me. Lois looked shocked and I apologised quickly, gesturing for her to pick up her story.

Roger was notoriously shit at managing the staff here; who were mainly women. He left pretty much all tasks that involved interacting with them to me citing it was "good for my development" as a reason for me to pick up the shit he didn't want to do. Just like dealing with any horrendous complaint was "good experience" and he was actually doing me a favour passing angry or irate customers to me. Somehow, over time, this meant a huge portion of my days were spent listening to my colleagues' personal lives and woes. After Lois had trotted off, Hannah came in and proceeded to show me about 800 photos of her child's haircut. I was exhausted by 9am when we finally opened up. I made my way to the meeting room at the back of the building, wondering what Roger wanted at such short notice. I wondered whether we would be the latest in branch closures. As part of the bank's cost-cutting strategy and digital vision, branches were being culled up and down the country. We were no longer the sales hubs, now the emphasis was on 'responsible' lending. The banks didn't give a shit that branches were relied on heavily by small businesses and the older generation.

Roger confirmed my suspicions that the meeting was to discuss branch closures. It was the neighbouring branch though and not ours that was for the chop. There were seven roles that would be lost from this closure and two roles would be moved to our branch. All the staff at both branches would have the option to preference for voluntary redundancy. Including me. Roger was preparing me as he was aware that there would be a lot of unrest and questions on the back of the announcement made this afternoon, and reassurance and support would obviously fall to me. For my development of course.

The announcement was made, just before lunchtime, and I spent the rest of the day, in between customers and complaints, reassuring colleagues and listening to their concerns. Roger was predictably nowhere in sight. I had a text from Luke, looking to solicit any insider information on who would be applying for VR. I replied honestly that I didn't know and that I had no part in any decision making. By 5.30pm, I was physically exhausted, emotionally drained and my 'professional' smile was basically just me baring my teeth at everyone. The prospect of redundancy seemed much more attractive than it had that morning. I had sent messages to Steve and Andy with the news, but they were both clearly too busy with their important lives to respond. My phone beeped with a message as I dashed through the doors of the train. It was Jen.

"Read about more branch closures :(You ok? X x"

Ah, at least someone cared about my life.

Chapter 3

I met Andy, that evening, at a bar called Chester's for a comedy night. He was backstage with the other stand-ups, so I bought myself a jug of Mojito and sat up by the bar, popping out occasionally for an illicit cigarette from the pack I'd treated myself to after the awful day I'd had. Luke had kept up a steady stream of texts during the day and was also out and about that evening with the rest of the branch staff. The texts were growing increasingly flirty as the night went on.

Andy was up on stage at 9pm so I loyally put my phone away and turned to face the stage to give him my full attention. I knew all Andy's routines, one-liners and anecdotes off by heart, but I smiled and laughed the whole way through, feeling the same maternal pride as I do sitting through my kids' school concerts and sports games.

After he'd finished, Andy slid onto the barstool next to me. I realised I'd almost finished a whole jug of cocktails and ordered myself a glass of water.

"Well done, babe!" I congratulated him. "You were fab."

"Thanks." Andy beamed, fidgeting with his phone.

We chatted away about the other acts, but he seemed distracted. He was constantly texting on his phone and seemed keen to round up the night. I had given up my evening and used my only free babysitting card to be ignored, I fumed to myself, more irritated than upset. I gave up trying to make conversation and pulled out my own phone. I noticed a message from Luke asking if I fancied meeting up with the rest of the staff for a drink. The thought of making work-related conversation filled me with dread and I suggested we meet up alone. After a few texts back and forth, during which time Andy continued smiling down at his phone and ignoring me, Luke and I had established that we could meet up within twenty minutes at his tube stop and I could still be home by 11.30pm. I gave Andy the get out clause that he was clearly after, feigning tiredness, and slid to my feet, a little wobbly from the effects of the Mojito. Andy made some excuse about having to go somewhere and we parted ways.

Luke was waiting on the corner by the station entrance. My drunken face lit up into a genuine smile at the sight of him.

Luke was tall and slim, with thick dark hair that fell across his forehead, sexy green-grey eyes and a massive straight-toothed grin. He was dressed casually but immaculate in dark jeans and a plain t-shirt. He turned and watched me walk towards him; the corners of his mouth turning up in a sexy smile. I turned my face up to him, letting him kiss my cheek in greeting and, wordlessly, we walked together towards his flat. The tension was palpable and by the time we reached his place, I was feeling dizzy with the anticipation. The sex was fast and dirty. He pulled my hair and grazed his teeth over my neck and my shoulders. When it was over, I dressed quickly and leaned back down to kiss him slowly.

"I'm falling in love with you, sweetheart." He said solemnly as he lay naked and spent in his bed. He pulled me into his arms and held me against his chest.

We'd been sleeping together, on and off, for over a year now. Mainly off, but over the course of this time, we had exchanged a lot of texts, sharing things more intimate than just a bed. We talked about our lives, our hopes and dreams, and genuinely got on as friends. I had grown increasingly fond of Luke and loved spending little bits of stolen time with him whenever we could. I was under no illusion though that I was the only person Luke was seeing, and I held back from jumping into any romantic fantasy.

"Want me to walk you to the station?" He asked, as I broke away from his embrace and made my way to the door.

He made no attempt to get up and dressed. If he had to ask, he could fuck off.

"You're ok." I smiled instead.

I slipped my feet into my shoes and left, feeling nothing more than the beginning of a headache and a mild sense of disappointment.

As I waited for my train, I checked my phone. Steve should have got back to the house and relieved my mother of her babysitting duties but instead I had a text message.

"Babe, I'm running late! I text your mum, so she knows."

I groaned inwardly, knowing I would be walking into chaos

when I got home. I pulled my jacket around my shoulders and prayed that Steve would make it home before me, so I wouldn't have to deal with my mother judging me for being a bit drunk on a Wednesday, for the state of the house or for the fact the kids had had KFC for dinner. My train pulled up and I jumped on, head down tapping out a response to a message from Jen. From the corner of my eye I caught sight of something and looked up sharply. Any alcohol in my system drained away and my stomach dropped; now stone cold sober as my husband met my eyes across the carriage.

He rose to his feet and was next to me in the seconds it took for me to rearrange my features from guilty shock to a warm smile of delight.

"Hey babe!" He slung his arm around me and kissed me square on my unfaithful, cheating mouth. "Where've you been?"

"Hi babe," I smiled back. "I've been to watch Andy do stand up. He was really good. We went to some little pub after for drinks."

Steve squinted at me and I held my breath waiting for him to challenge my story.

"Are you drunk?" He laughed finally.

I nodded, relieved.

"Bad news about that branch," He said, referring to my earlier text. "Will that impact your branch?"

“Possibly,” I jumped on the subject gratefully. “There’ll be seven losses at the branch and it’ll create two vacancies at ours. Everyone at both branches has the option for redundancy though.”

“Good news for you, though, “Steve continued. “Your branch must be out-performing theirs.”

“Gutted for them though.” I frowned at his lack of empathy. These were real people with lives, bills and families. My salary might just be money for clothes, holidays and the Audi people carrier we barely used but this would really impact my colleagues in an already tough job market. “I quite fancy the thought of redundancy.”

Steve frowned . “Not really the best time for you to be thinking about that if we’re going ahead with buying the holiday let.”

I bit my lip and reminded myself that I’d just fallen out of a 28-year-old colleague’s bed so now was not the time for me to play my favourite role of “Ms Moral” up on my platform of choice “the soapbox”.

“Hmmm,” I mumbled, noncommittally. “Are you going to manage to fit in any of the property stuff this weekend?”

Steve had his heart set on buying an apartment near the golf course in Portugal as a rental property/ getaway for him. I had no real problem with it but was slightly nervous that we were already over-committed financially.

Steve argued that it was an investment. The apartment was big enough for us to use as a family, close to the beach and would comfortably pay for itself as a summer rental.

"Yep, I'll squeeze it in first thing Friday," Steve assured me. "That reminds me, can you manage to grab my dry-cleaning Friday as I'll be away." And then without pausing to let me answer. "Thanks, babe."

He grabbed my hand and pulled me to my feet as the train reached our stop. He gave my bum an over-familiar grab and we walked the short distance home.

My mother opened the door looking stressed and dishevelled.

"Hello, Suze," Steve the charmer swooped in and kissed her cheek, "Shall I drop you home or is Graham picking you up?"

"Thank you, Mum." I said gratefully, my eyes frantically surveying the hall and stairs for chaos, damage or bodies. "Were they alright?"

"Graham is on his way." She replied to Steve, ignoring me as she smoothed her coiffured ash blonde hair and reapplied her Estee Lauder lipstick in the hallway mirror.

"Kids alright?" Steve called from where he'd flung himself down on the sofa with the dogs, hand already on the TV remote ready to change over to Sky Sports.

"Yes, fine," My mother replied. "Little darlings."

Steve and I exchanged mock-shocked looks and I decided to use the distraction of my flustered mother to jump in the shower and wash away my sins; leaving Steve to schmooze until Graham, my stepfather, arrived to pick her up.

Matilda was curled up in the middle of our bed; blonde curls stuck to her head with sweat, wearing an inside out Tinkerbell nightie and a ninja turtle mask. I slipped Raphael's red mask off her sweet, sleeping face, plugged my phone in to charge at the side of the bed and loosened the covers around her.

Five minutes later, I was out of the shower, wrapped in a fluffy cream towel and feeling fresh. Steve was sat on the side of the bed, still dressed. Matilda was still fast asleep next to him and my phone was in his hand. My heart stopped.

Steve looked up and met my eyes, "Who the fuck is Luke?"

My whole body ran cold. The fight or flight animal instinct, that lives deep in our primal brains, was triggered and my mouth opened, and I spoke before I even knew what I was going to say.

"Luke?" My voice came out calm and breezy. "He's Andy's friend. Why? What did he say?"

My hands flew to adjust the towel on my head, nervous energy flooding back to my body.

Steve unplugged the phone and tossed it to me. His dark

eyes still narrowed and hard. I knew this sign though. He wanted to buy my bullshit and keep subscribing to our status quo. Part of me wondered why I continued to save myself.

"Fuck it," said the devil on my shoulder. "Tell him."

In my twisted fantasies, I relished the explosions this would cause to my picture perfect suburban life that I didn't deserve. My eyes rested on Matilda's sweet, cherubic face; her tiny body so innocent next to Steve's 6-foot, broad frame and I knew I couldn't do it to them. I scooped the phone up, struggling to keep my face nonchalant. It was just a WhatsApp message.

"Had an amazing time with your sexy body."

I theatrically rolled my eyes.

"He's one hundred percent gay, babe." I reassured Steve, turning and grabbing my lotion for my usual post-shower ritual. "He's joking. Some guy text him that earlier and we were all joking about it."

Steve said nothing but got up and started to undress. He gently picked Matilda up and carried her to her own bed.

He was back in bed feigning sleep by the time I'd finished drying my hair. I glanced at my phone and it was gone midnight. I slid under the covers and pressed up against my husband. His body tensed, and he shrugged my arm off him.

"Love you." I whispered, wondering if I really did.

Chapter 4

The next few days rolled into an emotional and physical vacuum; the demands of four children, two dogs, a sulking husband and a branch full of stressed and harassed staff slowly ebbed away at every last fibre of my strength and humanity. By Friday evening, after leaving work thirty minutes late due to an aggrieved customer who felt that the spate of branch closures was one, a personal attack on her following forty years of custom and two, a decision that I could personally reverse, I had had enough. I resisted the urge to scream at her that I was just a salaried performing sea lion and ushered her out of the doors when Kylie, one of the part time cashiers, had an emotional breakdown. I drew a few deep meditative breaths and pasted on my concerned face but, by this point, it was all I could do to not join in with her racking sobs.

I dashed to the school, looking forward to being chastised by the staff for my lateness, feeling guilty as I was no doubt keeping them from their own plans and families. On a positive, Jen, miraculously, had no plans that evening and as I already had Freya booked to babysit, we had made plans to meet up for dinner and drinks. I was looking forward to catching up with my friend, but the thought of getting ready and hauling myself into town on a Friday night was not appealing to me. Jen had millions of friends and was one of the few people who actually showed genuine empathy for the (self-made) busyness of my life, so I knew she would understand if I cancelled. A hot bath, a bottle of wine and my pyjamas was what I really needed in my life, but I was not, and would probably never be, the type of person to cancel on plans. There was some kind of subservience engrained in me from birth, which sucked the fun out of life and meant that I'd wasted possibly hundreds of hours at parties and events that I had been too polite to flake on.

Esther was raging that I'd booked a babysitter and had packed an overnight bag and flounced off to her friends for the evening. She point blank refused to even watch her darling siblings for me to run to the shop for half an hour some evenings. I was in no mood for this conversation after the week I'd had so I happily handed over £20 and made myself even later by navigating the rush hour traffic to drop her safely off. I rushed back to the house and got on with the arduous task of tweezing and painting myself beautiful. Matilda sat at the bottom of the bed chatting away. Steve had left for his "boy's" weekend in Portugal this morning, still not speaking to me over the Luke text. I'd been a dutiful wife up until he left; rushing around on my lunch hours that week to pick up toiletries he needed and his dry cleaning and even making his bloody dinner but to no avail. He tended to go in moods for up to a week after we'd argued, or I'd wronged him in any way, so I wasn't overly concerned although the guilt had settled in, so I had given Luke a wide berth since.

To be honest, I'd been thinking that the whole Luke thing had been going on a bit long. We'd been sleeping together sporadically over the last twelve months since a work night out, but it was the frequency and content of our communication that had been playing on my mind. While it had started as my usual needy desire for attention and validation from an attractive, younger man, it had escalated into deep and meaningful conversations, a few stolen nights away and some weird kind of friendship. Half the time, I didn't even like Luke; finding his respect for women (namely me) lacking. I knew deep down that my 'relationship' with Luke was merely a distraction from the mundane Groundhog Day that I was living and proof, in my mind, that I was still reasonably attractive to other humans. Luke was actually a really nice person, albeit one with a whole heap of issues. If I was single, there would be no chance, despite his good looks and charm, that I'd ever put up with his shit. As attention and validation was all I wanted, the arrangement had worked out quite well so far for both of us. I liked having Luke around but maybe it was time to quit while I was ahead. Jen would be able to offer me her expert advice that evening, I thought to myself as I squeezed into a tight black dress and finally hurried out of the house already late.

I walked into the restaurant, self-consciously tugging at the hem of my dress that had ridden up around my thighs from the serious pace I had put in to minimise my lateness. The restaurant had a cocktail bar vibe to it and I utilised the mirrored walls to tidy up my unruly, strawberry-blonde curls. There was a smudge of eye liner already underneath my pale blue eyes and I swiped ineffectively at it before giving up and surveying the room for my friend.

"Lucy!"

I turned towards the sound of my name to see beautiful Jen propped up at the bar, looking every inch the Goddess that she was. Her curves were squeezed into an emerald green silk wrap dress and her full red mouth was curved in a smile that lit up her face. She uncrossed her long, tan legs and got to her feet to greet me. I wrapped my arms around Jen and she squeezed me with genuine affection. As always, I felt a rush of love for this woman.

"Jen," I sighed happily. "I've bloody missed you!"

Jen and I had first met at a work party just before I left Forrester's. She was a few years older than me and our paths had never really crossed paths in our day jobs, however we had hit it off despite how different we were and hers was one of the few friendships that had grown over the years.

"I've missed you, too." Jen squeezed me again before going back to her seat and pushing a large glass of wine towards me. "What's new?"

I sipped the wine gratefully, "Thanks. Nothing really- same old. What about you?"

"Ok," Jen answered hesitantly, before leaning forward with a serious look in her big, dark eyes. "I've been offered an amazing secondment. In New York, Luce! Can you believe it?"

"Wow!" My eyes widened at this huge news. "That's amazing! Well done!"

“This is confidential, by the way,” She added sipping her own wine thoughtfully. “Don’t tell Steve.”

Jen worked for the bank that had recently taken over Steve’s company. I nodded in agreement that I wouldn’t.

“Tell me everything!” I prompted, delighted to see Jen’s career doing so well.

“So, it’s just for six months because there’s been a major fuck up with some of the integration. They know I won’t go permanently- obviously because of Coco.” Jen told me.

Coco was Jen’s miniature dachshund and her favourite being in the world. Jen had made better life choices than me and was happy at thirty-seven to be living in her beautiful, clean, quiet home alone with her dog. She had never succumbed to any marriage proposal and had never expressed any interest in having children herself. Jen’s personality was as magnetic as her dark, Mediterranean looks. Her father had allegedly been a waiter, her mother a Bohemian backpacker with a taste for recreational drugs. Jen hadn’t had a great childhood and had eventually been palmed off on her grandmother, Dorothy, who was an absolute angel of a woman. From the few things Jen and Dorothy had ever said, it seemed that Dorothy had ploughed everything into breaking down the barriers Jen had put up due to her formative years being a time of uncertainty and neglect. Dorothy was so, so proud of Jen, and particularly of Jen’s successful career. Jen was one of the youngest people, let alone women, to take her position in the bank. Jen was, in my biased opinion, that mythological combination of brains, beauty and charisma. She was friendly and genuine to everyone, but deeply private. I felt blessed that I was one of the few people who knew about Jen's past and about her dreams and aspirations. On paper, she sounded as made up as the concept of women being able to have it all. In reality, she was probably my favourite person in the world.

We finished our drinks and were seated at our table to order dinner. Jen rested her chin on her closed hand and surveyed me thoughtfully with her piercing brown eyes.

I smiled at her, a little self-consciously, "What, Jen?"

Jen's smile widened, flashing me a row of pearly white teeth and she held up her hands in a display of innocence. "I'm not staring!"

Jen's eyes danced in the low lighting of the restaurant, and I felt myself blush slightly as if we were flirting. Which we weren't. Why was I so awkward? I dropped my gaze to the menu and changed the subject to food. Once we had decided, we chatted about life in general before the subject came back around to Steve and Portugal. I told Jen about the property we were buying.

"Is that what you want?" Jen asked, her voice thoughtful not judgemental.

"Well, Steve seems to think it's a good investment," I chewed on my bottom lip, remembered I was wearing lipstick and stopped abruptly. I leaned forward and bared my teeth at Jen in an unspoken request for her to check them for lipstick. She leaned across the table, peered closely at my mouth and swiped her little finger across my right incisor before leaning back and nodding that the job was complete.

"And you?" Jen pressed on with the conversation and I shrugged in response.

"It's a nice place," I said finally. "It's just another financial commitment."

A fleeting look of something like frustration shadowed Jen's eyes but it was gone immediately, and she smiled brightly, "Oh we can definitely have a few weekends away together! Hopefully before I'm shipped off to New York!"

"Oh, I'd love to," I said happy that she hadn't pushed me into admitting I wasn't feeling confident about the purchase. "It won't be ready until August though."

"We're due a weekend away soon, though." Jen said firmly. "I know someone who will lend us a cottage in Cornwall. We can take the dogs."

"I'd love to," I repeated but this time with an apologetic look. "I don't know when I'll be able to though as Steve isn't speaking to me at the moment."

Jen raised her perfectly arched eyebrows questioningly.

"He read a message on my phone off Luke." I admitted

embarrassedly.

Jen looked surprised. "I cannot believe you are still shagging that man-child!"

My mouth dropped; usually she was the least judgemental of all my friends. I stayed quiet and waited for her to elaborate.

"Don't look at me like that, Lucy." Jen said, looking disapprovingly. "He's a liability. He's bound to cause drama for you one way or another."

"He won't," I protested. "He's not interested in anything serious."

"Really?" Jen looked sceptical. "He's bound to be falling for you."

"He's not," I shook my head. "I'm too old and have way too much baggage for him."

"You're not, Lucy," Jen sighed, her body language softening. She leaned over and covered my hand with hers. "I'm just sick of you wasting your time on dickheads."

I met her eyes and smiled softly at her. She ran her finger over my bare arm.

"You've got goose-bumps." She said, still holding my gaze.

I looked down at my arms and pulled my hand out from under hers, wrapping them around myself, suddenly feeling self-conscious. "Yeah, it's a bit cold in here."

Jen nodded and folded her hands in her lap.

"I'm going to cut it off with Luke," I said, feeling anxious that I'd annoyed her. "I just don't know how to do it without causing any drama."

"Just be busy," Jen said. "And still be friendly. And make sure you tell Steve we're going away!"

Jen unfolded her hands to reach for her wine glass and I reached across and touched her hand, wanting her approval.

I smiled. "I promise."

Jen entwined her hand back with mine and I looked down at our fingers linked against the shiny wood table. Moments passed and neither of us said anything but then the waiter arrived, and we pulled away to make room for the plates.

We fell back into an easy conversation and the subject circled back to work.

"Will your Gran have Coco?" I asked.

I would have happily had her, but Coco was happiest as an only dog.

"Yes," Jen nodded. "She said she would. I plan on coming back a few times, when I can."

"I would love to go to New York," I said. "It'll be amazing."

"You should come out and stay!" Jen exclaimed.

"If only!" I knew that our already stretched finances would never allow for me to fit in a solo trip away. Jen looked disappointed but didn't press the subject.

After dinner, we headed across the road to a bar with a courtyard out the back. It was heaving with beautiful twenty-something's but, as always, Jen "knew" someone so dragged me to the cordoned off area where there were some tables reserved. I caught the disgruntled looks of some of the gorgeous creatures who were eyeing me suspiciously as Jen and I were led over to a reserved table in the corner by an immaculate woman. A group on the next table, that I'm sure I recognised as from the X Factor called over familiarly to Jen, but she just smiled and waved and carried on her conversation with me. I felt a warm flush, which was probably just the alcohol running through my veins. I wondered, not for the first time, why someone as amazing as Jen would be friends with someone as plain and vanilla as me.

"He's cute." I nodded in the direction of a handsome bearded man who kept glancing over at Jen.

Jen scrunched up her nose and shook her head. "I'm not interested right now. Honestly, though, he's not that nice. It's the beard. They're deceptive. You could stick a beard on a potato and there'd be a queue of women waiting to get ghosted by him."

I laughed, and Jen smiled at my reaction.

"Anyway," Jen continued. "No men allowed tonight. I never get you to myself. Tell me everything. Even about Luke."

"There's nothing to tell. He's a nice guy but I know I need to end it." I shrugged, making it clear I didn't want to discuss it any longer.

"How's work?" Jen asked, sipping her drink.

"Awful," I admitted. "I hate it. Steve was really dismissive about me applying for VR and he's got a point as we're up to our necks in commitments. It would be hard to find something so local."

"Does he know how much you hate it?" Jen asked.

"We don't really talk about stuff like that anymore." I said, realising how pathetic that sounded as soon as it was out of my mouth. I couldn't bear the pitying look in Jen's eyes, so I rummaged in my bag for my emergency cigarettes.

"Ooh," Jen homed in on the cigarettes before I'd even pulled them out. "Let's have one, Luce."

I reached over to hand her one, but she dropped her face, indicating that I put it straight between her lips. I leaned over to light it and Jen reached up to cup my hands as I held the flame against her cigarette. I felt something flicker in the pit of my stomach and I couldn't take my eyes from Jen's lips. I was clearly more drunk than I thought, I shook it off and lit my own. We both inhaled deeply. Both ex-smokers who occasionally relapsed when we were drinking.

We ordered more drinks and Jen encouraged me to hypothesise about the different jobs I would do in a dream world, where I didn't have sole responsibility for four children and massive financial burdens. We always came back around to travel; where we'd go, what we'd do, and we huddled close together peering at Jen's phone screen as we searched various routes and destinations.

"One day!" Jen slurred. We were both pretty drunk by now. "You can stop running around after everybody else. Steve and Luke can fuck off; they're not having you! We'll see the whole world and you can do what you want to do instead of giving everything up for everyone!"

For some reason, this made my eyes well up with tears. Jen saw this and leaned forward to wrap her arms around me. She was one of the few people who really understood me. She understood how I struggled with anxiety and feelings of low self-worth. I constantly battled between wanting to be there for my children and feeling I'd sacrificed my career and ambition to do so.

"I'm fine." I managed to choke back the sob of self-pity that had built up in the back of my throat.

Jen pulled back and her dark eyes searched my face. The intensity of her gaze made my stomach knot and I felt that strange flutter of butterflies inside me. I blinked away the tears and forced my features into a wry smile.

"You're fine." Jen repeated and reached over to brush a single tear away from the bottom of my lashes. Her fingers lingered there, just above my cheekbone, for a moment and I felt frozen; my eyes locked on hers. Jen moved her hand away and turned as she did. The moment was broken and we both laughed a little self-consciously.

“Shall we go somewhere to dance?” I suggested, thinking I needed to sober up fast.

Jen nodded, and we unsteadily got to our feet to leave.

Chapter 5

I swung open the frosted glass door of the small meeting room, struggling to balance a stack of papers and the two Starbucks cups in my hands.

Roger watched me unhelpfully from his seat at the table, wearing his usual expressionless look.

“Sorry I’m late.” I said as cheerily as I could muster.

“Take a seat.” Roger got straight down to business as usual, no interest in pleasantries. “We’ll conduct your review and follow immediately with a preliminary review of the expressions of interest.”

I made a show of fanning out the papers on the table. Some of these were expressions of interest in redundancy, which technically and ethically I should have no access to. Fortunately, respecting colleagues’ privacy was much further down Roger’s list of priorities, way below delegating-everything-to-Lucy.

Roger prompted me to get started and so I reeled off numbers and other corporate bullshit. Roger stopped me from time to time to interject with his opinion. Even though I had been ripped to shreds countless times by Roger and past managers, I felt myself growing more and more anxious as we drew to a close. By the end of the conversation, Roger had used the phrase “bitterly disappointed” at least twice and I felt so deflated I was practically lying on the table. I heard my own defensive tone when I tried to justify how I had zero influence over the bank's measure of staffing costs and overheads, which our branch was failing to achieve.

"You need to understand," Roger said in his monotonous tone. "It is all our responsibilities to offer proactive solutions."

What he was saying was absolute nonsense. Was he suggesting I ring around the electricity company to see if we could get better rates? That I personally review salary guidelines and change this. These were both centrally-controlled, and I was so sick of this bullshit.

Roger continued speaking. The usual corporate crap flying out of his mouth "target strategic solution", "empowered for customer focus". I folded my hands in my lap and waited for him to finish as the blood simmered in my veins, working up to boiling point.

I reminded myself that, for the time being, I needed this job and I needed to just shut my mouth, write down actions and let it go. To distract myself from the furious woman inside, I pictured my inner monologue as a cartoon version of myself, but she was a real bad ass with a megaphone and tattoos. The thought of this made me smile a little bit and Roger frowned at my expression. I quickly nodded and started jotting random words down on my pad of paper, hoping he couldn't read from his side of the table what was just a shopping list. I had accumulated that many tips for managing my emotions over the years that I could probably write a self-help book. Or a blog. Esther said everyone 'blogs' now. Esther. I held on to that thought, remembering she had a geography trip to Iceland which would cost at least £1500 plus outfits. I one-hundred-percent needed this job, so I kept my head down and let Roger continue his critique of me. He needed no encouragement with this character assassination and, with the natural-born confidence of a white middle-aged man, droned on and on. When it was finally over, and my humiliation was complete, he gestured to the other forms I had printed off for him.

"I probably shouldn't be involved in this process," I said, hesitantly. "As it's open to me as well. Plus, people can give personal reasons and it might be confidential."

Roger gave me a look that implied I was clueless and took the papers, leafing quickly through them.

"If you want to progress," He said, a little sternly. "This sort of experience will support you. I trust that you will keep this confidential."

I nodded, my moral objections silenced by the implied promise that I could rise to branch manager if I were obedient.

"The following have expressed preliminary interest." Roger continued and read out a short list of names that wouldn't cover the seven jobs that needed to be cut between the two branch teams. "Who hasn't submitted anything?"

I listed all the staff in both branches that hadn't been

named already.

“Luke.” Roger held up his hand to stop me mid-flow when I came to him. “There have been some concerns raised about your relationship with him.”

My heart dropped, and I struggled to maintain my composure. Roger fell quiet, and the inferences of his silence told me that any rumours were a little more than a “you both take too long on lunch break”.

“That’s not true!” I said, hoping I sounded shocked and not guilty.

Roger took the list I had started to write down from my hands. “It will make it difficult for Luke to relocate to this branch with rumours like that.”

“Unfounded, malicious rumours?” I asked, absolutely furious and feeling panicked that Luke may lose out due to our ‘friendship’. It was bad enough that I’d clearly hurt Luke’s feelings over the last week as I’d tried to cool things off with him.

“Smoke. Fire.” Roger responded with casual arrogance and I felt myself explode.

“That’s bollocks!” I raged. “Whatever has been said is a malicious lie and you cannot make a decision like that based on hearsay!”

Roger didn’t flinch at my outburst. He surveyed the list slowly and tapped the top of his pen against one name.

"Leanne." He said, ignoring my outburst. "She would be an asset to the branch."

Leanne was my leggy, blonde equivalent from the other branch. Younger than me, she had been fast tracked on the company development programme, which was great for her. I'd heard some rumours of my own about her though, and some of them included Roger. I was pretty sure Luke had shagged her too. Not that I was jealous.

"Well, if you've made your decision," I said, gathering up my belongings. "I'll get back to work."

I didn't even wait for his response as I was so angry and incensed at the injustice of it all. I headed back to the back office, dropped my papers into the confidential waste bin and grabbed my bag.

Lois was dashing back to the counters and she caught a glimpse of my stony expression.

"You ok?" She asked, looking concerned.

"I need to pop out," I said to her, touched by her concern. "Can you tell the others if they ask?"

"Of course." Lois gave my shoulder a squeeze and I smiled gratefully at her and left quickly.

I stomped up the high street, still tightly wound up like a coil. I dialled Andy first, but he didn't answer so I tried calling Steve. Shockingly he answered.

"What's up, babe?" He answered.

I launched straight into my rant. "I've had the worst meeting with Roger. I cannot stand it any longer- "

"Oh nightmare," Steve cut me off, not sounding remotely interested. "I'm just on my way out of the office. Can this wait?"

"Where are you going?" I asked annoyed.

"To see a client," He answered. "Tell me about it at home."

I wanted to scream and cry that this couldn't wait, and I needed to vent now before I exploded with rage. Instead I made a noise in agreement. I heard a woman's voice in the background.

"Two seconds, Charl," Steve said, sounding muffled like he'd covered the phone with his hand. "Ok, see you later. Bye."

He ended the call, without waiting for my response. I felt my fury rise to critical levels. I stormed over to Pret but then changed my mind. I wasn't hungry. In that moment, I had a flashback to when I first started to feel uncontrollable emotion like this. I remembered being fifteen years old, standing in the queue for lunch in my pleated skirt and blazer, literally trembling with anger. I had had an argument with a friend (I think over a boy) and then immediately walked straight into our Head of year who'd proceeded to give me a very public and longwinded dressing down over my non-regulation earrings. I had had to hand over my

Tiffany drop earrings (a rare gift from my real dad) and take a detention slip, slinking off humiliated and alone. I remembered being very aware of how angry I was; almost like I was a bystander watching myself and feeling scared of what I might be capable of. Up until that day, my whole childhood/ teenage years, I'd been a good girl. I followed the rules. I internalised my emotions and hated confrontation. In that queue, on that day, I decided I wasn't following the rules and I just walked out of the school gates and went home.

Recalling this, as a grown woman, I made the same choice and I chose not to go back to work. I decided that I would cool down first and call Roger later. I headed to my house, grabbed my gym kit and was churning away miles and emotions on the treadmill within an hour. I felt the tension melting away with every mile I ran; my legs pounded out the frustrations of my life. After forty minutes, I slowed down, looking around to see whether the cross trainer was free. The flirty instructor, who on the rare occasions that I made it here usually gave me enough attention for me to feel the hefty monthly fee was worth it, was leaning against a cross trainer "instructing" a tanned, toned Goddess in a Lycra crop top and matching leggings. I opted for the furthest machine from the pair and was soon drenched in sweat.

The Goddess had been joined by an identical beauty, and they were keeping up a steady conversation while working out with ease. In comparison, it was all I could do to breathe. Probably all the "social" smoking I had been doing.

I had no intention of eavesdropping, but I had forgotten my headphones and their conversation was loud. At first, it was just key words like "lipo", "fillers" and "OMG"'s. The second Goddess started reading out a text message to the first one (still pacing on the machine).

"Charl's dropped out! Listen to this!" She trilled. "Soz ladies- have to cancel. Steve's whisking me away for the weekend. Have fun."

The first Goddess made a noise of disapproval. "Is that the married man she's banging? She's such a tramp."

"I know, right!" Goddess number two replied. "I'm so pissed off with her. I'm not going to reply."

The words "Charl", "Steve" and "married" swirled around my head as I weighed up the chance of this being a coincidence. I quit my work out and headed to the changing room to shower. It wouldn't surprise me. I had seen physical evidence several times over the past few years that pointed to Steve's infidelity. Despite my own guilty actions, I felt wound up at the thought of Steve carrying on with a colleague. Especially a high flying one. As I left the gym, I fired off an SOS text to Andy and Jen summarising the events of my day.

Jen replied straight away.

"Has he said he's going away? He's such a prick."

I typed out my response, "He hasn't said anything."

Jen fired back, "Text him and tell him you're going away with me this weekend. See what he says. Weekend away and ruin his plans. Winner!"

I was pondering her idea when Andy replied. I quickly filled him in on Jen's idea. Andy texted back his approval.

"Good idea. I can get us in the Manor Spa this weekend. Discounts too! Ask Jen if she fancies it."

This really appealed to me and I sent Jen a message. She replied quickly with a "thumbs up" emoji. I gave Andy the go ahead and text Steve to tell him I was going away this weekend. He called me back surprisingly quickly for someone who'd been too busy to listen to his wife's awful day earlier. I panicked and stared at my phone wondering whether to answer. It rang off and Steve texted a blunt "Call me back.". Fuck. I summoned up my emergency rations of bravery and pressed dial.

"Hello?" I said, a little timidly as he answered.

"What the hell are you throwing this at me last minute for?" Steve barked down the phone. "I had plans this weekend."

"Doing what?" I challenged, my irritation kicking in.

"I was going away with Greg." He answered, annoyed.

"Where?" I pressed on.

"Portugal." He snapped back.

"You were there not even two weeks ago!" I snapped. "You don't own the weekend. Plus, Andy has already booked it as a surprise, so I've got to go."

"I've booked the fucking flights." He spat furiously.

"Why didn't you tell me?" I asked, innocently. "Can you get a refund?"

"No, I can't." He growled. "You'll have to ask your mum to babysit."

"She can't do it." I replied. "She's at Emily's."

My sister and her family lived in Wales so logistically this was a no go.

"I can't believe you've done this." He told me.

"Done what?" I snapped back. "Booked to go away without consulting my spouse?"

"You're such a bitch," He responded. "You can sort your own child care. This is your problem."

With that he ended the call. I was furious now and at a loss for what to do next. My plan had backfired. Despite my horrendous day, I had felt uplifted the moment I thought about a weekend away with my best friends. I never spent any time away, unlike Steve, who's calendar was a social whirlwind of weekends away and nights out. Andy and Jen would be back working now, and so I dialled my little sister Emily for advice. Emily was horrified at Steve's behaviour.

Her own husband, Shaun, was a lovely, hands-on family man who worshipped the ground she walked on.

"I'm so pissed off, Em," I sniffed, on the verge of tears. "I don't think I want to be with him anymore."

"I wouldn't either!" Emily said. "Tell you what, Luce, why don't I come up and stay at yours with the kids? Finley is dying to go to London Zoo and Mum can spend time with all her grandkids at once!"

"Oh, Em!" I felt a wave of love for my kind-hearted only sibling. "I couldn't let you do that. Thank you though. That's so kind."

"Don't be silly!" Emily shook off my protests. "We're coming! We'll come up Friday night though. It'll be a bit of a squeeze but so nice to catch up."

I protested a while longer, feeling guilty that my self-pitying call had put this on Emily and now changed everyone's weekend plans. Emily was insistent and promised she would deal with my mother's annoyance at the new itinerary. I pottered around my house trying to distract myself from my thoughts and tried to feel excited again about not only having a night away with friends but at seeing my sister and nephews. I realised at 4pm, with horror, that I hadn't called Roger to advise him of the reason why I had gone home. I dialled his number, expecting a second lecture for disappearing after the meeting.

"Roger," I started, letting my instincts kick in rather than overthinking what I was going to say. "I'm sorry I left and haven't called."

"Oh, right." Roger sounded surprised, and I guessed that he hadn't been on to the 'shop floor' all day therefore assumed I was working. My lovely colleagues must have noticed and kept their mouths shut, I thought gratefully. All those hours of listening to their problems had its advantages.

"Yes," I continued. "And I'm awfully sorry but I've been feeling very unwell and have only just stopped being sick. This is the first chance I've had to call."

"There are procedures that you should have followed," Roger said tartly. "We will talk about this tomorrow."

No, we fucking won't. I wanted to reply. Because I had no intention of coming in.

"Ok, bye." I said instead and hung up the call.

That settled it. I wasn't going in for the rest of the week. That made me feel slightly better. All that was left to do now was to deal with that cheating, misogynistic arsehole I was married to. A notification popped up on my phone to tell me I had a voicemail from my mother. I groaned before deleting it unopened. There was only so much I could deal with in one day.

Chapter 6

Steve came home so late that night that I was asleep. I had hovered around all evening, waiting for the explosive confrontation that never came. He barely spoke to me for the rest of the week and I couldn't bring myself to start the conversation. On Friday morning, with no discussion around when he would be back, Steve took his overnight case and left the house before 5am.

"Are you actually just going to go without us talking about this?" I asked, bleary eyed from my bed.

Steve shook his head as if exasperated by my comment.

"You're really going to do this now?" He asked. "After you've ignored me all week?"

"I haven't ignored you!" I exclaimed. "You've been out until gone 10 every night and out of the house at 6am. When was I meant to have had this conversation?"

"Such a victim," He sneered. "You could have phoned me and disturbed me in work like you did Monday. It's not like I'm busy providing for this fucking house."

I was gobsmacked at his selfishness. "If you don't want to provide for us, how about you fuck off and don't come back?"

"Maybe I won't." He grabbed his case and stormed out.

I listened to the door slam, alone in my bed, and felt tears building up at his coldness. Just days ago, we'd been fine, but one conversation over who had the right to freedom that weekend, and we suddenly couldn't be further apart. He had no idea that I'd not been to work all week- calling in with a sickness bug. He had no idea that my sister and her family were staying here all weekend and my plans were going ahead without his support. After a week off work with my faux illness and no interaction with Steve, I was sick and tired of feeling sad and alone. I forced myself to get up out of bed and to start tidying the house before the kids got up for school. They were all buzzing that Emily, Shaun and their cousin, Finley, were coming to stay which made me feel a lot better about the mum guilt of leaving them tomorrow morning. I hadn't realised what a state the house was in and it took me all day to get it up to a hygienic standard. Another area in my life I was failing at. Emily and Shaun didn't arrive until late, which worked out fine as it meant I wouldn't have to see my mother, who I'd ignored all week. This would one hundred percent come back to bite me at some point, but I figured I would cross that bridge when I came to it. Emily was exhausted when she did arrive. She had her own Events company and had been working flat out over the past few months for peak wedding season. Emily sat up with me with a glass of wine, but I could tell she was exhausted and I feigned tiredness to give her an excuse to go up to bed. I had changed my bed for Emily and Shaun. Finley had happily jumped in Leo's bunk bed, delighted to be one of the "big boys". Luckily, Matilda had already fallen asleep or this would have caused ructions.

I settled down on the sofa, wrapped in a fluffy throw blanket, and tried to drift off to sleep. Despite all my protestations that I didn't care what Steve was doing, all I could picture was Steve and some faceless blonde laughing and kissing in the sunshine. I felt sick at the thought of him falling in love with a woman who was more interesting, more intelligent and more beautiful than me. All I had become to him was the frumpy mother of his children and a sub-standard housekeeper. I had been with Steve for sixteen years. We had four beautiful children together and while our relationship was definitely not healthy, I couldn't imagine life without him. This wouldn't be the first time we had split up. We had split up briefly before I had fallen pregnant with George and again when Matilda was just a baby. I had gone back to working full time as I had felt pressurised by work and Steve into coveting the assistant manager role. Without working full time, I would have had to take a step back and Steve had thought this would have been madness. I had already downgraded my career when I left my role as an analyst to work in the bank as a cashier. Why would I sabotage myself any more, was his attitude. Steve's lifestyle never changed to compensate for a fourth child. He was still a regular at after-works drinks, still made time for the gym and running most days and couldn't say no to a stag do or boys' weekend. I could barely cope with my work-life balance. Matilda was a good sleeper, thank God, but it was all the running around from work to nursery to school to activities. Steve still had the sexual appetite of a lion in mating season. (FYI, that's every 15 minutes over a five-day period). I was constantly exhausted, struggling to lose my pregnancy weight and could barely string a sentence together if it wasn't work or child related. Usually it's the man who cheats, if you believe everything you read, but to be honest if Steve had been bringing a woman home and having noisy sex with her in my living room every night, I wouldn't have noticed and if I had, I wouldn't have cared. As it was, it was me that cheated, not Steve. I built up a friendship with Paul, a dad from the school whose son was in George's year and also had a toddler and a baby. Paul's wife was a City hot shot and Paul had given up his job to be a stay at home parent. We had started a friendship over coffee at the soft play parties that seemed to be a weekly occurrence at that stage of our life and this had developed into meeting up at the park on weekends or after school with the children when our partners were too busy with their own lives to come with us. I relished the friendship and loved being with someone who understood, to some extent, what my life felt like. One day, Paul suggested we "go for a drink", just the two of us. I naively agreed but once out it became apparent that Paul was interested in me in a completely different way. I had had a particularly hard week, worsened by a gut feeling that Steve had been seeing someone. I had no evidence of this, but I just had that strong feeling inside that he was. I had asked him outright, but he had denied it, outraged with my accusations and stormed out of the house. He had stayed out all night, just long enough to teach me a lesson, and returned the following day after I had text him to apologise. So, when Paul started to flirt with me and touch my hand over the pub table, I had been flattered. I didn't really fancy Paul, but

I enjoyed his company and I loved the attention and when he suggested we go away for a night, I foolishly agreed. Paul looked delighted and had immediately gone on his phone to book a hotel room. I was taken aback by how quickly this had escalated but I didn't back out. We had had a snog in an alleyway behind the pub that evening as we parted ways, and I had been horrified to realise there was absolutely no sexual chemistry between us. Paul, however, must have thought there was as he left looking like the cat that had got the cream. He had text me that night, telling me how excited he was to sleep with me. I had felt awful and was desperately trying to figure out the best way to let him down gently. Unfortunately, Paul's wife was a keen reader of other people's text messages and found out about Paul's sleepover plans. She had sent me a message condemning me to the circle of hell that is reserved for women who sleep with married men. She also found out who I was married to and sent him details of our "affair". Steve had, understandably, been furious and had packed his bags and left. I had had no choice but to do what women all over the world do, so I rolled up my sleeves and continued to be a busy, frazzled working mum doing it alone. Steve went to stay with a friend, meaning his interactions with his children were minimal. We were even more over-committed and over-indebted back then due to my brief maternity periods and Steve couldn't afford a place of his own. This meant that the children could never stay with him and he would "pop" in to get them, as and when suited him. During this period, Jen was my rock. She knew I never had any child care and was constantly skint, so she used to turn up in the evenings with wine and takeaway and pretend that she would rather be in with me and my kids watching films than out on the town. She even bravely babysat for the first time, so I could go to my work Christmas party, coming over early to do my tan and nails as she knew I couldn't afford or fit in a visit to the salon. Steve and I had been living apart for two months and Christmas was rapidly approaching. The children had been besides themselves with excitement when we woke to a dusting of white, fluffy snow one weekend and had begged to go out in it. I had called Steve, unsure of how I would cope with a sledge, two children, a toddler and a baby. He had made his way over and it had been lovely to see him as excited as the children as he played outside with them for hours. The initial anger at my planned infidelity had died away and Steve and I had started to speak to each other in friendly tones again. The subject, as we walked home with the children late that afternoon, turned to Christmas day. Neither Steve nor I wanted him to spend the day without the children, just "popping in" on Christmas morning like a visitor and I invited him to spend Christmas eve at the house. After hours working together as a team to assemble bikes and a tonne of plastic toys, we had shared a couple of bottles of wine together and ended up in bed. Steve had forgiven me and had moved back in that week.

As hard work as our relationship was, and at times as one-sided as it felt, I wasn't keen to go back to that place where Steve had to schedule in any time with his children. I had no idea whether my belief that Steve was cheating on me and was in fact away with another woman was even true. I tried to put it out of my head and eventually fell asleep, waking up early to meet up with Andy and Jen for our weekend away.

Andy picked me up and we drove on to Jen's. I hadn't seen Jen since our night out although we'd exchanged plenty of messages since. Andy and Jen had developed an easy friendship, despite only knowing each other through me, and we all chatted away in the car on our way to the spa hotel. Neither of them mentioned Steve until we were almost there, and I realised with embarrassment that I hadn't told them that Steve had in fact still made it to his "dirty weekend".

"He still went?" Jen asked, incredulous.

Andy seconded Jen's disgust at Steve's behaviour. Both of them clearly convinced that he was away with a woman and not his friend as he had insisted.

"Well," I said, my face flushing. "I'm hardly innocent, am I? I can't really say anything if he is."

"That's hardly the same!" Jen exclaimed.

"Do you think it's serious then?" I asked, nervously. They both looked at me in horror as if I had lost my mind.

"I can't see a young, single woman wanting Steve's baggage." Andy offered from the driver's seat.

"I don't know what I'll do if it's serious." I said, sadly. Jen squeezed my shoulder from her seat in the back of the car.

"Shall we talk about something else?" She suggested kindly and I nodded gratefully.

We arrived at the Spa hotel too early to check in, but we had planned for this to make the most of the facilities and Andy had pre-booked some treatments.

"You two are sharing, is that ok?" Andy asked.

"Of course," Jen said. "As long as you don't mind missing out on all the fun!"

Andy gave a smirk and I blushed again. Jen laughed at Andy's dirty mind and we made our way down to the changing rooms.

The facilities were beautiful. The marble floors were heated and immaculately clean. Jen dumped our towels on some loungers.

Jen slipped off her white fluffy robe to reveal a tiny blue bikini over her tanned, toned body. She stretched her arms, struggling to knot her short hair on top of her head.

"Shall I?" I offered as several strands came untucked. I took off my own robe, conscious that I looked pale and curvy compared to Jen in my black one piece. Jen leaned her head back into me as I expertly tucked her hair up into a quick bun. I stayed where I was standing, after I'd finished, and Jen kept her head leant back against my chest reading to me from the drinks menu. At that moment, Andy walked out to join us.

"You pair look cosy!" He joked.

I stepped back self-consciously. Jen laughed and frisbeed the menu at him.

"What time did you book my massage?" Jen asked him, spreading herself out on the lounger.

"12." Andy confirmed. "I'm going for a treatment now. I'll see you pair in a bit."

Andy wandered off and Jen and I settled into companionable silence on our loungers. We ordered drinks from a waitress and after we'd finished them, Jen got to her feet.

"Fancy a swim?" She asked.

I followed her to the pool. We submerged our whole bodies and swam several lengths in the warm water before lying back and floating blissfully side-by-side.

"This is so nice," Jen sighed. "This is how life should be."

I felt a wave of peace and contentment wash over me as I floated, letting the water relax my permanently tense body. I felt hyper-aware of my body; the heat from the room on my face and the weight of my blonde messy bun, now weighed down with water. I breathed deeply, filling my chest, and closed my eyes to savour this feeling of serenity.

“The jacuzzi is free.” Jen interrupted my silence, and I opened my eyes and rolled onto my front.

The only other people using the facilities this early were a group of women who had exited the jacuzzi and were making their way towards the pool. I nodded my agreement and Jen dove gracefully underneath the water, emerging in front of me so close my chest was touching her back. In one fluid movement, she had scooped me up onto her back and started swimming towards the steps. I laughed delighted that, despite being a thirty-seven-year-old high flier, Jen could be as playful as a child. I felt very conscious of my bare legs wrapped around my friend, the intimate feeling of skin against silky-smooth skin. As she approached the shallower end of the pool, Jen skilfully dived under the water, holding on tightly to my legs so I was forced to go under with her. She let go of me and we both surfaced at the same time, wiping water from our faces. We were facing each other now and I stepped forward to regain my balance at the same time Jen did causing us to bump into each other. I was still laughing at being dunked under, but as our bodies lightly skimmed each other’s, the laughter died away on my lips. Jen watched my reaction change curiously and I dropped my gaze quickly. Jen took my hand, still beneath the water’s surface, and I held my breath at her touch.

“Come on.” She tugged at me and turned her body away now and I had no choice but to follow her. She kept hold of my hand until we were stood on the poolside and I felt a jolt of disappointment when she let go. We both slipped into the jacuzzi and I wondered, not for the first time, why I was so awkward. I started up a conversation, asking her about her upcoming job move, and we chatted with such ease and familiarity that I questioned whether I created some of these “moments” in my head. Some more people had started to arrive now, and a couple slipped into the jacuzzi. Jen slid closer to me and we exchanged annoyed looks that our solitary soak had been ruined, as the couple whispered and giggled to each other. Both their hands were under the bubbles and Jen nudged me, giving me eyes to suggest they were behaving inappropriately under the water. I pulled a disgusted expression at Jen quickly, not wanting the couple to catch me. Jen slung an arm around me and started nuzzling my neck in imitation of the couple. I turned away, half horrified by her blatant mockery of the petting couple and half a little uneasy at the way her skin felt on my neck and shoulder. Jen saw this had attracted the attention of the couple, who stopped what they were doing, unsure whether they were being made fun of or whether we were just an amorous couple like them. Jen buried her face in my neck, and I felt her body moving slightly as she hid her face to laugh. I couldn’t help but smile at this and I pulled away slightly, taking her by the hand and starting to get out. This time it was me that kept hold of her hand, keen to keep up the illusion of us being a couple so that we didn’t offend our Jacuzzi companions. We stayed like this as we padded over to our loungers, bodies warm and wet, and I realised that I was feeling happier and more relaxed than I had in a long time.

Chapter 7

Andy eventually turned up after we'd both been for our treatments. He offered no explanation for how long he'd been and brushed us off when we asked. Jen and I exchanged glances but didn't push it any further.

We had a light lunch with a few glasses of wine, sat outside on the terrace under a wide canopy. Andy regaled us with stories about some of his "celebrity" patients. Jen raised concerns about confidentiality, but Andy waved away her comments arguing that we didn't count.

"What's with all the mystery?" I asked him, confidence boosted after a few drinks.

Andy smiled secretively and said nothing.

"I heard you blew Lucy off for some guy the other week," Jen chipped in. "She had to settle for second best!"

Before I could protest, Andy raised an eyebrow and deadpanned, "Who? Luke?"

"Oh God!" Jen groaned jokingly. "I must be third choice now!"

I shrieked a protest and grabbed Jen's hand, clutching it to my chest while proclaiming that she would always be my first choice. Andy frowned slightly and, self-consciously, I dropped her hand and took a large sip of my wine.

Andy's phone pinged, announcing a message, and we all turned our eyes to the phone. Andy swiftly picked it up and held it close to his chest as he read the message.

"Oh wow!" I whistled. "You really are keeping him a secret from us!"

"You didn't tell me you were still shagging Luke." Andy countered.

"I would have if you had asked!" I protested. "And anyway, I'm not anymore."

"Oh really?" Andy challenged. "When was the last time you saw him?"

"Ages ago." I said stubbornly.

"Be specific." Jen joined in, and I crossed my arms defensively at their attack.

"What the fuck do you see in him?" Andy asked, seeing I wasn't prepared to elaborate on dates and times.

As bossy as Andy could be, I knew his attack came from a place of concern for me. I had, during the early days of my friendship with Luke, developed quite intense feelings for him, being an intense kind of woman. Andy had had to talk me down from my infatuation. He'd explained to me that Luke's behaviour; a bombardment of intense contact, followed by periods of slow responses and frequent cancelling of plans created uncertainty. Andy cited studies that showed that uncertainty of whether someone liked you had an aphrodisiac effect, explaining that I only wanted Luke because I wasn't sure of whether he liked me. This seemed so silly, but I had googled what Andy had told me, and the more I had thought about it, the more it made sense. Andy had told me to visualise Luke fitting in to Steve's shoes. Could I see Luke on a family holiday? Bowling? At McDonalds? If I'd asked Luke, I imagined his words would have been "Lol. No.". Andy was right, in reality, we wouldn't work. So, as easily as that, I had turned off the emotional ties and made do with enjoying the attention. This didn't change the fact that I was still incredibly fond of Luke as a person. I wouldn't say aloud to Jen and Andy and risk their scorn, but I could see some of Luke's behaviour was a defence mechanism, and he was as vulnerable as me in some ways.

"I don't see anything in him." I said, irritated at both of my friends. "I told you both, I'm not seeing him. He's a friend though and he's actually a nice person. Stop trying to deflect from your big secret!"

"I'm going to have a nap." He said, rolling his eyes and getting up from the table. "I'll be back later."

Jen and I stared at each other, unsure whether he was annoyed with me or genuinely going for a nap.

"Shall I see if he's ok?" I asked with concern.

Jen shook her head, "He clearly wants to be alone to talk to whoever he's seeing. Just leave him."

We went back to lounge poolside, to make the most of our time away. The plan for the evening was to have dinner and drinks- nothing to lively as none of us could bear the thought of travelling back feeling hungover. I wondered if Andy would bother joining us as he hadn't seemed interested in spending any time with us since we'd got here. I was leafing through a trashy magazine when my phone vibrated with a message. It was Luke.

"You free tonight?"

I tapped out a reply, "Am at the spa with Jen & Andy. Won't be home til tomorrow night."

"I saw your Instagram pic (heart eyes emoji). I'm not far from there- been to my parents. I'll stop in on my way home (praying hands emoji)." He replied immediately.

I glanced over at Jen and bit my lip. I t would be nice to see him, especially being as Steve was living it up abroad massaging lotion into Charlotte's chest no doubt. Jen caught me side-eyeing her and peered over her book.

"Why are you looking at me like that?" She asked.

"Hmmm?" I tried to look innocent. "I was just thinking."

"Thinking what?"

"Thinking nothing." I shut my mouth and sat back, pretending to leaf through my magazine.

Jen wasn't giving up that easily. "Who are you texting?

Steve?"

I shook my head and sighed, picking my phone back up and staring at the message, "Luke."

Jen rolled her eyes, "You're going to see him again, aren't you?"

Her accusatory tone really irritated me. So, what if I bloody well was? My husband was going to leave me. I thought that I deserved a tiny bit of fun with an attractive man.

"If Steve can do what he wants, why shouldn't I?" I replied.

Jen said nothing and turned away. After a moment, she got to her feet.

"I think I'm going to have a sleep." She said, picking up her robe and her book.

She didn't look at me as she said it and I felt a pang of guilt for upsetting her. She walked off in the direction of the changing rooms and I hurriedly followed her.

"Jen?" I called as I caught up.

She stopped but didn't turn around, her hand resting on a tanned, curved hip sulkily.

"Are you pissed off with me?" I asked hesitantly.

Jen turned around slowly to face me, lips set tightly. "Why would I be pissed off with you?"

“Because I know you and Andy don’t like Luke.” I said, feeling as if there was maybe another reason that Jen had for not liking the relationship between Luke and me.

Jen shrugged but her eyes were dark and hard, “I don’t have an opinion on Luke. It’s your life.”

I tried again, not wanting Jen to walk away without us resolving this.

“You seem annoyed with me. Please don’t be!” I pleaded. “Steve has fucked off. Andy is being weird. Even my mother is mad that I ruined her weekend plans. I can’t bear the thought of you being upset with me.”

Jen sighed, “I’m not annoyed with you. You can carry on and ruin your life with Luke?”

“Ruin my life?” I was incredulous. “How is it ruining my life? What do you want me to do? God, Jen, there’s nothing going on between us!”

“Between “us”?” Jen’s hard expression changed to shock.

I was confused by her reaction, “Not you and me. With Luke, I meant. You and me, us, we’re fine. Right?”

Jen visibly softened. “Yeah, we are. I just don’t want to see you hurt.”

I stepped closer and wrapped my arms around her, squeezing her tightly against me. Her skin still smelled like the cocoa butter she used, in comparison to mine that just smelled of chlorine.

"I won't get hurt." I said, still hugging her. I felt her body relax and her arms reached up and hugged me back, signalling our feud was over.

"I am tired though, Luce," Jen said as we continued our walk into the changing room. "I'm going to have an hour."

We both showered and dressed quickly before going up to our room. Jen slid the key card in the lock and pushed the door open. The room was small and cosy, with a king size bed taking up the majority of the space. Jen dropped her bag on the floor, peeled off her clothes and climbed straight into the bed, moaning with delight as her head hit the pillow. I realised I was stood awkwardly staring at her, bag still in hand so I turned away and busied myself with unpacking my toiletry bag and clothes for that evening. I went into the bathroom and when I came out, Jen was fast asleep. I peeled my own clothes off, hanging them up carefully rather than leaving them where they fell like Jen had. I pulled on a t-shirt and a pair of shorts and climbed into the bed next to my sleeping friend. I closed my eyes to summon sleep, but fragments of conversations and memories circled my mind. I felt very aware that through a thin layer of cotton Jen lay sweetly sleeping next to me. Her skin dark and smooth against the white bed sheets. I shook this thought away, not letting any feelings come too close to the surface lest I feel obliged to analyse what I was thinking and mess my head up further. I realised, as I started to drift off that I hadn't replied to Luke's message, but I pushed this away too and let sleep wash over me freeing me from my own incessant thoughts.

Chapter 8

I dreamt that I was in my garden. A string of twinkly fairy lights criss-crossed the whole length of the lawn and patio, and the part of me that knew I was dreaming thought this looked beautiful and that I should see if they sold them in IKEA or online. I was sat on the low wall gazing at the lights and basking in the solitude of the twilight. A caterpillar wiggled over towards me and he was the size of my hand, but in my dream, this was a perfectly normal size, so I was unbothered by this. I peeled a leaf from the ornamental cabbage plant (again, conscious me wondered if these were actually edible in the real world or whether I was dream-murdering the abnormally-sized bug) and I reached over and fed the cartoon-like creature. He chomped away, looking happy and I continued to peel leaves for my new companion. I became aware of a hammering noise that grew louder and louder. Puzzled, I looked around the garden for the source and my caterpillar stopped munching, also looking disturbed by the interruption. I was pulled slowly from the dream, back into consciousness, and I felt Steve's arm lightly over my abdomen and our legs entwined lovingly. The hammering had followed me from my dream and I struggled to open my eyes as I realised I hadn't dreamt the noise. I realised simultaneously that my cuddle buddy wasn't Steve and that the noise was Andy knocking the door. Flustered, I untangled myself and stumbled groggily to the door.

"Bloody hell!" Andy huffed as I pulled the thick wooden door open. "I've been knocking for ages!"

"Ugh!" Jen groaned loudly from the bed. "We've been napping!"

"We need to go for food!" Andy exclaimed, clearly irritated. "Our reservation is for 7, and it's 6.30 now."

"Shall we just cancel and go somewhere else?" I asked, knowing there was no way we'd be ready even though the restaurant was one of three on site. Andy had been keen to eat here as it had rave reviews and was booked up months in advance. He "knew someone" who could get us a reservation, as was the world of my friends.

"Nope." Andy said firmly. "I'm going down to the bar. You pair have half an hour."

With that he left, slamming the door on his way out. Jen was sat up now in the bed, rubbing her eyes sleepily. The sheet held up against her chest and her long legs out over the side.

"I can't believe we slept so long!" She groaned. "I'm going to be wide awake all night."

We rushed to shower and dress, applying minimal makeup and having to be creative with a can of dry shampoo and some hair grips. We barely made it down to the bar in time and Andy was frowning over a gin and tonic as we hurried in.

We walked the short distance to the restaurant and Andy was surprisingly pleasant and chatty, complimenting us both on our outfits. Jen was dressed in a simple black silk top and wide legged white trousers. Her dark bob clipped back from her face slightly (as we hadn't been able to tame her hair with the dry shampoo). I had my curls pinned up on my head (same issue) and had settled on a high necked black dress with a white floral print and a swishy skirt that ended above the knee with a strappy pair of black heels. We ordered wine and chatted as we perused the menu.

"I'm so glad we got here in time," I said as I tried to choose. "I'm so hungry!"

"I know we said we weren't going to have a late one," Andy started tentatively as we all devoured our delicious meals. "But do you fancy going somewhere after here?"

"I do." I said, through a forkful of tender stem broccoli, wanting to keep the peace and for us all to get on being as we'd spent the day apart and/ or sleeping.

"Yeah, me too." Jen nodded, and I smiled at her gratefully. "I know somewhere good we can go. It's only a short taxi ride away, I think."

Andy looked put out by this. "I really want to go to Joia. I've been there before. It's lovely."

"Ok," Jen agreed quickly. "That's cool with me."

I let out the breath I didn't realise I'd been holding. Jen and Andy could both be stubborn and forceful, and I was surprised at how easy Jen had compromised. After we'd eaten, we finished off another bottle of wine before heading to Andy's bar. It was fashionably understated and there was a fierce-looking brunette on the door, who looked like she had come straight from a modelling job, but she nodded Andy in as though they were old friends, even flashing him a warm smile. Andy beckoned for us to follow him and led us to the back of the room and up a narrow staircase, through a stained-glass door and onto a gorgeous terrace. Another hard-faced-but-ridiculously-attractive member of staff was guarding the terrace and I prepared myself to be sent back downstairs with the ordinary people. Again, Andy was greeted and shown to a table despite the terrace being packed with gorgeous, young people. I glanced around and was surprised to recognise quite a few people. I frowned trying to work how that was possible when Andy elbowed me sharply.

"Stop staring, Lucy!"

"Oh, sorry." I quickly averted my eyes and looked back at my friends. "Some of these people look familiar."

Jen laughed, and Andy joined in.

He smiled at me affectionately. "There's quite a few actors here."

"Oh." I said, dumbly, suddenly feeling very self-conscious in my mumsy outfit.

Jen and Andy fell into an easy conversation and I fumbled with my phone. I had another message from Luke and I noticed that Steve had posted some pictures of his holiday on Instagram. I looked at Steve's pictures first and was surprised to see he genuinely was with Greg, his friend. There was a selfie of them on the golf course.

"Look!" I exclaimed, a little high pitched with excitement. I held out my phone to them. "He is with Greg, Not with a woman!"

Jen and Andy turned to me, stopped their conversation and peered at the image I had thrust in their faces.

"Or Greg is there as well." Jen said, and I pulled my phone away annoyed by her patronising tone.

Andy raised his eyebrows in an equally condescending manner and they both turned back to their conversation, rudely ignoring me. Probably comparing celebrities here that they'd both shagged, I thought pettily. I sent Steve a peace-offering message asking if he was having a nice time and then had second thoughts about putting all my eggs in one basket and text Luke to tell him I was out drinking and see what he was up to. I put my phone down on the table and knocked back my vodka cranberry in one. I glanced around for a waitress to order another and noticed a commotion out on the streets below.

A broad, muscular man dressed in a white shirt was exiting a car and walking towards the entrance to the bar. About 5 or 6 people wielding big, professional-looking cameras were rushing towards him from the pavement outside the bar. He only needed to cover a short distance, but the paparazzi were running alongside his brisk walk, snapping and calling out to him. His head was bent, and he moved quickly. I couldn't make out who he was or what they were saying. He disappeared from my view and I looked up to see Jen and Andy had been watching too.

"Who was that?" I asked them.

"John Taylor." Jen said, before casually adding. "I used to date his brother."

Andy looked surprised. "Really? Wow."

John Taylor was a British film actor who usually played James Bond type roles. He was in his forties and a massive sex symbol. Steve bore a slight resemblance to him and more than once some mothers at the school had commented on this much to my amusement and Steve's delight. I went back to trying to attract the attention of a waitress when John Taylor appeared at the entrance to the terrace. The model from downstairs had accompanied him and was scanning the room for an available table. Her eyes fell on our prime spot and I imagined that she was trying to figure out how to evict us nobodies without making a scene, so she could seat John quickly. John followed her gaze and Jen, seeing him looking in our direction, lifted a hand to him. John squinted slightly and then a smile lit up his face and he waved away the hostess and walked over. My mouth dropped as he moved over to our table, but I quickly regained control of my reaction before I could show my friends up.

“Hi Jen.” He said, bending down and kissing her cheek. Up close, he was absolutely beautiful, like a chiselled God and he smelled deliciously masculine. I checked my mouth was still closed. It was, but barely.

“Hi John.” Jen said in a throaty purr, which she hadn’t been speaking in until John appeared. “Lucy, Andy, this is John. John, these are my friends, Lucy and Andy.”

I managed a “hello” and sat back mesmerised as he exchanged pleasantries with Jen. Andy soon joined in their conversation and I remained quiet, feeling a little star struck and very ordinary in comparison to my sophisticated friends. John took a seat next to me and a waitress appeared immediately.

“What are you drinking?” John turned to me, and I felt myself blush as I answered.

John seemed like nice and down-to-earth. He kept trying to bring me into the conversation, but I was too nervous and could only give basic responses. I caught Jen frowning at me and I excused myself to look for the ladies’ room. Alone in a cubicle, I checked my phone. Steve was clearly ignoring me as my message was unread despite him being online within the last ten minutes. Luke had replied though and asked where I was. I typed back “Joia” and he responded straight away.

“That’s a bit pretentious for me. I’m about 10 mins away at the pub by my parents’ house. Fancy popping over? The house is free tonight (winking face emoji).”

I considered it but couldn't bear to look rude to my friends. I washed my hands and headed back to the table, determined to try to join in with the conversation. As I took my seat, delighted to see a more drinks on the table, Jen was saying she couldn't believe John was still single.

"I can't believe you are!" John responded, his dark eyes crinkling at the corners. Up close, I noticed he had a sprinkling of grey at his temples. This made him look even sexier and I mused on how unfair it was that men can rock grey hair and wrinkles whereas women are condemned to being non-sexual beings the minute they get either.

"Or me!" Andy joked, and they all laughed. John grinning widely at Andy across the table.

"Are you single too?" John turned to me and I felt my heart racing with nerves.

"No, Lucy's living the dream," Andy saw my panic and slid in to save me from social awkwardness. "She's got a husband, a boyfriend and four kids!"

John kindly ignored the first part. "Wow! Four children? You look amazing!"

"Thank you." I smiled shyly. John started asking questions about them and I answered easily, feeling more comfortable. At some point over the next half an hour, several more drinks were consumed, and I had my classic jigsaw memory. I never get black-out drunk where I forget everything, but I had often got to an inebriated state where

I lost several chunks of the night. Usually crucial parts.

I woke up back in my hotel room, fully dressed and feeling like my head was about to explode. A sixth sense urged me to go back to sleep until I was ready to cope with the memories and the fall out of the previous night, so after slugging the water and paracetamol that some angel had left on my bedside table, I fell back in to a groggy, unsettled sleep.

Chapter 9

I surfaced a few hours later. Blearily, I forced my eyes open and winced at the shaft of light streaming in through the open curtains. I was alone in the king-sized bed, still fully dressed, still feeling like absolute shit. I struggled to sit up and glanced at my phone, which was unhelpfully dead. I groped around for the charger and plugged it in before sitting back exhausted from that small movement. I took another swig of the warm, bottled water and wondered how long I could suppress the urge to pee. The answer to this was not very and so I stumbled into the bathroom. I returned to my spot in the bed, feeling a little more awake, and then with sheer horror, a vague timeline of the evening started to trickle back into my consciousness.

I remembered meeting John Taylor. I remembered drinking vodka like it was water. I remembered dancing with Andy and being aware that Jen had gone. I remembered this made me very emotional. I remembered seeing Jen with John and being even more emotional. There was an argument and I had left. Oh God, I had called Luke and I had met up with him. Everything else was a blur of vague images and darkness. I had no idea how I ended up here or where Jen was.

I realised that it was almost midday and we should have left the hotel by now. Jen's things were still strewn over the dressing table and so I could be quite sure that they hadn't abandoned me here to die of shame, alone. I turned my phone on and checked for messages from Andy, ignoring all other messages and missed calls, not ready to attempt to piece my night together just yet. Andy's most recent message said they had paid to keep the room on until 1pm, and they were at the spa. I decided to shower and get dressed before attempting to face whatever consequences were awaiting me. As I was leaning against the shower wall, twenty minutes later, pitifully weak under the jets of hot water, trying not to die of my hangover, I heard the door open and Andy calling out to me. I made a noise that passed as a greeting and forced myself out of the shower, into a towel and back into the bedroom.

"You look like shit, Lucy." Andy said cheerily.

I led back down in my towel and covered my face with my hands. "I feel like it."

Andy said nothing, clearly enjoying my suffering.

"I was a nightmare, wasn't I?" I asked finally.

"Yeah, a bit," Andy agreed. "I've come up because I need to warn you that Jen is furious with you."

"Oh God!" I wailed. "I don't remember everything."

"You accused her of shagging John. In front of him." Andy continued. "And then you stormed off. Jen followed you, but you jumped in a taxi. We thought you'd come back here but you didn't. You wouldn't answer your phone and when you eventually stumbled back here at 4am, Jen was on the verge of phoning the police. You threw up in your own bag and fell asleep."

"I am so sorry." I groaned. "I ruined your night. I am such a mess."

"I forgive you." Andy said good naturedly. "You were pretty funny up until the point you flew off the handle at Jen and legged it. I knew you had been texting Luke, so I wasn't that worried about you."

"I went to his parents' house." I told Andy, feeling ashamed.

"That's nice," Andy deadpanned. "Meeting the new in-laws already. With Steve not even cold in his grave."

I managed a bitter laugh and reached for my clothes. "Right, how much of an apology does Jen need?"

"A fucking huge one." Andy laughed and turned to leave. "Pack your stuff up and if you need to be sick, do it now. If you're sick in my car, you're walking home."

Jen appeared ten minutes later, with a face like thunder.

"Are we ok?" I asked in a small voice.

"Fine." Jen replied, in a tone that indicated we were clearly not.

I dropped the last of my belongings into my overnight bag and turned to face her.

"I am so sorry, Jen," I apologised. "I was an absolute dick."

“Yeah, you were.” She nodded stonily.

“Did I ruin things with John?” I asked, not wanting to mention it but knowing I needed to address the issue.

“John?” Jen spat out, her tone now furious. “I fucking told you last night, there’s nothing between us.”

“I don’t remember, Jen,” I said, my eyes filling with tears. “I just know I kicked off at you and left.”

“John is a friend.” Jen said firmly but her voice softening. “I’m really hurt that you had a go at me for “going off” with him and then you just fucked off! I was literally smoking on the terrace and buying a round of drinks- you made out like we were gone for hours.”

“Oh.” In my head, I remembered that it had felt like hours. “I’m sorry. And I’m sorry I just left.”

“I wish you had told me where you were going.” Jen said. “I was really worried.”

“I know.” I felt ashamed of myself. “I really am so sorry.”

Jen moved around the room in silence packing up her own things. She stopped what she was doing and sat down on the bed next to me. I held out my hand to her and I was relieved when she took it in her own.

“I’m just so sorry I ruined everything.” I said honestly.

“You are forgiven.” She replied finally, caressing my hand

with her long fingers. “On one condition.”

“Anything.” I promised gratefully.

“Stop being a doormat to that arsehole.” She said firmly.

“Steve?” I asked confused.

“I meant the other one,” Jen said, letting my hand go and getting up. “But any idiot really.”

“Ok.” I said not wanting to press the issue. Jen continued packing up her clothes and I flicked through my messages. I had a timeline of events through the back and forth exchange to Luke, and I cringed as little bits of memories came back to me as I read them. I had gone over his just for sex and practically demanded a taxi when it was over. He hadn’t messaged me to see if I was home safe so there was a strong chance I’d pissed him off at some point too. Steve had eventually replied to my text from the previous night. I clicked on it to read his response.

“Lovely thanks, babe. See you Sunday x”

He’d even signed off with a kiss after our bust up. That was typical of Steve though. We often had huge arguments and a few days later he would just accept my peace offering as if nothing had happened. I felt a little guilty now that I’d jumped so quickly to the assumption that he was cheating on me and had demanded he cancel a weekend with Greg. Putting myself in his shoes, I could see how unreasonable I may have come across as.

I typed out a quick reply, "Can't wait to see you x".

Jen emerged from the bathroom and glance at my phone in my hands before looking away.

"You ready?" She asked.

We made our way down to the car and were back in London a few hours later after a quiet, subdued journey home. I made my way into the house, anxious to see my children but with a mild sense of dread knowing my mother would be there waiting for me. Emily had already warned me that she had insisted that Emily and Shaun leave after lunch to ensure they were back in Wales at a reasonable time. Emily had tried to protest that she was happy to wait for me but my mother, a real force to be reckoned with, had waved away Emily's insistence and assured her that she would look after my brood.

The front door was unlocked, and I dumped my bag by the stairs. A clattering of paws came skidding across the wooden floorboards as Hermione, closely followed by Ron, came to greet me. My mother glanced up from Price Drop TV with a perfunctory "Hello Lucy".

She got slowly to her feet, giving the impression that she was a little old lady not a fit, athletic 60-year-old who ran more miles every week than Steve and I combined. She gathered up her handbag and her trademark Hermes scarf, as I stood awkwardly in the doorway.

"Were the kids ok?" I asked, wondering if she'd sedated

them as I couldn't hear their usual racket from upstairs.

"Fine," She nodded. "Graham has just taken them to that burger place. I took the dogs out instead. You know I can't bear that food."

I nodded dumbly. I was dying to kick off my shoes and sprawl on my sofa. Preferably with some cuddles from my children. I sent up a silent prayer that Graham would be back soon, so my mother would leave.

"The house is a mess." My mother said, filling any silence with criticism as she tended to. The dining table was covered in a Lego castle and some homework. The floorboards always showed up any paw prints/ foot prints in sunlight. It looked fine to me. I shrugged and wandered off into the kitchen to check if there was any more evidence of my domestic failure. The kitchen looked fine. I'd cleaned it Friday before Emily came, and it looked exactly the same. I volunteered this information to my mother.

"Oh, I know Emily kept it clean!" My mother huffed. "But look at those tiles!"

I rolled my eyes and put the kettle on. "Thanks for looking after them. Do you want a coffee?"

"No thank you." My mother sniffed, disgruntled that I hadn't responded to her critique of the cleanliness of my house. "Graham will be back shortly."

I really had nothing to say to my mother when I was

hungover and irritated. I felt a surge of relief when Graham finally turned up; my children spilling excitedly out of the car. I hugged them all to me tightly and waved off my mother before shepherding them all back into the house.

"Mummy!" Matilda wrapped her arms tightly around my legs. "Please don't leave us ever again!"

"Didn't you have fun with Auntie Emily?" I asked surprised.

"Yes of course," She lisped. "But you should have been here too. I had to sleep with Essie, didn't I, Es? Because I missed you so much."

"Yeah, she did." Esther nodded, clearly annoyed by this.

"And I missed you, Mum." Leo volunteered.

They trailed me to the sofa, even Esther and George, and bombarded me with stories of their weekend and tales they needed to tell on each other. I used all my influencing and negotiating skills to get them to agree on a film to put on and we all squished up on the sofas for the afternoon in our pyjamas. One film led to a movie marathon and I ordered takeaway for our dinner, feeling only slightly guilty that they'd had McDonald's followed by Papa John's in the same day. It was late by the time I realised that I hadn't timed a shopping delivery and we were out of everything that was needed for the kids' breakfast and school lunches. The supermarket would be shut now, and I couldn't bear the thought of having to get the kids dressed and out to the 24-hour petrol station. I checked the flight times online to see what time the flight back from Portugal was this evening, hoping Steve would pick up some bits on his way home. There was nothing showing on arrivals from Gatwick. I checked Heathrow. Nothing. He wouldn't fly from Luton, would he? I scanned scheduled arrivals- nothing. I text him a quick list, assuming he'd maybe arrived already in which case he'd be home soon. It was gone 8pm now, and I summoned up all my strength to oversee some quick showers before hustling them off to bed. Exhausted, I apologised to the dogs for not walking them and tucked myself up in bed to await my husband and my shopping delivery. I was craving a diet coke and a bar of Dairy Milk and had added these to the list. I sat up, flicking through my phone, when Matilda appeared in the doorway, thumb planted firmly in her mouth and carrying an arm load of soft toys. My heart melted a little and I moved over to indicate she could jump in with me. She messed about tucking all her toys in and by the time she had fallen asleep, I was crammed right to the edge of the bed. I could hear some noises from the other children's bedrooms, so I slipped out of bed and did my nightly rounds, turning off iPads and doling out kisses. I untucked Matilda's toys and propped them up against the bedside table, but couldn't bear to move her back to her own bed even though I knew Steve would be annoyed when he came in. He still hadn't replied to my text and I started to feel agitated. I read a few chapters of my book while I waited but by 10pm I decided to phone him. He answered straight away, and I could hear a noise in the background like he was at the pub.

"Hey," I whispered, trying not to wake my daughter. "Where are you?"

"Can't hear you, babe." He practically shouted in my ear. "I'm just stopped off with Greg for one. Football is on."

"Are you coming home?" I asked, immediately annoyed that he must have been back for a few hours and coming home to his family hadn't crossed his mind.

"Yeah, in a bit." He replied. "What do you want?"

"I sent you a list." I said, crossly shutting my book now it was clear I wouldn't be waiting up for him.

"Ok, I'll see if I pass a shop." He said casually.

"You won't "pass" a shop," I told him, my annoyance quickly growing into anger. "There's nothing here for the kids in the morning."

"You can nip out in the morning." Steve said, not reacting to my tone.

I couldn't even begin to explain how inconvenient this would be, so I just ended the call, turned my phone on to silent and tried to fall asleep. Just as I was dropping off, the sound of heavy footsteps startled me awake before my bedroom light flew on announcing Steve's arrival.

"You're in bed early." Steve said, flinging his own bag down on the floor.

"Have you had a nice weekend?" I asked, my tone more sarcastic than I meant to be.

Steve turned his head sharply at my tone and a flash of something like guilt crossed his eyes before he looked away. "Yeah, good. You?"

"Yeah, good." I nodded, remembering that I had equal, if not more, reason to feel guilty.

"Are you moving her?" Steve nodded at our sleeping child. "She's too wriggly."

"Aw leave her," I shook my head protectively. "She slept with Esther last night because she missed us."

Technically she'd only said she missed me, but I didn't want to be petty.

"She can go on your side." Steve said, back in full sulk mode. I pulled my little princess over on to my pillow wordlessly and turned my back to him. Steve huffed and puffed a bit more before he reached for the remote control for the TV. I gritted my teeth. Was he fucking seriously going to put the TV on?

"Steve!" I hissed, from between gritted teeth. "Don't put the TV on. You could have gone to the bloody shop if you're this awake."

"You could have gone to the shop," He countered like a petulant child. "You're the one who wants stuff!"

“I want fucking bread and coco pops, do I?” I sat up now, furious.

“They were on your list!” He spat back, ignoring my earlier request and flicking the TV on so the whole room was lit up by the fucking huge screen he had mounted on the wall even though I didn’t want a TV in here.

“My list? Steve!” I genuinely couldn’t believe the audacity of him. “They’re your fucking kids!”

He shook his head and stared at the TV, ignoring me. His phone lit up with a message and he glanced at it before clearing the notification. The same flash of guilt passed over his face as I thought I’d seen earlier.

“Who’s that?” I asked, blood boiling now and my anger building up to rage. He continued to ignore me, and the words flew out of my mouth before I could stop them. “You can just fuck off and go and fucking live with Charlotte if that’s what you fucking want!”

Steve tensed at my words and I watched the telling sign of his jaw harden. He remained facing forward staring at the screen and that told me everything I needed to know. He could easily have posted an old photo of him and Greg, I realised feeling foolish. He’d been on about a hundred golf weekends with Greg and I knew for a fact Greg was a notorious cheat, who Steve had openly covered for many times in the past, laughing off my disgust at his friend as prudish.

"Do you hear yourself?" Steve finally responded, his voice icy cold. "You're crazy."

"You were away with Greg, were you?" I asked, sitting up in bed and struggling to keep my voice level so I didn't disturb Matilda. "There was nobody else with you?"

"No." Steve frowned at me. "You're the one with dodgy texts off men, not me. Don't try to turn this shit on me."

I was too upset to feel remotely guilty, even though I was aware there was truth in what he was saying. "Can I see your phone?"

As soon as the words were out of my mouth, I regretted them. I didn't want to be "that wife". The accusatory psycho that didn't let their husband live any form of social life for fear that they'd find a better offer. The bitter, jealous woman that Steve had always praised me for not being. Steve looked at me with sheer disgust.

"What is wrong with you?" He said finally, shaking his head slowly as if in disbelief. "You're unbearable to live with. Constantly pushing me away."

"Me?!" I exclaimed incredulous that he was turning this on me. "How can I push you away when you're never here?"

"Alright, Mother-of-the-year!" He spat back. "Where were you this weekend? Not making fucking arts and crafts with your kids, that's for sure! What did you get up to? Shagging all the branch staff? Or the dads from the school?"

Any discussion I wanted to have about my suspicions that Steve was having a relationship with a colleague was pointless now.

"You know I wasn't." I said hurt at his accusations and insults.

"I don't though," Steve said turning away from me. "You started this. I honestly don't know how much longer I can put up with the shit you give me."

Steve flicked off the TV and turned his back to me. He was breathing deeply within minutes.

By now, my body was trembling with rage. I waited for the adrenaline to drain away, unused, and watched every hour tick away on the clock as my mind did its favourite thing of running through far-fetched scenarios as I imagined life without Steve. I finally fell asleep at about 3am. When I woke, groggy and confused, it was 6.30am and Steve was gone. I got up exhausted and drained, feeling the familiar heaviness clouding me again as I tried desperately to feel ready to tackle the week ahead alone. Starting with figuring out what to feed my children from my empty cupboards.

Chapter 10

The week rolled by in a blur of work, end of term school events and passive aggressive silence from my husband. I hadn't spoken to Andy or Jen either which was rare, but I was still too conscious of the tension from the weekend (with Jen) and the secretiveness (Andy) to reach out to either of them.

Work was an absolute nightmare. I'd been off sick the previous week, so Roger turned up the usual tones of disappointment in everything I did from the standard "subtle" to "high". I was exhausted from a combination of walking on eggshells whenever Steve was home, keeping up with the flurry of activity and the high emotions of the children now the end of term was approaching and the constant nagging of my anxiety, which was at record levels.

A combination of delays on my line, a forgotten violin which meant we had to turn around and go back to the house, a dog that had thrown up and a very public meltdown outside the school (Leo, not me) meant that I walked into work over thirty minutes late on the Friday. I rushed in throwing apologies to the other staff and dumped my handbag in the back office, typing in my log on details quickly to check my appointments for the day. Roger appeared out of nowhere like The Ghost of Careers Past and loomed over me. I kept my head bent over the PC, hoping that if I ignored him he would disappear.

He cleared his throat and I cringed at the sound of the rattle of phlegm.

“You’ve missed an appointment.” He told me, just as it flashed up as overdue on my screen.

Ah, fuck! I bloody well had too. I never accepted early morning appointments just because things always came up or I was usually covering on the tills for one of the other staff who were prone to “running late”.

“Sorry.” I said. “I’ve had a nightmare morning-“

“Hmmm.” He interrupted me. “Not very professional, is it?”

“No.” I said dumbly. “Who covered?”

“There was nobody available.” He said. “I told Lois to send the customer away with apologies.”

“Couldn’t you have seen her?” I asked. This would have been the logical explanation. The company made a huge song and dance about “all hands on deck” to cover for busy periods and sickness. Roger also regularly parroted this ethos at us whenever he declined leave requests for school events, medical appointments and holidays.

“I’m extremely busy.” Roger said, slightly outraged at the concept of him interacting with the unwashed public/ our customers. “I’ve been picking up work due to your absence as well you know.”

“Right.” I said, chastised.

"I will be documenting this," Roger continued. "These are not the values and behaviours we expect from someone who is meant to be a role model to the other staff. I've also spoke to HR about this."

He'd had time to speak to HR but not time to conduct a half hour financial review with a customer. Nice.

"Sorry." I repeated, just wanting him gone now so I could quietly die of the shame of my dressing down.

"I'm really not sure if this is the right role for you," He said, my humiliation not quite completed. "We'll be welcoming new staff to the branch soon and one of those will be stepping back from her role as assistant manager to come here. How do you think she will feel? Knowing she offers a higher standard of work and behaviours?"

Was he fucking kidding me? Was this a threat to demote me? I was pretty sure he couldn't do that.

"Oh." I said, rising to the bait. "The jobs are official now, are they?"

Roger frowned at me. "Not yet. If word gets out, I will be holding you accountable."

Of course you fucking will, I fumed inwardly. I said nothing and pressed print, locked my workstation and collected my calendar from the printer.

I went to my next appointment, popping my head through the door to the row of cashiers to ask Lois to try to get her lunch break at the same time as me. I usually brought food with me as we were so short staffed I would either end up covering breaks or I had a list of errands I needed to do. Lois gave me a nod and I felt mildly happier, knowing I could have a rant and getting some of the last week's frustrations off my chest.

My first appointment went off without a hitch, and I scored a great loan rate for refinancing for a lovely young couple, who were clearly struggling under the weight of life's expenses. I ran over slightly for my next appointment and I groaned inwardly when I recognised the customer as a notoriously difficult man, who fancied himself as a bit of a financial expert, double-checking everything and determined to prove that somehow the bank was ripping him off with his various products. Despite his intellectual superiority over us mere bank staff and our combined incompetence and criminal behaviour, he continued to bank with us and regularly review his products. He was probably blacklisted from all the other High Street banks because he was such a pain in the arse.

"Good morning, Mr Davey," I turned up my professional smile a notch. "Sorry for keeping you."

"Wasting my time as well as my money," He tutted. "I should start charging you."

I smiled in what I hoped was an apologetic manner and led the way to the interview room that I'd been allocated. I logged into the work station and sat back in my chair, placing my hands on the table in what I hoped was an open gesture.

“So what can we do for you today?” I said pleasantly.

“I told all this to the girl that I spoke to when I booked the appointment.” He replied. “Why should I waste my time and go through this again?”

“I’m awfully sorry, Mr Davey,” I said flicking through the notes. “It’s just been booked in as a general review.”

He moaned on and on about the dreadful staff and customer service, wasting ten minutes of the appointment. I looked pointedly at my watch.

“Mr Davey,” I interrupted him, not wanting to but knowing if I didn’t get some actual work done now he would be leaving this appointment with nothing achieved or I would be ridiculously late for my next appointment which would throw my whole day out of sync. “I am sorry for the inconvenience you’ve experienced, however now you are here, shall we look at which products were concerning you?”

“So now you’re going to interrupt me?” He asked, looking disgusted.

“No, Mr Davey,” I tried to look apologetic. “I’m just keen that we get this resolved for you as efficiently as possible.”

“Ha!” He almost shouted triumphantly. “Efficient! That’ll be a first. It’s an absolute disgrace the way this bank is run.”

I gave up trying and let him rant on about my incompetence until he had exhausted the subject.

"I did ask to only have my appointments with the manager." He continued. "You are not the manager, are you?"

"I'm the assistant manager." I told him.

"I asked if you were the manager." He repeated, pompously. "It's a yes or no question. Do you understand that?"

"Mr Davey," I was getting seriously annoyed now. He had wasted nearly half of his appointment and I wasn't getting grief off the rest of my customers and missing lunch for this idiot. "We're not really getting anywhere. I can either talk you through your current saving products and the range that we have available or I can terminate this appointment and reschedule it for when you're ready to actually discuss what we're here to talk about."

I watched, with equal parts horror and fascination, as Mr Davey's face turned a bright puce colour. His nostrils flared in outrage at my words and I wondered if this would be the day that I received a punch in the face from a customer.

"Get me your manager. Now!" He demanded, standing up and towering over the table between us. I felt my own face drain of colour.

"Mr Davey," I tried to keep my tone calm despite trembling inside. "I was simply suggesting that if you didn't want to utilise the allocated time to review the available products then maybe now wasn't a great time for us to discuss this. You seem unhappy with our service, and I understand that some things can be frustrating-"

"No!" He roared. "You are frustrating! Manager! Now!"

Through the window in the door, I could see my colleagues' heads turning in this direction as well as a few customers. I tried again to placate him, but he was simmering with rage and I left the room, closing the door firmly behind me.

Lois hustled over. "Are you ok?"

"It's Mr Davey," I told her in hushed tones. "He kicked off the minute he got here and now he's demanding to see Roger. He's going to complain about me."

My voice wobbled a little and Lois guided me away from the shop floor to give us privacy.

"Where's Roger?" I asked nervously.

"Oh, Luce, he would go mad if you land Mr Davey in his lap!" Lois said, her face draining of colour with worry. "He can't handle normal customers let alone that..." I thought she was going to swear for a moment which would have been very unlike Lois, but she stuttered for a moment before finishing her sentence. "Horrid man."

The door to the staff room opened and we both turned towards it in slow motion. My heart was in my throat now.

"You look like you've seen a ghost!" Luke walked out of the staff room and surveyed our faces.

"Oh thank goodness!" Lois let out a sigh of relief. "We're looking for Roger."

I ignored Luke; my mind unable to multitask and perform civilities while I was in full panic mode. Luke frowned at my terrified expression and stepped closer, putting a hand gently on my arm.

"Roger is on a call with his boss in the glass office." Luke said. "It's important as he's just cancelled a mortgage appointment with me to take this call. What's the matter?"

Lois looked at me for permission and I nodded my consent; half-relieved that Roger was occupied and half-horrified of having to go back and deal with Mr Davey alone. Lois explained what had happened.

"Ah, Mr Davey," Luke nodded knowingly. "He's awful. I'll deal with him."

"You can't!" I exclaimed, grabbing Luke's arm to stop him. "He's demanding to see Roger."

"I'll tell him Roger's not here and I'm acting manager." Luke shrugged and started off again.

I had to practically jog to catch up with Luke's long strides.

"Luke!" I forcibly turned him to face me. "Seriously, please don't. It's not worth the shit you'll get."

"Lucy," He pulled me against his chest and placed his lips gently on top of my head. "We're all losing our jobs anyway. I know I'm not getting one, so I don't give a shit about what Roger says. If anything, he should thank me for dealing with it for him."

He released me as quickly as he had embraced me and made for the small bank of interview rooms. Lois stared at me in shock. I realised how that must have looked and I blushed furiously.

"What shall I do, Lo?" I asked mortified.

"Just get on with your appointments," She said, looking as worried as I felt. "I think Luke will deal with it."

I did as I was told, although I was barely able to concentrate as I watched through the window in the door. I eventually saw Luke walk out with Mr Davey, stopping to shake his hand before he left. Luke turned towards my interview room after Mr Davey had left and gave me a cheeky thumbs up and a wink. I jumped on the first excuse to leave the room, feigning the need to check a detail on a change to the way credit records were updated. I rushed out towards the staffroom hoping that I hadn't missed Luke and found myself up against his chest for the second time that day.

"Woah, you're keen!" He joked, grabbing hold of my wrists and taking a step back.

I was still too pent up to laugh. "Everything sorted?"

“Yes, of course,” He smiled. “He’s such a chauvinistic dickhead though.”

“Ugh, I know!” I agreed. “Thank you so much. I’ve already had shit off Roger today. I couldn’t cope with anymore.”

“You’re welcome, sweetheart,” He gave me that lazy, sexy smile. “I’m heading back to my branch now that Roger’s wasted my time by being a no show. You can buy me a drink after work to say thank you.”

I couldn’t help but smile back at him. “If I had a babysitter, I would.”

“Next week then?” He said, slipping his grip from my wrist to my hand. “Give you chance to sort something? “

“Ok.” I nodded. “I’ll text you.”

Luke gave me another smile and left. I rushed back to my customer grateful for Luke’s intervention. He was right about one thing; in all reality he wouldn’t have a job when the decisions were finalised. That sucked. The way the culture had been over the last few years, he was probably better off out of it. A lump sum pay-off and the chance to actually work for a human being would be nice. The deadline for redundancy was today. I felt overcome by an urge to put my name forward. Screw what Steve wanted. I was so miserable in this job and I knew it would be even worse when Leanne was here with her eye on my role and her hand on Roger’s crotch. There would be days when I was late to work because I was juggling an actual life, and there would be days when customers kicked off and complained for no reason. That wasn't going away, and I had a feeling that every little thing I did would be under the microscope for the whole time Roger was at the helm. I mulled this over for the rest of my day, receiving some strange looks from customers as I got muddled and distracted on more than one occasion.

I confided in Lois over lunch and her eyes widened.

"Wow, really?" She seemed more surprised than I had expected. "What has Steve said?"

"I think we're going to break up, to be honest." I told her, dropping my eyes to my lap, not wanting to see any pity in her eyes.

"Lucy!" Lois looked shocked. "I had no idea!"

I shrugged. "It is what it is, Lo. I'm going to fill that form in and send it off now before I change my mind."

Lois, flustered, tried to talk me out of it but something had clicked inside me and I knew I was going to do it. Not only was I going to do it, but I knew, in my heart, the bank would be happy to lose me. But not as happy as I would be to be free. I rushed to fill the form in and emailed it to Roger and the HR rep, as requested. Roger sent a short email confirming receipt, not even bothering to ask what had prompted my change of heart at the eleventh hour. I left work at closing time and felt like a weight had been lifted from my shoulders. I strode confidently towards my train, shoulders back and head held high. My phone in my hand reminded me that I should share my news with someone. Not Steve, obviously. I didn't think Andy or Jen would be as delighted as me, but I knew someone who would. I fired off a text to Luke and he responded straight away. A row of celebration emojis and a "WELL DONE BABE. PROUD OF YOU". I beamed from ear to ear as I travelled to the school.

"You look happy, Mum." George said as we walked home together.

"I am." I grinned. "Let's get Esther and go out to celebrate."

"Is Dad coming?" Leo asked, peering up at me.

"I hope not," George quipped. "I want to eat before midnight."

The moment I had sent that email to Roger a huge portion of my anxiety felt like it had evaporated. I felt trepidation at the thought of telling Steve what I had done. Our relationship was currently at its most rocky and I had a feeling that my reckless move may tip the balance and send it crashing down irreparably. The sensible part of me rolled this risk around and around my mind but there was no regret or fear, just excitement at the prospect of a change and a fresh start. For my job and my relationship.

Chapter 11

The subject of my redundancy application finally came up on Sunday. Steve had been predictably late home Friday, spent Saturday ferrying the children around football and hockey matches before he went out for "a few drinks with the boys". I woke up Sunday morning to an empty bed and a 3am text saying he couldn't get a taxi and was staying at Greg's. I very much doubted this was true and wondered whether he had gone out with the intention of spending the whole night with Charlotte.

I pottered around before I readied the children for their swimming lessons; more annoyed that Steve's absence meant I had to drag them all along rather than just the two who had lessons. This meant I had to endure not just two hours sweating poolside but sulking older children and spend a fortune in spare change from the vending machines to bribe their good behaviour. As I was just getting to "losing my shit" levels of impatience with the children, Steve rocked up.

"Hi!" He called cheerily, not looking like he'd been out drinking all night.

"Yes!" George shouted triumphantly. "Dad's home! Can we stay here now?"

I nodded at George but purposely avoided looking in Steve's direction.

"I'm jumping in the shower." Steve said, kicking off his

shoes and walking upstairs.

George dived back on to the sofa and turned his Xbox game back on. Leo and Matilda loitered by the door, swinging their swimming bags.

"Two minutes!" I called to my obedient youngest. "I'll just get my purse."

I dashed up the stairs and into my room to retrieve my handbag. I could hear the water blasting in the en-suite and Steve's clothes were kicked off in a pile on the floor. I stepped over them in irritation and catch sight of his phone tossed casually onto the bed. The screen was lit up showing he had just received a notification. I picked up the phone; something I wouldn't usually do but the memory of him doing the same to me was still fresh in my mind. The screen showed he had, indeed, received a message. From Charlotte. I glanced at the closed bathroom door and again at my bedside clock. Before I realised what I was doing, I had swiftly pocketed the phone and was back down the stairs and strapping my children into the car.

While my youngest child practised her doggy paddle, I bought an hour's silence from my younger son with a handful of coins and full, unrestricted access to YouTube via my own phone. I had cunningly kept enough coins back to be able to offer Matilda the same deal when it was time for them to switch places. I only had to try twice before I cracked Steve's passcode and I mentally high-fived myself on my detective skills. I scrolled through his thread of messages and read his relationship with Charlotte play out until the current day. He had indeed taken her to Portugal. Greg had coincidentally been out there with his brother-in-law, so it was the perfect cover. He had stayed over hers last night after they had been out for a meal. Their most recent communication was this morning, Steve's last message sent moments before he must have started his shower.

Steve: Didn't want to leave!

Charlotte: Come back then.

Steve: I wish :(Tuesday?

Charlotte had replied with an affirmative, but Steve would never know this, as I had his phone and I wasn't sure whether I was going to give it back. I stared at the messages, reading and re-reading them. I flicked through the rest of his private correspondence noting that he also had a Kelly and a Sam that he was exchanging occasional flirty messages with. I wondered if Charlotte knew this or she thought she was on to a good thing with lovely, unhappily married Steve. I opened Steve's Instagram app and searched for Charlotte's profile. In all fairness to Steve, she was attractive, I thought to myself, feeling oddly detached from the situation. The latest picture she'd posted was a full length shot; body angled slightly away from the camera as if the photographer had caught her unaware (yeah, alright!) as she stood barefoot in a tiny black bikini looking out at impossibly white sand and a turquoise ocean.

Her figure was predictably fantastic; long slim legs and a high, round bum barely covered by the scrap of bikini. Her blonde hair was loose and flowing over her shoulders. I noticed Steve had 'liked' the picture and from the date, he had probably taken it too. I waited for the stab of rage or jealousy, but it didn't come. I felt nothing except tired. Tired of living like this.

I put the phone away. I didn't like invading his privacy like this. I didn't want to be in a relationship where I did things like this. I knew I needed to have this conversation with him. My first concern was not that I was about to lose my marriage but that I would have to have this conversation with him at some point. I couldn't keep burying my head in the sand. I spent the rest of the swimming lesson alternating between taking an interest in my son swimming and chatting to my daughter.

I arrived back at the house, debating whether to broach the subject with Steve or leave it to a more suitable time when George raced to the door waving a colourful piece of card and looking agitated.

"What's the matter?" I asked him, dumping the bags of wet towels and swimwear in the kitchen.

"Harvey's party!" He exclaimed. "Quick, Mum! We're going to be late!"

Shit! I knew I'd forgotten something. I took the invitation from his hand, scanning the details. Great. I needed to be at the same bloody leisure centre I'd just left for George to play indoor football. I rummaged in the cupboard for a spare birthday card, that I stockpiled for this exact reason, and found a crumpled £10 note at the bottom of my purse. Present sorted.

"Right, shoes on! Let's go!" I called to George.

"Where are you going?" Steve looked up from the sofa, where he was flicking through the sports channels.

"Mum forgot I had a party." George told him disloyally.

Steve gave George a little look as if to say "typical Mum" and turned back to the TV.

I ignored him and called to the others. "Leo, Matilda! I'm taking George to a party. Are you coming or staying here?"

"Staying here!" They both chorused from upstairs.

Steve turned back around. "Can't you take them? I was going to go to the gym for an hour?"

"No." I replied bluntly. "I can't."

I didn't bother telling Steve I'd be straight back as I didn't need to stay to supervise George. If it messed up his selfish life, all the better. As soon as I'd dropped George off, I decided I couldn't bear to go back home and so I resorted to a failsafe coping technique and sent Luke a message, asking him what he was up to. I loitered in the car park waiting for a response but when my phone pinged with a notification, it was a message from Jen.

We hadn't spoken properly since the Spa weekend.

"Hey Lucy. I've got a date for New York. Only a month and I'm off! Hope you and the kids are ok. X x" The message read.

I felt a pang of happiness that she'd still wanted to share this with me.

I replied straight away, "Wow- so soon! Fancy a coffee soon?"

She texted back straight away "Now?" and I calculated that I had plenty of time to get there and back to the local Pizza Hut that George and his friends were heading to after football, so I drove over to Jen's.

We chatted easily, and I offered to come over in the week and help her to start to pack up. She knew someone in work who would rent her flat while she was away and so wanted to get all her personal belongings in storage at her Gran's. I realised the time was pushing on and I'd have to move quickly to get back in time for George.

"Awww!" Jen said, pretending to pout when I said I needed to leave. "All I've done is talk about me- I haven't heard how you're doing!"

"Exactly the same," I waved dismissively not wanting to moan on about Steve and his cheating as I always did and then remembered. "Oh actually, there is something! I completed a preference form for voluntary redundancy."

"Oh my God, Lucy!" Jen's mouth dropped. "Do you think you'll get it?"

"I don't know," I shrugged. "Roger thinks I'm a twat, so probably. I really have to go, or I'll be late to get George and I was bloody late dropping him in the first place."

Jen grabbed her shoes. "I'll come! Just to pick George up so you can tell me."

I was pleasantly surprised by how much interest Jen was showing in my life, much more than my own husband ever did. I told her everything on the way; from how I'd been feeling in work to the latest with Steve.

"What are you going to do if you get redundancy?" Jen asked excitedly.

"I don't know," I said honestly. "But I do know I'll look for something that I actually want to do- not just something that pays the bills."

"You should!" Jen agreed. "You're so clever and good with people- you could do anything."

I flushed and waved away her compliment. "Even if I don't get it, I'm definitely going to start looking for another job. It's draining my soul at the bank."

"And what about the other thing?" Jen asked, less enthusiastically this time.

"Steve?" I asked.

She nodded, and I sighed. I knew I was probably having some kind of weird delayed reaction, but I couldn't bear to think about it.

"I don't know. I know I need to have the conversation with him, but he'll just turn everything so it's all my fault. Plus, it's the kids that'll miss out if he leaves."

"How will they?" Jen asked frowning.

"You know what it was like when we split up before and he just saw them here and there." I shrugged, already exhausted by the subject of my relationship.

"Sounds about the same as he does now," Jen said dryly. "The man's got less responsibility than me. And I've only got a dog."

I pondered Jen's words and recognised that there was definitely truth in what she had said.

"Right," I said pulling up outside Pizza Hut, cringing as I saw some boys from George's class leaving already with their mums and dads. "I'll be two minutes!"

George and I got back in the car and Jen tactfully turned the conversation back to what careers she thought I'd be good at.

"Are you getting a new job, Mum?" George asked, looking interested.

"Maybe." I said noncommittally. George joined in with Jen's

suggestions until the pair of them let their imaginations run away and started listing ridiculous jobs and we were all laughing as we dropped Jen off.

"Come and see me in the week!" Jen ordered as she gave me a quick kiss on the cheek.

"I will!" I promised.

When George and I finally got back to the house, Steve was pacing the kitchen looking agitated. He looked the image of George had when I'd come home earlier, and I felt a rush of genuine affection for my husband despite everything that had gone on. After all, he had contributed genetically to my beautiful babies. The affection was followed by a pang of sadness that we just couldn't seem to make our marriage work.

"You've been ages!" Steve said accusatorily as I put my bag down and switched the kettle on.

"Mum's been with Jen," George told his dad. "Me and Jen think Mum would make a really good YouTuber if she gets her re- re-"

He looked at me searchingly to help him with the word he was looking for.

"Redundancy." I prompted him automatically.

"You're not going for redundancy." Steve said, crossing his arms across his body and leaning against the one kitchen drawer that I needed to open.

"I am." I said, surprised that I actually felt very calm despite knowing that he was going to kick off.

"You'd better be joking." He responded, his tone furious now.

"I'm not." I walked away and started loading the washing machine.

Steve had followed me into the utility room and stood across the doorway. His jaw was clenched, and I could see the muscle in his cheek twitching like it always did when he was angry.

"I can't believe you would do something so selfish!" He burst out.

"What does it matter to you?" I asked coolly. "I know you're seeing someone."

"Don't you dare turn this back on me!" He was yelling now, and I put my fingers to my lips, concerned about the children hearing him. "No! I won't be quiet! You really have taken the piss this time. Can you tell work you've changed your mind?"

"I'm not going to." I said firmly, standing up and switching the machine on. "If you can go away for weekends with women from work, I can make my own decisions about my career."

Steve opened his mouth to protest but I cut him off.

“Don’t.” I hissed, feeling angrier about him trying to control my working life than I did about his whole affair. “Just do us both a favour and get your stuff out of this house. You live like you’re single and I’m sick of it. We’re done.”

I stormed back into the kitchen, feeling the adrenaline racing now I’d done this. I stuffed my feet into my shoes and grabbed my bag.

“Kids!” I hollered, in my ‘we’ve got to leave this house in two minutes’ voice that I saved for every morning before school. “We’re going out! Move!”

The two youngest responded to my urgency, and I sent Leo back upstairs to get Esther and George. Steve blocked the doorway, “Where are you going?”

“For dinner.” I replied evenly. “Don’t make a scene in front of the kids.”

“Are you coming, Daddy?” Matilda asked, jamming her feet into sparkly wellies. I didn’t bother telling her to change them. They would do. I looked at Steve for his response. He looked back at me with eyes full of anger and ignoring Matilda’s question marched upstairs. Matilda gave a comical shrug at his rudeness. I remembered I still had his phone and quickly slipped it out of my bag, leaving it on the stairs. I went out to the car and waited for the eldest to come out.

“Dad!” I heard George call up the stairs. “Mum found your phone! It’s on the stairs!”

With that, George slammed the front door behind him and we headed out. By the time we had found somewhere we could agree on and eaten, it was getting late as I pulled back up to the house. I approached the house cautiously half-hoping Steve would be gone, but half-wishing he would be there begging for my forgiveness and willing to change. I opened the door slowly and instinctively I could tell he was gone. I checked his wardrobe and saw that he'd taken about half of his belongings. I sat down on the edge of the bed and the finality of it finally dawned on me. I waited for the tears of sadness to come but they didn't. I felt the same as I had when I'd selected redundancy. Scared but free.

Chapter 12

Steve maintained a radio silence during the next week and, with the exception of a few questions, the children seemed unperturbed by his absence. I powered through the week at work; the usual irritations and stresses barely registering on my scale now I had a potential finish line in sight.

I had spoken to Jen a few times over the week and updated her on Steve's departure. Jen had checked in via messages and the occasional phone call, but she had been manic tying up loose ends in work and I had nothing new to add to the conversation anyway as Steve's absence was no different to when he was living with us. If anything, my life was easier without the added stress of wondering whether he would be around to help out with the activity run and without constantly feeling like I was walking on eggshells around his mood-swings. Andy's once-religious 8 am phone calls had been scarce over the last month and he was no closer to revealing the secret distraction behind this, but I'd given him an update and he'd been an absolute angel; popping over midweek with his arms laden down with takeaway, remembering all the kids' favourites. Despite Andy's insistence that I must want to talk about the split, I honestly had nothing to say on the matter. I had been exhausted and sad for so long in my marriage that this break felt like a relief. I knew that at some point I would feel the full loss of our 15+ years together and that it would no doubt hit me like a tsunami but until then I was welcoming distractions. Andy was still playing his cards close to his chest.

"I know you're seeing someone!" I had protested as I tried to draw him into conversation on the subject. "Come on, Andy! I tell you everything."

"There's nothing to tell," He had replied demurely. "He's just a really nice man and I promise you will meet him soon!"

I had begged for a name, a photo, an address, a job title, absolutely any tiny morsel of information on the man who finally had my best friend smitten but Andy had dodged my questions until I sensed his annoyance. After he had left, I realised that I was feeling irritated at Andy for his secrecy. I had never kept any secrets from Andy, despite this opening me up on more than one occasion to his disapproval. Whatever he was hiding from me, he could carry on. I was no longer interested, and I was no longer sharing my own business with him.

Not that I had any 'business'. My life was a whirlwind of work, school run, kids, with little variation. Luke had eventually responded to my Sunday text two days later with a "Sorry, babe, just seen this." I'd had just enough dignity left in my reserve to not respond. We hadn't even spoken about my drunken visit to his parents' house and I was still none-the-wiser to whatever had happened. He hadn't chased me for the drink he'd been insistent on when we'd last seen each other in work either which made me wonder whether he'd moved on to someone else in the interim. By Friday, I was fed up, bored and lonely, faced with a weekend of no adult company and a never-ending wheel of the kids' weekend activities, I finally shed my first tears since the break-up. I didn't want to burden Jen as I knew she was chasing her tail to get everything ready for her move and I would rather cry on my own all weekend than text either Andy or Luke.

Andy, who seemed to have a radar that detected whenever he had pushed me as far as our friendship could go without us falling out indefinitely, called just as I was drying my red, puffy eyes after my pity party-for-one.

"Hey babes!" He called cheerfully. There was background noise like he was at a station.

"Hi." I said glumly.

"What's wrong with you?" He asked without a trace of empathy.

"I'm just enjoying wallowing in my own misery." I replied, trying to be flippant now I'd cried out my loneliness.

"Cool." Andy said, ignoring my response. "Are you ready to talk about me now?"

I laughed, despite myself. He was such a dickhead sometimes, but he did make me laugh.

"So," He continued, encouraged by my response. "I know you're in a mood because you think I don't trust you..."

He tailed off and I know he was waiting for me to protest and insist that I trusted him. I stayed silent, refusing to let him off the hook.

“Lucy?” He said. “I think your phone is broke.”

I laughed again, “Stop it. Yes, I’m in a mood with you. Continue with your point, please.”

Andy cleared his throat dramatically. “As I was saying, I am willing to forgive your moodiness if you can accompany me out tomorrow night. I promise I will tell you everything you want to know about my life.”

“I don’t want to know anything about your life,” I told him sulkily. “And I think you’ve forgotten that I can’t go anywhere as my estranged husband is not currently in contact.”

“Just phone him and tell him to have the kids,” Andy said, sounding annoyed. “Fuck’s sake, Lucy, stop being a martyr!”

“Oh, what a great idea!” I replied sarcastically. “Why didn’t I think of that?”

“You can be sarcastic and feel sorry for yourself all you want,” Andy lectured me. “But you haven’t even asked him.”

“I’m not begging him to look after his own kids.” I said feeling an after-party of pity coming on. “I can’t come to whatever it is you’re doing. End of.”

“Fine.” Andy responded clearly irritated now. “If you won’t even make the effort, don’t bother.”

“I won’t.” I said firmly. Andy ended the call without bothering to say ‘goodbye’.

I indulged myself in my second cry of the day and decided that as the children were all in bed at a decent hour, I might as well just sleep off my low mood. I changed into my pyjamas and padded downstairs to let the dogs out before turning in for the night. I ushered them both out into the garden and scrolled through my phone as I waited. I clicked in and out of my last message to Steve wondering when he would finally get in touch when another message popped up on my phone. I had my fingers on the touchscreen and accidentally went into the message. I cursed myself when I saw it was from Luke and he would see that I’d opened it immediately.

“You ok, babe?” It said simply.

I felt that, since it would show as read, I had no choice but to reply to avoid looking like I was being petty over his late response.

“Yes thanks. You ok?” I then added a kiss on the end, so he wouldn’t think I was in a mood with him.

“What you up to?” He replied immediately. I replied, and we chatted via text for a while.

“I saw Lois earlier,” He messaged, after a while. “She said you’ve split up with you husband.”

I replied confirming this, feeling betrayed by Lois, who was the only person in work I'd mentioned this to.

"Why didn't you tell me?" Luke responded quickly.

"Why would I?" I replied, equally fast.

"You know I've wanted a chance with you for ages."

"You had your chance." I typed, before furiously backspacing and replying. "We've only just split up last week."

I wasn't in the mood for small talk and I intended to cut the conversation off and stick to my original plan of going to bed when Luke phoned me. I stared at his name flashing on the screen. This was not how Luke and I interacted! Why was he breaking the rules? I answered the phone hesitantly, expecting him to be drunk to be calling me up like this. Surprisingly, he wasn't. He was at his flat and told me he was just phoning to see how I was doing. For some reason, probably the rapport we'd built up on the side of our fling, I felt more inclined to tell Luke about what had happened and how I'd been feeling than I had with my friends.

"Do you fancy some company?" Luke asked, when I'd finished offloading.

"I can't," I told him, genuinely feeling disappointed after what had been a really nice chat. "I've got the kids. And will always have the kids."

"Let me come over," Luke pressed. "I promise I won't try anything on. Just as a friend."

I felt awake now after our conversation and I glanced at the clock. It was only 9pm. Esther was sleeping at a friend's and the others were fast asleep. I trusted Luke not to try anything on if I asked him not to and who knew when Steve would have the kids for me to socialise. I could be waiting until Matilda was a teenager to be able to make any plans. Tentatively, I agreed after insisting that it was in the capacity as friends. Luke agreed and hung up.

When he arrived, I had purposely stayed in my pyjamas without a scrap of makeup; not wanting him to think I'd gone to any effort. His eyes lit up and he grinned widely at me when I opened the door. I tilted my face up towards him to allow him to kiss my cheek, but he ignored it and, instead, swept me up off my feet into a powerful bear hug.

"What was that for?" I laughed when he placed me gently back down and let me go.

"Because you look so cute." He smiled, kissing the top of my head as he said it.

"Cute?" I wrinkled my nose at him and he laughed.

I invited him into the kitchen, as I thought the bar stools at the counter were safer territory than the cosy sofas where one thing could easily lead to another. We chatted easily about work at first and how we had both submitted requests for redundancy at the last minute. It was now just a waiting game. We talked about what we wanted to do next and the subject finally swung around to my break up.

"You didn't tell me things hadn't been great." Luke said, leaning forward, his eyes full of concern.

"I wouldn't have been shagging you if they had been great, would I?" I countered, trying to be flippant.

Luke raised his eyebrows at my words and said nothing.

"I don't want you thinking I'm going to get all needy now I'm single," I continued when Luke didn't respond. "I know we're not like 'that'."

"Like what?" Luke asked, frowning.

"Serious." I answered, feeling awkward that we were having this conversation in my kitchen. "I know you see other people, and I'm fine with that-"

"I'm not seeing anyone." Luke cut me off, still looking serious.

"No," I waved my hand trying to find the right words, so Luke knew I wasn't expecting anything from him. "What I mean is, that you and me aren't anything and I'm fine with that-"

"Really?" He cut me off again. "Because I really like you, Lucy."

"No," I shook my head at him. "You don't. You text me as and when you want. You don't want anything serious and that's one hundred percent fine with me."

"I text you as and when because I try to distance myself from you," Luke said, still serious, reaching across and taking my hand in his. "Because I've got feelings for you. You know that."

"I don't." I insisted. "I don't want anything serious, Luke."

"You tell me that all the time," He sighed, turning my hand over in his and running his thumb over my wrist. I shuddered involuntarily at the sensation and the corners of his mouth turned up as he watched my reaction. "And I respect it."

"Right." I felt a little turned on as he continued to stroke the sensitive underside of my wrist, his sexy green eyes gazing intensely into mine.

"I'm not seeing anyone else," He repeated. "And I won't. Unless you don't want to date me properly. When you're ready, of course."

"Luke," I sighed. "I do. It's just-"

I should have cut this off then and there. I liked Luke. A lot. But I had been in a relationship since I was 20 years old. I had children and potentially a change in careers coming up. The right thing to do would be to spend time on my own before jumping into something new. Plus, it was more than likely, based on experience, that everything Luke was saying to me was utter bullshit. After an emotionally difficult week, my raging hormones were more than happy to swallow this though and my overriding urge was to fall into Luke's arms.

"Luke," I tried again. "I like you. A lot. It's just not the right time."

Luke dropped his gaze and I felt my heart pull at the sight of his sad expression. Just as quickly, he recovered and smiled at me warmly. "Honestly, babe. It's fine. I totally respect that. Let's talk about something else."

I'd been on the verge of working up to ask him to leave as it was getting late, but I felt bad at hurting his feelings, so I made us both coffee and changed the subject back to general chit chat. There was a gentle knock at the door and I jumped, startled. The reality hit me that I was sat in my pyjamas drinking coffee with a twenty-eight-year-old hottie in my marital home. My face must have displayed my fear as Luke got to his feet.

"Is that your husband?" He asked, sounding a little concerned.

"I don't think so," I answered uncertainly. "I'll check."

I went into the hallway and peered through the security window. I made out the outline of a tall woman, but her face was turned down looking at the phone in her hand. She suddenly looked up and our eyes met through the glass panel.

"Lucy!" She exclaimed, and I felt my body flood with relief.

It was Jen. I swung the door open.

"I've been phoning you!" She exclaimed, walking straight in

without hesitating.

"My phone is on silent," I said dumbly. "I thought you were Steve or his new woman!"

"Bringing him back now she's realised what a dickhead he is." Jen said dryly.

I laughed. "What's up anyway?"

"I was dropping some stuff over Gran's. I've been phoning you to see if you were in!" She said, kicking off her work heels and making for the kitchen. "I know it's late but do you fancy-"

She made a noise of surprise as she walked in and saw Luke sat at my counter, nursing a coffee.

"Oh," She said awkwardly. "I'm sorry. I'll come back-"

"No!" I exclaimed, slightly too loudly. Luke and Jen both looked at me, startled by my tone. I tried again. "No need. Jen, this is my friend, Luke, from work. He just popped in for a coffee. Luke, this is my friend, Jen."

They said a polite hello to each other. I caught Jen eyeing up my pyjamas and I looked away guiltily.

"I was just leaving." Luke said, getting to his feet and smiling politely at Jen.

"Please don't!" Jen reached over and placed a hand gently on his arm, turning up the wattage of her smile to charmingly dazzling. Luke smiled back at her and opened his mouth to protest but Jen beat him to it. "I'm just picking up my suitcase."

I tried to give Jen a pleading look to let him leave but she held my gaze, steadfastly not backing down.

"My suitcase, Lucy?" She repeated. "Sorry I've burst in like this. I did try to call."

"Do you want to come up and get it?" I asked, trying to send Jen a telepathic message to stay.

"Can you?" She asked.

Luke was still stood up, looking back and forth uncomfortably at our awkward exchange. I disappeared up the stairs to retrieve the suitcase from the back of my wardrobe. When I reappeared, Luke and Jen were both looking more comfortable. Jen was draped over my kitchen worktop, leaning forward as she chatted to Luke. He was clearly getting an eyeful of her breasts straining beneath her silk shirt.

"You should consider it," Jen was saying to him. "It would be great for anyone's career."

"Sounds amazing," Luke replied, not even looking in my direction as I dragged the suitcase into the room. "What's the partner company?"

Jen handed Luke her phone. "Here, give me your email and I'll send you the details."

Luke took the phone off her and tapped in his details, looking pleased. He handed the phone back and I bristled with jealousy as I watched them giving each other shy smiles. Jen looked radiant and I couldn't help but compare myself to her; Jen looking sexy and sophisticated in her suit and me dishevelled and puffy-eyed in pyjamas.

"Ladies," Luke said smoothly. "I really do have to run. Lovely to meet you, Jen. Lucy, I'll see you in work."

I followed him out to the hallway and he gave me a quick hug, landing another kiss on my forehead. He put his mouth close to my ear. "Text me later."

I told him I would and shut the door firmly behind him, walking back into the kitchen to my friend.

"Sorry about that!" I tried to smile breezily.

Jen looked back at me with a slightly frosty smile. "It's my fault. I shouldn't have assumed I could just turn up now you're a free agent."

"Jen!" I objected. "It's not like that."

Jen waved her hand dismissively. "It's fine. And it's late."

She picked up the case and pecked me on the cheek. "Thanks for this. I'll see you in the week, yeah?"

I had no choice but to nod as she swished out of the kitchen and through the door, closing it herself gently. I sat back down and sighed into my now cold cup of coffee. Why did I feel lonelier than ever?

Chapter 13

After an eventful few weeks, the next week was thankfully calmer. Apart from messages from Luke that had increased in frequency, the only adults I spoke to were customers or colleagues. This was the penultimate week in school and there was a run of activities scheduled. It was George's last few weeks of Primary School and, despite having been through all this with Esther already, I felt overcome with emotion every time I thought about my little tearaway growing up so fast.

George had been feeling uncharacteristically sentimental and we spent the Friday evening going through old photos that he asked me to drag down from the attic.

"When is Dad coming home?" George asked, tracing a finger over a photo of Steve, toddler Esther, baby George and a younger, prettier me beaming happily.

"Don't know," I said, trying to sound casual, and moving swiftly on to the next photo. "Why don't you text him?"

Despite Esther and George having contract iPhones, the concept of using them to do anything as basic as send a text or, even worse, answer a call from their parents was unchartered territory to them. I flipped between feeling glad that Steve was remaining elusive as it meant I didn't have to deal with any conflict and alternately feeling furious that he thought that little of his responsibilities that almost two weeks had passed with little more than a text to say he'd be in touch when he had sorted somewhere to stay that he could bring the kids. I knew that he was alive as I regularly (maybe obsessively) checked his latest time online and I'd also noticed he was regularly updating his social media "stories" with glimpses into his fun, carefree life.

Esther had been suspiciously silent on the matter and when she opted to stay in on a Friday evening, I knew I should start to worry. As tempting as it was as a mother to ask her what was up, I knew from experience I had to wait for her to open up to me in her own time.

At 8pm, we were sat around the living room eating room eating yet another takeaway in our pyjamas. Esther would usually eat her food and immediately make a beeline for her bedroom, but she dragged a fleecy blanket over and sat next to me, draping her long, skinny legs over my lap. I tried my hardest not to look pleased as this would cause her to retract any sign of warmth towards her mother. It didn't take long for the other children to grow bored of the film and wander off.

"Shall we watch something else, Mum?" Esther asked as the credits rolled on the film we were watching. I handed her the remote to choose.

"Shall we watch something funny, so you don't get sad and cry?"

I glanced at my daughter from the corner of my eye; unsure how to react.

"I don't get sad and cry." I said levelly but I smiled so she would know I wasn't offended.

"Yes, you do," Esther poked my shoulder with her foot. "All the time."

"Not all the time!" I protested, squeezing her toes playfully. "I'm just more emotional than most people."

"Ha!" Esther laughed. "You're the most emotional person in the world!"

"I'm just too pure for this cruel world!" I held a hand theatrically to my forehead and Esther rewarded me with another genuine laugh.

"Seriously though, Mum," She side eyed me, her tone solemn. "I know you and Dad are breaking up and I'm here if you want to talk about it."

I felt my eyes fill up with tears and my heart ached at her sweetness.

"Thank you," I smiled grateful for this beautiful girl in my life. Her blonde hair was piled up, in its naturally curly, untamed state on top of her head. She was all long, skinny limbs and if she hadn't been wearing Unicorn pyjamas, she could easily have passed for 15/16. She made me feel so proud of how kind and thoughtful she could be, despite the odds being stacked against her having two idiots like Steve and I raising her.

"It's ok, Mum," She looked down at her lap self-consciously. "Mum, has he met someone else?"

I froze, unsure of how to respond. What did I say to that? I didn't want to treat her like a child and risk alienating her, but I didn't want to upset her when I didn't know whether Steve's relationship was even serious.

"I don't know." I finally answered.

"These things happen," She told me with all the wisdom of a savvy teenager. "Olivia's mum ran off with her personal trainer."

"Poor Olivia."

"Yeah," Esther continued. "Her dad smashed up her mum and her boyfriend's matching Range Rovers."

I made a noise between a sob and a laugh in response. Esther smiled at my response and, encouraged by my reaction, decided to share some more stories of Debauchery in Suburbia.

"The worst was when Freddie Davison's mum caught his Step-Dad shagging the au pair in Tignes!"

"Oh my God, Esther!" I spluttered. "Don't say 'shagging'."

"Oh shush, Mum!" She tutted at me but looked pleased with herself. "I'm not a little kid."

"I know!" I burst into the laughter I'd been trying to contain despite feeling empathy for Freddie's mother's awful ski trip. "I'm your mum though! Don't say that!"

"Oh Mum!" Esther shook her head at me. "You're so tame! That's what happens when you're a child bride!"

I smiled at her mockery of me. "What about you though? How are you feeling about everything?"

Esther shrugged. "It doesn't really make any difference. He's never here."

I didn't know what to say to that, but I could tell she was hurting.

"I'm not doing the whole hideous weekends doing family things with him," She continued. "I'm busy with my friends."

"Right," I said, not sure what to say. "Dad does really love you, you know that?"

"Ssh," She pointed at the TV signalling that our deep and meaningful conversation was over. "Watch the film."

As always, my brain reserved the right to dwell on this as soon as I slipped into bed that night. I flicked through various social media pretending to myself that I was just browsing but I was scouring my feeds for signs that Steve was out living his best life while I was trying to carve some semblance of normality for his children. Although if I was honest, I had been doing this alone for years while he just popped in to our family home to shower, sleep and join in with an occasional family activity when it suited him. Thankfully there were no hashtag-loving-life posts from him that evening and I felt my anger simmer down to a mild sense of injustice.

I woke up the next morning still exhausted from tossing and turning all night stressing over every poor decision I had made in my life that had led me up to this moment. As I reached for my phone, I noticed Andy had sent me a message at 3am that morning. I sat up in bed to open it. We had exchanged a few messages since he'd hung up on me the previous week, but our friendship had definitely dimmed a few notches recently, which made me feel sad. As much as Andy annoyed me at times, he was my best friend and I missed him. I clicked on the picture he'd sent and nearly fell out of bed in shock. It was a photo of Andy with John Taylor. John was nuzzled up against Andy, kissing his cheek. Andy was pouting at the camera in his typical selfie pose and he'd keyed a line of text across the picture "So this is my mystery man... Now can we be besties again?" I dialled Andy's number with hesitating. He must be winding me up, I thought as I listened with impatience to the phone ringing.

"Hiya babe!" He answered, surprisingly chirpy for someone who'd been up until the early hours.

"What the fuck, Andy!" I burst out as soon as I heard his voice. "You're not serious. Don't lie- I swear, I'll kill you!"

Andy laughed at my outburst and I heard a man's voice in the background.

"Lucy." Andy said, responding to whoever he was with.

"Andy!" I said impatiently. "Swear on your life."

"I swear on my life." He said, still laughing.

I was quiet still unsure whether to believe him as I had fallen victim to many of Andy's elaborate tales over the course of our friendship.

"Are you still there?" He said after a few moments had passed.

"I don't know whether to believe you!" I admitted. "You wind me up all the time."

"Well," He countered. "If you actually made the effort to come out with me, you could see for yourself."

"Don't start that again." I joked. "Why didn't you tell me before? You're rubbish at secrets!"

"I know!" Andy agreed. "I wanted to tell you. Anyway, I need you to come out with me later so can we be friends now?"

"Yes, we are friends," I smiled. "But I can't come out as I've got my kids."

"Please," He pleaded. "Just try. I need to tell you stuff."

I realised that, in all my own dramas, I had neglected my super-needy best friend. I racked my brain wondering who would be prepared to babysit for me. I was desperate to find out Andy's gossip and to verify his mysterious relationship wasn't just a massive wind up.

"I promise I'll try," I said, meaning it.

"Ok," Andy said, satisfied with my answer. "Oh, and you can't tell anyone."

"Ok." I agreed.

"Anyone!" He emphasised. "Even Jen or your mum."

"Oh!" I said surprised. "Ok, I won't."

"Phone me in a bit and tell me if you get a babysitter." Andy ordered, ending the call.

I sat in bed for a while after we'd hung up, pondering this bombshell. I spent a few more minutes googling John Taylor. He'd been in loads of films and TV programmes and he lived quite locally. There was no mention of any wife or kids but there was also nothing that indicated he was gay either. Maybe that's why Andy had felt he had to keep things low key. I was so intrigued to find out more about how Andy had come to be dating a Hollywood superstar that I felt bolstered to try Steve as my first port of call for the children. I fired off a casual text before getting up and going downstairs to let the dogs out. They both surveyed me with sad eyes, clearly feeling the neglect now they were missing out on their morning walks.

"Sorry." I apologised to them. "I promise we'll do something today with you."

They went out into the garden without responding to my good intentions. I flicked through my contact list, scanning the names for potential babysitters as I wasn't holding out much hope for Steve to even get back to me, let alone agree to having his own children. Leaving them with Esther was absolutely out of the question and if I couldn't find anyone, I would just have to risk Andy's wrath. I narrowed my search down to two Mums from the school who had older daughters who I knew babysat occasionally for other parents and fired off messages, keeping my fingers crossed for luck. I hustled the kids up and we got ready for a day of driving from ballet to football training to a hockey match, and I came through on my promise to Hermione and Ron by whisking them around the park with the three youngest huffing, puffing and moaning in tow. The day went by in such a whirlwind that I didn't have a chance to check my messages until later that afternoon. The two potentials had declined; with one girl having plans and the other already engaged in a babysitting job that evening. Steve, unsurprisingly, had not responded and I felt a surge of disappointment and resentment at having to let Andy down again. I walked back into the house, dogs and kids all muddy, hungry and bad-tempered, when my phone rang. Steve's name flashed up on the screen. I felt a pang of hope and swiftly buried it before Steve could shatter it himself.

"Hello?"

"I just read your message," Steve said coolly, not bothering with any pleasantries. "I'm staying at a friend's, so I can't have them to stay. You know this."

"Well," I said levelly. "Can you have them here? I won't be late."

This meant I would have to deal with the awkwardness of having Steve in my house when I got in, but it seemed like I didn't have any other option.

"It's not ideal," Steve said in a snide tone. "But as I haven't seen my children since you threw me out of my home, I would like to spend some time with them."

"You can see them whenever you like." I said, trying to keep my own tone polite.

"I can't though, can I?" Steve spat back, sounding furious.

I didn't know how to respond to this in a way that would avoid a full-blown argument, so I said nothing.

"Where are you going?" Steve asked. "Got a date?"

"Just for dinner with Andy." I replied as calmly as I could muster.

"What time will you be home?"

"Not late," I said quickly. "About 11? Unless you want to stay with the kids overnight."

I wanted to give him as many options as possible to maximise the chance of his cooperation. If he went for this, I had no idea where I would stay but I'd figure something out.

"I can't stay," Steve shot back. "I'll be over at 6."

"Great, thank you!" I said gratefully, jumping up and down in silent celebration. I hung up and danced around the kitchen before phoning Andy to relay the good news.

Andy applauded my bravery, as despite his strop the previous week, he knew how difficult Steve could be. Andy, clearly alone now, was able to fill me in on a bit of the background over the phone. His voice was bursting with happiness as he told me that he had met John a few months back backstage at a comedy club.

"That night I came?" I asked, shocked.

"Before that," He admitted sheepishly. "His brother does amateur stand up."

"The brother Jen dated?" I asked trying to thread all the pieces together.

"Yes." Andy confirmed.

I thought hard about this. "You knew Jen knew John, did you? When we "bumped" into him."

Andy laughed. "Aw Lucy, I really wanted to tell you. He's so lovely and kind. And he can cook."

"And he's gorgeous!" I added, joining in with Andy's infectious laugh. "I am really happy for you, Andy. You sound like you're really happy."

"Now I've told you everything," Andy continued. "Can John come with us tonight? I really want you to meet him!"

"I met him already," I said, and as star struck as I was, I felt too embarrassed of my previous behaviour to have to face John again and I had been hoping for some time alone with my best friend. "Plus, that'll be weird, me third-wheeling."

"Ask Jen to come." He said.

"It's short notice." I countered.

"Third wheel then." Andy challenged back.

"Fine," I said, admitting defeat. "I'll ask her but otherwise I'll crash your date alone. Where to? What time?"

Andy gave me the details smugly now he'd got his own way. "See you later, beauty!"

Chapter 14

The handover with Steve was as awkward and fraught with tension as I'd predicted. The children were genuinely pleased to see him though, so I sucked up my own reservations and pasted a smile on. I promised myself that I would make more effort to speak to Steve civilly about how best to make these arrangements so none of them missed out on a proper relationship. I felt only the tiniest stab of sadness for our marital breakdown when I saw him and quickly shook it away, before dashing out of the house as quickly as I could.

Jen had agreed to come. Andy had sworn me to secrecy and had insisted that I claim Andy and John were "just friends". I felt uncomfortable lying, even by omission, to Jen but I didn't have the energy to challenge Andy and I figured that Jen would work it out for herself during the evening, if she hadn't already. I met up with Jen at a bar across the road from the swish eatery Andy had booked for our cosy foursome. This was another friendship that had felt more than a little fraught lately and I had been surprised that Jen had agreed to come out, knowing how busy she'd been lately trying to get everything ready for her move. We had spoken several times after she'd walked in on me entertaining a colleague in my kitchen, just general chitchat, but this was the first time I'd seen her. Whatever I do tonight, I told myself, I cannot mention Luke and I cannot get drunk.

Jen was nursing a tall glass when I walked in.

"Can I get you a drink?" I asked, kissing her cheek in greeting.

"I'm not drinking," Jen said, holding up her glass to show me it was water. "So much to do still, so I can't be hungover tomorrow."

"I'm not drinking either after last time." I smiled sheepishly.

Jen smiled back and we both laughed, which I took as a good sign. We chatted about New York and the kids; neither of us mentioning Luke or Steve. I was hoping she wouldn't mention Andy and John's friendship, but she did. As I'd hoped, she suspected there was more to it without me having to confirm or deny anything. We made our way over to the restaurant and the night went well. John was lovely and charming; laughing off my apology for my drunken behaviour and telling stories of his own drunken escapades that made mine pale in comparison. Jen and Andy chatted animatedly about her upcoming secondment to New York. When the bill came, John reached for his wallet, but Andy waved him away and insisted on paying for us all. After dinner, Andy tried to convince Jen and I to stay out for drinks but we both declined. Andy made us both promise that we'd do this again before Jen left for New York and we all headed out to get in our taxis. Jen was going in the same direction as John and Andy, so they sent me off in the first car and I sat back in my seat smiling happily at how well this evening had gone. I had just one more hurdle to overcome when I got home.

I politely knocked the door gently to announce my return before walking in. The house didn't look like the usual bombsite it always was after I'd been out, and Steve was sat watching a film with Esther, with George fast asleep in the crook of Steve's arm. I felt a little tearful at the scene of domestic bliss.

"Hi, good night?" Steve asked, looking up as I entered the room.

I nodded, surprised at his friendly tone. "Yes, thanks. You?"

"Lovely." He said. "Leo and Matilda have only just gone up. George wasn't far behind them."

"Oh, bless him." I sat tentatively on the edge of the opposite sofa.

"I'll take him up now and be off," Steve said shifting his weight to get up.

"Dad!" Esther protested. "Please can we just watch the rest of this?"

Steve opened his mouth to protest but I stood up first. "I'll go and get ready for bed if you want to finish this."

Esther gave her dad a pleading look and he relaxed back onto the sofa. "There's only 10 minutes left."

When I came back down, Steve was stood up with George in his arms.

"I'll carry him up," Steve said. "He's huge! I won't be able to do this in another year!"

"Thanks," I said gratefully, feeling the tears of nostalgia creeping back up on me. "I can't pick him up anymore."

Esther followed her dad upstairs and I heard Steve chatting to her for a few minutes before he came back down. He appeared at the bottom of the stairs, smoothing down the front of his t-shirt a little self-consciously.

"Right," He said. "Goodnight."

"Oh!" I said, remembering I had planned to try to make some kind of civil parenting agreement. "It's George's last week so he's got that Leaver's concert. Can you make it?"

"Thursday?" Steve nodded. "Yeah, I got your text. I'll see you then, but I was hoping to see the kids before."

"Oh, ok," I said, pleasantly surprised. "Anytime is fine."

"Tomorrow?" Steve asked, looking so hopeful that I felt like crying.

"George has got his football match at 1 but you can take him if you want. You'll have to take the car."

"Great!" Steve looked genuinely pleased. "Thanks! See you then!"

He left, and I locked up and went up to bed, feeling a whole range of emotions. If only Steve had been that enthusiastic, when we were together, about spending time with his family. I concentrated on my breathing, willing myself to fall asleep before I fell back into the cycle of having second thoughts.

I was prepared to feel gloomy and morose about our split the whole next day but there wasn't time. I was awoken early by my house phone ringing. It was Jen.

"Why are you phoning my house?" I asked, half-asleep and confused.

"Because you didn't answer!" Jen exclaimed.

"My phone is on silent," I responded. "What's the matter?"

"Have you seen the news?" She sounded practically frantic.

"No!" I felt my heart start to race. "What's happened?"

"I'm coming over!" Jen said, ignoring my question and hanging up.

I scrolled through the news, scouring for what she could possibly be alluding to, but nothing jumped out at me.

In less than twenty minutes, Jen was at my door. She was dressed casually in jeans and a white t-shirt, but she looked like she'd run a marathon. She marched into my kitchen and flung her bag down, clutching her phone to her chest.

"Jen, what's happened?" I asked, my eyes wide with concern.

Jen said nothing but thrust her phone in the direction of my face.

Her phone was open on the celebrity section of a tabloid newspaper. It was a paparazzi shot of John holding the car door open for Jen. I clicked on the surrounding article and saw Jen had been identified as "City high-flier Jennifer Nicholas" and they had featured a professional looking headshot from Jen's LinkedIn profile. The story told how Jen had been dating John Taylor for a few weeks and there was a grainy image of John and Jen laughing on the smoking terrace of Joia, clearly taken from across the street.

Jen burst into a furious rant. All directed at Andy.

"Andy is such a fucking prick! He knew exactly what he was doing dragging us out, so he could cover up his fucking relationship." She spat, angrily. "I've got fucking photographers hanging around my bloody flat now too, just when I've got a million things I need to do!"

"What's Andy go to do with this?" I asked, confused. "They've clearly just taken the picture and got the wrong end of the stick."

"Fuck's sake, Luce!" Jen was pacing my kitchen now, her hands waving expressively as she raged. "You can be so bloody naïve! Andy has basically tagged you and me along with him both times, so he can out in public without his boyfriend being outed!"

"John's personal life is nobody's business," I said with

feeling. “He shouldn’t have to talk about his relationships.”

“That’s not my point!” Jen wailed. “I don’t give a shit what he does to avoid speculation but now my personal fucking life is being flung all over that shitty paper!”

I could see Jen’s point now. “I’m sure Andy and John didn’t mean for this to happen.”

“Really?” Jen raised her eyebrows at me. “John is photographed a hell of a lot. Yet the only time he’s out with his new boyfriend, there’s two women conveniently with him. What a coincidence!”

“Have you spoke to either of them?” I asked.

“Andy’s phone is off.” Jen fumed. “I need you to go over there and sort this out! I can’t afford for this to jeopardise my career!”

“What?” I frowned. It wasn’t like Jen to be this dramatic.

“Think of all the shit I’ve done in my life, Lucy!” She put her head in her hands, in despair. “Imagine if there’s any low life kiss-and-tells off the back of this.”

Some of Jen’s more risqué antics flashed through my mind. “Shit!”

“Imagine my Gran or my boss reading that I’d snorted coke off the drummer from Power’s tits!” Jen groaned in horror. “Or when I shagged my old boss, who’s now a bloody FTSE 50 CEO. Why the fuck was I such a wild child!”

“I’m sure they wouldn’t sell stories on you.” I reasoned, searching for my emergency packet of cigarettes that I hid at the back of the cupboard for emergencies.

“No,” Jen agreed. “It’ll be people like the reality TV couple that I had a threesome with. Which is fucking mortifyingly embarrassing!”

I could see Jen’s dilemma and we both stared glumly into space picturing worst case scenarios.

“Right,” I said, trying to take control of the situation. “Can you stay here with the kids and I’ll try to get hold of Andy?”

Jen nodded, practically ripping the cigarettes from my hand and heading to the back door. I tried Andy’s phone, but it went straight to voicemail just as it had for Jen.

I drove over to Andy’s, not sure what else to do as I had no idea where John lived. His car was parked outside, and I ran up the steps to his front door. He swung the door open and I could tell immediately he was going to be on the defensive.

“It’ll all blow over,” He said coolly when I updated him on the reason for my visit. “Tell Jen to stop stressing.”

“Is John here?” I asked, shouldering past Andy and into the house. I was annoyed by his flippant response and I wasn’t about to have this conversation on the doorstep.

“She’s really worried about any media interest in her life,” I said, trying to appeal to Andy’s better nature. “She’s got enough going on at the moment."

"You're both being dramatic." Andy said. "It'll blow over by tomorrow."

"What if it doesn't?" I continued. "Is John going to address this?"

Andy shrugged. "I'm on my way out. Trust me, it'll be fine."

My heart sank at his lack of concern for Jen. I couldn't go back and relay this to Jen. She'd be furious.

"Andy," I started, trying to choose my words diplomatically. "Did you only invite Jen and I to the spa and to dinner in case John was photographed?"

A shadow crossed Andy's eyes and I knew, without him saying anything, that Jen's theory was right. If he hadn't set out to deliberately watch his own back, the thought had at least crossed his mind.

"No!" He looked angry now. "I'm not talking about this now."

"Can you at least tell me what John's going to do about this?" I exclaimed exasperated. "I don't think you understand how upset Jen is."

"I'll ask him and let you know." Andy gestured towards the door and followed me out. I watched him get into his car and drive off without a backwards glance.

I returned home, and Jen was in the kitchen with my now-awake children. She looked a lot calmer than she had when I'd left and was making pancakes with Matilda sat up on the worktop next to her.

"How did it go?" She asked as I walked in, not turning around from the frying pan.

"Ummm," I hadn't counted on having an audience when I had to relay the conversation I had just had. "He's going to speak to John to see what he's going to do and let us know."

"Did you tell him that I know this is his fault?" She asked in a calm, even tone. She aggressively flipped a pancake and I could tell from her body language that she was furious. Matilda clapped her pancake-flipping skills and Jen rewarded her with the first of the batch.

I sat down and waited silently until she was finished feeding my pride of starving children. After what felt like an eternity, Jen and I were left alone in the kitchen.

"What were Andy's exact words?" She demanded.

My heart sank as I knew that even if I omitted the worst of it there would be no happy outcome from this. I gave a brief overview of the short conversation with Jen butting in to request more details, specifically "Andy's exact words". When I had finished speaking, she sat down and exhaled heavily.

"Screw him!" She said decisively. "I'd like to see how he likes it when I point any media in his direction!"

"Jen!" I was shocked by her venom. "Let's just see what John says first."

She pursed her lips, "I wouldn't really. But not because I've got any loyalty to Andy."

Jen moped around my house that morning, distracting herself with the kids and a few more cigarettes. Eventually, as we were sat side by side on the sofa, I received a text from Andy.

"John's PR have put out a statement. Should be online. All sorted." I read it out to Jen.

"Good," She said, immediately pulling out her phone to google this. "I know it'll die down, Lucy, but I'm going to feel on edge for weeks now. And I'm not speaking to Andy until he apologises."

I reached over and gave her a hug, feeling her relax in my arms. Her glossy dark hair fell across my face and I closed my eyes as I inhaled the coconut smell of her shampoo. She twisted slightly so her head rested on my shoulder and, without thinking, I pressed my lips against the top of her head. Jen let out a little sigh.

"Thanks for always being there." She said.

"You're always there for me, too." I tried to ignore the butterfly sensation in my stomach but now I had acknowledged it, I felt very conscious of the way we were cuddled up on the sofa. Jen looked up at me from under her long, dark lashes. Her head still against my shoulder meant her face was just inches from mine. Her full, dark lips parted slightly as she gave me a little smile and, from nowhere, I felt an almost overwhelming urge to kiss her. I held back; unsure of why I was suddenly feeling like this and scared of losing yet another person in my life. Jen seemed to sense my hesitation and she dropped her own gaze. She shifted slightly away and then turned, looking me straight in the eye, her mouth opening to speak.

A knock on the front door followed by the door opening caused us both to jump.

"Hello?" It was Steve.

I felt my heart speed up and Steve walked into the living room seconds later.

"Hi." He said. "You pair look cosy."

We both laughed awkwardly, and Jen got to her feet.

"Don't go." Steve waved a hand in her direction. "I'm just picking the kids up for football. Are they all coming?"

I called them down and they all agreed to go, even Esther, clearly enjoying the time with their Dad.

"I've got to go anyway," Jen said, as she hugged the children goodbye. "So much to do."

“I’ll come and help.” I offered.

Jen looked pleased and, after waving the kids off, we set off to hers to spend a few hours packing up boxes before dropping them over to her Gran’s. There was no awkwardness and, by the time I got back home, the memory of ‘that moment’ felt like it had been all in my head.

Chapter 15

The next week was the usual end of term chaos. I outdid myself in work and was late every day due to various mishaps and mayhem in my highly-strung household. I had booked the Thursday off months before as it was the last day of term and George's leaving concert. I had the first two weeks of the school holidays booked off so when I finished on the Wednesday afternoon, even Roger keeping me behind late for a 'documented' lateness conversation couldn't burst my bubble of excitement at being out of the office.

I was the expected emotional mess all day on George's last day. Steve took my hand at one point, as the class performed a medley of songs, and I had failed to hold back a noisy sob. The gesture took me by surprise and I forgot my maternal blues temporarily as I stared ahead feeling like my hand was clamped between two bricks. Steve quickly dropped it and I flashed him an awkward smile of gratitude.

Steve had shown some more interest in parenting since the weekend and it had crossed my mind that maybe the romance had turned stale between him and Charlotte without the added illicit thrill of the secrecy. As much as I had wanted this relationship to fail, I didn't want Steve to come crawling back and end up falling into the same old routine of arguing and affairs, so I was almost pleased to see him fire off a quick text to her when I glanced over his shoulder as we were waiting outside George's classroom after the concert. Almost. I was torn between wanting a fresh start after years of feeling unappreciated and being terrified at the prospect of all this change. The announcement for redundancy was only a week away now and this had been playing on my mind. My head was battling between exhilaration at the thought of never having to put up with Roger again and panic that I would be jumping from the frying pan into the fire. I had started to doubt myself; whether I was overreacting, out of frustration, and sabotaging my own future by quitting both my job and my marriage. Things had been frosty with Andy, so I hadn't even had the chance to talk my muddle of worries and second thoughts over with anyone.

As Steve left that evening, he hovered in the hallway as if he was building up to saying something. I dumped the bags in the kitchen and turned to him.

"Everything ok?" I turned on a friendly, professional smile as if he were one of my customers.

"I was just wondering," He started. "We didn't really talk about what plans you had for the school holidays."

I reeled off the dates I was off work and any clubs/ activities the kids were booked into for the duration of the six weeks.

"Wow," Steve said looking impressed. "I can't believe you remember all that."

“I do this for thirteen weeks of every year.” I replied nonplussed. I wanted to add that I couldn’t believe that he didn’t, but I left it at that.

“I was hoping to take the kids over to Portugal for the last week,” He continued a little hesitantly. “Would that be ok?”

“What? On your own?” I asked in shock at him volunteering to actually have all four of them on his own.

“Ummm,” He looked down at the floor and I realised the cause of his nervousness. “My friend might come, if that’s ok with you?”

“Oh.” I said, now it was my turn to look down at my feet. I had no idea how I felt about this and wanted to buy myself time to process how I felt. “Have you asked the kids?”

“No,” He shook his head, looking refreshingly vulnerable for once in our whole relationship at deferring to me. “I was waiting to see what you said first.”

“Will you still take them if they don’t want to meet your, ummm, friend?” I asked, genuinely interested to see whether he would.

“Of course.” He flushed slightly, and I wondered if he would. I guess we’d soon see.

"To the apartment?" I asked, feeling a little stab of regret that he'd be playing happy families in what should have been our holiday home.

Steve nodded, and I could see him growing more and more uncomfortable by the minute.

"Can I use it?" I asked, suddenly. I watched his expression change to one of surprise.

He took a moment to recover, "Oh, yes, of course. I haven't listed it as a rental yet so it's free."

"Can I take the kids there next week?" I asked, feeling spontaneous and spurred on by the redistribution of power in our relationship. It had always been me deferring to Steve. He had never asked me for permission in my life.

"Oh." It was his turn to look surprised. "On your own?"
I nodded. We had nothing booked and a holiday in the sunshine would be amazing.

"If I can get flights," I said. "Although there'll probably be ridiculously expensive now."

I realised as I said it that they definitely would be if there was anything available at all and immediately felt disappointed.

“Shall I have a look?” Steve offered, pulling out his phone. He sat down at the kitchen table and started searching before I could reply. After a few minutes, he gave me a thumbs up.

“Going out Tuesday but coming back on the Monday?”

“How much?” I asked.

Steve waved his hand dismissively. “It’s ok, I’ve got it.”
He pulled out his credit card and started filling in the fields to book. He paused and turned to me. “So I can book mine then?”

I was momentarily taken aback but I wanted the holiday, so I nodded.

“Can you just check with the kids that they’re ok about your ‘friend’ going first?” I said, trying to sound reasonable.

“I kind of mentioned it to Essie already.” He admitted looking sheepish.

I felt a prickle of annoyance. So he was probably only asking me as a formality. I would have been interested in his reaction if I hadn’t been so easy going about it.

“Ok.” I said coolly. I turned away and busied myself with emptying the school bags. Steve finished what he was doing and forwarded the confirmation straight over. He left not long after that, after making arrangements to take the kids to his parents' Saturday for a sleepover.

I felt a little out of sorts and opened a bottle of wine to reward myself for surviving an emotional day. The children went to bed at a reasonable hour, exhausted by the end of term pandemonium. As the bottle grew emptier, I felt myself grow more morose and lonely. I found myself dwelling on Steve's keenness to involve Charlotte in his family life. I couldn't picture anyone ever slipping into my daily routine like that and I wondered if I was destined to grow old on my own.

Luke and I were still in frequent contact, but I had a feeling he was seeing someone new again as he hadn't pushed me to see him. I had the children constantly anyway so there was slim chance of me ever dating anyone properly. I pondered downloading a dating app, but it felt pointless and I knew that I couldn't handle the rejection if I did put myself out there. I was feeling crappy enough as it was without putting my heart on the line. I was pretty tipsy by this point, so I broke one of my cardinal rules and sent Luke a late night, desperate text. As soon as I sent it, I was consumed with regret. I would be checking my phone and his social media now every two minutes and agonise over his lack of response. I decided to text Andy as well to distract myself. That was another relationship I was feeling unsure of.

Andy must have been feeling some form of responsibility for our mini bust-up over the Jen/ John thing as he replied straight away by calling me.

We hadn't spent any time together for ages and we were on the phone for over an hour. Andy told me the full story about how he'd started seeing John. He still didn't want to admit that he'd used Jen and I as a cover, but I could tell by his tone that he felt remorseful and a little frustrated by how difficult dating someone in the spotlight was. Andy confided that he was finding it a bit difficult living in a bubble and not being able to do 'normal' things but he waxed lyrical about how great John was and how they just 'clicked'. It was lovely to hear the happiness in his voice as he talked about his new relationship, but I felt concerned about how everything would work out as time progressed because of John's job keeping him in the public eye.

Andy seemed really interested in how I was coping with the redundancy announcement imminent and my recent marriage separation. I admitted that I was still 'talking' to Luke but it was not anything serious.

"You should start seeing people, though," Andy encouraged me. "You've got to live your life. You're not getting any younger."

I laughed at this. "Thanks, Andy! I just can't be bothered with the hassle. I just feel like any rejection would crush me right now!"

As we chatted, I heard a message come through and I checked it while still on the phone to Andy.

"Luke's just messaged me!" I told him, omitting the part where I had drunk texted him first.

"See! You can still elicit interest. What did he say?" Andy asked, and I could tell he was trying to be positive as he had never had anything nice to say about Luke and certainly wouldn't be encouraging me.

"Just asked what my plans are this weekend?" I said, feeling a little twinge of excitement that he might actually want to do something with me and I would have real adult plans for when Steve took the kids to his parents'.

"Do you need a babysitter?" Andy asked, and I felt a rush of love for him.

I explained that Steve was having the kids all day Saturday until Sunday evening and Andy egged me on to text Luke asking him out. I did as he told me and then questioned him on his change of heart.

"You obviously like him," Andy replied. "And I just want you to be happy for once."

I blinked back tears at his sweetness. Andy stayed on the phone until Luke replied and cheered when I proudly announced that I had an actual date Saturday.

"Luke is a bit of a flake though," I told him, feeling worried about how I would react if he let me down. "Can you be on call to listen to me cry Saturday?"

Andy laughed at my honesty. "Lucy, if he lets you down, I will drive to his house and kick his ass and then I will cancel my own plans and take you out myself."

I laughed at this. "Promise?"

"I promise." He said, and I believed him. "Come over for Sunday lunch and we'll debrief!"

I agreed and went up to bed excited at the prospect of having a date lined up, a holiday booked and my friendship with Andy back on track.

When Saturday came, Luke was still maintaining a steady level of contact. I held my breath for most of the day waiting for a last-minute cancellation, but he even chivalrously texted an hour before our arranged date just to say he was looking forward to seeing me and I felt my stomach butterfly a tiny bit with excitement. I was going on my first real date in over fifteen years! After dressing, doing my hair and makeup, I stared into the mirror frowning. I hated what I was wearing. I looked old and desperate; squeezed into a tight black skirt with a silky coral camisole. I stripped off and kicked the clothes away with frustration, yanking open my wardrobe door and staring into it in the hope that the perfect outfit, that combined sexy, womanly and effortless, would jump out at me. It didn't. At that moment my phone pinged announcing a message. I snatched it up, half-hoping it was Luke cancelling so I could bow out of this date before I made a fool of myself or got my feelings hurt. It was Jen.

"Packing is killing me! Fancy a sleepover buddy?"
I hadn't told Jen about my date, despite us speaking via message several times that week. I had justified this to myself as it just wasn't something that had come up in conversation, plus I had been almost certain that Luke would cancel. I felt something niggle at me that felt suspiciously like guilt. I knew Jen wasn't Luke's biggest fan and I didn't want to risk annoying Jen so close to her departure. She had enough stress right now, I told myself.

"I would have loved too," I replied. "But I'm going out though with colleagues. I'm glad you texted- I need your fashion guidance."

Jen responded immediately, and we exchanged a few more messages as she solicited information from me on my venue and advised me accordingly on appropriate attire which would, in Jen's words, make me "look hot!"

I thanked her and dressed quickly, pleased with her advice. I was still messaging her as I got on the train on the way to my date and I filled her in quickly on Portugal.

"I wish I was coming!" She texted.

“Come out for a few days?” I replied spontaneously, thinking how much fun that would be but also knowing it was an empty gesture as Jen had two weeks left until she headed off for at least six months, but in reality, probably longer, to New York.

“That would be amazing!” She replied. “I’ll have a look at flights and let you know!”

I was bursting with excitement at the thought of Jen joining us on holiday next week. I was daydreaming about lounging poolside with my friend with four impeccably-behaved children splashing happily in the water when I almost walked straight into Luke without seeing him.

“Hey!” He put his hands on my shoulders to stop me hitting him square in the chest and I jumped in surprise.
I blushed deeply.

“Lost in your own world?” He laughed, bending to kiss me on the cheek.

I turned an even deeper red and told him I had been thinking about my holiday.

“You’ve got a place in Portugal?” He asked, looking impressed.

I nodded, taking my purse out to pay for the drinks we’d ordered. Luke waved my attempt to pay away and handed his own card over to the barman, scooped up both our drinks and carried them over to a table.

"We should go away for a dirty weekend." He joked.
I laughed, and we fell into an easy conversation. After a few more drinks, we headed to another bar and spent hours on the dancefloor flirting and laughing. Luke was amazingly attentive. Steve had never been able to resist the urge to check out any other attractive women within a mile radius whereas I noticed Luke didn't so much as glance at any of the much younger, more attractive women in the bar. Luke noticed that I started flagging around midnight, despite my attempts to dance through the pain of my now-throbbing feet. He pulled me through the crowd and pressed his lips to my ear.

"Shall we call it a night?"

I nodded gratefully and let him lead me out onto the street. He expertly flagged down a cab and gave the driver my address.

"Just one stop?" The driver asked. Luke looked at me hesitantly and the almost shy look in his sexy green-grey eyes caused my stomach to butterfly slightly. I nodded, and he pulled me closer to him. I was definitely more drunk than I had thought and, as I cuddled up to him, his hand caressing my thigh and my head resting against his chest, I felt myself growing drowsy. The journey seemed to take forever, and Luke had to rouse me from my half-slumber when we arrived. He paid the driver and I fumbled with the keys at the door.

The moment we were through the door, Luke pulled me into his arms. We stumbled, kissing passionately and pulling off each other's clothes as we almost fell up the stairs. I fell against the wall as Luke ripped my top up and over my head. He circled his arms around me to stop me falling further and lifted me up against his chest as he navigated our way into my bedroom. We fell onto the bed and I covered his smooth, naked chest with my mouth, working my way down his tight, taut abdomen. I struggled to remove his belt and he raised his hips, letting me pull away his clothes. His erection, now familiar to me, strained against the waistband of his tight, designer underwear. I rolled them away and took his smooth length in my mouth.

Luke groaned in pleasure and buried his hands in my hair. I looked up through my tangled mess of curls and watched him watching me. The sensation got too much, and Luke signalled for me to stop to let him regain control. He pulled me up onto his chest, circling my nipples with his tongue and sliding his hands down my body. I slid easily onto him and rocked back and forth, feeling myself building up quickly.

Luke pulled me up and off him, flipping me over onto my back with ease and sliding back into me. I wrapped my legs around his waist and pulled him in deeper. His change to the position had knocked me off my stride, I realised with mild irritation. After fifteen years with the same man (discounting my occasional quickies with Luke) I had developed some shortcuts to ensuring I always had a good time. If this was going to be a regular arrangement, I needed to leave satisfied. I slid down the bed, taking Luke back in my mouth for a few minutes before pushing him onto his back. I rode him hard; my hand pressed firmly down on his chest and his hands in my hair kissing me hungrily. He moaned that he was close, and I bit down on his lip, ordering him to finish. I was dripping in sweat by the time he came deep inside me and I felt my own orgasm crash over me. Luke pulled me into his arms and I let him hold me before I got up and deftly disposed of the condom. I wondered if Luke was going to leave now but when I got into my bed, he took me back in his arms and asked tentatively if he could stay. I kissed him gently and rested my head against his chest in agreement. As I lay in his strong arms, my eyes growing heavy, I realised how much I had missed having someone to cuddle up to. Luke drifted off before me and I shifted slightly to give him space, but he moaned gently in his sleep and pulled me closer, and I felt a little flutter of happiness which floated through my body as I fell asleep.

Chapter 16

After a lazy morning of tired, hungover sex, I felt a twinge of regret that I had to send Luke away to meet up with Andy for lunch. Luke asked if he could see me again Monday before I went away, and I was genuinely gutted that I had to decline as I didn't have any childcare.

Andy had moved lunch from his place to John's. I drove through the gates of his Georgian brick home and crunched up the gravel drive filled with a combination of excitement and nerves. A handsome, blonde spectacled man answered, and I wondered whether John had actual house staff like something out of Downton Abbey. I managed to stutter that I was here to see John and the man greeted me warmly.

"Hi Lucy!" He said warmly. "I'm James, John's brother. I've heard so much about you."

I smiled shyly, following him into the house. Andy and John were in the kitchen, both of them working away at different stations to prepare the lunch. I could tell from the array of utensils that John took cooking as seriously, if not more so, than Andy, who did nothing half-heartedly. I hid a smile at the seriousness on both their faces. Maybe they really were a match made in heaven. James saw my smile and he laughed.

"They didn't even hear the door." He confided, and he clapped his hands causing them both to jump.

"Hi!" I smiled brightly at them. Andy gave me a half-wave,

but John wiped his hands and walked over to greet me.

"We're running a bit behind," John apologised. "We had some last minute creative inspiration and had to run out to get different potatoes."

"We're wild." Andy chipped in dryly from his chopping board.

James took me by the arm. "Lucy, come and have a sit down with me while they finish up."

"We won't be long!" John promised, returning to his own pots and pans.

"They take this way too seriously." James said laughing as he led me into a tastefully decorated sitting room.

James was lovely and charming at chatted away as we sat and waited. I felt a little uncomfortable at being babysat by John's brother and wished I'd cancelled to spend the day in bed with Luke.

"You know my friend, Jen, don't you?" I asked, politely realising I hadn't said much and not wanting to appear rude.

"I do." James replied, smiling wryly. "She was the one that got away."

"Really?" I asked, feeling a twinge of something that felt a little too close to jealousy for my liking.

"I was head-over-heels," James grinned sheepishly. "I've

never met anyone like her."

"She's pretty special." I agreed, with equal parts pride and guardedness.

I wanted to ask how serious they had been, but I held back, feeling like I'd be betraying Jen to nose into her private life.

"I thought I was going to marry her." He continued, clearly a big fan of sharing but answering my unspoken question. "Haven't met anyone who came close to her."

Andy walked into the room at that moment, carrying a tray of coffee.

"Is James telling you about how hard his single life is?" Andy laughed, and James joined in.

"Don't listen to him!" John followed Andy into the room. "He's got a string of women on tap! In fact, Lucy, don't look him in the eyes or you'll be next."

They all laughed good-naturedly, and I regarded James in a fresh light. He was very attractive, although very different to his brother. John was film-star handsome, but James was undeniably sexy in a very upper-class kind of way. He wouldn't have looked out of place on the cover of a magazine. I wondered why Jen had ended it with him. I made a note to myself to ask her.

James ended up staying for lunch as John and Andy had gone overboard with the cooking. It turned out that cooking wasn't the only passion they shared, and John was genuinely funny, kind and caring. I felt a surge of happiness that Andy might just get his own happy ever after.

"Jen might be coming away for a few days." I mentioned as the subject had turned to my upcoming holiday with the kids.

"Was everything ok with Jen?" John asked, looking genuinely concerned. "I'm so sorry that the media jumped on that cropped shot. I didn't even think!"

Andy shot me a look and I frowned in response.

"I think everything was ok," I said, tentatively. "She hasn't said anything and there hasn't been anything in the news that I know of."

"Luckily that American boy band scandal hit when it did," James said dryly. "Well, lucky for your friend, and John, anyway."

"Yeah," I agreed, feeling increasingly uncomfortable at the conversation. "I think it's all fine now. No harm done."

"Have you spoke to her?" John asked, directing this at Andy.

Andy shook his head. "We're not that close. She's Lucy's friend."

I tried to keep my face neutral despite feeling annoyed at Andy's response. If we'd been alone, I would have reminded him of all the nights out we'd had as a threesome and how well they both got on, but, being as John was present and I couldn't say anything without making Andy look bad, I bit my lip and said nothing.

"Really?" John looked like he didn't quite believe what Andy was saying. "I'd have thought you would have got on really well with her. From what I remember she's quite like you, Andy."

"Is she?" Andy asked, batting John's question back with one of his own. A classic Andy technique.

John could clearly read Andy's annoyance at the subject, but he persevered.

"Funny, ambitious, good looking." John reeled off, giving Andy a little smile as he did.

Andy couldn't help but smile back and I was impressed to see John knew the secret art of diffusing Andy's moods already.

"Lucy," John turned his attention to me. "Is Jen upset in anyway with Andy and I?"

I was useless when put on the spot. I flushed a little and shook my head. "No, I don't think so..."

"That's a yes." John interrupted. He turned to Andy. "Andy, you know her better than me. You'll have to reach out. It's our bloody fault for not thinking!"

Andy gave a tight-lipped smile. "It's fine, John. There's been no harm done."

"I know that it's come to nothing!" John exclaimed. "But I don't want you to fall out over it."

I started to worry I was going to have to sit here and witness them have an argument. James, on the other hand, looked completely nonplussed as if they were discussing their Sunday lunch.

"We haven't fallen out." Andy repeated, a little coolly this time.

John raised his eyebrows in response to Andy's tone and Andy got up.

"I'm going to check on the dinner." He said, turning away and leaving.

John turned back to me, looking a little embarrassed.

"Sorry, Lucy," He apologised. "I'll just..."

He gestured to the door as if to follow Andy and I nodded, dying inside at the thought of there being a huge scene over this.

James looked at me, when they'd both left the room.

"They'll be fine," James said confidently. "They'll sort it out now. Is Jen single?"

I nodded, wishing he'd change the subject. I felt conflicted enough as it was, without speaking about Jen to an ex. I could hear raised voices in the kitchen and I held my breath waiting for it to all kick off.

"What's she up to these days?" He pressed on, oblivious to the argument taking place across the hallway.

"She's doing well," I said politely. "She's off to New York on a secondment soon."

"Really?" James' face lit up. "I spend a lot of time out there with work."

Of course, he fucking did. They were all super-important Business-class regulars. His persistence in talking about Jen was starting to get on my nerves.

"Who do you work for?" I asked, skilfully turning the conversation, knowing that if he was anything like Steve and his awful colleagues, he would relish the opportunity to talk about himself.

As we'd been talking, I realised I could no longer hear any raised voices; just the sound of pots and pans. The smell of roast beef floated into the room and my stomach growled in response, interrupting James' response.

"I'm starving too!" James said, grinning at my rumbling abdomen.

"Sorry!" I exclaimed. "I'm a bit hungover and all I can think of is food."

"You're in for a treat then," James laughed. "John is an amazing cook. I didn't think he'd ever meet anyone who matched his culinary expertise until Andy rocked up."

Andy came through to call us for lunch, with a sheepish smile at me that told me all was well with him and John.

"Ok?" I asked, giving him a pointed look.

"I will speak to Jen," He said quietly to me, so James wouldn't overhear. "And I am sorry."

I gave his arm an appreciative squeeze and followed him through to the kitchen, where a farmhouse-style table had been set informally for lunch.

John and Andy waited for us to be seated and carried over dishes of vegetables and potatoes. Andy passed me a plate loaded with delicate slices of mouth-watering roast beef and I accepted it gratefully.

"Oh, this smells like heaven!" I moaned appreciatively. We helped ourselves to the vegetables and I tasted their last-minute potatoes.

"What do you think?" Andy asked, proudly and I gave him a thumbs-up through my mouthful.

"She's hungover," James volunteered. "You could have fed her a McDonald's and she'd be loving it."

I laughed and protested that the potatoes were well worth the wait.

"Oh yes!" Andy chimed in. "Tell us about your date!"

“It was nice.” I smiled shyly.

“Where did you go? What did you do?” John pressed.

I filled them in briefly, with Andy interrupting to give an edited background story of how I worked with Luke and had always secretly fancied him. Andy, kindly, deleted the part where I’d been sleeping with him on a casual basis whilst married and also kept his opinions about how Luke was unworthy to himself. I gave him a little nod of thanks which I knew he understood. We exchanged a smile of solidarity.

“Did he sleep over?” Andy asked.

I smiled shyly again and was rewarded with applause from my fellow diners.

“Good for you, Lucy.” John congratulated me. “Got to get back in the game! Are you seeing him again?”

“He asked to see me tomorrow,” I told him. “I can’t though so I’ll see him when I’m back from holiday.”

“I’ll babysit.” Andy offered immediately.

“Can I babysit too?” John asked, looking enthusiastic.

John Taylor was now offering to babysit my kids! I felt momentarily dumbstruck by how surreal this moment was. I was eating lunch and joking with a major A-list film star in his home and he was actually trying to wingman me with the hot twenty-eight-year-old I was dating!

"You can't come to Lucy's!" Andy shook his head at John. "She'll be splashed across the papers next. Suburban MILF and the film star!"

"I'll come in disguise!" John protested. "As the milkman."

"Nobody has a milkman anymore!" Andy laughed. "You could be the window cleaner!"

"You wouldn't want to," I insisted. "My children are like wild animals!"

"They can't be any worse than my niece and nephew," John joked. "We have them over all the time when I'm home."

"They're not!" Andy said, leaning forward and spooning the last of the potatoes onto my plate. "John's niece and nephew are real little monsters. Your kids are pretty good, Luce, there's just loads of them!"

"They are monsters!" John agreed, not at all offended by Andy's description of his kin. "Ruby drew in marker pen all over the wall on the landing- I'll show you after."

"Not my kids!" James cut in quickly. "That's our other brother."

"Are you the one that does stand-up?" I asked, remembering that's how Andy and John had met.

"Yes," John nodded. "He's pretty good too."

James denied this but looked pleased with the compliment.

"You haven't done anything for a while." I commented to Andy.

"I know," Andy shrugged. "It's fitting it in. We've been busy. I will do some soon."

"You can't be offering to babysit for me then," I said. "If you're that busy."

"That's different," Andy insisted. "I want you to get out there and date someone."

"Plus, we're practising in case we decide to have kids!" John grinned.

They both laughed but I could see that there was some truth in this in the way that they smiled at each other. They looked at each other with such affection and the love between them was almost tangible. I felt a little bubble of happiness that maybe Andy had found his soulmate, and maybe the tiniest glimmer of hope that it wasn't too late for me to be that happy too.

Chapter 17

I spent Monday in a whirlwind of panic as the reality kicked in that in less than twenty-four hours I would be boarding a low-cost airline alone with four children and our luggage. Steve popped over Monday evening and continued his run of friendly and helpful behaviour, giving me clear directions to the apartment and instructions for everything there as well as taking the kids out for dinner while I did some last-minute packing. Luke had been texting me all day, clearly angling for an invitation over when the kids went to bed, but I had too much still to organise. I couldn't face having to pull out my A game to impress him and I didn't feel we were at the stage, after one date, where I could reveal my true, hideous, stressful self. Jen was still undecided as to whether she could spare the time to come and out, as much as I had been looking forward to having some adult company, I completely understood and told her the offer was open if she changed her mind.

The kids were relatively well behaved in the airport. The logistics of having four children caused me to panic slightly as I tried to cram them into seats dependant on who would need the most supervision to prevent us getting kicked off the plane and who would cry if they weren't sat by me. I offered up a prayer of thanks for Esther, who maturely took charge of Matilda and entertained her/ fed her Pringles and Haribo for the entire flight, so I could stop George and Leo kicking the back of the seats in front as they whinged about the lack of leg room like the middle-class brats they were. Emily was heading out to stay with my parents for the first week of the school holidays and as I broke up the first fight between my sons, I chastised myself for not going with them to Spain and being foolish enough to tackle this trip single-handedly.

When we arrived in Portugal, I realised with horror that I'd completely overlooked the fact that most taxis would only fit four people in. I had taken for granted the availability of bigger cabs in London plus my home advantage of knowing the public transport routes. With a little help from google, I bravely commandeered my gang onto a bus. I had had the foresight to pack lighter than usual and I felt a glimmer of pride as we headed to our destination. If Steve were here, he'd be huffing and puffing and getting annoyed with the kids by now. Although he'd have definitely booked a car.

We ended up getting off the bus a little prematurely and I kicked myself for jinxing us with my smug thoughts earlier. The sun was blazing, and I couldn't quite figure out which direction we needed to walk in to get to the complex. Leo and Matilda were starting to flag, and Esther surveyed me with an expression of contempt as she watched me frowning over Google maps.

"Are we there yet?" George moaned impatiently.

"I'm thirsty." Matilda chipped in.

Leo piped up, seconding Matilda.

I shot a look at Esther, telepathically willing her not to add fuel to the potential mutiny.

"I think I remember this place," Esther said, ignoring my pleading eyes. "The golf course is miles away."

This set off more protests from my traitorous children. I took another look at my phone and pasted on my most confident expression as I spurred them on in what I prayed was the right direction. I dragged the suitcase and led the way; beads of sweat starting to form on my forehead. It was pretty hot. I started to worry that the kids would burn or dehydrate. George and Leo walked behind me carrying their own bags, and Esther brought up the rear, dragging a small wheeled case behind her with her little sister clinging to her back.

After about half a mile, I noticed a turning up a hill that looked familiar.

"Oh!" I pointed excitedly. "This is the way, isn't it?"

George agreed with me confidently that this definitely looked familiar. While Steve was a regular at this complex, we'd only been as a family twice. I could call him and ask him, but I didn't want to admit defeat this early on in both the holiday and my life as a single mother.

We crossed the road and made our way up the hill. It was a lot steeper than I remembered, but that was probably because Steve had driven us this way, not forced four children to lug their suitcases in the midday July sun. I glanced back, guiltily, to see how the children were faring. George and Leo had lagged even further behind, level now with Esther, who had given up piggy-backing Matilda.

"Mum!" Esther called to me, looking hot and cross. "You'll have to carry her. She's too heavy and she won't walk."

I stopped, panting slightly and waited for them to slowly catch me up. They were all red and sweaty, and I realised I hadn't even put any lotion on them yet.

"Not much further!" I said in an encouraging tone. "You're doing great!"

"How much further?" Matilda whined, her blonde curls stuck to her face with sweat.

"Not far." I avoided giving a definitive answer as I couldn't be one hundred percent sure whether it was another ten minutes or another half an hour. Probably more like an hour at this rate.

"Carry me." Matilda demanded, hanging off my leg.

I hefted her onto my hip, grimacing at the added load and felt my knees almost buckle as we set off again.

They walked unbearably slowly, and I felt ready to pass out with the exertion of lugging Matilda and the suitcase up the hill. Esther kept tripping on the uneven paving in the unsuitable flip flops she had insisted on wearing. She swore loudly with frustration and dragged her case off the kerb, proceeding to continue her journey in the road.

"Please walk on the pavement." I warned her, too tired to pick her up on her bad language.

"There's hardly any cars." She countered, picking up speed to prove her point.

At that moment, Leo tripped on the pavement, sending him flying forward onto his knees. He promptly burst into tears and I hurriedly released Matilda and the case to rush to him. His knees were skinned and bleeding. I hugged him close to me as I frantically searched for a tissue or a plaster in my bag.

Patched up and still sobbing, I tried to heave him up onto my back.

"Matilda?" I asked, feeling desperate. "Could you carry Leo's bag please?"

"No!" Matilda was hot and bothered now. "It's too heavy!"

She flung the bag I was trying to pass her on the floor and burst into tears, sitting down on the pavement in a show of protest. Leo clung onto my back even tighter, fearful that Matilda's tantrum would win over his bloodied knees. George and Esther both sat down on the kerb in solidarity with their little sister.

I felt a wave of helplessness rush over me and fought the urge to sink down next to them and burst into tears. I turned my back to my children long enough for me to take a few calming breaths and blink back the tears of pity that were threatening to spill over. Nobody prepares you for the moments when you are forced to be the only adult. They should teach this before you're allowed to take your baby home from the hospital. Or better yet, paste this warning over condom packets as advertising for a child-free life.

"Right!" I said, summoning my inner-Jen as unfortunately giving up was not an option. "We'll make it to the top of the hill. There's a shop before the apartment and I'll get you drinks and ice creams."

Matilda scrambled to her feet and Leo bravely slid off my back and picked up his own bag.

"Both?" George asked suspiciously before he committed to this truce.

"Both." I confirmed.

George and Esther joined the others on their feet. Esther gave me an icy stare but after years of receiving these from Steve it rolled off me without the desired impact.

We climbed the rest of the hill slowly and steadily. I sang a few songs, changing the lyrics, to make them laugh and distract them. Esther looked disgusted, but the others laughed and made up songs of their own. By the time we reached the crossroads at the top, I was dripping in sweat. I was relieved to see the shop as I'd been beginning to think I had imagined its existence. I duly came through on my end of the bargain and we sat in the shade with the drinks and ice cream to catch our breath.

Sun lotion applied and slightly placated, we continued with our journey. My phone signal was patchy and so I had used my extremely basic grasp of the local language to obtain rough directions from the lady in the shop. We walked on in the blistering heat and had been going for another twenty minutes when I felt the mood shift back to tired and miserable.

We walked past the bus stop that we should have alighted at, and the feelings of failure returned to me. I wanted, more than anything, to be a strong, independent woman who could tackle something as simple as taking her own family on holiday without getting lost and killing them from heat stroke. I blinked away the second lot of silly, childish tears, but surveying my hot and tired children, I knew I was failing them.

Just as I was ready to phone Steve (if I could get a signal) and beg for him to solve this, the complex appeared, like a mirage on the horizon, and I almost danced with relief. The apartment was easy to find once we reached the block and Steve's instructions were thankfully clear and concise. We abandoned our cases and changed quickly into our swimwear and were poolside within half an hour of opening the apartment door. There was a poolside bar that served snacks and I ordered more drinks and plates of fries to tide the children over until later. I sank, exhausted and relieved, onto a sun lounger, keeping one eye on the children as I sipped an icy cold beer.

The complex WI-FI kicked in and I had a stack of messages come through at the same time. Emily and my mother had both texted to check we'd arrived, as had Steve. I responded to them, confirming that we were here, and all was good (editing out that my failure as a responsible adult had caused us nearly an hour of traipsing in nearly thirty-degree heat). Two more messages came through; Jen asking for a picture of the complex to tempt her into abandoning her priorities for some sun-seeking and an explicit picture message from Luke. I sent Jen back a selfie of me in my bikini holding a beer. I was tempted to ignore Luke, but I looked quite nice in my bikini, so I sent him the same picture I had sent Jen.

"Wish I was there to rub your lotion in." Luke replied immediately.

We chatted via message for a while. The redundancy announcements were due on Thursday and as much as we'd both said we hated our jobs and wanted it, I could tell Luke was feeling as nervous as me with D-day looming.

"I've booked Friday off," He messaged. "If I get VR, I might jump on a flight and come and join you."

I assumed he was joking and sent back a quick, "That sounds amazing! I wish."

I put my phone down and concentrated on devouring the plate of chips in front of me. Matilda had climbed out of the pool and was sat dripping cold water over my towel.

"What's the matter?" I asked her, wrapping her up in her own towel.

"Dad always plays with me in the pool," She said, grumpily. "George and Leo won't play my game, and Esther is boring and won't come in."

I hated going in the swimming pool when we were away, unless it was scorching. I was much more at home in the sea. That had been one advantage of Steve; despite being either absent or moody, he doted on Matilda and would play whatever game she demanded of him. Nobody else in the family would play with her as she had a habit of changing the rules to suit her own purposes. I had been worried that she would carry this trait into her school life, but her teachers had reassured me that she wasn't a sociopathic monster in school. Those weren't their exact words, but I read between the lines.

"What do you want to play?" I asked, draining the rest of my beer now it was apparent that I would have to get in the cold pool.

"Mermaid-zombies riding on unicorns." Matilda declared.

"Do we have a unicorn?" I asked, wondering whether the shop sold unicorn floats as I'd been hoping to buy some inflatables and leave them at the apartment ready for Steve's trip.

"No," Matilda frowned at me. "You're the unicorn."

"What if I want to be a zombie-mermaid?" I joked, taking her hand and tentatively dipping my toes into the pool. I winced at the coldness, let go of my daughter and jumped in. Esther shouted at me crossly as I'd splashed her with the freezing water, and I hid a smirk.

"Mermaid- zombie!" Matilda corrected me from the poolside. She dropped the towel into a puddle of water and jumped fearlessly after me. I caught her, and she climbed up onto my shoulders. We splashed about, laughing and playing, until, one by one, the children clambered out of the pool cold and sleepy. I decided that we should have a siesta and we gathered up our soaking wet towels and made our way up to the apartment.

After a few initial arguments, they finally reached a compromise on the sleeping arrangements, with the boys taking the twin beds, Matilda bagging the double bed with me and Esther opting for the privacy of the sofa bed. I pottered around and unpacked the suitcase, before heading onto the balcony with the beer I'd brought up from the pool. I shut the door behind me and dug out my secret stash of cigarettes, lighting one up and exhaling as I leant over the railings. The apartment looked over the golf course, acres of rolling green fringed by dark green forest that I knew dropped off to the sea beyond. I stared out, enjoying my moment of solitude with the sun beating down on my face. I extinguished the cigarette in the empty bottle of beer, planning on burying the evidence at the bottom of the kitchen bin. My plan was to walk down to the beach a little later for dinner and stock up on essentials for breakfast and snacks on the walk back. The children would be happy enough to chill at the apartment in the evenings with their iPads and I could sit out on the balcony with a bottle of wine and the book I'd being dying to read.

The walk down to the beach was a lot easier than our journey to the apartment, thankfully, and we had a lovely dinner al fresco before paddling in the sea. I bought as much food and drink for the apartment as I could carry, and Matilda was beside herself with excitement when she spotted an inflatable unicorn. This led to Leo and George also demanding novelty floats and the sun was almost setting by the time we trekked back lugging a unicorn, a crocodile and a giant inflatable pizza slice. Esther was too cool to want an inflatable, but I caught her eyeing up the unicorn and would have put money on it that I'd be buying her a pool float the next day. We all went to bed early, exhausted by the day, and I was fast asleep within minutes of laying down.

We headed to the beach in the morning and spent a leisurely day alternating between digging in the sand, splashing in the sea and snoozing under the parasol I'd bought. I made them come back to the apartment before they showed any signs of being tired, careful to not repeat another disastrous journey when they were tired and hot. We stopped for lunch on the way and I talked them into another siesta when we got back to the apartment, promising that we'd hit the pool in the afternoon and have dinner on the balcony.

Everything just felt easier and more relaxed when the sun was shining, and the skies were blue. I daydreamed how nice it would be to live here. My go-to dream, even as a child, had been to live in a white-washed villa somewhere. I pictured myself cycling along the beach on my way to some little job that didn't require a suit and meetings. Being so close to the beach made my soul happy and I basked in the time alone with the children. I felt grateful to Steve for making this happen and I hoped that he would enjoy his time away with them as much as I was. I wondered, fleetingly, whether it would be different or awkward for the children having their dad's new girlfriend around, but this was something I guess they'd have to get used to if Charlotte was going to be a permanent fixture in his life. I just hoped that Steve would appreciate his time with the kids and not be side-tracked by his bikini-clad new blonde.

Jen had messaged a lot, still not sure whether she could afford to take the time out to come over, and I promised her that we'd definitely arrange a weekend away here in the future, most likely after her stint in New York was complete.

Luke messaged me on Wednesday night. I had sent him a "good morning" selfie of me and when I didn't get a response all day, I wondered if he was slipping back into his old, elusive habits. I hadn't asked him if he was seeing anyone else, but I realised that he could well be as we hadn't made any promises of commitment to each other. I was drinking the last of my wine after a simple, homemade meal of bread, cheese and local meats when I opened his message.

"Good luck for tomorrow." It said. "Text me when you find

out x."

I was annoyed that it had taken all day for him to respond to my message but half-grateful that he hadn't given me any of his "just seen this" bullshit.

"Good luck to you too." I replied. "Let me know as soon as you find out!"

Roger had been annoyed that I wasn't coming in for my face-to-face meeting and had wanted to delay telling me until I was back in the office. I had made some noise about checking with HR and he had relented and promised to phone me. I felt nervous at the prospect as I was pretty sure that they would be happy to pay anyone off who willingly asked for it rather than make involuntary cuts. I vowed that I wouldn't stress out and ruin my holiday but would start job hunting on my return as, if successful, the leaving date was scheduled for 1st September.

Despite my insistence that I'd be cool and calm, I was a bag of nerves all day Thursday until the phone call finally came after 2pm. Roger waffled on, with his usual long-winded spiel and I found myself growing more and more agitated waiting for him to get to the point.

"Your request for redundancy," He finally told me. "Was agreed. Your leaving date will be 31st August."

He continued talking, a warning about maintaining standards and non-disclosure until the rest of the announcements had been made. I cut him off, faking a poolside crisis, and ended the call, desperate for silence to be able to process the news. So that was it. I was free from my job. I would have a small lump sum that would last me until Christmas, providing Steve didn't cut off his share of the bills. I exhaled slowly to calm my racing heart. My first thoughts were to share this, and I dialled Jen's number.

"Have you heard?" She answered breathlessly, as if she'd run to answer her phone.

"Yes!" I exclaimed. "I've got it!"

"Oh my god!" She shrieked excitedly. "I'm so happy for you. How do you feel?"

"Amazing!" I answered honestly. "And a bit scared."

"I promise you," Jen said. "It'll be fine."

"I'm just scared now that I won't find anything before the money runs out." I admitted.

"You will!" Jen replied emphatically. "Anywhere would be lucky to have you."

"Thank you." I said gratefully. "Are you in work?"

"Yes," She said. "I just almost vaulted over my desk to get my phone as I knew it would be you. I just had a feeling."

I laughed, picturing her doing this. "All ok at work?"

"Yeah, just busy," She sighed. "Andy phoned me by the way."

“I thought he might.” I filled her in briefly on an exaggerated story of how remorseful Andy was.

“I’ve forgiven him,” Jen said, her voice slightly cool. “But if he tries anything like that again…”

“He won’t!” I said quickly.

“Are you having a lovely time?” Jen asked, changing the subject.

“Yes, it’s beautiful here,” I told her. “We’re having an amazing time.”

“I wish I could come,” Jen sighed again. “I don’t think I’m going to be able to, and I feel bad about leaving Coco when we haven’t got much time left together.”

“It’s ok,” I said, feeling gutted but genuinely understanding. “We’ll come again. Just the two of us.”

“Definitely!” Jen agreed. “I’ve got to go back to work but phone me later. I’m so happy for you.”

I thanked her and promised to call later. I stared at my phone when she hung up and realised how disappointed I was that she wasn’t coming out. I had loved spending time with the children but in the evening, they preferred to retire to their electronics and it was a bit lonely sat on the balcony sipping wine with no adult company. A message from Luke popped up and I shook myself out of my thoughts to read it.

“Leaving!!!!” He had written. “You?”

I sent a reply confirming my own news and congratulating him. I ordered myself a wine at the bar, in lieu of champagne, and led back on my sunbed toasting myself and my future. Half an hour had passed when another message came through from Luke.

"Just found flights to you tomorrow night. I'm coming to see you!!!!"

I spluttered on a mouthful of wine and almost dropped my phone. I jabbed a chipped fingernail at the call option and waited, heart in mouth, for him to pick up and tell me he was joking.

"Hey babe!" He answered the phone, sounding upbeat. "Are you excited?"

"Ummm," I had panic dialled him and had no idea how to start this conversation if he wasn't joking. "You were joking, right?"

"No," Luke said, his tone changing slightly. "Why? Don't you want to see me?"

"Of course, I do," I replied automatically and then kicking myself for my words. "It's just a bit awkward because of the kids."

"I'll sleep on the sofa," Luke said easily. "I totally get that it's too soon to be parading me around."

"It's only a little apartment," I said feebly. "And Esther is on the sofa at the moment."

“Can’t she jump in with you?” He asked, sounding a little annoyed. “Or do you want me to book myself a hotel room. I don’t mind but I did have a look and most places are full as its peak season.”

“When are you flying home?” I asked, chewing my lip with worry.

“I thought you’d be happy I wanted to come and see you,” Luke replied, sounding hurt. “I’ll just cancel my flights. It’s only a few hundred pounds I’ll lose.”

“No!” I protested, immediately feeling guilty as he’d clearly misread my signs somewhere along the lines. I remembered the reply I’d sent him at the beginning of the week which had more or less told him I wanted him to be there. “I was just wondering how long you’d be here.”

I wondered if any of the other apartments were vacant and I could speak to the lady who managed the rentals to sort something out.

“I’ve got a flight back Sunday evening.” He said, still a little huffily.

“The kids are quite full on,” I warned him. “So, we won’t have any alone time.”

“I’m not coming out there just to shag you!” Luke responded with indignation. “I don’t think this was a good idea.”

You’re telling me! I thought, gobsmacked that he now

seemed to be annoyed with me.

“Luke,” I tried to reason with him. “You know I would love nothing more than to have you here with me.”

“But?” He cut in, a little sulkily.

I didn’t want him losing the money he’d paid and what I was saying was true. I did want to see him. Despite us only having been on one date, I had known him for years, so it was probably no different from Andy or Jen coming over, I reasoned to myself. I was also a little scared of ruining the chance of a relationship before it had even had chance to start.

“But nothing!” I said brightly, even though I was still filled with doubt. “I can’t wait to see you!”

“You sure?” Luke asked a little suspiciously.

“Yes!” I replied, sounding even more enthusiastic this time. “I was just worried that it would be hard keeping my hands off you.”

Luke laughed, and sounded genuinely pleased now. “You’ll have to keep those hands to yourself, babe. I want to make a good first impression.”

We chatted a while longer and I gave him the details of how to get to the apartment. By the time he hung up, he sounded happy and excited to see me. I went back to the bar for another wine. I drank it quickly, standing up, and ordered another one. How the hell was I going to explain this to the children.

Chapter 18

I tried to focus on the positive. Luke clearly thought enough of me that he had happily spent a few hundred pounds to spend a measly two nights in the company of me and my children. Steve was planning on forcing his new significant other onto the children for a whole week, so I was hardly the worst mother ever for subjecting them to not even two full days with someone who was technically just a colleague and a friend. The time would have had to come when Luke would spend time at my home, and maybe even move in, all going well in the future. Dating in your thirties was probably always a bit more rushed.

It niggled away at me though that this choice felt like it had been taken out of my hands. Despite what Steve chose to do, I knew, in my heart, that it was too early to be adding another change to the children's lives. I bounced back and forth between looking forward to having adult company and wishing I'd put my foot down and made it clear that this week was for me to spend time with my kids. Luke and I could have even arranged to come out for a weekend on our own. It was too late now, and I had to work up to telling the children.

I started to form the sentence a few times but backed out. Over dinner, I told the children that I'd be leaving the bank and looking for a new job when school started.

"Why?" Leo asked, looking thoughtful.

At last, the perfect segue. I explained about the

redundancies and how I really wanted to do something different, although I wasn't sure what yet.

"A few of my colleagues are also leaving," I continued tentatively. "One of them, Luke, is in Portugal this weekend. I said he could stay at the apartment."

"Why?" Esther's head snapped up from her phone and she regarded me with suspicion.

"He's thinking of buying an apartment out here," I brazenly lied, losing my nerve under Esther's judging look. "I said he could have a look at ours."

"So why does he need to stay?" She repeated, setting her phone down and crossing her arms.

"It's just polite to offer." I shrugged, going back to my salad unable to maintain eye contact with her.

I made a mental note to text Luke to back up my lie.

"Is he your boyfriend?" George asked, swinging on his chair and looking interested.

"Ummm, no," I answered uncertainly. "Not really."

"Oh my God, he is!" Esther practically shouted, standing up and banging her chair against the table.

"Esther," I warned her. "He's not my boyfriend. He's my friend. And he's really nice."

"If Dad gets to have a girlfriend, Mum can have a boyfriend

if she likes." George defended me.

"I've got a girlfriend." Matilda chipped in, shovelling bread into her mouth.

"Have you?" I asked, glad of the diversion. "Esther, sit down and eat your dinner."

Esther sat back down, with a face like thunder.

"Yes," Matilda continued, the centre of her own world. "Hannah is my girlfriend and we're going to get married."

"Aw," I said, ignoring Esther's sulk. "That's cute."

"It's not cute," Matilda shook her head at me. "It's serious business, marriage."

"Right." I nodded solemnly at her. Maybe that's where Steve and I had been going wrong.

Matilda dominated the conversation for the rest of the meal, telling us in detail about her wedding plans and her subsequent career as a Unicorn keeper. As I was clearing up, I pulled Esther to one side.

"I know you're not happy," I said quietly. "Just say whatever you need to say now."

Esther shrugged at me. "It's your life, Mum. And I don't want you to be old and lonely, but it's sly throwing it on us like this."

"Es," I turned her to face me. "I swear to you that this is last minute. I did invite Jen, but she couldn't come. Luke seriously just told me today that he was coming. I can show you the text."

I was improvising now, and I prayed that she didn't accept this offer as I had loads of dodgy texts that I needed to delete from the thread first. Fortunately, she just nodded and gave me a little half-smile.

"It's fine, Mum." She turned back to her phone and I exhaled in relief.

The next day, I let the kids make all the decisions to make up for being the worst mother ever. This meant that we had McDonald's for lunch and spent all day on the beach. Luke's flight was due in at 9pm, so I was hoping the kids would be fast asleep by the time he arrived. Esther had begrudgingly agreed to sharing a bed with Matilda and I, and I was hoping I'd have enough time to do a quick tidy up after they'd gone to bed.

Predictably, nothing went to plan. Everyone was wide awake, and the apartment was a mess when Luke knocked the door at just after 10pm. Matilda flew off the sofa bed, that I'd been desperately trying to make, and flung the door open before I could stop her.

"Hi." She said confidently.

"Hi," Luke smiled. "Is your Mum there?"

"Yes." Matilda answered, still blocking the door.

I rushed up behind her and scooped her out of the doorway.

"Hi!" I smiled, a little flustered.

He grinned at me and I took a moment to appreciate how good looking he was, dressed in chino shorts and a dark t-shirt, his bag slung over his shoulder.

I opened the door wider and ushered him in, introducing him to the children. The older three greeted him with polite but disinterested hello's before heading into their bedrooms and closing the doors. I offered him a drink and we went out on to the balcony. Matilda followed eagerly.

"She'll get bored and leave in a bit." I whispered to him.

We sat down with our drinks on the balcony. We were both silent for a moment and I realised how awkward this weekend could potentially be. Not for the first time, I cursed myself for letting this happen by being a doormat.

"How was your flight?" I managed finally when the silence got too much.

"It was alright." He replied, taking a sip of his wine.

I waited for him to continue the conversation. He got up and leaned on the railings.

"It's lovely here." He said, staring out at the dimly lit golf course.

"My mum said you're going to buy a house here." Matilda

said, jumping into his vacated seat.

"Did she?" Luke frowned, and I made eyes at him which I hoped he'd interpret as we'd discuss this later. Matilda swung on the chair for a few moments and then, thankfully, wandered back into the apartment.

Luke turned around and smiled at me. "Come here."

I glanced over my shoulder to check she was really gone before I let him pull me into his arms. He kissed me deeply on the lips and I tried to relax into his embrace, but I was too anxious about one of the kids walking in.

"So, I'm going to buy a house?" He raised his eyebrows at me as I pulled away and took my seat again.

I sighed. "I just didn't want to force a new boyfriend into their lives. They're going away with their dad and his girlfriend at the end of the holidays and it's a lot of change for them."

"Boyfriend?" Luke asked in a serious tone.

I felt myself blushing furiously. "You know what I mean."

Luke laughed and took my hand, pulling me back to my feet. "No, I like the sound of that."

He kissed me again. His lips gently probing at mine and I felt myself start to relax and respond. He wrapped his arms around me.

"We'll see how this weekend goes," I warned him. "This is what my life is like, and it's not pretty!"

Luke laughed again. "They seem like good kids. I'm sure it'll be fine."

We had a few more drinks and the awkwardness seemed to melt away. I pointed out the direction of the beach to Luke and he stared out thoughtfully.

"The kids are too young to be left on their own, are they?" He asked.

"Yes." I told him in a slightly sharp tone.

"Oh, ok," he said, looking taken aback. "I don't know, do I? It would have been nice to go for dinner and drinks with you."

"Next time," I said, softening a little and leaning forward to kiss him gently. "We can go down there tomorrow night, but obviously I'll have the kids."

"That sounds nice." He said, reaching over and holding my hand.

He seemed surprised when I showed him where he would be sleeping and then turned in the direction of my own bedroom.

"Aren't you going to jump in with me?" He asked, pouting a little.

I shook my head. “No! I told you I can’t.”

“Just for a minute?” He pulled back the covers, revealing his muscular thighs in tight boxers.

“Can you put some shorts on?” I asked, feeling like such a frumpy mum the moment the words were out of my mouth.

Luke laughed and then immediately looked confused when he realised I wasn’t joking. He fumbled around in his bag and slipped on a pair of jogger shorts.

“Happy?” He asked, a little sarcastically sitting down on the edge of the bed.

Not really, I felt like answering. Instead I nodded and crept back over, feeling guilty at the atmosphere already. I slipped onto his lap, facing him and wrapped my legs around his back. I slid my hand down his chest, feeling his muscles tense under my fingers. I trailed tiny, soft kisses down the side of his face and neck slowly.

“When we come back here,” I whispered seductively in his ear. “I promise I’ll show you a good time.”

I trailed my hand along his thigh, stopping before I went too far. I kissed him again, on the lips this time, flicking my tongue between his lips and he groaned in my ear.

“Such a tease.” He reached to grab me as I slipped off his lap. I turned and gave him a smile, blowing him a kiss.

“Goodnight Luke.”

I climbed into my own bed and lay awake for most of the night, conscious of Luke on the other side of the door. I was so annoyed at myself for letting Luke into my real life. Not only did I have to worry about psychologically damaging my darling children by subjecting them to my "boyfriend" this early on in the separation but I was also now forced to let Luke see the unsexy, stressed out Mum side of me too.

The next day went more smoothly. We spent the day at the beach, which meant Luke could lie and sunbathe a few feet away from us while I dug holes, supervised any sea swimming and reapplied sun cream every ten minutes. Luke declined coming for lunch with us, claiming he wasn't hungry, and I agreed to meet him back at the apartment. I panicked that he had maybe realised that he had bitten off more than he could chew trying to date a mother of four. I said nothing though and gathered up our belongings to make the short walk over to a beach front restaurant that served chicken nuggets.

"He's actually quite fit," Esther told me as we ordered our food. "Well done, Mum, you little hottie."

"Esther!" I laughed, slightly mortified.

"No," Esther shook her head, grinning at me. "I mean it, Mum. I thought you'd just get a really ugly, fat, old boyfriend but you've done good."

"He's not a proper boyfriend." I warned her. "Don't go getting excited. I could still end up with some old grandad."

"That's fine as long as he's rich," Esther winked at me. "With a dodgy heart."

We both burst out laughing and I was relieved that Esther didn't seem effected by this monumental fuck up of mine.

Luke didn't come back to the apartment until later that afternoon. We'd foregone our usual siesta for a lounge around the swimming pool. Luke strolled up at about 5pm, just as I was ushering the children out of the pool.

"Hey!" I smiled hesitantly, unsure whether he had considerately been giving me and the children our own space or whether he was finding this so difficult he couldn't bear to come back.

"Hi." He smiled and went to kiss me, before remembering at the last minute that I was surrounded by my children and pulling away.

"What've you been up to?" I asked politely.

"I fell asleep on the beach, grabbed some food and went for a walk," He then winked at me. "I went to see some apartments."

George frowned at him. "Why did you wink at my Mum?"

Esther gave a snort of laughter and Luke looked at me in panic. I laughed at his expression and just shook my head, ignoring George.

"We're going to go up for a couple of hours, get changed

and then go for dinner if you'd like to come?" I invited him.

"I'd love to," He smiled back then looked at George expectantly. "Is that alright with you?"

"Yeah," George shrugged. "Just don't wink at my Mum."

Luke laughed this time and chucked his towel down on a sunbed. "I'll be up in a bit. I'm just going to have an hour down here."

I smiled gratefully at him, appreciating that he was trying to not impose too much on my time with the children.

We went back down to the beach to eat, and when Luke tentatively slipped his hand into mine I let him, feeling a genuine little flutter at the gesture. After dinner, we had a few drinks by the beach while the children played on the sand in front of us. The sun was setting, and Luke was holding my hand discreetly under the table.

As moments go, I thought to myself, this was quite a lovely one.

Luke let go of my hand and pulled out his phone. "We haven't had a holiday selfie."

I smiled at him and let him pull me close for the obligatory picture.

"Put a filter on it," I ordered when he showed me the photo. "I look old."

Luke glanced over at the kids to check they weren't looking and, on seeing that the coast was clear, kissed me on the lips. "You look beautiful."

I cuddled a little closer to him, feeling happy that he seemed to be fitting into my world.

By the time Luke left, on Sunday afternoon, to get his flight back home, I felt relaxed and confident that we could make things work back at home. All I had to do now was find a job that I actually liked, and I could live my own happy ever after.

Chapter 19

My spirits were, amazingly, still high when we finally got home late Monday night. I was physically exhausted by the time I dumped the bags in the hallway but mentally and emotionally I felt stronger than ever.

Steve had texted offering to bring the car to pick us up from the airport, which was nice of him, but I was determined to continue my run of independence. Mainly though, I was conscious of the children mentioning Luke when I was trapped with Steve in a people carrier and couldn't escape any questioning. I politely declined, and Steve replied asking if he could have them for the day Saturday. I jumped on this and offered him the option of staying overnight (without me) but he already had plans. I felt a little miffed at this. I had got over the whole Charlotte thing pretty quickly, which I felt Steve owed me some gratitude for. For all Steve knew, I was a lonely, broken-hearted wife. He at least owed me a few nights off. Spending time with Luke while I had the kids with me had been easier than I thought it would be, but I had a feeling Luke would get tired of having to fit into my family plans if I couldn't manage regular 'alone time'. Instead of brooding on this and feeling miserable and hard done by as I usually would, I resolved to speak to Steve about this sooner rather than later.

Luke had maintained a steady flow of contact after he'd left which gave me a warm, fuzzy feeling, knowing that I was wanted. He was keen to spend some more time together and I had already sent Andy a pleading message, first thing

Tuesday, asking when he could fulfil his best friend duties and help me get laid by babysitting.

My good mood was also aided by knowing that I didn't have to walk back into work for another week, and that when I did I would be on the final countdown to leaving. There weren't enough words to describe the joy and freedom I felt at the thought of never having to don that uniform and that fake smile again.

The only fly in the ointment was Jen's leaving date creeping closer. I would have to compete with the time difference and her no-doubt fabulous new life in New York to maintain our friendship. Wild nights out and lazy nights in would be a thing of the past. With Andy settled down and my redundancy imminent, my only social life would be the occasional boozy nights with my 'mum' friends where the topics of conversation varied diversely between children, husbands and other mothers. If things didn't work out with Luke, I would be a real loner without Jen around.

Andy replied to my plea offering his services for Friday. I was over the moon with this as I had been expecting to be palmed off with a Wednesday or a Thursday that nobody (namely Luke) would want to go out on. I messaged Luke immediately with the good news.

"Hey babe," He replied a few hours later. "Can't do Friday. Out with the boys. Saturday?"

I sighed, frustrated, and replied that Friday was my only free night. Luke read my message at 4.04pm according to my iPhone. After staring at my phone for what felt like hours waiting for a response that didn't come, I threw my phone down on the sofa and left it there in annoyance.

I went back to my phone half an hour later when my disappointment had lifted slightly. I picked my phone up expecting a reply from Luke but there was only a missed call from Jen. I flopped down on the sofa and called her back.

"Hi." I said brightly when she answered. "What's up?"

"You didn't tell me Luke came to Portugal!" Jen exclaimed, without bothering to say hello.

There was an accusatory edge to her tone.

Shit, how did she know? I wondered, panicking slightly. Maybe Andy had told her. We had spoken via message a few times, so I had no excuse not to tell her, but I had held off, worried about how she would react.

I tried to play it down slightly, feeling guilty for my lie-by-omission. "It was really last minute. I forgot to tell you."

"You forgot to tell me?" I could hear the disbelief in her voice and my guilt climbed another few levels.

"I was hoping to see you, so I could tell you what happened," I continued, praying she wouldn't be upset with me. "When are you free?"

"When are you free is probably the better starting point?" Jen countered, still cool but I could feel her thawing.

“Friday?” I offered my only night on a platter to placate my friend.

“Steve’s having the kids on a Friday night?” Jen asked incredulously, her annoyance with me temporarily forgotten.

“No, Andy.” I told her.

“It’s like a parallel universe!” Jen exclaimed. “If you come over mine Saturday and help me with more packing, you’ve got yourself a date. Obviously, the kids can come.”

“I love you!” I declared, grateful that she had forgiven my shady behaviour. “Steve’s actually having the kids in the day so how about I come and help you, and then we have a takeaway at mine Saturday night. Coco can come.”

“Deal,” Jen agreed. “We won’t get wasted Friday then- dinner and drinks.”

We finalised our plans and I dialled Andy’s number to find out what he had said so I could get my story straight without digging an even bigger hole.

“I didn’t say anything,” Andy said when I got hold of him. “I spoke to her to apologise for all that stuff from before, but we don’t talk really. Only via you. Has he tagged you in anything?”

I hadn’t thought of that, but I hadn’t had any social media notifications. Andy put me on handsfree while he checked my various profiles.

"Yes," He confirmed after a few moments of silence. "On Instagram. It doesn't come up though, so she must have looked at your tagged photos."

I was glad Andy was savvy with things like this as I honestly had no clue.

"Can I delete it?" I asked, opening the app and seeing the notification that I'd missed.

Andy talked me through how to remove it from my profile. I stared at the photo for a few more moments.

"Actually," I said, changing my mind. "That's pretty cute that Luke's put that photo on. I might leave it there."

Andy laughed. "Up to you. Anyway, John and I are definitely on for babysitting Friday. I made you a promise and I won't let you down."

"John's coming?" I asked shocked.

"Is that ok?" Andy sounded surprised at my tone.

"Oh yes, of course," I said quickly. "As long as he doesn't mind."

"Of course not." Andy replied. "See you then."

The moment I hung up the phone I flew into a panic. John was coming to my house. I paced through the house, trying to view each room through the eyes of a super-rich film star. I wondered aloud whether I would have time to completely redecorate the living room by Friday.

Esther heard me muttering and stared at me in alarm.

"Mum, are you ok?" She asked with concern.

"I've been meaning to decorate for years!" I wailed in frustration, more to myself than in response to my child. "Now it's too late!"

"Too late for what?" Esther regarded me with equal parts suspicion and acceptance as if she had been waiting for this breakdown since the break-up.

"The house!" I exclaimed, throwing my hands up in the air. "Andy's babysitting Friday and it's a state in here!"

I spotted a scuff on the wall and made a beeline for it, scrubbing at it furiously with the sleeve of my cardigan.

Esther was watching me as if I was losing it. "So? Andy's been here millions of times."

"I know." I said abandoning the mark when it became apparent it wouldn't budge. "But his boyfriend hasn't."

"Oh crap!" Esther morphed into a mirror image of her panic-stricken mother. "That man from those films? Oh God, he'll think we're animals, Mum!"

I almost laughed at Esther's face, realising she was as prone to over-reacting as me. I made a note to myself to dilute my crazy as it was definitely shaping my kids.

"Ok." I sat down and switched on my problem-solving mode. "Realistically, we need to decide what we can change by Friday?"

Esther took a seat next to me and together we surveyed the room, eyes narrowed identically in scrutiny.

"Can we replace the sofas?" Esther asked uncertainly.

"No." I answered, but regarding the huge grey sofas and instantly wishing they were more chic and minimalistic.

"That wall?" Esther pointed at the patterned feature wall that was meant to compliment the rest of the room.

"I don't know how long that would take." I admitted.

Esther pulled her phone out and started googling. "No, that'll take a few days."

"Shall we just go and look for some inspiration?" I asked, warming to the theme of making some physical changes to my home.

We spent the rest of the day cruising various furniture and DIY stores and we spent the evening rearranging furniture, switching soft furnishings and erasing scuffs and fingerprints from walls throughout the house. We'd even bought wallpaper and hired a steamer, but I decided that this would have to wait until after Friday as I didn't want John to have to walk into an even worse state.

By Friday morning, I had started to come down from my

positive start to the week. I knew I was feeling a little insecure about things with Luke as, although he'd kept up contact, he hadn't made any attempt to reschedule a date or even asked to come over. Not that I wanted him to come over, as I was still of the opinion that it was too soon, but he'd been keen to spend the weekend away with me and then, nothing. Steve had also gone from showing a glimpse of his humanity to parading his high life on social media, and I'd seen a tagged picture of him and Charlotte on Instagram (only now I was in the know, thanks to Andy, that these even existed). Steve looked like a dick in an expensive blazer and jean combo that screamed 'trying to be young'. Charlotte was practically clinging to his chest, doing that awful pouting thing and, in my opinion, had accessorised hideously.

As much as I had distracted myself for the last month since Steve had packed up and left, I still had periods where I felt sad and hurt over our separation. Despite knowing about Charlotte, actually seeing an image of them looking happy and in love felt like a stab to my heart. I spent at least an hour obsessing over the picture and morbidly going back to scrutinise every detail. I treated myself to a little cry in the shower and then resolved to not look at it again.

I almost welcomed the nerves that I felt about John coming over this evening with Andy as it was a welcome distraction from my low mood. I'd mentioned my little social media stalk to Andy when we had spoken that morning and he had instantly tried to make me feel better about it.

"Everyone looks at their ex's new partner or their new partner's ex," He assured me. "Just give yourself a daily stalking limit so you don't obsess over it though!"

"Really?" I asked, doubtful that Charlotte was currently pouring over photos of me online.

"I promise." Andy said confidently. "Why are you faltering now? It's Luke, isn't it?"

How the hell did Andy read me so well?! I admitted that Luke had been full on and now he'd backed off a little.

"You need to get on a dating app or something," Andy warned me. "Luke's fine for a rebound but we both know he's too flaky for anything long term."

Part of me knew what Andy was saying had some truth in it, but, at the same time, Luke wouldn't have come out to Portugal if he hadn't wanted something serious. Or posted a picture of me on his Instagram.

I voiced my thoughts and Andy shot me back down. "Why didn't he jump on the chance to see you tonight?"

"Shall we just leave this before I end up crying?" I said, feeling tearful.

"Sorry, Lucy," Andy apologised. "I'm probably just being hard on him because I don't want you to get hurt."

"It's fine. I'll see you tonight." I sniffed. "Thank you, though. I know you're just looking out for me."

Not only did I have the image of my husband and his attractive, successful new girlfriend tattooed onto my brain but now I was almost certain that Luke had lost interest in me. All this negativity circled around in my head until I received a message from Luke at 5pm, while I was just thinking about starting to get ready for that night.

"Miss you too much." The message read. "Cancelled with the boys. What time are you free?"

My heart skipped and sank at almost the same time. This is what I wanted from him, but it was too late to cancel on Jen. I called him to break the news.

"Hello?" Luke's voice was barely audible over the background noise.

"Can you hear me?" I asked, trying to make out what he was saying over the echoes.

"Babe?" There was another muffled noise and the line went dead.

Frustrated, I texted him. "Can't hear you. Can you phone me when you've got signal? I've got plans now that I can't change." I added a sad face emoji for good measure and pressed send.

No response came, and I continued getting ready, feeling a little gutted that I'd miss out on seeing him. He finally called me half an hour later.

"I can't believe you've made plans," He said when I

explained that I was seeing Jen. "I cancelled a night out just to see you."

"I know," I said sadly. "If I could change mine, I would."

"Why can't you?" He asked. "You can see your friend anytime."

"She's moving abroad next week," I said. "I can't cancel on her."

"Shall I come over yours?" He asked. "You can fake a headache and come home early?"

"I'd love to," I smiled wryly. "But my kids are here with the babysitter."

"I thought they were going to their dad's?" He asked, sounding a little annoyed now.

"Tomorrow," I told him. "But only in the day."

"Ok, I'll see you then," He said in an almost identical sulky tone to the one Steve had frequently used when he didn't get his own way. "Glad you phoned before I got home. I can go straight to the pub now."

"I've promised to help Jen pack tomorrow," I apologised guiltily. "I'm really sorry. I'll try to sort something next week."

Even as I said this, I knew I had little chance of making this happen, especially as I was back in work.

Luke made an exasperated noise. "I don't know why I bother. I'll see you whenever."

Frustrated, I flung my phone down and lay down on my bed. It wasn't long before the self-pitying tears had turned to full blown racking sobs, muffled by my face in the pillow. It just felt like nothing would ever go right for me. If I hadn't been seeing that absolute idiot maybe I'd have made more effort and my husband wouldn't have left me in the first place. Had I really thrown it all away for him? I felt so foolish and angry with myself.

I was red-faced, un-showered and still lying on my bed when Esther called up the stairs to announce Andy's arrival. All I wanted to do right now was crawl into bed and never face anyone again. I didn't feel like I had the strength in me to get up, but the thought of Andy or, worse, John finding me crying and pitiful was almost worse than the knowledge that I was destined to die alone bitter and miserable. I called down that I wouldn't be long and then raced to repair the damage to my swollen eyes in record time.

I emerged, not so much a beautiful butterfly but a passable moth, dressed casually in a shirt dress and sandals. I politely kissed John, gushing my thanks for his kind offer to babysit. I could see Andy regarding me suspiciously as I thanked him too. I left before he could grill me, knowing that I would break down within minutes of any interrogation.

The tears kept creeping back on my journey to meet Jen and the more I tried to push them away, the harder the wave of sadness came crashing back. I searched in my bag for my sunglasses, despite it being quite an overcast day.

"Lucy!" Jen spotted me as she waited at our designated meeting point opposite the restaurant.

I waved and walked over.

"Why are you wearing sunglasses?" She asked, peering at me curiously as she leant in for a hug.

The minute she pulled me towards her, the crescendo of misery burst its banks and I collapsed in a sobbing heap in her arms.

Chapter 20

Jen whisked me into a nearby bar, dragging me into the toilets. I allowed myself to be manhandled; too overwhelmed by my own emotions to care about the people turning to stare. She snatched up a roll of toilet tissue from a cubicle and lifted my sunglasses from my face, mopping at my make-up smeared face. She must have realised that there was no point while I was still hysterically sobbing as she dropped the wad of tissue in the bin and wrapped her arms around me again.

"It's ok," She murmured, stroking my hair like I was a child. "Let it out, Lucy."

I couldn't have stopped if I'd wanted to and I cried and cried until I finally felt purged. As the racking sobs slowed to a mere sniffle, Jen went back to work with the tissues, wiping the smudged eye liner and mascara as best as she could manage.

"Are you going to tell me what's happened?" She asked finally.

I felt a little silly and self-conscious now the outburst was over, and I glanced around the room at the other women, washing their hands or re-applying already flawless makeup.

"Shall we just go home?" Jen tried again.

"What about dinner?" I asked in a small voice, wanting nothing more than to go back to Jen's away from the general public.

"I'm not even hungry," She shrugged. "We can get takeaway anyway."

"But you're all dressed up!" I protested. My voice then broke and another ridiculous sob broke free. "And you look so beautifuuullll."

Jen's hand flew to her mouth as if I was the saddest thing she had ever seen. Which I possibly was. "Oh, my poor Lucy! Come on! We're getting out of here."

She ordered a taxi on the app on her phone and, while we waited, she ordered two large vodkas which we drank standing up. As the alcohol coursed through my bloodstream, I felt fuzzy, exhausted and grateful to Jen for taking charge. I was also extremely conscious that I was ruining her night, so I tried to paste on a brave face and talk her out of cancelling our dinner by explaining I was just having a delayed meltdown, brought on by Luke turning out to be the douche that Jen had told me he was. I waited for her to pull out the "I told you so" but instead she hugged me again.

"Oh, that's so shit," She looked genuinely sympathetic. "Neither of them ever deserved you. We're going home and we're going to get shit-faced and have a proper cry."

"Are you ok?" I asked, immediately concerned at Jen wanting to cry too.

"I will be," She gave my hand a squeeze as we drained our glasses and made our way out to the waiting cab. "I just feel really sad to be leaving."

"I'm such a bad friend," I felt myself welling up again as we slid into the car. "It's been all about me and my drama when you've got so much going on!"

"Lucy!" Jen exclaimed at my tearful expression. "We're not allowed to do this until we're safely behind closed doors."

I laughed at this and slipped my hand into hers gratefully.

By the time we got back to hers, I was feeling a little bit better although that consisted of empty numbness as opposed to rock bottom despair. Jen stripped off her shoes and dress and threw on a pair of comfortable pyjama bottoms and a vest top. I took off my shoes and flopped down on the sofa.

"Shall we drink first or order food?" She asked, hovering by the fridge.

"Drink!" I ordered, knotting my hair up on top of my head now we'd abandoned our plans.

Jen poured us both large glasses of wine and we clinked them together in a silent toast to us.

"What are you going to do?" Jen asked, sitting on the opposite side of the sofa to me and stretching out.

"There's nothing I can do." I shrugged feeling hopeless.

"Ok," Jen considered this for a moment. "What do you want to happen?"

I shrugged again.

"Do you want to get back with Steve?"

"He's with someone." I sniffed, taking a huge gulp of my wine.

"That wasn't my question." Jen said pointedly, and I shook my head straight away.

"No." I said, realising as I said it that I didn't.

Jen tilted her head to the side questioningly.

"We should never have got back together." I realised. "I've been on eggshells around him and his moods for years. I'm better on my own. Except I'm not happy on my own."

"Why aren't you happy on your own?" Jen probed, sitting up a little and leaning forward.

I shrugged. "It's just lonely, isn't it?"

Jen gestured to herself and her apartment. "Is it?"

I flushed, not wanting to offend her. "Not for you, Jen. You're strong and confident. You've got an amazing career and you're not needy like me!"

"Why did I want to come back here to put on my pyjamas and have a pity party then?" She asked, topping up both our glasses.

“Really?” I asked uncertain whether she was just trying to make me feel better.

Jen just seemed to always have her shit together. She was beautiful, successful and she had an amazing social life. I didn’t believe she’d ever allow herself to be walked all over and left heartbroken by someone.

“Really.” She looked at me, her face serious.

“What’s going on?” I asked, feeling worse about Jen’s sadness than I did about my own.

“It’s just everything and nothing,” She waved my concern away flippantly. “I’ll get over it. Honestly, I’m just hormonal and feeling guilty about leaving Coco.”

“Coco will be fine.” I reassured her.

We both turned our gaze to the little dog lying forlornly in her basket, giving us sad eyes.

“I’m making her worse,” Jen admitted. “I’ve just been crying every time I look at her this week so she’s picking up on my sad vibes.”

“It’ll fly by,” I promised. “And she’ll be so spoilt at your Gran’s. And I’ll visit.”

“Oh my God, will you?” Jen’s face lit up like a child at Christmas.

Shit. I'd meant I'd visit Coco at Jen's grandmother's house. I realised straight away that that was not how Jen had interpreted it though. I couldn't bear to kick her while she was down and so I smiled back and nodded, while furiously trying to calculate how far my Avios points would take me.

"That would mean everything to me!" Jen continued, looking delighted.

Coco noticed the change in her mother and hopped up onto the sofa between us, wagging her little tail.

"I wish you could come," Jen said apologetically to Coco. "But you would hate the flight and you'd have to go in the hold."

"I'll visit her too." I promised.

Jen sighed with happiness, leaning back against the sofa. "Honestly, Lucy, you don't know how much that means to me. When do you think you'll be able to come?"

"I guess it'll depend on when Steve can have the kids." I said, feeling guilty at my own hesitation.

If I was on my own and not a financial mess, I would be over there like a shot.

Jen pulled her phone out and started typing away. "Did you say Steve was taking the kids away?"

I nodded, "Last week of the school holidays."

"Perfect!" Jen exclaimed excitedly. "I'll have been there a

couple of weeks by then. I'll find flights."

I started to worry and wondered how to tell Jen I couldn't afford it. She was so determined when she got an idea in her head. She was so naturally assertive and proactive. It was no wonder she had done so well in the business world.

Despite my last conversation with Luke probably being the end of my budding romance, it crossed my mind how annoyed he would be that I was using my one guaranteed child-free week to spend more time with my friend.

"It'll be my last week in work," I told her. "I don't think I'll be able to get it off."

"Just don't go in." She said breezily and then turned to look at me. "Actually, you're right it's selfish of me to expect you to miss your last week and give up a whole child free week to hang around an empty hotel room all day when I'm working. Especially if you're still with Luke."

"I doubt I will be after today." I shrugged, surprised but grateful for her consideration. "That's what he's been a dick about today."

I told Jen an abbreviated version of the story. How Luke had declined my time saying he had plans and then expected me to cancel my own plans to see him at the last minute because he'd had a change of heart. As I told her, I felt a little sheepish at admitting how thoughtless he'd been. Jen was so kind and so non-judgemental that I opened up further and explained how he had booked flights last minute to Portugal, despite my reluctance for him to meet the kids so early on.

Jen did her best to disguise the fact that she clearly thought this was out of order and gave me a sympathetic smile.

"It might just be hard for Luke to understand how someone with children has different priorities," She started diplomatically. "Have you tried talking to him about it?"

"You understand." I said, fed up of trying to excuse the shitty behaviour of the men in my life.

"That's different." Jen looked pleased at my recognition though.

"How?" I asked. "You've gone out of your way to fit into my life, even when it was inconvenient."

"That's because I love you." She smiled at me and I felt a familiar little flutter at her words.

"Is it?" I felt my face growing warm at her words and my heart quicken.

"Yes," She lifted Coco into her lap, smoothing the little dog's face. "And if Luke understood your priorities, maybe he'd be a bit more appreciative of your time."

"Maybe." I said, seriously doubting this. I didn't understand why Jen was being so encouraging of my relationship with Luke. She'd had nothing good to say about him before. I vocalised my thoughts.

"It doesn't matter what I think of him," She shrugged. "I'm not going to be here for you. You'll be going through a lot over the next few months: new job, a separation, God knows what else Steve will throw your way. All on top of the stress of navigating the kids through life. You said yourself that you get lonely."

"I wish I was confident enough to be happy on my own," I admitted. "It would probably solve half my imaginary problems."

Jen laughed at this. "Be on your own then. It'll be good for you."

"I'm too weak and needy." I joked.

Jen shook her head, a little exasperated. "What do these Steve's and these Luke's bring to your table anyway?"

"Just sex and stress." I replied after thinking about it for a minute.

"You need to decide whether the half an hour is worth the headaches and the heartache," Jen said. "You know you could easily be your own fucking Prince Charming."

I smiled at that, knowing she was right. I fell from relationship to relationship. Even before Steve, I'd always had a boyfriend. Maybe being on my own was the answer to my stresses.

"You always make me feel like I can do anything." I said gratefully to her. "You should be a motivational speaker. Or my life coach."

Jen laughed at this. "You do the same for me."

"No, I don't," I protested. "You never need me like I need you."

"Stop being down on yourself!" Jen tipped the last of the wine in our glasses and shook the empty bottle at me to show me we'd drained it already. "You've built me up before every date, every job interview, every trip I've taken. You've been my cheerleader."

"That's just what friends do."

In contrast to husbands or boyfriends I'd had that had always made me feel smaller and less capable. Jen went on dates occasionally but despite us being friends since I was pregnant with George, there had only been two people that she'd been serious enough with for me to actually meet. When they'd broken up, Jen had always been remarkably nonplussed about it, citing her independence as being more important to her. She'd had marriage proposals from more people than I'd slept with and, despite always declining, she managed to break people's hearts gently, so all her exes still counted her as a friend.

"Shall we have a cigarette?" She asked, gesturing to the balcony.

We went outside. It was getting dark now as we'd been sat chatting for ages. We stared out at the city lit up around us.

Jen sighed. "I wonder if I'll miss this view."

"I will come out to New York." I said suddenly spurred on by Jen's words to do more for myself.

"Really?" Jen's face lit up hopefully.

"Yes." I nodded. "It'll be amazing."

"Thank you!" Jen covered her mouth with her free hand and I could see her big dark eyes filling with tears of happiness.

Coco chose that moment to wander out onto the balcony and, with a doggy sigh as if she knew we were talking about Jen leaving, sunk to Jen's feet.

Simultaneously, both of us welled up with tears and, before long, we were a crying heap on the tiles. Jen clutched Coco to her and I wrapped my arms around Jen. Coco licked at Jen's tear stained face as if she wanted to comfort her, which made us both cry harder at the sweetness.

"I love you so much." Jen whispered, smoothing Coco's floppy ears back from her face.

Her sweet exchange with her dog made my heart hurt. Jen sat on the floor between my legs, cradling Coco to her own chest. This was the kind of love I wanted, I realised. Someone who felt the same way as me about things, who loved animals and crying, who I could look like crap with and not care. Jen was right. I could be my own hero. I had Jen to meet all my emotional needs and Andy to remind me to stand up for myself and to take my car for its MOT. I said as much to

Jen and we both laughed.

"I'm going to have to go home soon," I told her, gutted to be leaving. "I promised I'd be back by 11. I'll come back in the morning."

Jen looked gutted and, for a moment, I saw that she was just as vulnerable and capable of loneliness as I was. She just hid it better.

"Unless," I started hesitantly. "You and Coco want to come over. We can go for brunch in the morning before we come back here to do your packing."

Jen paused as if considering this. "I will come. And Coco, as long as you don't mind her sleeping in her basket in your bedroom. It's going to be hard leaving you, Lucy."

"Of course," I smiled back, getting to my feet, determined to stay positive and not burst into tears for the third time that night. "Come on. Let's make the most of each other for the next week!"

Chapter 21

We did make the most of the next week, even though we were both manic; Jen finalising her move and me working and juggling the kids. Jen and Coco stayed at mine for the weekend. There was none of the awkwardness I felt went Luke had spent two nights with me and the kids, as Jen was easy going and genuinely seemed to like being around my family.

Luke hadn't called or texted so, feeling empowered, I refused to go begging and apologise for not prioritising him over my friend. I had been too busy having a good time with Jen to even feel more than a temporary pang of sadness.

Esther had insisted she was too old for childcare and so was spending the holidays in the house or out with her friends. I was, obviously, a nervous wreck which led to more dressings down in work as I kept nipping out to call and text her throughout the day.

I had made Steve aware that Esther was staying on her own and asked him to be on standby "just in case".

"Just in case what?" He'd asked, looking a little annoyed as if I was being ridiculous.

"I don't know!" I answered defensively. "She's only thirteen. Lots of things could happen."

"If you're that worried, you shouldn't have said she could!"

Steve retorted.

"What could I do with her?" I exclaimed. "Bring her to work with me?"

"You're finishing soon," Steve shrugged. "Just don't go in."

It was pointless trying to get through to him, so I said no more on the subject and just hoped for the best.

As I had sensed with my motherly intuition, the crisis came Wednesday as I was missing another lunch hour to cover for our short- staffed cashiers so Hannah, who was expecting another baby, could leave early for her twelve-week scan. It had been manic all day in work and I hadn't had time to check my phone every half an hour. As I grabbed a coffee from the back office to keep me going until the end of the day, I checked my phone and my heart almost stopped when I saw a stack of missed calls from Esther. I dialled her number and waited, breath held in panic.

Finally, Esther answered.

"What's the matter?" I burst out as soon as I heard her voice.

"Ella is being a cow," She said sulkily. "So, I need you to come and get me."

Esther had had plans to go shopping with her friend Ella and I'd left her with enough money to shop and buy lunch.

"Where are you?" I asked, feeling relieved that she was just being dramatic.

Esther named an out-of-town shopping mall, and I gasped in horror.

“How the hell did you get there?” I exclaimed. “That’s like an hour away! Is her mum there?”

“Her older cousin brought us.” Esther said defensively. “I’m not going home with her. I hate her.”

“You’ll have to.” I told her, feeling annoyed at both Esther for going so far away without clearing it with me first and with myself for thinking she was responsible enough to be left on her own when she clearly wasn’t.

“She’s not answering her phone.” Esther said in a small voice and I could tell she was on the verge of tears.

“Can you phone her cousin?” I asked, immediately feeling guilty when I heard how upset she sounded. “I’m in work and it’s at least an hour to get to you.”

“I don’t know his number,” Esther sniffed. “And he’s really weird. That’s why I had an argument with her.”

“How old is he?” I asked, horrified.

“Seventeen.” Esther admitted. “I’ve tried to phone Dad and he’s not answering. Dad would come and get me.”

If I left now, I knew Roger would stop Hannah going to her appointment. My priority though was my teenage daughter and her safety.

"Have you got charge on your phone?" I asked, desperately trying to work out what to do for the best.

Esther confirmed that she did.

"Ok, give me five minutes," I assured her. "I'll figure something out."

Esther promised to listen out for my call and hung up. At that moment a text from Jen came through. I opened it distractedly.

"I'm driving past yours from Gran's," She had written. "Is Esther in? Can I take some more of those boxes out of your shed?"

I dialled her number, thinking it would be quicker than texting her. I explained Esther wasn't in and my predicament.

"I'll have to drop the boxes to you later, if that's ok." I apologised, keeping one eye on the door to the bank floor. The moment Hannah left, I would have to make a run for it.

"Oh my God," Jen gasped. "Don't worry about the boxes. I'll go and get Esther for you."

"I couldn't ask you to do that!" I protested. "I'll just have to leave work."

"No." Jen insisted. "I've got Gran's car today to move the last of my things, so I'll go. Text me Esther's number so I can arrange to meet her. I'll bloody wipe the floor with her friend's cousin too."

“Thank you!” I exclaimed. “Thank you so much. I’ll call her now.”

I kept my phone in my pocket, even though this was against the policy in work, and kept an eye on it until Jen texted me to confirm that she had Esther and they were on their way back home. It was only then that I felt the panic die away.

By the time that I got home, Esther was over her fright and was back to being sulkily defensive. I sent the younger children into the living room and went straight up to her room. I tried to drive home to Esther the risk she had put herself in.

“You’re thirteen years old!” I wailed in a high-pitched tone that I couldn’t help. “Anything could have happened to you!”

“It’s fine,” Esther shrugged moodily. “Ella said sorry. She thinks her cousin is a bit weird now and we’re just not going to bother with him again.”

Oh my God, I couldn’t cope with this. I had told Esther that I was proud that she had got herself out of a situation where she’d felt uncomfortable despite the peer pressure she’d felt from her friend, but inside I was still shaking at what could have been. I walked away, feeling myself seething with fear and anger. I would call Ella’s parents later when I had calmed down. I wandered into the kitchen to pour myself a well-deserved wine when I saw a huge bouquet of flowers on the kitchen table. I peered at the card.

It simply read “Sorry. Luke.”

“Who put these flowers here?” I yelled up to Esther, not being able to face another trip up the stairs. Now the adrenaline had left me, I was exhausted.

“Jen.” Esther shouted down. “They were on the doorstep.”

The cynic in me wondered what Luke was apologising for: railroading me into allowing him to gate crash my family holiday, dropping me for his mates, expecting me to cancel my plans or going in a mood and not texting me for over five days. Maybe all the above. I sat down to drink my medicinal glass of wine and appraised the bouquet. It was a big arrangement and they were pretty. I felt myself thawing slightly the longer I looked at the mass of lilies and roses. Knowing that Luke didn’t like to put himself ‘out there’ emotionally, I appreciated that he must be sorry to have pulled out a stereotypical romantic gesture like this. I reached for my phone to call him to thank him and accept his apology.

Even as I scrolled through my contact list, I felt a little niggle at the back of mind reminding me of the conversation Jen and I had had over the weekend. I couldn’t imagine Jen being swept back up just because someone sent her flowers. On the other hand, I could imagine how awful it would feel to have such a lovely gesture as sending flowers rejected. The thought of hurting anyone intentionally made me break out into a cold sweat. I would just phone him and thank him, I decided. I would be able to gage whether he understood that his behaviour was not ok and then I’d be able to make an informed decision as to whether we could move forward from this. Decision made, I felt proud of myself for not compromising my own principles and I made the call. Frustratingly, it went to voicemail. I left him a message simply saying, "Thank you for the flowers. Call me back." I called Jen instead to thank her properly going out of her way to rescue my wayward teenager. Jen was as concerned as I was about Ella's cousin's inappropriate remarks that had caused Esther to walk away. I reassured Jen that Esther was ok and thanked her again for her help. I waited for her to mention the flowers, but she didn't, so I left it.

"Will I see you before you go?" I asked in an almost pleading tone.

"Of course!" Jen exclaimed. "I promised we'd see John and Andy too so shall we make it a foursome. Obviously, something a little more private after last time! If Steve's a dick about having the kids, we can always just have a takeaway at yours. "

When we'd come back to the house Friday night for an impromptu sleepover, Jen and Andy had been fine despite it being the first time they'd seen each other in person. John had claimed he had had a lovely time babysitting although Andy had moaned that he was exhausted from juggling four children and two dogs, which made me laugh as he was always implying that his life was way more stressful than mine. I almost hoped that Andy and John would start a family, so I could rub my hands with glee at Andy suffering through parenting problems like school runs and sleepless nights.

“I’ve had Freya, my emergency baby sitter, on a retainer specifically for this occasion!” I promised. “I wouldn’t miss seeing you for the world.”

My phone beeped with an incoming call and I saw Luke’s name flashing up on the screen.

“Luke’s phoning me back.” I said aloud, without thinking.

“Ok,” Jen said in a bright tone that rang a little false in my ears. “I’ll speak to you later.”

Without waiting for a reply, she ended the call. Oh shit, I hadn’t meant that I wanted to go. I pressed the accept button automatically.

“Hey,” I said in a similarly cheery tone to the one Jen had just used on me. “Thank you for the flowers.”

“That’s ok,” Luke said, sounding a little sheepish. “Sorry I was in a mood.”

All the rehearsed ‘strong, independent woman’ lines that I’d had on the tip of my tongue earlier seemed to evade me and I heard myself reply with a feeble, “Oh that’s OK. I understand.”

What the fuck, Lucy! I chastised myself. You need him to understand that it wasn’t ok.

“It’s just hard,” Luke started. “Because you’re never free and I’m not used to having to make plans so far in advance.”

"Right." I nodded, getting ready to give him my spiel. "The thing is-"

"But I get that your life is crazy hectic," Luke cut me off before I could even get started. "And I've had a think about it. Even though it's difficult-"

He was recognising that my life was busy and could be difficult. That was a start.

"Because I'm used to girls, like, my age," He continued. "I don't want to be without you, babe. I think I'm in love with you."

I'd heard this before from Luke. It was harmless then as I just figured that it was his go-to pillow talk. I felt slightly conflicted at what he was saying but hearing someone tell you they're in love with you does give you a warm and fuzzy feeling.

"Aw," I replied, not knowing what to say. Then feeling guilty. "Me too."

"Shall I come over later?" He asked. "When the kids are in bed?"

"Today's not great," I admitted apologetically. I updated him on my day's events.

"Ah nightmare," Luke said after I'd recounted my panic and Jen's amazing rescue. "Tomorrow then. I don't want to wait until Friday to see you."

"I can't, Friday." I interrupted. "I'm seeing Jen as it's her last night."

Luke said nothing, and I felt my stomach knot at another potential argument.

"No worries," He finally said breezily. "Maybe Saturday if you're free."

"Yes," I said quickly, exhaling the breath I'd been holding. "Definitely."

We chatted for a while longer and I hung up feeling half-relieved that Luke was finally acting mature about my logistical challenges and half-agitated, but I couldn't quite put my finger on why. After all, Luke wasn't a parent, so I could hardly expect him to understand my panic over Esther. I silenced the little voice chirping away at the back of my mind that Jen had understood. That's not helpful, I told my inner voice, and forcefully turned my mind back to the present.

Luke came over the following evening and ended up staying. I had intended for him to go home but one thing led to another and we ended up falling asleep. I ushered him out of the house at 6am, praying that the kids wouldn't have noticed. None of them said anything and I spent all day Friday smiling to myself in work. Despite Luke's shortcomings, he was just so sexy, I thought, as I remembered our adventurous antics the previous night.

All that was left to do now was to bid my lovely Jen farewell.

Andy and John had wanted to showcase their culinary talents, so I picked Jen up and we headed out of town to John's house. Andy had been spending a lot of time at John's despite this increasing his commute into work every day. I didn't think I would ever be so in love that I'd happily sit in standstill traffic for two hours every day, but, then again, I was unlikely ever to bag myself a film star.

"Let's try and keep this upbeat," Jen said to me as we got out of my car. "No tearful goodbye's. I'll see you in a couple of weeks."

"I'll try." I promised in a joking tone, despite feeling a tiny bit emotional already.

John was a perfect host again and they'd definitely gone overboard on the food to make up for Jen and I insisting we weren't drinking. By the time we left, Jen and I had both popped the top buttons on our jeans and were groaning at how stuffed we were.

"Andy looks so happy." Jen commented. "They both do."

"It's lovely, isn't it?" I agreed. "To see them so in love."

"That'll be you next." Jen said, staring straight ahead.

"Or you." I said, watching for a reaction out of the side of my eye.

Jen smiled. "Not me. How's things with Luke?"

"Alright." I said hesitantly, not wanting to talk about him and risk souring what had been a lovely night. I changed the subject. "Why not you though?"

"Just alright?" Jen did that thing she does when she doesn't want to answer by pretending she hadn't heard.

"You heard me!" I laughed. "And yeah, just alright. Your turn!"

Jen flashed me a guilty grin. "Why just alright? And I don't know. I'm just not feeling anyone. I can't be bothered to date- it just seems like such a waste of my time."

"Well you are busy," I replied. "Are you just of the mind that if you meet someone, you meet someone."

"Why just alright?" Jen repeated, but with a teasing tone. "And yeah, I just think if it happens, it happens. I don't need anyone."

"You're so wise," I sighed, wishing I was as strong as Jen. "I don't think Luke is 'long term material', do you?"

"Doesn't matter what I think, Lucy," Jen smiled to show she wasn't being shitty. "As long as you're happy, right?"

"Right," I agreed and then added, feeling a little self-conscious. "If I'm honest, I think I might be rebounding."

Jen nodded, and she gave me a little smile.

"You already know that though, don't you?" I could read Jen like a book. "Smart arse."

Jen laughed at that. "You know I'll be there for you, whenever."

I reached over and squeezed her hand. "Same."

Jen stared straight ahead, and I kept her hand in mine.

"Remember we're not getting emotional." Jen warned me, and I could hear her voice break a little.

That set me off and I choked back a full-blown sob. "Sorry."

We both laughed as I took the turning into Jen's street.

"I'm jumping out!" She exclaimed. "I'm not saying bye! I'll text you tomorrow!"

Jen threw the door open before I'd even pulled the car to a complete stop and flew out onto the pavement.

"I love you!" I called. "Text me!"

"I love you too!" We were both laughing at the lengths we were going to avoid a heart-breaking farewell. "Go, Lucy! Go!"

She slammed my door shut and made her way to the entrance to her building. I sat and watched her, feeling almost paralysed to the spot. As she fumbled with her key fob to open the doors, she glanced over her shoulder and saw me still sat there. I put my fingertips to my lips and blew her a kiss. She reciprocated the gesture and paused. For a moment I thought she was going to turn back but she turned back, pushed open the door and was gone.

Chapter 22

After that night, I barely had time to dwell on how sad I felt to see Jen go.

Steve "couldn't" have the kids for the next few weekends as "something" came up last minute. After his initial efforts to be nice, he had slipped back into his usual selfish ways and, on the few occasions I saw him, he seemed stressed out and on edge. If I'd had time to reflect on it, I'm sure I would have felt smug that his life with his new attractive girlfriend clearly wasn't as great as he'd thought it would be. As it was, I was too busy juggling the kids, work and my own new attractive (and needy) boyfriend.

School holidays were always a little bit challenging. The children (with the exception of Esther) were all attending various summer clubs, but they seemed to have stacks of energy when they got home which resulted in late nights and moody mornings dragging them out of bed. I tried to compensate for palming them off at clubs by planning lots of "fun" activities for weekends and some evenings. It wasn't even halfway through the holidays and my energy levels were as depleted as my bank account.

Work was horrendous. Now that I had my leaving date circled and underlined on my calendar, Roger was even more obnoxious than usual; checking up on nearly everything I did as if I was going to pocket the day's takings and do a runner. I had leave left and had requested the last week off to tie in with my trip out to see Jen. The rule was only two people could be off at the same time and so he had no choice but to authorise the majority of my leave, however two people were already off on the Monday and he was point-blank refusing to approve this. There was no chance in hell I was coming in, but his pettiness left a frosty atmosphere between us.

Things with Luke were going ok. Luke had jumped headfirst into job hunting and was scouring the internet daily for jobs far and wide. I was still pondering over what it was I *really* wanted to do after so long doing what I felt expected to. Andy had offered to help me with my CV once I finished work. John was heading off to the US for filming and so Andy was keen to make me his pet project to pass the time. Luke couldn't understand why I was being so lax about finding something, but then Luke didn't have a successful, estranged husband paying his mortgage and the majority of his bills. After racing back to work when most of my offspring were still fresh out of the womb, I thought it might be nice to just kick back and enjoy them for a little bit. All my career-focussed friends thought I was crazy with the exception of Jen, who agreed with me that life was too short to be unhappy. I felt no sense of urgency but maybe that would change when my redundancy started to run out and Steve started talking money.

Another thing that Luke couldn't get his head around was that I liked spending time on my own. I was just beginning to learn that Luke was all or nothing. What Andy had described as "Reward Uncertainty" as a tactic to hook gullible, lonely women, such as myself, in seemed to be part of Luke's genetic make-up. He was either all over me; texting, calling, wanting to see me; or missing presumed dead. To be honest, I think I preferred it when he was the latter. After his five-day sulk and subsequent apology, Luke had been extremely attentive. To the point it was getting on my nerves. When we were together, we got on as well as always. I fancied him, and he was fun to be around. I had described our relationship as a rebound to Jen but there were more than a few fleeting moments, when Luke and I were together, where I thought I could see a future. He insisted on coming over most evenings to spend time together, which was just as well as Steve hadn't had the kids much, but I felt myself thinking back nostalgically to all those nights I'd lounged on my sofa with a glass of wine and trashy TV shows alone, while my husband was out shagging his colleagues. I didn't feel like I could say no to Luke as it was sweet that he wanted to spend time with me when I usually sent him home at bedtime (there was more than one accidental sleepover) plus I was rarely able to go out on dates due to my non-existent childcare and the only week I had away from work and the children, I'd booked to go to Jen's. Luke had been really mature about this, but I could tell he was disappointed.

Steve's holiday with the children was fast approaching. I was torn between not wanting to place my precious angels in the hands of the moody prick and his girlfriend (who he still referred to as "his friend" on the few occasions we spoke about the trip) and being terrified that he was going to cancel, and I wouldn't be able to go to New York. I had signposted this to Jen and she had forced me to speak to my sister to make a back-up plan.

The school holidays raced by, instead of dragging like they usually did. Lois had kindly arranged leaving drinks for the week before my trip as I would miss the joint night out for the few of us who'd opted for redundancy. I would have preferred to slip away with as little fuss as possible, but Lois had gone to loads of effort and I felt obligated to act grateful. I'd given Steve loads of notice of the date, but he was dragging his heels. Probably because he was taking them away less than a week later and thought that counted as his annual quota of parenting. I'd pulled out every tactic possible to get him to agree including, I'm ashamed to admit, telling him in front of the children that if he didn't have them I'd miss the *party* that work were putting on *especially* for *me*. My loyal tribe picked up on my emphasis of the key words and duly chimed up.

"Dad! She can't not go to her own party!" Leo had got the ball rolling.

"Daddy!" Matilda gave him her best cross look.

George and Esther gave him judgemental looks waiting for his response.

"I had plans." Steve said sulkily.

I could tell he was softening under the pressure from the kids though, so I waited silently, letting them do their worst.

"What plans could possibly be more important?" George

scoffed.

The others waited for his response.

"It's fine," Steve answered finally. "I'll have to have them here though. Don't be late."

I'd have to give Luke the heads up that he wouldn't be able to come back here afterwards. He wouldn't be happy, but the alternative was not an option.

Most of the staff from both branches turned up for leaving drinks. Roger obviously opted out. He never came out, except for the mandatory Christmas do where he'd sip one drink all night and disappear by 10pm. I was surprised that Leanne had shown up as we hadn't had many interactions despite doing the same roles at different branches. I assumed that Leanne was grateful that I'd chosen redundancy as it left my role open for her to transfer into and maybe had decided to come out to wish me all the best. I made pleasant, but slightly awkward, small talk with her at the bar before excusing myself and heading over to Luke who had just arrived.

Luke and I were no longer a secret as a few colleagues had seen his Instagram picture of us in Portugal. I walked over to him with a wide smile on my face and went in for a kiss. Luke turned his face and let me brush his cheek lightly with my lips before pulling away.

"Hey," I smiled still brightly, although a little confused about the brush off. "Everything ok?"

"Great." Luke gave me a polite smile but avoided making eye contact. I wondered if he was just trying to play the extent of our relationship down around colleagues or whether he was annoyed that I had to leave early and alone.

"Do you want a drink?" I asked politely, holding up my nearly empty wine glass.

Good etiquette indicated that this was a sign for Luke to offer to buy me a new drink but instead he glanced fleetingly at my hand and shook his head.

"No thanks," He replied equally politely. "Just going to go and catch up with the team."

He made a beeline over to the congregation of staff from his branch, leaving me stood on my own. Confused by his coolness, I wandered back over to my own colleagues. There were definitely two camps being created this evening and I stuck by Lois' side feeling a little embarrassed by his obvious distance.

Lois and I headed to the toilets. I was sat in a cubicle, phone in hand deliberating whether to text Luke asking what was going on when I heard a voice from another cubicle.

"You are so going home with him!" A familiar voice was laughing. "He can't take his eyes off you!"

"We'll see." Came the cool reply that I recognised as Leanne's voice.

I instinctively knew they must be talking about Luke. I calmly pushed my phone back in my bag and went out to the sinks. I spent a ridiculously long amount of time washing my hands, waiting for Leanne and her colleague to emerge from their cubicles. Lois had clearly heard what they were saying and had come to a similar conclusion as she stood next to the hand dryer, with a nervous expression on her face. Leanne emerged, flipping her long hair over her shoulder; all legs in a tiny, black playsuit. She glanced at me and had the decency to look embarrassed. The next cubicle opened and her colleague, Jess, joined her.

"He's so fucking hot," Jess said, oblivious to my presence. "Is he still with that 'Mum'?"

Leanne made a non-committal noise and shot Jess a glance.

"Who's fucking hot?" I asked in a friendly tone which was out of sync with the hard look in my eyes.

Jess noticed me for the first time and hid a smirk. "Oh. No-one you'd know."

"Luke?" I directed the question at Leanne.

Leanne tried to look smug and haughty, but I could see the panic in her eyes. "Luke? God, no! He's such a fuck boy. I couldn't imagine anything worse."

I heard Lois intake a sharp breath and I waited for a feeling of anger at Leanne's put down. When it didn't come, I realised I really didn't care. I didn't care if Luke was shagging Leanne and I certainly didn't give a shit what Leanne thought of me.

"Really?" I gave her an openly contemptuous look. "You would suit each other."

Leanne frowned slightly, unsure of how to take this. I laughed, turned on my heel and swished out. Lois followed quickly behind me.

"Are you ok?" She asked with concern as soon as we were out of earshot.

"I am," I nodded, feeling absolutely fine. "I kind of got stuck with Luke and just want him off my hands now so I can concentrate on my life."

Lois appraised me and, on seeing that I really meant this and wasn't just putting on a brave face, pulled me in for a quick hug. "Good for you, Lucy. I'm not really fussed on him, but everybody needs a rebound."

I laughed at this and headed back to the bar to get drinks for Lois and I. Out of the corner of my eye, I could see Jess whispering animatedly to the staff from her branch. A few of them glance over in my direction and I gave them a cheeky wave. Lois laughed at this and clinked her glass to mine.

"Lo," I said, draining my glass. "I've had a lovely time and I'm so grateful to you for arranging but I think I'm going to call it a night."

Lois hugged me again. "I'm going to miss you."

"I'll miss you too," I said truthfully. "But not all the bitching and politics. We'll definitely keep in touch though, I promise."

I said my goodbyes quickly and with as much warmth as I could muster, purposely including Leanne, Jess and Luke in my little round of hugs. Luke didn't even have the decency to make eye contact and I almost laughed at his uncomfortableness.

I made my way home feeling empowered and like a strong, independent woman. I didn't want a man hanging around and bringing me down, distracting me from my own needs and wants. I'm sure there were relationships out there that were mutually supportive and beneficial. Maybe I was just not great at finding those. I would one hundred percent be having this conversation with Luke at the next opportunity. That's if he didn't just ghost me and go AWOL as was his favourite move based on past experience.

I arrived back at my house and breezed in, not bothering to knock. I heard raised voices in the living room and immediately quickened my pace. Steve and Esther were having a full-blown argument; Steve pacing, red-faced and angry, Esther sat arms crossed and huffy.

"What's going on?" I asked, looking from Steve to Esther with concern.

"Her attitude!" Steve huffed at exactly the same time as Esther pointed accusatorily at her father.

"His attitude!" She fumed.

Steve sat back down; his body language mirroring his daughter's. I almost laughed at the sight of him behaving like a petulant teenager.

"I'm not going to Portugal with his bloody girlfriend." Esther burst out. "And you can't make me."

My heart sank. I was hoping they were arguing about something easily resolvable like an appropriate bed time or her phone bill.

"You bloody well are." Steve responded. "And stop swearing."

The irony was completely lost on Steve and I tried to keep my face calm and neutral.

"Why don't you want to?" I asked evenly. "It's clearly important to your Dad. And I would like you to go."

"Only because you want us out of your hair, so you can swan off with your mate." Esther countered.

"Not at all," I said in my best therapist tone. "I want you to be able to have a lovely holiday with your family. This means a lot to your Dad."

"No, it doesn't," Esther was starting to get upset now that she was off the defensive. "He just wants me there to look after the kids, so he can shag his girlfriend."

“Esther!” I gave her a warning look. “That’s not true.”

Steve looked extremely uncomfortable.

“He can choose!” Esther sniffed. “Me or her!”

Steve’s jaw tensed with irritation. “I’m not being blackmailed by a child!”

I gave him a look of pure contempt. I knew Esther. All he had to do was let her think she was winning and she’d feel guilty and back down. Why the hell couldn’t he see that the more stubborn he was, the harder it would be to reach a compromise.

“I’m not coming then.” Esther shot back.

“You went with your Mum’s boyfriend!” Steve hit back. “How’s this any different?”

“Because he wasn’t there the whole time!” Esther exclaimed. “He slept on the sofa and he didn’t hang around us all day pretending to be in our family.”

I flushed slightly at the mention of Luke. “So, would you feel better about going if you had time on your own with your Dad?”

Esther shrugged. “I don’t care.”

I looked at Steve trying to telepathically communicate to him that she certainly did care, and this was his chance to put things right.

“See!” Steve threw his hands up in frustration. “She doesn’t care. She’s just doing this to be awkward.”

I felt like banging my head against the wall. He was intolerable sometimes. Most of the time.

“Just go, Steve,” I sighed. “I’ll sort this out.”

Esther shot me a look. “I’m not going, Mum.”

“We’ll talk about this after.” I said to her, keeping my tone light. “Shall we just go to bed and sleep on this?”

Esther nodded, got up and, without saying anything to her father, went up to her room.

“You need to start backing me up.” Steve hissed at me. “She runs wild.”

“You could do a better job, could you?” I laughed bitterly. “You’ve made that ten times worse than it needed to be. Tell Charlotte to phone me. I’ll sort it, ok.”

Steve frowned, surprised at my request. “Why?”

“Just do it.” I sighed exhausted. “I’m going to bed. Let yourself out.”

And with that I left him, seething with fury in my living room.

Chapter 23

Steve predictably didn't ask Charlotte to call me, or maybe he did, and she chose not to. I left Esther to sleep on it but the next day she was still stubbornly sticking to her guns. I tried every tactic in the book over the next two days, but the day of their planned departure was looming and after 48 hours of solid negotiation with a wilful teenager I was at my wits end.

After a particularly terse conversation with Esther which left me red-faced and furious, I locked myself in my en-suite and phoned Steve.

"She's not backing down." I launched into my reason for the call without bothering with any pleasantries. "You need to speak to her. Nicely. She doesn't respond well to ultimatums."

"That's your fault." Steve snapped. "She's a bloody spoiled brat. Charlotte says-"

"Charlotte says fucking what?" I interrupted, feeling my blood boil. "Do you know what? It doesn't matter what Charlotte says because Esther is not her fucking daughter! She's yours! And you need to put your kids first for once in your selfish, fucking life!"

"If she doesn't want to come," Steve said coldly. "That's fine with me."

"If she doesn't come," I seethed, raging with anger at him.

"The others won't either. I'm telling you now, you need her on side. You can either get this right by swallowing your pride and putting yourself in your daughter's shoes, or you can carry on acting like an arsehole and lose all the respect of your children. Your choice."

I didn't wait for his response. I ended the call and threw down my phone, my whole body shaking with fury. Then I had second thoughts, scooped the phone back up and turned it off. They were meant to be going the day after tomorrow; less than 48 hours before my flight to New York. As pig-headed as Esther was being, I was not going to force her into going. I could actually empathise with everything that she was going through and I was plagued with guilt at my part in the disruptions in her life. What I had said to Steve wasn't a threat either. As much as my children wound each other up and fought like cats and dogs, they were a team. Leo was so much more reserved than the other three and I know that he was having nerves about being away from me already. None of them had ever been away for more than a few days and I knew the moment Esther told them she wasn't going, Leo would fall apart. Matilda would be lost without someone to share a bed with, as she could barely sleep alone at home and always had to share when we were away. I couldn't see Steve kicking Charlotte out of bed to co-sleep with a five-year-old. My heart felt like it was breaking, just thinking about having to send my kids to another country where I couldn't be there to protect them. I had been counting on Esther, the leader of my squad, to take care of them as selfish as that was. I felt awful that I'd been counting on Esther to shoulder the responsibility for her siblings. All because I couldn't trust Steve to do the right thing by his kids.

I sunk onto my bed, head in hands, despairing of what action to take. I knew the right thing to do was to encourage my children to have a relationship with their father, to trust Steve to do the right thing and exercise my parental control and insist that Esther go on this holiday. My heart ached thinking about this. I had never been an authoritative parent. I didn't know the answer to most things, let alone everything, so it just felt hypocritical for me to force my own wants or beliefs on the children, aside from the common sense ones to keep them alive/ out of trouble/ prison: "brush your teeth", "don't run carrying scissors", "don't hit people", "don't steal", "don't say fuck in school", those kinds of things. This is probably where I'd been going so horribly wrong and ended up with a mutiny on my hands.

If Steve didn't come through, I literally had no idea what I'd do. Not about New York. I wanted to see Jen but, when it came down to it, my children were my whole heart and I wouldn't go anywhere if they needed me. I meant I'd have no idea what to do if the other children refused to go. I was so torn between thinking that I should let Steve assert his own parental authority and feeling that I should protect my children's right to have a say in their own lives.

I was still sat on my bed deliberating when there was a gentle knock on the door. Esther walked in, wrapped in a fleecy dressing gown despite it being August.

"Are you ok, Mum?" She asked in a small voice that was a million miles away from the screaming match we'd had less than an hour earlier.

"I'm fine," I nodded, sitting up. "Are you?"

"Yeah." She climbed up on the bed next to me.

We both stared ahead not looking at each other.

"Am I ruining your trip by not going?" She asked finally.

"What?" I looked at her, surprised. "No! Not at all. If it's going to take you a while to get used to Dad having a girlfriend, that's your choice."

I said this automatically and regretted it the moment I did as I was basically consenting to her not going. I hadn't even decided whether my gut instinct was the right one to follow yet.

"It's not fair that Dad gets to have a life," Esther said quietly. "And you don't."

"I've got a life, Esther." I tried to give her a jokey smile, but she wouldn't meet my gaze.

"You know what I mean," She shrugged. "Where's Luke? You haven't seen him for ages."

"I'm not going to bother." I shrugged, joining in with the teenage closed-off body language.

"You broke up?" She asked, looking interested.

"Kind of." It was my turn to avoid eye contact.

"Mum." Esther turned her body now towards me, forcing me to make eye contact.

"He's just a bit of a..." I shrugged again, feeling uncomfortable having this conversation with my daughter.

"Dick?" Esther filled in the blanks. "What happened?"

I gave an extremely edited version of the leaving drinks, just explaining that he'd been a bit weird, so I had ignored him and hadn't heard from him since.

"Oh my God!" Esther exclaimed. "He actually ghosted you! What a child! What is he? Like twelve?"

I laughed at her reaction and she saw that I was amused and not upset and joined in too.

"Mum," She said after we'd finished laughing at Luke (and, I think, my) expense. "I've thought about it. I don't want to go on holiday with Dad and his stupid girlfriend."

"I don't think she's stupid." I interrupted, trying to be mature.

"Anyway," Esther continued. "I don't think it's fair that the kids are there alone without me. So, I'm going to go. But I still love you more than Dad."

My heart melted at her kindness and how she'd put her siblings before her own emotions.

"You love us the same," I told her, but my lips turned up in a smile. “You’re just annoyed at Dad at the moment. This is a very kind thing of you to do for the others.”

“I know,” She gave me a little grin, back to a cocky teenager. “I’m so mature.”

“I love you, Es.” I smiled back at her and I felt tears prickle at the back of my eyes.

“Love you too.” Esther slipped off my bed and left the room now it was getting sentimental.

I put my head down on my pillow and allowed myself to have a little cry to purge all the pent-up emotions and the guilt of what Steve and I were putting these children through.

Time flew by, as it always does when you want it to slow down, and I packed my children off on their holiday with a heavy heart and a brave face. I remembered my own goodbye to Jen; how she insisted on it being short and sweet and replicated her fleeting goodbye in order to prevent myself crying like a baby. My last official (not counting the Monday that I was going AWOL) work day had been and gone. I’d been so hung up on the children’s first trip abroad without me that I hadn’t even felt the slightest emotion all day. I had ticked off all my “last’s” in my mind as I went about my usual work day; the last time I’d walk in to the branch as an employee, the last coffee from the horrible vending machine, the last customer I’d serve. I had discreetly emptied my locker of any personal items and emailed any work or appointments to Lois “just in case”. I gave Lois a wink as I did this, and she gave me an exaggerated sad face back. I felt a tiny twinge of something, but this was more to do with how much I liked Lois than any regret at leaving. I almost forgot to tick off "last time leaving" as I was in such a rush to get out and pick up the children for our pre-holiday dinner together. It's crazy how you can spend so much of your life and so much of your emotional energy on someone or something, and then just walk away and feel nothing. I wondered if this was how Steve had felt leaving me. Like my years at the bank were to me, was I just an inconvenience or a wrong turn in Steve's life? I mulled this over in my head as I tried to distract myself from the slightly lost feeling I had now the kids were safely on their way to the airport.

If you could go from loving someone so much, living with them, eating, sleeping and raising kids with them to them meaning nothing to you, to you not even giving them a second thought; what did that say about love. Was it just a social convention that we're tricked into conforming to? An evolutionary adaptation that we've grown out of? Was I destined to be alone forever? Did I even care? I spent a few hours dwelling on this, running it over and over in my head. I wished that I wasn't so insecure as to always want someone in my life. Andy was always either in a relationship or at the very least seeing someone, but Jen had always been perfectly happy on her own. Obviously, she'd been in relationships and dated people since I'd known her, but she was never actively seeking anything when she was single. Maybe being beautiful and intelligent helped you to feel complete in yourself and above any judgement from others.

I decided that maybe I should let this be my fresh start. New job, new single status, new me. I laughed out loud at the cheesiness of my thoughts and dragged my melodramatic self out with the dogs for a few hours. A brisk walk around the local common with the sun shining down was good therapy for my bleak introspective mood. I even managed to convince the lazy dogs to increase their usual snail pace and was able to jog a few laps of the park before Hermione gave up by sitting down and refusing to budge. It was moments like these that made me grateful for sticking to lap dogs as I scooped her up and endured the indignity of carrying my idle pooch back through the suburbs to our house. I pottered around the house, doing some last-minute cleaning and packing. I shut the dogs in the kitchen in order to drag my suitcase out in my bedroom, as the sight of a suitcase usually induced abandonment sulking from both of them. As I was stood over the piles of clothes trying to figure out what I might need, I heard a sound downstairs followed by Ron's bark.

I assumed that he had worked himself up into a state at being shut in the kitchen and knocked something over. I threw down my armload of tops and padded down the stairs quickly to chastise him.

My heart almost stopped in shock as Luke stood in my hallway, looking sheepish and glum.

"Hi." He said simply.

I was speechless for a moment, waiting for my heart rate to return to normal, and as it did I searched for an appropriate verbal response. I bought myself a moment by leaning past him to open the door and let the dogs into the hallway. They both rushed out, sniffed Luke suspiciously before settling at my side.

"What are you doing here?" I asked quietly.

Luke reached forward to touch me lightly on the arm and I flinched away from his touch. He pulled his arm away quickly.

"I miss you." He said, his sad expression turned up to its highest setting.

"You've ignored me for a week!" I exclaimed, gobsmacked at his audacity.

"You know I find all this hard." He answered pitifully.

"All what?" I asked.

He shrugged. "Just the way you never want to spend time with me."

Oh my God. Was he actually serious?

"I told you what I've had going on." I replied evenly, despite feeling furious inside that he'd turned up at my home and let himself in after ignoring me for over a week. "This just isn't going to work."

He stared at me. His eyes sparkling with tears of hurt.

"Please."

His voice cracked slightly, and he looked so vulnerable that I couldn't bear to look at him. I turned away and walked into the kitchen. He followed me.

"Why are you doing this?" I asked, filling the kettle.

I then changed my mind and reached for the wine bottle instead. I offered him a glass and he accepted. We sat side by side at the kitchen table and I waited for him to respond.

"I love you." He said feebly.

I almost rolled my eyes, but I felt sorry for him and held back.

"You can't just ignore me for days and then turn up like this."

"I was upset." He said, not looking me in the eye.

"Why?" I asked, feeling frustrated. I had a ton of packing to do. I really didn't need this right now. "We were fine and then you just got shitty."

"I just feel that you always put everyone else first." He replied, turning to look at me.

"Like who?" I asked, taking a huge sip of my wine.

"Well, obviously your kids." He then added quickly. "Which is fine. But your friends too."

"Why don't you talk about this, rather than sulking for days?" I challenged him.

"You don't understand how difficult you can be." He

responded.

“Me?” I asked incredulously. “How am I difficult?”

“You make me feel bad when I want to spend time with you.” He replied, a pout on his face.

“So why are you here?” I asked coolly, despite being furious at how he was turning this on me. I had just enough self-esteem left to leave Leanne and the likely string of other women out of it.

“Because I want us to work out.” He replied.

“This is my life,” I sighed finally. “I’m busy. I want to spend time with my friends. I want to spend time on my own. I just haven’t got the time to commit to a relationship.”

“Can we just be casual then?” He asked, reaching over and touching my thigh with his hand.

I moved my leg away. “I don’t think that’s a good idea.”

I stood up, waiting for Luke to follow. He reached forward and put his hand on the back of my neck, gently pulling me towards him.

It was so tempting to just go with it; to let him sweet talk me back with an occasional romantic gesture and his smooth moves but then what? It was painfully embarrassing to admit the truth but, I’d basically saddled myself with a younger version of Steve. The ridiculousness of it hit me as he gazed smoulderingly into my eyes and I choked back a laugh, more at the situation I'd got myself into than at poor Luke's attempts to woo me back into bed.

"Luke," I stepped backwards and shook my head regretfully. "I'm sorry but I can't."

His face fell a little, but I wasn't falling for it.

"Are you seeing someone else?" His eyes narrowed suspiciously. "Are you back with your husband?"

Part of me wanted to scream with frustration but I just shook my head instead.

"I'm not." I said firmly. "I would like it if we could be friends, but I think you should probably go now. I've got a flight to catch first thing."

It was Luke's turn to look like he wanted to scream with frustration, but he quickly regained his composure and gave me a fleeting hug.

"Don't let anyone treat you badly." He said as I opened the front door to let him out.

"I don't intend to." I replied and shut the door, still smiling at the irony.

Chapter 24

I boarded the plane the next day full of excitement. I couldn't remember the last time I'd flown alone. Any flights, with the children, were a stressful drama of kicking legs, sticky hands and numerous changes of clothes.

I settled into my seat and enjoyed some much-needed R & R. I watched films, read my book and sipped copious amounts of wine in peace, feeling almost decadent with the luxury despite being sandwiched between two other travellers in the economy section.

Jen was at work when my journey was finally complete, so I jumped into a taxi feeling joyously free and happy. I sat back in the backseat of the car and enjoyed the sights of New York as the driver whizzed me to Jen's hotel. Jen, as always, had thought of everything and the attentive staff at reception greeted me and whisked me up to her suite. Jen had given me a quick hotel room tour via Facetime, but I was not prepared for the luxury of her home from home. I walked into the immaculate living room. It was a corner suite with stunning views over the city. I stood at the window gazing out in awe.

Jen's company must be spending a fortune on this place, I thought to myself as I ran my hand over the shiny glass surfaces. I knew Jen had a good (translate well-paid) job but we never would have dreamed of discussing salaries. I assumed that she earned similar to Steve but, looking around at the suite, it was evident that she was doing extremely well for herself. Out of curiosity, I googled the cost of a suite here for one night. I gave a sharp intake of breath at the result. I googled her job title and the word "salary" next, gasped again and closed the internet window quickly as I suddenly felt intrusive. Wow though. I wondered if Andy knew she earned more than him. That would piss him off, I thought laughing to myself.

I wandered through the open door into the bedroom, carrying my bag through with me to start hanging up the few clothes I'd brought with me. I quickly realised that there was only one bed; a white King Size that dominated the gorgeous bedroom. It was definitely a "lived in" room with items of clothing strewn around, a heated brush left plugged in and various, probably confidential, documents fanned out over the desk in typical Jen style. The mother in me couldn't cope with the chaos and I quickly tidied up before hanging up my very average outfits next to Jen's fabulous trousseau. I noticed a folded cream sheet of paper propped up against the night stand with "Lucy" scrawled across it. This bedside drawer was devoid of any clutter unlike its twin and I assumed, with a silly sense of happiness, that Jen had allocated me a 'side' of the bed. I sat on the bed and unfolded the note.

"Welcome to New York!" Jen's familiar scratch spoke to me from the paper. "Can't wait to get home and see you! I'll be back by 6 and I've made us reservations for dinner. If you're not tired, ask concierge and they'll point you in the right direction for a walk. Or get room service. Love You!"

As I read the words, I could hear Jen's voice in my mind. I realised I was still smiling widely and staring at the words minutes after I'd finished reading. I put the note down and pondered on what to do next.

I didn't feel tired and I calculated that I could go for a quick walk and then get room service and have a nap before Jen got back. I changed quickly; refreshing my deodorant and makeup lightly instead of showering. I made my way down to the front desk but decided that I'd try to figure out my own route and just refer to Google maps if necessary.

I stepped out onto the pavement and turned my face towards the blue rectangle of sky peeking out from between the imposing buildings. I strolled leisurely towards Central Park, enjoying the feeling of anonymity amongst the hustle and bustle of tourists. I felt a wave of tranquillity wash over me; unknotting the ingrained tension from my shoulders and my back as I walked unhurried.

My mind turned to the future and I let my imagination run away as I dreamed up far-fetched scenarios where my career choices took me from travelling the world with famous movie stars (after being discovered at one of John and Andy's dinner parties of course) to running a chic, little boutique hotel next to the sea and then to a vineyard in France where I checked on my produce barefoot, looking bohemian and youthful.

I smiled to myself, amused at my own fanciful projections and my renewed sense of optimism. Truth be told, I didn't need an exotic, exciting career to be happy. I wanted to be able to hold my own financially and do something remotely rewarding that I enjoyed.

I'd only planned to go for a short walk before returning to the hotel for food and a sleep, but my high spirits carried me on further and further as I weaved my way through the park, with no destination in mind, just taking in the sights and people-watching. I stopped at a café for a drink and by the time I reached the hotel, my curls were a sweaty, frizzy mess and my shoulders were an unflattering pink from the warm sun. I abandoned my plans for room service as it was now almost 4pm and I could feel exhaustion kicking in. I knew that without napping, I'd be irritable and bad company later. I helped myself to some crisps and tucked into these sitting on "my side" of the bed still in my jeans, my sweaty t-shirt peeled off and tossed on the floor.

Next thing I knew, I was aware of the sound of running water and I jolted awake with a start. It took me a moment to realise where I was, and I blinked hard trying to relieve my sleep heavy eyes. Jen was stood, wrapped in a fluffy, white towel, in the doorway to the bathroom.

"Morning, sleepy head!" Jen laughed, walking over and hopping up onto the bed.

"Oh no!" I gasped. "Is it the morning?"

Jen laughed again. "No, I'm joking! It's 6.30pm."

I struggled to sit up and turned to give Jen a hug before

realising I was half-naked and covered in Pringle crumbs. I tried to back out of the hug, but it was too late, Jen was fully committed.

"You're clean!" I protested, shying away. "I'm gross and sweaty!"

"I don't care!" Jen wrapped her arms around me and squeezed me to her. I savoured the sensation of her damp skin and soft towel against my naked chest, but then, conscious of my own feelings, I pulled away blushing.

"Can I use the shower?" I asked.

Jen frowned slightly as if confused by my strange behaviour but nodded.

"Thanks." I smiled, trying to act natural. "We'll have a proper catch up as soon as I've woken up."

"I'll show you how to turn it on." Jen offered, following me into the bathroom. "It took me ages to figure out the best combo."

I waited next to the huge shower, looking at the various chrome nozzles and awaited Jen's instructions.

Jen was explaining and jabbing at various buttons when I realised I wasn't taking anything in except for the sweet scent of the body lotion on her skin. I must have been staring as she broke off what she was saying and followed my gaze to her bare shoulders.

“You ok, Lucy?” She asked, looking half-amused, half-perplexed.

“Sorry,” I mumbled. “I’m so tired. I’m like a zombie.”

Her expression changed to one of concern. “We don’t have to go out. We can get room service and chill here.”

I shook my head quickly. “No, I’ll be fine once I’ve showered!”

Jen moved over to the huge mirror and started opening various jars of creams and potions. I waited for a few moments until it became clear that she wasn’t leaving.

I self-consciously pulled my jeans off, stepping into the shower. I tried a few nozzles, wishing I’d listened and squealed loudly when I was hit by a torrent of freezing cold water.

I saw Jen’s reflection jump in surprise at my scream from the corner of my eye.

“You didn’t listen, did you?” She asked me in mock exasperation.

I laughed, despite the fact that I was hopping around trying to stay out of reach of the icy blast. I turned several of the controls, desperately trying to stop it. Jen crossed the room and opened the door. She leaned past me and turned a switch, that in my defence didn’t even look like it was part of the various buttons. The water quickly changed from shockingly ice-cold to soothingly warm.

“Hotter?” She asked, very matter-of-factly for someone who’s arm was millimetres away from brushing the soft flesh of my naked stomach.

“Please.” I nodded, realising I’d been holding my breath since Jen had opened the shower door.

Jen twirled another notch. “Try this.”

Jets of hot water shot out from concealed vents around the two walls, massaging my back and legs. I couldn’t help but let out a groan in delight at the feeling, shutting my eyes in ecstasy.

“So good!” I stretched under the water and when I opened my eyes, Jen was paused at the door; her eyes on my face and an affectionate smile playing at the corner of her lips. I met her eyes and it was her turn to flush slightly, dropping her gaze and then recovering her composure so quickly that I couldn’t be sure that I hadn’t imagined it in the first place.

“It’s the best, isn’t it?” She said quickly. “I’m definitely getting one of these at home.”

“Oh yes!” I agreed, tilting my head back so the water cascaded over my face. “I’ll be moving in if you do.”

Jen grinned at me and shut the door, returning to her post at the mirror.

By the time I could finally bear to tear myself away from the best shower ever, Jen was back in the bedroom dressing.

"What shall I wear?" I asked. Jen was wearing a strappy dark grey dress and looked like a model.

"Whatever," Jen shrugged. "You always look amazing."

"I don't." I protested, adding some defrizz serum to my wet curls quickly before they took on a life of their own. "I've hardly brought anything."

Jen stopped what she was doing and walked over to the clothes I'd hung in her wardrobe. She flicked through them; her eyes narrowed in concentration. She selected a floaty knee length skirt, slinging the hanger over her arm, and then retrieved a slinky navy silk top from her own jam-packed rail.

"Ta Dah!" She announced, looking proud of herself as she passed me her selection.

I dropped my towel, trying not to be self-conscious and pulled on underwear before trying the outfit.

"Wow!" I appraised my reflection. "That look great. You could be a stylist!"

Jen beamed at my words. "I could be! Thank you. You look beautiful, Lucy!"

Something in the tone of her voice made me blush again and I wondered why I was suddenly so conscious of everything Jen did and said. As if my life wasn't already complicated enough between my estranged husband and my unemployed status, my destructive self had decided now was a good time to develop a crush on the one constant in my life. I needed to stop acting so ridiculously and pack away all these thoughts, as I couldn't bear the thought of risking my relationship with my funny, thoughtful, lovely friend.

Romances came and went, as well I knew, but I wanted Jen in my life forever. I forced a smile on my face and reached for the hair drier.

"Thanks, Jen." I grinned. "Help me do my hair or we'll never make dinner?"

Dinner was amazing. We ate at a rooftop restaurant overlooking the city. Jen updated me on everything that had been going on in her life which, at the moment, was mainly work. She loved the job and the city and talked animatedly about her plans to visit a few places on her bucket list while she was in the States. I listened enviously, feeling proud of her achievements and delighted at her happiness.

"So, is it still just for six months?" I asked, sipping on the delicious cocktail in my hand.

"Probably." Jen replied but looked unsure.

I pressed her for more details, wondering, with shock, if maybe she would love it here so much that she wouldn't want to ever come home. Her company were clearly enamoured with her, evident in the way they were throwing money at that hotel suite. Jen brushed off my questions and I made a mental note to pick this up another time as something was clearly playing on her mind that she didn't want to share right now.

"So how are you getting on being actually single?" Jen asked casually.

I had updated Jen on everything that had happened with Luke, but I felt too embarrassed to bring up how he'd ignored me at the leaving drinks and then turned up at my house. For a split second, I considered lying rather than having to vocalise what a doormat I'd been. I knew in my heart though that I would never deceive Jen and I sighed loudly, putting down my glass.

I explained how I'd felt manipulated by Luke from how he'd railroaded me into letting him stay at the apartment to how he'd turned up at my house uninvited after ignoring me for days. I watched, out of the corner of my eye, as Jen's mouth set in a hard line, feeling my heart sink that she was disappointed in me. I voiced this concern and Jen shook her head quickly.

"Oh, Lucy! No, of course I'm not disappointed in you!" She reached across the table and took my hand. "If you want to sleep with Luke, go for it. Just don't let him mess you around or hurt you."

"Oh, God!" I half-laughed. "He certainly couldn't hurt me! I told him that I wasn't interested in a relationship and asked him to leave. He seemed a bit gutted but I'm honestly over any feelings I thought I had for him."

“You asked him to leave?” Jen looked pleased, squeezing my hand. “Good for you if that’s what you want. I’ll always support whatever you do as long as you’re happy.”

I smiled gratefully at her. “I think I just need to be on my own. Be an independent woman like you for a bit.”

She laughed at this and took a sip from her drink.

We both fell quiet, staring out at the dark sky lit up by thousands of lights in high rise buildings around us.

“I would have loved to have a late one tonight.” Jen said finally. “But I need to go into work early to make sure I can finish at a reasonable time to make the most of your time here. I hope that’s ok.”

“Yes, of course,” I nodded. “It’s been lovely here, but I could do with an early night.”

Jen insisted on paying despite my protests and we made our way back to the hotel in silence. Jen was attentive, checking I knew where everything was and that I had everything I needed, but seemed distant. She disappeared to the bathroom and came out wearing cotton pyjamas, which was probably the most un-Jen-like outfit I’d ever seen.

I was sat up in bed, flicking through my social media. Luke had sent me a message telling me to let him know if I ever felt ready for a proper relationship. I sent him back a “blowing kiss” emoji as I didn’t want to get drawn into any deep and meaningful conversations; I just wanted to draw a line under my attempt at a relationship with Luke. Steve had uploaded a picture of my four beautiful children smiling at the beach. My heart ached a little at the sight of them and I studied their faces until I was satisfied that they all looked like they were having a good time. Jen climbed into the bed next to me and I put my phone back down.

"Do you mind if I turn off the lights now?" She asked.

"That's fine," I agreed. "Thanks for tonight, Jen. It's so good to be here."

"It's so good to have you here." She smiled and turned off the lights. "Goodnight, Lucy."

Chapter 25

There was something about being around Jen that just made me feel more myself than I did without her. I was the first to admit that I was an anxious, insecure mess at times; always doubting myself and existing in a tangle of my own worries. When I was with Jen I felt relaxed and comfortable in my own skin.

The next few days were (obviously discounting the births of my children in case anyone is judging), without a shadow of a doubt, the most blissful and contented of my life. By day, I saw the sights of the city and indulged myself with some shopping and, at night, wined, dined and conversed with Jen into the early hours. We laughed more than I'd laughed in years and never ran out of things to talk about or tired of each other's company. Jen's passion and enthusiasm for life sparked my own newly-found optimism and ideas for my new career spiralled and spun as we egged each other on to live our best lives.

"You haven't said whether you're seeing anyone?" I asked one night, after we'd been out for cocktails and were sat up in bed flicking through our phones and munching Pringles in companionable silence. Jen's phone had beeped several times as her fingers flew across the touch screen seemingly keeping up a quick-fire conversation with someone.

Jen paused, looking up from her phone. "I've been on a few dates but I'm not looking for anything."

"No?" I asked, feeling a little twinge of envy.

Jen shrugged. "You know when you just can't be bothered with all that crap?"

"Oh, yes!" I said, thinking of Steve and all his lies. "I'm so done with people's crap."

"So, is it really over with him?" Jen asked, raising her eyebrows and putting her phone down. It beeped but she ignored it.

"Steve?" I frowned, confused. "He's on bloody holiday with a woman, so yeah, of course."

"Ah." Jen said, nodding. "I thought you meant Luke."

"Oh," I laughed. "I think I've forgotten he existed already!"

"And there was me thinking he was my competition." Jen laughed.

I felt my pulse quicken. "Your competition?"

Jen nodded, still chuckling to herself.

I waited, breath held, to see if she'd elaborate but she didn't say any more. Jen rolled onto her side and we were facing each other; eyes on each other's faces and silent. I felt frozen, unable to turn away but unwilling to take my eyes from her. I felt a surge of desire to kiss her soft, full lips but I held back; terrified that I might ruin our friendship.

Jen looked relaxed; head against the pillow and a contented smile on her lips.

“What are you thinking?” I asked finally when the tension felt too heavy and I couldn’t bear the loaded silence any longer.

“Honestly?” Jen raised an eyebrow challengingly.

I swallowed nervously. “Honestly.”

“I love you.” She said simply.

A swarm of butterflies burst into flight in my stomach and I felt my heart ache at the tenderness in her voice.

“I love you too.” I said.

“Like how you love Andy?” Jen asked. “Or how you love Steve?”

There was no malice or insecurity in her voice and, without our phones lighting up our faces, we were cloaked in almost darkness, the kind that makes deep conversations easier. I swallowed again and thought before I answered.

I loved Andy like a brother. He drove me crazy, but I could honestly say that I would do anything for him if he needed me. I loved Steve as the father of my children. He hadn’t given me butterflies for years but that was to be expected; no marriage was all goose bumps and romance after routine and life got in the way. I knew Steve was physically attractive, but I didn’t particularly like him. Maybe that was the problem. When we’d fallen in love, we were both young and ambitious, but over the years as we’d grown up, our interests and personalities had changed. Steve liked sports and his yuppy friends, I liked laughing and travelling. We had little common ground any more. I didn't find Steve easy to live with nor supportive of my own needs.

I answered Jen with an honesty that left me feeling more vulnerable than ever before.

"Neither."

Jen tilted her head questioningly. A lock of dark hair fell forward covering her face as she moved. I reached forward and brushed it back with my fingertips. Jen circled my wrist with her finger and thumb, and held my hand, gently but firmly, against her chest above the bedsheet.

"Neither?" She repeated.

"I love Andy like I love my sister," I told her, wondering if she could hear the thumping of my heartbeat. "And I care for Steve as the kids' dad."

"And you love me differently?" She prompted.

I could sense a nervousness in my always-confident and self-assured friend. This spurred me on. That and the numerous cocktails sloshing around in my system.

"I think so." I nodded.

Jen lifted my hand to her lips, pressing her mouth gently against my fingertips. I felt myself stir with desire.

"Tell me." Jen almost whispered. "Things have changed between us, haven't they?"

"What do you want?" I thought my heart was going to break free from my chest. I was terrified of saying something that would ruin our friendship but equally terrified of letting this moment pass and never knowing what could be.

"I just..." Jen started tentatively, and I saw, even in the darkness, a shadow of something in Jen's eyes. She dropped her gaze before continuing. "I just like you. A lot. Like 'want you around' like you."

"I am around." I smiled, trying to lighten the mood out of sheer nervousness.

Jen smiled, but her smile was tinged with sadness which made my heart ache.

"You and I live such different lives." Jen said quietly.

"I know," I nodded. "The kids-"

"Not the kids." Jen shook her head, cutting me off. "I love your kids. You know that."

"What then?" I asked, back to wondering whether I was imagining the chemistry I felt between Jen and I. Surely someone as amazing, charismatic and successful as Jen couldn't like me like that.

"You've just got to work out what you want," Jen shrugged. "Marriage. Job. Life."

"I will." I affirmed, actually meaning it. "I will get my life sorted."

I paused and then bravely added. “And then what?”

“Then what?” Jen repeated. I knew that she knew what I meant.

“Us.” I said with more confidence than I felt. “What do you want to happen?”

Oh God. I couldn’t believe I just asked that.

“It doesn’t matter what I want.” Jen sighed. She dropped my hand and rolled onto her back, shutting her eyes as if in frustration.

I took her hand and pulled her back towards me. She looked as surprised as I felt at my assertiveness.

“It does matter.” I said fiercely, every nerve in my body feeling alive. “Jen, I would never hurt you.”

“I’ve heard that before.” Jen gave me a wry smile but didn’t pull away. I could feel her heartbeat racing like mine.

I’ve read this wrong, I thought terrified. I’m drunk and this isn’t going to end well.

Jen must have seen my expression change, even in the darkness, and she leaned forward and gently kissed my lips. I kissed her back slowly, sliding my arms around her and pulling her close. The kiss was soft and cautious. Jen slid her fingers into my hair and I pulled away slightly, to look at her. Just seeing her face and the way she was looking at me, I felt my heart soar. Jen rested her face against mine for a moment and then pressed her lips softly along my jawline. I lifted her chin with my thumb and kissed her lips again. She kissed me back and this time it was with a growing hunger that sent waves of desire shooting through me. I kissed her with a passion that grew stronger with every second, pushing her onto her back in my yearning to get closer. She responded, running her hands from my hair down the length of my body. We were still separated by the bedsheet and she pulled away, pushing it off her and pulling me back in one fluid motion. She pulled my top away and her mouth found my nipples. I moaned loudly at the sensation and buried my hands in her thick hair. Jen worked her way down my body with hungry kisses and my whole body trembled with anticipation. She paused as she traced her tongue across my stomach and I pulled her back up to her kiss her mouth fervently. I slid the straps of Jen's top down her shoulders, trailing hungry kisses down her neck and running my hands over her perfect breasts. I cautiously slipped my hand further down her body; my fingers resting under the waistband of her pyjamas. Jen arched her back against my touch and I tugged at her bottoms, pulling them down and away. My fingers stroked the soft, naked skin between her legs and I felt her growing excited with my touch. I ached to taste her and pulled back from our kiss to work my way down her curves. As I flicked my tongue lightly over her, Jen groaned with pleasure. Jen writhed against my lips and tongue before, eventually, pulling me back up to her; simultaneously burying her tongue in my mouth and her fingers in my own wetness.

We explored each other with a longing and passion I had

never felt before. Every touch sending shivers through my body and I felt my sole purpose was to show Jen how beautiful she was. Jen's body responded to my touch in a way that gave me more pleasure than my own orgasm. We made love for what felt like only minutes but must have been hours.

We woke in the morning, still tangled together, and I felt a jolt of fear that Jen would regret this as a drunken mistake. Jen opened her eyes and, without any hesitation, gave me a lazy smile and snuggled in closer. My whole heart surged with joy and I honestly thought I would die of happiness in that moment.

The remaining days of my holiday, I felt alive. Alive like I'd only been half-living up until now. I don't know how loving someone so wholly and so openly could make you feel so free. There was none of the self-doubt and the anxiety that had always plagued me in other relationships. The vulnerability of loving her made me feel stronger, somehow. That was the thing about Jen. She inspired me. And knowing Jen was beside me, I felt I could face anything.

On our last night, Jen whisked me off for a sunset boat trip to the Statue of Liberty. She admitted, on the way, that she had wanted to book a private boat, but it was too short notice. I laughed, more delighted at her intentions than I would have been with the whole VIP experience. We stood close together, packed in with the other tourists, staring out at the iconic silhouette of the city. I had never been a big romantic, but, as we cruised by Manhattan at sunset, all I could think about was holding her hand.

Jen seemed to read my mind and slipped her hand into mine.

"'It's so pretty." I squeezed her hand, wishing I had the words to tell her how magical this moment was to me.

"I love this city." She smiled. "I would love to live here. Wouldn't you?"

"If only." I kept my tone light, but a shard of worry pierced the moment as the reality of our incompatible lives hit me.

"One day." Jen stepped backwards, wrapping her arms around my waist and resting her cheek against mine. "When the kids are grown up."

My stomach flipped as she allayed my fears, without me even saying a word.

"Sounds perfect." I replied. "As long as you're with me."

"Yeah?" Jen gave me a pouty, little smile that did crazy things to my insides.

I turned and kissed her slowly in response, not caring about the other tourists around us.

The closer it came to me leaving, the more bittersweet our time together felt. After taking in the views, we had reservations for dinner.

"Would you rather go back to ours?" Jen asked hesitantly as we exited the tourist attraction. "Maybe get room service? I just want to be on our own tonight."

"Yes." I nodded. I had been thinking the same. I loved how in sync we were.

We headed back to the hotel. Inside, we kicked off our heels and peeled off our clothes, throwing on fluffy robes and climbing into bed.

"I don't want to go." I said, lying in Jen's arms after we'd made love, then eaten and then made love again.

"I don't want you to go." Jen replied, rewarding me with a kiss. "But you get to start a new career!"

"Hopefully that will make the time go quick." I sighed.

"I hope so." Jen gave me another delicious kiss and I ran my fingers lightly over her shoulders, watching the goose bumps rise at my light touch.

"How long have you liked me?" I suddenly burst out and then blushed at my lack of sophistication.

"Forever. But you were never single." Jen answered, not remotely phased by my geekiness. "How long have you liked me?"

"Forever." I smiled back. "I've had a crush on you since we met though, I think."

"Ha!" Jen laughed. "Me too."

"No way!" I protested.

We had met at a work Christmas party. I couldn't find Steve and had been pregnant-sick (as opposed to Christmas party sick) in a plant pot on the terrace.

"I was a mess," I laughed. "Remember you looked after me because I couldn't find Steve?"

Jen opened her mouth as if to say something and then closed it again.

"What?" I pressed. "You were going to say something?"

Jen shook her head, but she looked hesitant. "You looked beautiful with your pregnant glow."

"It wasn't a glow!" I joked. "It was sweat from throwing up! So embarrassing. You leant me your throw and sat with me all night pretending you cared about my boring life."

Jen laughed. "I did care! I was interested in your baby stories!"

"Really?" I asked sceptically.

"Yeah," Jen nodded thoughtfully. "I was at a crossroads. I hadn't long had an abortion and I was really torn over whether I'd done the right thing."

I tried to hide my surprise; I had thought that I knew everything about Jen's life. I'd always assumed that Jen had never wanted children and had respected her individuality in a world where we blindly follow convention, without ever feeling the need to ask her. Jen having an unplanned pregnancy, like I had, would never have crossed my mind.

"That must have been tough." I pulled Jen closer. "Do you want to talk about it?"

"I was seeing this guy. He was a dick. The end." Jen shrugged.

"So, did he not want a baby?" I asked, concerned.

Jen shook her head. "No, he did. Turns out he was married though."

"Oh God!" I gasped. "That must have been awful. You had no idea?"

Jen shook her head again. "He told me he was getting an amicable divorce. I was just a naïve idiot."

"Do you definitely not want one?" I asked. "A baby, I mean?"

Jen looked surprised. "No, definitely not. I liked the life I was living."

"And now?" I asked, knowing instinctively that I would support Jen in anyway but, at the back of my mind, worrying about the impact of my kids on our relationship.

"I really like the life I'm living," She leaned over and kissed me gently. "And I like your kids so stop stressing. I just don't want a baby."

I smiled, loving how she knew what I was thinking. "I love you."

We fell asleep, wrapped in each other's arms, but as I drifted off, despite my bubble of happiness, there was a nagging doubt in the back of mind wondering how sophisticated Jen would fit into my messy life.

Jen woke me in the morning, shaking me awake gently.

"Lucy!" She called and even in my semi-conscious state my heart both lifted at the joy of waking up to her and sank at the realisation that tomorrow I would be waking up without her.

"Good morning." I opened my eyes and tried to imprint her sleepy, bed-headed image in my mind to take it back home with me.

"You're so beautiful." Jen smiled at me and I saw her dark eyes were shining with unshed tears.

"I think we should say goodbye here." I told her suddenly, realising how emotional a goodbye was going to be. "It's going to be hard."

A tear spilled over Jen's lower lashes and that was all it took to set off my own tears.

We cuddled up in bed, alternating between crying and laughing at our sentimentality.

"So, what happens next?" I asked after we'd finally cried out all our tears and were getting ready for my departure.

"Are you asking me 'what are we'?" Jen smiled.

"No!" I blushed and shook my head before changing my mind. "Well, yes, actually."

"I don't want to see anyone else." Jen replied, pulling me close.

I rested my head on her shoulder and she kissed the tip of my nose affectionately.

"Are we telling people?" I asked shyly.

"Like?" Jen prompted.

"Andy?"

"It's up to you." Jen replied.

"Well, it's not," I batted back. "He's both our friend."

"He's your best friend though." Jen countered.

I wrinkled my nose up at her, giving up on Andy. "What about the kids?"

"There's a lot we haven't talked about." Jen wrinkled her nose up in imitation of me. "You can tell the whole world."

Jen pushed me away gently, holding me at arm's length and letting her eyes travel over me slowly before pulling me close again for one final kiss.

The telephone rang announcing my car to the airport. Jen hung up the phone and I could see the determination on her face to hold it together.

“Text you later?” I managed a brave smile.

Jen nodded. “I love you. I’ll see you later.”

I gave her a fleeting hug and backed away quickly before I crumbled. I grabbed my bag and with one small glance back, I left.

I carried that image of Jen with me nearly 3500 miles, all the way home; Jen stood in the centre of her plush hotel suite. Her usually immaculate dark bob still wavy from the shower, her feet bare and dressed simply in a t-shirt and jeans. She looked so vulnerable and real; I could feel my heart aching at her beauty.

The journey home was cloaked in sadness, but I was excited to see my children and fired up to tackle the next stage of my life. I felt like I’d shed my old, tired skin on this trip and emerged a stronger, brighter version of me. I felt ready to take on the world.

Chapter 26

Almost nine days without their mother was clearly an eternity for the children. They were wild with excitement to see me and I launched straight into hugs and stories of their alleged neglect/ harm at each other's hands.

"George hasn't brushed his teeth the whole time!" Matilda exclaimed gleefully.

"Esther has been horrible." George volunteered after I'd emptied my bag of Duty Free sweets and chocolate. "And she was rude to Dad and Charlotte."

I glanced at Esther and she had the decency to look away guiltily.

"Snitches get stitches." She hissed at her brother stomping off up the stairs. But not before she'd had time to scoop up the cosmetics and headphones I'd bought her, I noticed.

"Don't leave us again." Leo sniffed into my leg.

Steve was hovering around in the background and I saw his expression change to one of annoyance. He'd been staying at my house with the children.

"Did you pick the dogs up?" I asked although it was evident from their absence that he hadn't.

"Didn't have time." He shrugged. "I need to speak to you about Esther."

"Did you have a nice time?" I asked, ignoring his request.

I had been travelling for hours. I was exhausted and in desperate need of a coffee and a shower.

"Yes, lovely." He nodded, stuffing his hands in his pockets. "She was really out of order at times."

"Steve," I put my hand up to stop him. "Any chance we can talk about this another time? I've just got back. I need a coffee."

"There's no milk." He said.

"Aw!" Matilda stamped her foot. "I was going to have Coco Pops."

"You can't have that for lunch." I said on Mum Autopilot.

"We haven't had breakfast." Matilda fired back shooting an accusatory look at her Dad.

I noticed that they were still in their pyjamas despite it being midday.

"They had lie ins." Steve shrugged oblivious to my irritation. "Anyway, your daughter-"

"No." I cut him off firmly. I could picture what Esther had been like and I wasn't getting involved. "Unless 'My Daughter' murdered someone, I'm not interested right now. She's a teenager. She speaks to me like shit. You deal with it whatever way you see fit."

Steve opened his mouth to speak but saw my expression and clearly thought better of it. He grabbed his bag from the bottom of the stairs.

"Right," He huffed. "I'll be off."

I slid my feet back into my shoes, knowing there was no way I could relax until I'd picked up the dogs and done a quick food shop. I finally took in the scenes of devastation around me. There were toys littered everywhere, dishes in the sink and all the kids' holiday clothes had been dumped on the floor in the utility room. I used my finger and thumb to hook up a pair of swimming shorts and half a beach poured out onto the tiles. I groaned and dropped them back down, turning and shutting the door on the mess. It would keep.

"Right!" I yelled, engaging my military tactics. "Get dressed! Brush your teeth! We're going out!"

I cleared as much as I could up in the half an hour it took for George to find a pair of socks and decided against showering myself in fear I would fall asleep on my feet. Esther and George both wore matching expressions of contempt on being marched around the supermarket, dropping back twenty paces at all times to avoid being seen with me. In all fairness to them, I did look like shit. After a whirlwind tour of the shop and a trip to the kennels to pick up the dogs, I wheel-spun through the McDonalds drive-thru and we were back at the house in record time.

Once I'd made the coffee I'd been craving, I finally got around to breaking one of Steve's house rules and let the dogs on my bed for a team nap. Matilda and Leo dragged blankets and iPads in, and I sunk into a blissful daytime doze. I drifted in and out of sleep for a few hours and came around to Matilda brandishing my phone in my face.

"'S the matter?" I slurred slightly as I tried to make out what she was showing me.

"Jen phoned." Matilda said, tapping the phone screen.

I felt a silly flutter at the mention of her name. I struggled to sit up under the weight of Matilda's elbow on my chest and Hermione sprawled across my legs.

"I'll phone her back now." I said, yawning widely.

"I talked to her." Matilda told me. "She's gone now."

I took the phone off my daughter and checked the call log. Matilda had been on the phone for thirty-four minutes. I could feel my smile widening and tried to suppress it; I was acting like a love-struck teenager.

"Tell me about your holiday." I said to Matilda, sliding an arm around her.

We'd chatted briefly about it in the car, but I was keen to build up a bigger picture to ensure my children weren't psychologically damaged from the experience.

"Was ok." Matilda shrugged. "Esther was nice to me."

"That's good." I nodded. "Did Esther have a nice time?"

Matilda chewed on her lip thoughtfully and I could tell she was trying to work out whether it was ok to tell me something. I waited. Matilda was rubbish at keeping secrets.

"Daddy was grumpy at Esther and Esther said Charlotte was a cow." Matilda confessed finally.

"To her face?" I asked trying to hide my horror.

"No." Matilda shook her head and I felt relief that my kids hadn't disgraced me in front of the replacement. "She said it to Daddy."

"Right," It was my turn to chew my lip thoughtfully. "Did Esther have a nice time at all?"

"She played with me a lot," Matilda offered. "That must have been fun for her. And she got to be in charge when Daddy and Charlotte went out."

I frowned at that. I barely let Esther babysit at home, let alone in a foreign country. I made a note to bring this up with Steve. I opened my mouth to continue my investigations when my phone started to ring. It was Andy on Facetime.

"Hey!" I answered, holding the phone at arm's length so he could see Matilda was here and not say anything inappropriate.

"Hi!" Andy's smiling face filled the screen. "Hi Tilly!"

"Hi Uncle Andy!" She beamed. "I've been on holiday!"

“I know.” Andy answered. “Did you have a nice time?”

“Yeah.” Matilda replied noncommittally. “I already told Mum and Jen about it though so I’m tired of talking now.”

Andy laughed. “Oh, I feel your pain. All I’ve done today is talk, talk, talk.”

Andy paused and looked pointedly at the camera. I knew him well enough to know this was a segue and he was about to tell me what he’d “talk, talk, talked” about.

“Babe?” He raised an eyebrow. “Are you listening?”

“I’m all ears!” I laughed. “I had a nice holiday too, by the way.”

“Sssh!” He hushed me theatrically. “Your time will come.”

I laughed at his rudeness. Literally nothing could bring me down. “Andy?”

“Yes, Lucy?” He grinned, knowing I was playing along.

“What did you talk, talk, talk about all day?” I smiled affectionately.

Matilda, used to Andy, rolled her eyes and wandered off.

“Oh, y’know,” He gave a fake-coy smile. “Just general chat to the lovely people from Lifestyle Magazine.”

“Shut up!” I sat up straight in the bed and peered suspiciously at him. “Don’t wind me up now- tell the truth.”

"Swear!" He held up his pinky finger in a childlike gesture to me. "It's all public! John never does interviews, but he wanted to control this."

"Ah!" I gave a little shriek of excitement. That was definitely a sign it was serious! Not that I'd doubted it. "Congratulations, Mr Film Star's Fella!"

"Ha!" Andy laughed but he looked delighted. "I'm officially moved in by the way."

"I thought it wouldn't be long!" I was smiling so hard I felt my cheeks ache. "I am so bloody happy for you!"

"We just need to find you someone perfect now!" Andy sighed with happiness. "Oh! And a job! I haven't forgotten-we're doing CVs this week."

I opened my mouth. I desperately wanted to tell him I'd found someone perfect already. I then shut my mouth self-consciously. It was too late though as Andy knew me too well.

"Oh my God!" Andy clapped his hand over his mouth. "You've either got a job-"

I shook my head, laughing.

"No?" Andy frowned. "You're not back with that dick?"

"Which one?" I countered.

"Good point, well made." Andy deadpanned. "No, seriously, Lucy. You're not back with Luke?"

"Noooooo!" I shook my head again. "I promise I'm over that phase!"

"Not Steve." Andy said decisively.

"Definitely not." I agreed.

Andy looked thoughtful for a moment and then I recognised the penny start to drop. He opened his mouth and then closed it again.

"Who?" He asked suspiciously.

"Guess." I said, suddenly feeling too shy.

I could almost see Andy's mind working, trying to make the pieces fit. I suddenly had the urge to change the subject. I wanted to hold it close to my chest for a little while longer like a delicious secret. Just the thought of being with Jen made me feel all warm and fuzzy. New York had been so magical and special; nobody would be able to appreciate how special and I wasn't ready to have my sparkle dulled.

"Anyway," I said quickly. "It doesn't matter! When can I read your article? Are there photos? Send me the link!"

"I know what you're doing," Andy said suspiciously. I could tell he was dying to send me the link though and get my feedback (compliments). "I'll send it now. Two seconds."

The screen paused as he went into his messages and I exhaled quietly. My phone pinged with an incoming message and Andy appeared back on my screen.

"Oh my God!" He burst out. "It's Jen! You and Jen!"

I froze, and my silence answered Andy's educated guess.

"I knew it!" Andy exclaimed. "You pair have been flirting for ages!"

"No, we haven't!" I protested.

"Yes." Andy was on a roll now. "What happened? How? Don't tell me about the sex though. You're a mother- that's obscene!"

"Ew!" I laughed, grateful that Andy was making a joke and knowing he was trying to put me at ease despite this bombshell. "I can't talk to you about sex, you witch! That'd be like talking to my step-dad about it."

"So, did you just 'do it' or is this like 'a thing'?" Andy asked.

"It's 'a thing'." I confirmed, and I felt my mouth turn up into a smile. I couldn't help but grin every time I thought of Jen and I covered my mouth with my hand, conscious of wearing my heart on my sleeve.

There was a noise in the background and Andy turned away from the camera.

"Hi babe!" He called, probably to John. "Guess who Lucy's sleeping with?"

"Andy!" I shrieked. "No!"

"What?" Andy turned back to his phone. "Is it a secret?"

"Well, no," I replied flustered. "But we're not going to do Lifestyle Magazine just yet! It's early days!"

Andy laughed at this.

"And," I felt a surge of confidence and pride. "I'm not 'sleeping with' her. It's more serious than that."

"Sleeping with who?"

Esther's voice came from the open doorway and my head snapped up to meet her eyes in surprise.

At exactly that moment, Andy's voice boomed from the phone.

"Jen!" He was hollering in response to something John had asked. "She's in love with Jen!"

Andy's words echoed in my ears but all I could focus on was Esther's face as I waited, in what felt like slow motion for a response.

George suddenly appeared behind Esther's shoulder.

"Jen?" He pumped a fist in the air before walking off. "Better than Charlotte! Go on, Mum!"

Up until that moment, I had watched every range of emotion filter across Esther's face as she tried to process yet another parental bombshell in a (probably) psychologically damaging short period of time. Her big blue eyes crinkled up first and I felt my heart restart as I recognised the expression split-seconds before a genuinely happy laugh left her mouth.

"Better than Charlotte, Mum!" She laughed, repeating her brother's sentiments.

"Ah! I needed to talk to you about that, apparently!" I remembered.

"Right after you've talked about your romance?" Esther raised an eyebrow.

"Who's the parent here?" I tried to look authoritative.

"God knows anymore!" Esther threw her hands in the air and sauntered off before I could stop her.

"Lucy!" Andy pulled my attention back to my phone. "Dinner tomorrow! Bring the kids. Me and John want to know everything."

"A signed copy of Lifestyle and we're there." I gave him a wink before hanging up.

Not even home twenty-four hours and it was all public knowledge. I hugged the blanket close to me, feeling a shiver of delight. And this was just the start.

Chapter 27

With the time difference, I managed to Facetime Jen that evening. I only realised once I'd finished chatting to Andy that she'd called me during work, her time, and my heart fluttered at how sweet she'd been to endure over half an hour of Matilda's rambling when she must have just been checking in on me after my journey home between meetings.

"Hello, beautiful." Jen's gorgeous face filled my phone screen.

"Hey," I beamed at the sight of her. "Sorry I missed your call."

"Matilda and I had a lovely chat," Jen laughed. "She's so funny."

"You must have the patience of a saint." I told her.

"It was nice to talk to her." Jen replied. "How was their holiday?"

"Mostly ok," I confided. "Esther was a bit of a nightmare for Steve and his girlfriend though."

"Well," Jen reasoned. "It must be hard for her. I'm sure Steve can understand."

"Really?" I raised an eyebrow.

"No," Jen laughed. "I bet he's been a right arsehole about it. I was being polite as I don't want to be the new girlfriend who hates the ex."

The ex. My stomach butterflied in excitement at Jen describing herself as my 'girlfriend'.

"Everyone hates the ex," I joked. "So, it's fine."

"What are you up to?" Jen asked.

"We're going over Andy and John's for dinner tomorrow."

"Oh!" Jen's face lit up. "He just sent me a link for that feature- have you read it yet?"

"Yes, I did!" I nodded. "Pretty big news. Our Andy's a celeb now."

We both laughed at this.

"Were you going to mention anything to Andy?" Jen asked hesitantly.

"I kind of already did." I admitted. "Is that ok?"

"Oh, Lucy." Jen's full red lips turned up into an even wider smile. "Of course, it's ok. Am I a massive weirdo that I want to shout it from the rooftop? I'm dying to tell my Gran!"

My smile now rivalled hers. "God, I love you."

"I love you." She responded and we both giggled self-consciously at how ridiculously love-struck we were acting. "I'll take a lunch break tomorrow and call you. Is 8am, your time, too early?"

"No, that's perfect." I would have woken up at 3am if it

meant I could see Jen. It crossed my mind that the next five months would be difficult, but I was determined to make it work as I'd never felt happier.

The kids were due back in school the next day and I had a million errands to complete but I didn't feel the usual pre-school stress. The uniform, bags and shoes had been sorted weeks ago and now I wasn't working I had all week to pick up last minute extras and shopping. Nobody complained, as they usually did, when I told them we were going out for dinner. I wasn't sure whether this was due to them being so happy to be reunited with their mother or for the bragging rights of being able to tell their friends they'd been to a film star's house.

John had the foresight (I knew for a fact that Andy wouldn't have thought to do it) to keep lunch simple to cater to the kids' range of fussy tastes. John had left the WIFI password chalked on a board in his orangery and dug out a few token board games (just in case my family turned out to be lovely and wholesome in anyway).

"Ooh!" Matilda pulled out Twister from the pile. "Can we play this?"

"Twister?" I gave Andy a loaded look and he laughed out loud prompting queries from my innocent children as to what was so funny.

"Come through to the kitchen and give us a hand?" Andy gave me his own loaded look and I sheepishly followed him through, bracing myself for the inquisition.

John was lining up plates on the table and looked up excitedly. "Are we going to grill Lucy on her private life?"

"We certainly are!" Andy clapped his hands together.

"My brother will be devastated!" John joked.

I laughed, despite feeling shy at the thought of having to discuss my relationship. I hadn't had a problem with talking about Steve or Luke, but this felt different. I stayed quiet, not knowing what to say.

"Has this 'romance' being going on a while?" Andy pressed me for details as him and John whizzed around with their various pots and dishes. He exchanged a knowing glance with John.

"No, it hasn't," I replied. "And I can see you looking at each other."

Andy grinned, "We had a bet on."

John looked mortified. "Andy! Sorry, Lucy!"

I laughed. "Really? On what?"

"On how long this has been going on." Andy had zero shame.

"And what did you bet?" I asked, genuinely interested to know whether he'd seen this coming before I had.

"I can't answer that." Andy winked. "You'll lie so that John wins just to spite me."

I would have as well.

"So?" Andy looked at me expectantly.

"Just since New York." I answered.

"Nothing before?" He frowned.

"Lunch is ready." John said, changing the subject when he saw I was getting flustered.

"Just give us the highlights before the kids come in!" Andy pleaded. "We're happy for you. We love Jen."

I felt my ever-present blush deepen but fortunately, George chose that moment to wander into the kitchen. The children were impeccably behaved, and I was impressed by John's patience with them. At the back of my mind, I'd been expecting them to turn into little savages and to have to cut short the visit.

"I can't believe you're starting High School tomorrow!" Andy addressed George, as we were getting ready to leave. "I can remember when your mum was pregnant with you."

Andy and I both exchanged looks, remembering the hormonal nightmare that I'd been.

"That was when your mum met Jen." Andy continued, and I gave him a warning look.

It was one thing that the children were aware of my new relationship, but I didn't want Andy making it weird.

"Are you free to help me with my CV this week?" I cut him off before he could continue his reminiscing.

"Next week?" Andy offered. "John is away in the US, so I'll need the company."

"Whenever you can fit me in." I replied, before hustling the kids back into the car.

I didn't feel like I was in any rush to find a job. I had a few months' grace, thanks to the redundancy pay-out, and I quite fancied making the most of my time off. Most importantly, I wanted to work out what it was that I actually wanted to do.

Chapter 28

After a few weeks of actually being at home, I soon changed my mind. The children had all settled back into school quite well and I was feeling bored and restless. Days were dragging; partly because I was pining for Jen and counting down the days until we could be together.

I had started applying for some jobs but with no real urgency as nothing I saw was jumping out at me. After my years away from being an Analyst, the only things I was really 'qualified' to do were entry level or High Street bank roles. There was an entry level Analyst vacancy at Steve's company, but I would rather die penniless in the gutter than have to bump into him or Charlotte at the lifts every day.

Steve was back to seeing the kids when it was convenient to him. He still hadn't got himself a permanent home but, on a positive, he was still paying all the bills, so I kept my mouth shut. Not that it mattered really, Andy was keeping a low profile now he was publicly linked to John and Jen was away, so I had nowhere I wanted to go. The children didn't seem bothered that they weren't seeing their dad on a regular basis as their weekends were so full up of their own activities and social lives that they were barely home except to eat and sleep. Steve hadn't mentioned Esther's bad attitude since I'd cut him off and I had a feeling that all wasn't as rosy as he made out on his social media (it came up in my feed, I wasn't actively looking any more).

The time difference made speaking to Jen difficult. She was

only five hours behind, but she worked long hours and networking was a must in her line of work. I soon developed my usual anxiety, adamant that she'd grow bored of me and meet someone else, but as soon as her face lit up my screen on our daily FaceTime calls, all my worries evaporated. I never pictured myself as this sappily romantic, but I lived for our conversations. I genuinely loved talking to her, hearing about her day. All the little, mundane things were interesting and fun. I was head-over-heels.

I was gushing about my new relationship one morning in early October to my sister, when I realised she wasn't being the usual captive audience that she was meant to be.

"Em?" I cut myself off mid-sentence. "Am I boring you?"

It was on the tip of my tongue to protest that this was exactly how she had been when she started seeing Shaun when I heard her sigh.

"Sorry, Lucy," She said, her usually cheerful voice sounded tired. "I'm just distracted at the moment."

"Sorry!" I apologised immediately. "I just assumed you weren't working this morning. I'll call you later."

Emily ran her own business and did the majority of her work in the evenings and weekend. Our regular chats had been the best part of my stint of unemployment. We'd grown apart a little since she'd moved to Wales and I'd had all the kids, and it had been lovely to reconnect.

"No, it's not that." Emily responded quickly. "I was listening. Honestly, I love that you're so happy."

"So, what's up?" I asked.

"Don't tell Mum," She made me promise. "I've started IVF treatment. We're going to try to have another baby."

"Oh, Em!" I exclaimed. "That's so exciting."

She'd had a hard time getting pregnant with Finley and after several heart-breaking miscarriages, Emily had been through the gruelling process of IVF. I knew, from the attempts they had before Finley, that it was a physically and emotionally draining process for them.

"Is there anything I can do?" I asked, thinking back to how tired and stressed out she'd been the first time around. Shaun was away on a short-term contract and I could hear in her voice that she needed help. "Look after Fin for you to get some rest?"

"I wish!" She joked, back to her usual self. "No, it's fine. I'm just nervous. And hormonal. And tired."

"I'll come down!" I offered immediately, without thinking about the logistics. "I can help."

"No!" Emily protested.

"Without the kids!" I chipped in quickly, and I noticed, with a smile, that she didn't protest that time.

"If you can." Emily said tentatively.

I text Steve asking if he could pick up the kids from after-school club and have them for the weekend. Steve was overdue a visit to his parents and I was over-the-moon when he agreed.

It felt amazing to be on my second solo trip in the space of a few months. As much as I loved my kids, I had forgotten how delicious the freedom of just being by myself was and it was lovely to spend time with Emily. After juggling four boisterous kids, keeping Finley entertained was a walk in the park, and it felt good to pay Emily back for all the times she'd helped me out. The stress of the treatment was clearly taking its toll on her, and I brushed off her objections and spent the Saturday night hand-stitching butterflies onto fifty napkin holders.

"I can't believe you do this!" I said to her, threading the needle for about the millionth time as I lost the thread yet again. "I thought event planning was just booking things."

"It's doing whatever it takes," She replied dryly from her seat on the opposite sofa. "That's why I'm so busy. Because I'm bloody good!"

"You better chill out on the bookings then," I warned her. "You shouldn't be working like this. You need to start taking it easy."

"I will." She promised. "I'm booked up until the summer though."

"I'll be back to help whenever I can," I told her, meaning it. "Anything for my favourite sister."

She laughed. "I'm your only sister. And, anyway, you'll be busy with your own job soon."

Andy had done a great job with my CV and I had signed up for alerts with a few job sites, but I hadn't made much more progress than that. I thought about this as I drove home on Sunday and resolved to start taking my job-hunt more seriously.

It wasn't even 9pm by the time I got home but the nights had started drawing in already and every light in the house looked like it was on. I knocked tentatively before walking in; still feeling a bit weird about my estranged husband being a visitor in what was technically our home, especially as he was still paying the bills. The dogs rushed from the sofa with a clatter of paws to greet me, but the living room was empty. I could hear the kids, or at least their consoles/ videos, blaring from upstairs and I hesitated at the bottom of the stairs, assuming Steve was upstairs with one of the kids and not wanting to interrupt any paternal bonding. I surveyed the mountain of bags and shoes piled at the bottom of the stairs and rolled my eyes. I grabbed a handful of the still full sports kits and pushed open the kitchen door.

"Oh!" I exclaimed, surprised to see Steve sat at the table talking into his phone in a stressed out, hushed tone. "Sorry- I thought you were upstairs."

Steve glanced up at me before looking away and speaking

back into his phone. “Look, she’s back now. I won’t be long.”

I felt a prickle of irritation at him and, instead of leaving the room as I would have done to let him finish his conversation, I stubbornly set about emptying the bags noisily. I caught Steve shoot me a look of annoyance and I continued my banging around.

“No,” Steve was sighing into the phone. “It’s not...”

He was cut off by whoever he was talking to, presumably Charlotte. He drummed his fingers on the table in agitation as he listened to what sounded like an earful. I covered my mouth to hide my smirk.

“I’ll be home now.” He said finally. “Babe?”

He dropped the phone and exhaled noisily. It seemed Charlotte had hung up on him. Good for her.

“I thought you’d be back hours ago.” He turned his attention to me with a scowl.

I maturely ignored him and turned my attention to the counter full of dishes and cups, slamming them into the dishwasher.

“You’re fucking welcome.” He said sarcastically as he got to his feet.

I spun around and gave him a look of pure contempt.

“I’m fucking welcome?” I deliberately rolled my eyes. “You

want me to be grateful that you're looking after your kids?"

"How can I have them when I'm staying in the spare room at Greg's?" He spat out. I could see the annoyance on his face.

"You're not though!" I laughed bitterly. "You're living with Charlotte. I don't know why you're still peddling this shit! The kids have met her. What's the problem with having them there?"

Steve flushed angrily. "I'm not living with her. I just stay there a lot. And she's got a one-bedroomed apartment so it's not practical."

"Steve," I felt any confrontation drain away all of a sudden and I just felt sorry that this is what we'd become. "We can't go on like this. Can't you get somewhere? We've got some money, surely."

Steve shook his head in exasperation. "We're maxed out after buying that apartment and having the kitchen and bathrooms done last year."

I looked at him in surprise. I'd just assumed that we were still quite comfortable. I knew that we weren't loaded and that our lifestyle depended on me contributing a monthly income but hearing Steve saying that we were 'maxed out' came as a shock. The fact that he'd gone ahead and bought the apartment had irritated me but now it seemed downright infuriating.

"Why did you get the apartment?" I asked, trying to keep my

voice calm and not accusatory.

Steve turned away from me as if he was finished with the conversation. "I'm not talking about this right now. I'm still paying most of the bills here. Once that stops, I'll be able to get a place."

I nodded dumbly. I hadn't expected him to bank roll me forever and this just hardened my resolve to find something quicker so that I could keep my redundancy money back as a safety net.

"Can you just let me know what you think is reasonable, so I know what I'm working with?" I asked quietly.

Steve looked at me, my softness surprising him as if he'd been ready for me to protest at this. "Yes, of course."

"Thanks for coming over." I said feeling increasingly uncomfortable.

Steve gave me a little smile. "That's ok. It's good to see them. I miss them."

I felt a stab of guilt as if this was my fault that I was keeping him away from the kids due to my financial inferiority. I gave a half-smile back.

After Steve was gone, I settled the children down and whizzed through the house tidying up as I went. I showered and changed quickly before falling into my bed to facetime Jen as was part of our routine. It would be difficult once I was working again so I was making the most of being able to see her via the magic of WIFI. You could practically set your watch by our daily catch ups.

"Hey beautiful!" I felt the familiar butterflies as Jen popped up on my phone screen.

"Good morning." Her face lit up in a genuine smile of delight. "How did your trip to your sister's go?"

"Yeah, good," I nodded. I debated whether to tell her about my conversation with Steve as I always felt conscious to not bang on about the ex. "Are you in bed?"

Jen nodded and then held the camera up to reveal her full body. She was sat up on the edge of her bed wearing something silky, black and tiny. "Like my pyjamas?"

"Wow!" My eyes almost popped out of my head. God, she was perfect.

Jen grinned happily at me.

"Where was that when I was there?" I groaned, only half joking.

"I just bought it," She gave me teasing smile. "I'm updating my sleepwear ready for when I'm home."

"Tease!" I pouted. "But I can't wait. Only eleven weeks to go!"

"And counting!" Jen sighed. "Was Steve ok having the kids this weekend?"

"Yeah, he was..." I started.

"But?" Jen could see by my face that there was more I wanted to say.

"It's not ideal him not having his own place," I told her. "I thought he was doing it deliberately because he was living with Charlotte, but he's said a few things this evening about how we're financially up to our eyeballs. I need to get my arse into gear and get a job."

"Really?" Jen looked surprised. "Why the hell did he buy that apartment then?"

"It's mortgaged." I replied. "And the rentals just about cover that. It's just expensive having kids. Esther's off to Iceland with school in a few weeks- that's cost about a million pounds. Steve pays most of the bills here so hopefully when I find a job, I can take over a few and he'll free up some cash each month to get a place."

Even as I said it, I was estimating the cost of running another place. Especially in London. I couldn't see Steve being able to even afford a bedsit if we didn't find a way of lowering our monthly expenditure.

"Just don't go rushing into any old job and making yourself unhappy again." Jen warned me. "You know I'll help in any way I can."

I smiled gratefully at her, but I would never expect her to foot any of my bills.

"I won't rush into anything." I promised. "It'll be fine."

"Good." Jen propped her own phone against the nightstand and pulled off her silky camisole revealing her full, pert breasts. "I need to start getting ready now. I'm off out for food, but I just thought I'd try these on for you!"

"Oh my God!" I moaned in frustration. "I can't survive the next few months without you."

She gave me a cheeky wink and stood up to slip the tiny shorts off before kicking them away.

"Are you getting into bed now?" She asked leadingly.

"Uh yes!" I replied, propping up my own phone and pulling my extremely unsexy pyjamas off.

"Fuck it," Jen got back onto her bed and leaned forward seductively. "I think I'm going to be late!"

Chapter 29

I kept my promise to Jen and didn't rush into any old job. Unfortunately, I also kept my promise to myself and had been scouring the internet and sending out applications and CVs left, right and centre since the day after Steve had voiced his financial concerns. At first, I had been quite picky; only searching for analyst roles similar to my earlier job. It had been the juggling and the culture I'd struggled with, not the actual role, whereas now all the children were in schools with good after-hour childcare. I was fussy about the companies that I chose to apply for; scouring their corporate websites for their values and googling real employee reviews. I found an amazing vacancy for an analyst for a human rights charity and I kept my fingers crossed for weeks that I would hear back from them.

Nothing came, not even a standard "Thank you for your interest but..." email. I felt a little disheartened as I had really pictured myself working for that company and the location was perfect. I had applied for four other similar roles for different companies and had been praying that I got something back from the charity first, so I wasn't in a position where I had to decide whether the 'bird in the hand was worth 2 in the bush' but, as it was, I heard nothing from any of the companies. Disappointed and very much aware that I was now eating into my redundancy pay, I dug deep into my reserves for a bit of resilience and expanded my search to include other jobs. A few branch roles for other banks cropped up in my searches but I dismissed those, hoping I would find something before I had to resort to anything like my last job. I even roped in Andy to vet my covering letters and any applications I sent. Jen checked over my CV when she could see my confidence faltering but assured me that it was looking good.

I waited patiently for something to come back from this next lot of applications but after a week I'd just had a few "thank you but no thank you" emails and radio silence from the rest. Somehow the days were going so slowly; just a loop of groundhog days of me filling my time while the kids were at school; going to the gym, doing housework and walking the dogs. Despite the slow days, the weeks seemed to be racing away and I was excited at the prospect of Jen coming home for Christmas and then only a few more weeks until she came home for good at the end of February. My redundancy pay was also racing away at an equal speed. I tried to hold my nerve and ignore the dwindling balance. Steve had mentioned, on more than one occasion, that we both needed to see solicitors and make formal arrangements around maintenance. I had made noncommittal responses to this which he'd accepted but he had text me a follow up regarding this and I knew I could only fob him off so many times before he went ahead and changed our set up. He was still seeing the children sporadically and looking more and more stressed out every time I saw him. I knew, via the children, that he wasn't taking them to Charlotte's apartment and she hadn't gone to dinner, bowling or the cinema with them on the few occasions Steve did see the children. His social media life was pretty low key too although she'd 'liked' a recent picture he'd shared so I was assuming that they were still on. Even though I still thought he was a dickhead, it still wasn't fair that he was throwing all his money at my house and kids and leaving himself with nothing. I brushed off the latest round of rejections and opened up a new job search, widening my criteria.

Esther's week in Iceland with the school had been and gone. I'd spent a fortune on kitting her out in designer cold weather clothes as she'd shot up again since last winter and she was now almost taller than me. Her attitude, since going back to school, had been hideous and, as much as I missed her while she was away, we were all glad of a break from her moods. I'd been optimistic that I'd have found a job by the time she'd come home. In my head, this would allow me to skim away a decent salary to top up my diminishing savings and start the Christmas shopping and then be able to take over some bills in November to cut Steve some financial slack.

Steve had arranged to take the children to a Fireworks display and he arrived at the house to collect them. Andy was away visiting John in LA and I had zero plans, except for putting the TV on loudly to distract the dogs from any noise. We had an unspoken agreement that the car stayed with me, but he could take it whenever he had the kids as this was more convenient than using public transport and he had no reason to need a car of his own, never mind the added expense.

"What are you up to tonight?" He asked, loitering awkwardly in the kitchen as he waited for the children to put their hats, gloves and boots on. They were getting ready at their usual snail pace and I offered him a cup of coffee out of politeness when it became apparent that Esther wasn't going anywhere until her hair was finished.

"The usual," I gestured at the kitchen around me. "Just chilling in the house."

"You're not dating anyone yet?" Steve asked, not making eye contact as if he was embarrassed to ask.

"Oh." I was surprised as the kids were aware I had started a relationship with Jen and I had assumed they would have mentioned this to their dad. "I thought you knew- I'm with Jen."

Steve's mouth dropped open and I would have laughed at the confusion on his face if I hadn't felt so uncomfortable talking about my love life to my separated husband.

"Jen?" He repeated incredulously.

I nodded.

"As in Jen? Your friend?" He repeated again.

"Yes." I said.

"Really?" He frowned, peering at me as if he didn't believe me.

I nodded again but frowned back at him. "Is that hard to believe?"

"How long has that been going on?" He asked and there was

a suspicious note to his tone.

“Since I went on holiday in August to see her.” I replied, wishing the kids would hurry up now.

“I didn’t know.” He replied.

“Sorry,” I shrugged. “I thought the kids would have said something.”

“The kids know?” He asked sounding shocked.

“Yes,” I replied coolly, not liking his tone. He hadn’t been this interested when Luke had been on the scene, however briefly. “Is that alright with you?”

I could hear the sarcasm in my voice as I asked the question and I expected Steve to rise to this however he flushed slightly and apologised.

“Oh, of course, sorry.” He almost stuttered. “I just had no idea you were...“

“Bi?” I raised an eyebrow challengingly and he nodded. “Who knew, hey!”

“Well, I’m happy for you,” He said, ignoring my challenging tone and recovering his composure. “Is it serious?”

“I think so.” I gave him a little smile, feeling bad for jumping into defensive mode so quickly.

“Any plans to move in or?” He continued, and I could see his brain ticking. He was clearly aware that she was doing well financially. I wondered whether he was seeing this as an opportunity to pass the financial responsibility of this house on.

"No, none." I told him firmly. "It's still early days and I've got the kids to think of. She's still in New York until the end of Feb."

"But it's serious, you say?" He asked again.

"Yes." I frowned at his question. "Why are you asking?"

Steve shook his head. "I'm just surprised, that's all. She was never one for settling down, was she?"

Where was he going with this? I wondered. I had initially thought he'd been surprised that I was in a same sex relationship, but it was sounding like he was more surprised that I'd bagged someone attractive and successful. I should be offended but I just wanted the awkward conversation over with.

"Ready!" Esther interrupted us as she came down the stairs, twirling her perfectly styled loose waves around her finger. She stood before us waiting expectantly for our compliments.

"Your hair looks nice." I said dutifully.

"Beautiful." Steve gave her a little squeeze and tugged on the cream knit headband that she was wearing in lieu of a hat.

"Dad." She gave him a warning stare. "If you mess my hair

up, you'll be the one waiting and everyone will miss the fireworks."

We all laughed at that and Steve called the rest of the children to go.

"Do you want to come with us?" Steve asked me suddenly.

I was taken aback. "Oh, thanks but-"

"Oh yes, Mum!" Leo's face lit up and he grabbed my hand. "Please come!"

"Oh, no," I shook my head. "I have to look after the dogs. Ron doesn't like the firework noise. He'll freak out."

"Don't be silly, Mum," Esther frowned at me. "Just leave the TV on in here like you always used to. Come on, grab your coat. It'll be nice for us all to do something."

I looked at Steve pleadingly for help to back out of this, but he was nodding along with the kids.

"Come on!" He gave me a friendly grin and I felt myself swept up by their insistence.

It was actually nice to stand out in the field watching the firework display and the looks on the children's faces as they oohed and aahed at the flashing lights and colours. Steve bought us all hot dogs to eat on the way back to the car and it was only when I was back at the carpark that I realised I'd missed Jen's call by a few minutes. I would have called her on handsfree, as I sometimes did on the weekend if I was out and about with the kids, but I felt too self-conscious to around Steve and so I text her instead.

"Just leaving the firework display! Went on longer than I thought :(Shall I try you when I'm home or are you still working?"

Jen texted back a few minutes later. "Got post-work dinner and drinks. Will be too late, your time, by the time I'm back ☹ How come Steve didn't take them? Knobhead x."

Well, this was awkward. I cursed myself for going.

"Kids insisted I go with them <grimace face emoji> so sad I didn't get to see you. Phone me when you wake up. I love you x."

I waited for a response, but none came. I hoped she wouldn't be annoyed that the first time I'd missed our one of our calls it had been because I was with Steve.

"Is that Jen?" Steve asked, clocking me glancing at the phone in my hand.

"Yes." I nodded and then changed the subject, so he wouldn't ask any more questions. "How's everything with Charlotte?"

"Alright," He shrugged, and I knew Steve well enough to know, from his expression, that things maybe weren't that great. "She's doing well at work."

"That's good." I said, forcing an upbeat ring to my tone. "Any plans to move in together?"

Steve shook his head.

"Ah ok," I wished I hadn't asked. "Hopefully I'll be working soon, and we'll be able to sort out the whole money thing."

"Hopefully," Steve gave me a wry smile to know he wasn't being sarcastic. "I'm looking forward to having a permanent residence again. Greg and Alicia have been great, but it'll be a different story when the kids are home from school."

Greg and Alicia's children were both at an elite boarding school. Greg and Alicia had spent the summer travelling with their uber-cultured children, but I could imagine it would be a bit awkward if Steve was still hanging around when they came home for Christmas.

"Oh right," I felt awful that he was technically homeless. "We'll have a proper chat soon and sort something out."

"If we could." Steve sounded almost grateful and, in that moment, I realised that I might have to consider those bank jobs after all.

I offered to drop Steve off at the station, but he declined and insisted on driving us back to the house. Matilda remembered something she desperately needed to show her dad, despite it being well past her bedtime and I stood awkwardly in the kitchen waiting for him to leave.

"Could we maybe talk about money now?" He asked, when he'd finished looking at Matilda's drawing.

"Now?" I asked surprised. "It's late."

"Right, yeah." He nodded but took a seat anyway.

I felt a surge of annoyance. I felt bad that he didn't have a home and that things weren't going great with Charlotte, but he'd already dragged me out to the fireworks which meant I'd missed Jen's call and now I was practically going back to square one job-wise because he was financially irresponsible. I felt my body tensing and my heart quickening. He was stressing me out now, just like when we were together. I took a deep breath, trying to calm my prickling nerves.

"Is there something..." I started, but I was cut off by a loud bang and a panicked scream.

Steve and I turned towards the noise and our parental instincts kicked in. I flew up the stairs with Steve close behind me.

Leo was stood on the landing, screaming; his eyes fixed on the floor of his and George's bedroom. As I reached him, I saw the source of his panic and my heart stopped.

George was led at an unnatural angle at the base of his bunk bed. His body folded up and his eyes shut like he was sleeping. I leaned over him and shook his shoulders.

"George! George!" I heard my own terrified voice in my ears like an echo.

I pressed my ear to his nose and mouth, praying to hear and feel his breath.

"George! George!" I shook his shoulders with urgency. Why

wasn't he waking up?

I felt a pair of hands pull me away.

"Don't move him. Call the ambulance." Steve thrust a phone at me and bent over our son. I watched frozen as Steve started checking for a pulse.

"Lucy! Now!" He shouted.

Trembling, I snapped out of my trance and made the call. I repeated everything the operator was saying back to Steve and eventually he snatched the phone back off me.

"He's breathing." I heard Steve say. "But he's still unconscious. It looks like he fell from the top bunk."

Time seemed to slow down, and it seemed like an eternity before I heard sirens wailing and blue lights flashing through the blinds. Steve greeted the paramedics, clearing me and the frightened children from the landing. I stood, uselessly, looking on as they stretchered George away.

"Go with him, Luce," Steve nudged me after him. "I'll sort the kids and follow you down."

I could see the sheer fear and panic in Steve's face and I rushed after the paramedics, watching as they hooked my little son up to the machines and placed an oxygen mask over his mouth. I clutched his tiny hand and offered up prayers that he would wake up. Please, please, please wake up and be ok.

"He's waking up." The paramedic said suddenly, and I almost jumped in surprise at his voice. I had forgotten, in my silent prayers, that he was here.

George's eyes fluttered, and the paramedic stopped him from trying to sit up.

"It's ok," I soothed, moving so George could see my face. "You're in the ambulance. You hit your head. It's going to be ok. It's going to be ok."

I repeated this mantra over and over as the tears streamed down my face, clutching his hand tightly. Please let him be ok.

Chapter 30

If time had passed in slow motion at the house, everything sped up once we reached the hospital; time moving in a blur.

The ambulance doors opened up to the drab, grey hospital building, the automatic doors lit up by fluorescent strips and the rotating blue lights of the line of ambulances. The paramedics sprang into action, clicking metal and whizzing the stretcher off down an endless, colourless corridor. I ran alongside; conscious of not obstructing the flow of incoming patients in identical metal beds but prioritising keeping myself in George's eye line. My heart was racing, and my mind was whizzing trying to process this surreal scenario.

The paramedics wheeled George's stretcher into a bay and spoke quickly and calmly as they handed my son's care over to a young woman, with a messy ponytail and a stethoscope strung around her neck. She leant over George, speaking softly but clearly, and as I listened to him respond to her questions, I felt I could finally stop holding my breath.

"Are you Mum?" She asked, turning finally to look at me.

"Yes." I swallowed nervously.

"Can you tell me what happened?" The doctor asked; her pen poised ready to take notes.

"He, he fell." I stuttered. "From his bunk bed."

"He was unconscious?" She asked. "Straight away?"

"I think so," I nodded. "We were downstairs."

"They say he regained consciousness in the ambulance?" She scribbled something down and then directed her cool, grey eyes at me.

"Yes." I nodded.

"Can you tell me how long he was unconscious for? Ten minutes? Fifteen?"

"Yes." I nodded again, uselessly.

"Yes, what?" She frowned.

"Ten minutes, maybe." I racked my brain, but I hadn't had a proper grasp on time since we had heard Leo screaming.

"This is important." Her lips were pressed in a thin line and I felt the same pure fear as when I had seen his still body. The terror had subsided when George had woken up but seeing the seriousness on the doctor's face brought it rushing back.

"The ambulance came quickly," I answered, in a panicked tone. "No more than fifteen minutes."

I could see the concern in her eyes as she glanced at George and went back over to him; shining her torch in his eyes and ears.

"He will be ok now?" I struggled to keep the hysteria out of my voice for George's sake.

He was led on the bed, strapped in, looking pale, tired and so vulnerable that my whole chest ached with love for him.

“George is showing positive signs.” She turned and gave George an encouraging smile as she said this.

George tried to give her a polite smile back and winced immediately. “Ow, my head hurts.”

“We’ll get you something for that,” The doctor addressed him directly before turning back to me. “Fifteen minutes is a long time to be unconscious. We need to rule out any bleeding or other injury to the brain.”

I felt my blood run cold at her words.

“We’ll get George admitted to the ward and he’ll be a priority for further tests.”

I nodded dumbly, stroking George’s hand with my own, blinking back tears of fear. I could have been waiting in that cubicle for a minute, an hour or a whole day. Time meant nothing as I clutched my son’s hand, feeling useless and helpless with nothing in my control. George drifted in and out of sleep. Every time his eyes closed I felt a fresh wave of panic. I feebly asked the doctor whether I should be trying to keep him awake and she waved away my concerns, with a quick glance at her watch.

“It’s gone midnight. He’ll be tired.”

This surprised me as I felt we’d only just arrived and, for the first time, I thought of Steve. I should call him.

As if he had been summoned by my thoughts, Steve came, flustered and out of breath, through the curtains that separated George's bed from the patient next to him. He rushed over to George and I watched the fear in his face grow as he took in George's sleeping face.

"It's ok!" I reassured him quickly. "He's been awake. He's just sleeping."

"He's ok?" Steve repeated, and I could see the hope in his eyes.

I repeated what the doctor had told me; how he was showing positive signs, but they were concerned over the length of time he had been unconscious.

Steve's face drained of colour and I thought for a moment he was going to faint. He clutched the railing of the bed, his knuckles deathly pale.

"Sit down." I ordered hurriedly pushing a plastic chair towards him.

Steve sunk into the seat. He lowered his head into his hands and sat still for a few minutes. When he finally looked up, he seemed to have aged about ten years. I could see every line and wrinkle etched into his face under the harsh lighting.

A nurse pushed through the curtain, breaking the silence.

"Are you Mum and Dad?" She asked.

We both nodded, and Steve got to his feet slowly.

“We’re going to take George down for some tests now.” She told us. “You can both come.”

The nurse bent over my sleeping son. “George? George?”

He stirred but didn’t open his eyes. She tried again, and I moved to her side.

“George?” I called. “It’s time to wake up.”

He opened his eyes at the sound of my voice and peered up at me groggily. “Mum?”

“It’s ok, darling,” I soothed, gently stroking his hair. “Remember you fell and hit your head?”

George crinkled his brow sleepily as if trying to remember and finally nodded.

Steve and I released simultaneous sighs of relief.

“This lady is going to take you for some tests to make sure you haven’t hurt yourself.” I said gently.

“Ok.” George nodded, but I could see his eyes were heavy with sleep.

“Hello, George.” The nurse beamed. “My name is Amy and I’m going to come with you while we hook you up to a machine to get a closer look at your head.”

He nodded again but more awake this time. Steve peered around the nurse and spoke directly to George.

"Hey," He smiled, looking relieved to see George conscious and responding to questions. I could see Steve's eyes were full of unshed tears and my heart physically ached at the sight. "How are you feeling?"

"I'm ok, Dad." George gave his dad a brave smile.

"Right, then." The nurse clapped her hands together authoritatively. "Let's see where my porter has got to and we'll get you down to be looked at."

We followed George down to the MRI scanning suite and another doctor briefed us as George was prepped to go in.

"His responses are looking good but we're going to go ahead and get a closer look because of the length of time he was out for."

Steve and I both nodded and watched helplessly as George was wheeled away. Anxiety coursed through my body; my chest tightened, and I fought back against the incoming panic that threatened to overwhelm my body.

I needed to be here, in this moment, for my son. I told myself furious that my body was about to betray me when I needed to remain cool and calm for George. I flexed my clammy hands over and over, repeating this thought to myself until the panic ebbed away enough for me to catch my breath. Steve and I waited, in silence, for our child to be returned. Time still meant nothing to me and eventually the door opened. Another member of hospital staff emerged with George still on his bed.

"They'll take you up to be admitted to the children's ward." The same doctor we'd seen earlier followed them out. "The scan didn't show any obvious injury that would concern us, but we'll want to have a good look and the detailed report will be sent up to the ward doctors."

I nodded, knowing they had to err on the side of caution and we followed the bed up to the children's ward. The colourful corridors, decorated with cheery cartoon characters, made my heart ache again at the thought of all the poorly children who passed through these doors.

Another nurse greeted us and explained in sympathetic but firm tones that only one of us would be able to stay. For a second, I was scared that Steve was going to insist on staying but he nodded at me and the dread I felt at being away from my child was replaced by grateful relief.

"Right, mate," Steve leaned over and gave George a gentle kiss. "I have to go but I'll be back in the morning."

George nodded. "Bring my phone please, Dad."

Steve and I exchanged smiles at this.

"Have you got your phone?" Steve asked me.

I looked at my empty hands in surprise. "No, I didn't bring anything."

"Take mine." He handed me his phone. "My PIN is 011102. What's yours?"

I already knew it was Esther's date of birth, but I keyed it in anyway and gave him my own code. Steve went to leave but paused at the door.

"I'll just see if there are any vending machines," He said, reaching into his pocket for his wallet. "I'll get you a drink."

He darted off before I could protest and came back a few minutes later with two bottles of water. George was dropping off to sleep and Steve smiled affectionately at the sight of him. He pulled me to his chest and I rested my head against his heart, feeling exhausted now the worst seemed to be over. Steve gently pressed his lips against my forehead and I leant into the familiarity of his touch.

"I'll see you in the morning." He said and left.

I sunk into the chair next to George's bed, completely depleted of energy and watched him sleep. I dozed in fits and starts. The beeping of the machines and the regular observations throughout the night stopped me from sinking any deeper into sleep. George slept well; waking up when stirred every other hour much to my relief.

The morning came, and Steve arrived at the same time as the breakfast trolley. I rose from the hard-backed chair stiffly, rubbing my eyes with the back of my hand.

"Hi Dad." George's face lit up and Steve smiled joyfully at his son's reaction. We both laughed in delight when George followed this up with a request for his phone. Steve handed it over.

"Do you want to go and get a coffee?" He asked me.

I realised I was dying for a wee and I nodded gratefully. Steve passed me a £10 note and gave me directions to the coffee shop. By the time I returned brandishing two large coffees, George had demolished his juice, toast and cereal and was sat up playing a game on his phone.

"He looks alright, doesn't he?" I smiled, feeling more positive.

Steve agreed, looking equally happy.

"I didn't ask," I realised suddenly. "Who's got the kids?"

"Jan, next door," Steve replied. "She saw the ambulance and came straight over to offer. She said she'd come back this morning and wouldn't take no for an answer."

"I better go back," I said, glancing at George. "She's done enough for us."

"He looks like he's going to be ok," Steve agreed. "I'll phone you if there's any change."

Steve handed over the car keys, along with comprehensive directions to find the car in the multi-storey. I kissed George tenderly and said my goodbye's. He barely glanced up from his game and the normality of his behaviour made my heart fill with hope.

Chapter 31

The children were being well-behaved for Jan. Steve had assured them that George was going to be ok and the added bonus of a day off school had them all in good spirits. I thanked Jan for her kindness and made a note to arrange to send her flowers before rushing upstairs for a quick shower.

I had barely glanced at my phone but as I dried off, throwing my still damp hair up into a bun, I realised I'd missed Jen's morning call. I reached for the phone I'd tossed onto the bed and realised, with dismay, that I had been too preoccupied with George to swap back with Steve at the hospital this morning.

I tapped in Steve's passcode and, ignoring the temptation to open his notifications, I texted my own phone number.

"Doctors really happy with George :)," Steve replied from my phone. "You had message and missed call from Jen ;)."

I looked at the time and groaned. She'd be in work now. I tracked down the 'family' iPad and logged into my email account, firing off a quick email explaining what had happened and that Steve had my phone and I had his in the confusion. I kept the iPad close to me as I pottered around, hopeful but not expecting a reply as I knew there was little chance of her checking her personal emails during the day, if at all. I hustled the kids into the car, ready for visiting hours, and stopped at the shop to buy George some of his favourite treats. Steve and I then performed a smooth hospital switch, remembering this time to swap back phones. Steve took back charge of the kids and the car, and I settled back into the hard-backed chair to wait out the Doctor's decision.

"Fingers crossed, you'll be home tonight or tomorrow." Steve said as he gave George a hug.

"Will you stay with me for a bit?" George asked. "At our house."

"Yes, of course, mate." Steve ruffled George's hair affectionately.

I bit my lip, knowing I should set them both straight but, seeing George's happy face, I couldn't bear to be the one to shatter their little moment. I would find an appropriate moment to speak to Steve, although, when I thought about it, we should probably take it in turns checking up on George throughout the night for the next few days. I'd read in the pamphlet the Doctor had given us that concussions can last a while.

As it was, George was discharged the next morning. I spent another uncomfortable night in the chair but, despite the nurse insisting that he'd be fine, I couldn't bear the thought of leaving him on his own. Just the thought of him waking up in the night alone in a strange place made my heart hurt. Exhausted but happy, George and I were met by Steve for the short drive home. He'd packed the others off to school and we laughed at his impression of their disgust at having to go back to their usual routine.

I'd not been able to call Jen, on the ward, but I'd text her to check she'd read my email and she sent a lovely message back full of concern for George. I'd assured her that he was looking good and that I'd let her know as soon as we were home. I texted her in the car to say he'd been discharged and she replied immediately with a smiley face emoji. I saw Steve glance over at my phone in my hands and he looked away quickly as I caught his eye. Back at home, I made George up a bed on the sofa and flopped down next to him.

I woke with a start to see it was getting dark and heard Steve's familiar laugh from across the room.

"How long have I been asleep?" I asked, stretching out from the ball I'd been curled up into.

"It's 9 o'clock." Steve answered. "I picked the kids up, made dinner and they're all in bed now. George is sleeping in our bed."

He flushed slightly when he realised what he had said. "Sorry, habit. Your bed."

I tried to laugh but it came out sounding as awkward and unnatural as the situation.

"Thanks," I said quickly, keen to change the subject. "At least I'll be wide awake all night to check up on him."

"Do you want to watch a film?" Steve asked. "I made food for you- it's in the top oven."

"Oh thanks," I was starving. "Are you, uh, sticking around?"

“I hope you don’t mind,” Steve looked uncomfortable. “I kind of told George I would and I don’t want to let him down. But if it’s not ok…”

“No, it’s fine.” I said, although I wanted to object.

I went upstairs, checked on the kids, changed into the most un-sexy pyjamas I owned and went into the kitchen to warm up the lasagne that Steve had made. I ate it standing up in the kitchen as I loaded the dishwasher, but I was amazed to see the school bags had been emptied, the dogs had been fed and there was a wash on.

“Thanks for doing all that.” I said, gesturing to the kitchen as I came back into the living room.

Steve was flicking through the films on the TV and looked up at me.

“That’s ok,” He said. “Sorry I didn’t do more when we were together.”

I sat down on the opposite sofa, not knowing how to reply to that.

He selected a romantic comedy and I looked up in surprise.

“You don’t like these films!” I exclaimed, forgetting the awkwardness temporarily.

Steve grinned sheepishly. “I know, but you love them.”

“We can watch something else.” I protested. “Honestly, I

don't mind."

"No, it's fine," Steve turned the volume up a few notches and then set the remote controls down decisively. "I'm all for expanding my tastes."

We sat back in silence and I surreptitiously watched the clock on my phone, wondering how I could excuse myself to make my nightly call to Jen. I excused myself, just before 11pm, and headed upstairs. George was fast asleep, and I went into my en-suite to make the call, shutting the door firmly behind me.

Jen's face filled my screen and we both grinned at each other like idiots.

"Oh, Lucy!" She exclaimed. "How is he? How are you?"

"He's ok." I smiled gratefully at her. "And I'm fine. So sorry I've not been in touch."

"Don't be silly!" Jen shook her head. "He's your priority. I'm so glad he's home and he's ok. That must have been so scary."

"It was," I admitted. "I'm glad Steve was there as he knew what to do and I don't know what I would have done with the other kids otherwise."

"Where's George now?" Jen asked.

"He's sleeping in my bed." I told her.

"Oh," She looked relieved. "I did wonder why you were

calling me from the bathroom."

I laughed but then realised I would have to tell her. "It's a bit awkward, but George made Steve promise he would stay."

I watched Jen's expression carefully, but she kept her face neutral. "Oh, right. Will be good to have a hand with the school run and all while George is recovering."

"Yes," I nodded grateful that she was trying to be understanding even though I could tell that this was hard for her to hear. "It'll most likely only be tonight as I'm sure he'll be in a rush to get back to Charlotte."

Jen nodded and didn't say anything.

"Work ok?" I asked, trying to fill the silence and I watched as the light came back on in Jen's eyes.

"Oh God, yes!" She exclaimed. "Remember that London meeting?"

I nodded, remembering her saying something about a big meeting.

"So, they're restructuring back home, as always, and the Global Trades are looking to expand here which means I'll be getting some of the London team over too." She beamed, and I could tell that this was a big deal. "It's going to be so much work but I'm so excited about it."

"Wow." Her excitement was infectious and, despite the fact that I didn't really get what she was talking about, I was genuinely delighted for her. "Well done, Jen."

"The only crap bit," She gave me an apologetic look. "Is I might not be able to take the full 10 days off over Christmas."

"Aw, that's crap," I felt disappointed. "But you'll still get some time off to come home?"

"Oh yes." She nodded. "Even if it's only for a few days."

"Good," I smiled at her. "I miss you so much. I can't wait to have you with me."

"Me too," Jen sighed. "I am so horny too."

I laughed at her lack of self-consciousness. "I might die of frustration if you don't come back wearing those sexy pyjamas."

"Are you going to meet me at Arrivals wearing a matching set?" Jen teased.

I groaned. Oh, I really was dying for her. "Yes, we won't make it home. I'll be tearing them off in the short stay."

"I'll hold you to this." She laughed at this. "Unfortunately, my working day isn't over just yet. Phone me tomorrow."

"Will do," I said, wishing she could talk longer. "I love you."

"I love you." She ended the call and I headed back downstairs.

Steve was sat in silence flicking through his phone and I

realised he'd paused the film to wait for me.

"Oh, sorry," I apologised. "I didn't realise you were waiting for me."

"That's ok," He smiled up at me. "Were you phoning Jen?"

I nodded and sat back down waiting for him to un-pause the film. He didn't though. He put his own phone down and regarded me thoughtfully.

"So, the whole Luke thing?" He asked. "Was that just a rebound?"

Why was he asking about Luke? I wondered. Why didn't he feel as awkward as me having this conversation?

I shrugged. "He was more a mate than anything, I guess."

"He texted you when I had your phone." Steve said.

"Did he?" I asked surprised. "I didn't see any messages."

"I'm really sorry," Steve looked embarrassed. "I read it, so the notification would have cleared."

I picked up my phone and scrolled down until I found it. My eyes skimmed over it quickly. He was just asking about whether I'd found a job and if my friend in New York still worked for the same company. I flicked through the previous thread of messages that ranged from flirtatious to indecent and tried not to show my annoyance at Steve's invasion of my privacy.

"I didn't read any of yours." I gave him a pointed, and very judgemental, look.

"Really?" He looked surprised. "Sorry, I shouldn't have."

"No," I agreed. "Thanks for being honest though. I think I'm going to go up to bed."

Steve looked crestfallen, but he nodded.

I replied to Luke, when I was in bed, glad that he was reaching out and happy to hear from him after all this time. He replied briefly saying that he had an interview for the company and wished me luck with my own job search. I was wide awake now and decided to spend the time productively, throwing out a wider job search and completing more applications. I'd had more rejections by email and I was very conscious that Jen's career was going from strength to strength. If I didn't find something soon, the only thing I'd have to talk to Jen about would be the school run and the latest reality TV programme.

Chapter 32

Steve went back to work the next day and I was hoping this would mean we would be back to normality. He appeared at the door at 6pm and the children actually cheered to see him. He was carrying a heavy gym bag, a hold all and a suit bag. I frowned at his luggage.

"Did you carry that all on the tube?" I asked, hoping he would interpret this for what I was really trying to say which was 'what the fuck are you bringing that here for?'.

"Greg dropped me off," Steve said, not meeting my eyes. "Can I just hang it upstairs out of the way?"

I wanted to ask him how long he was planning on staying as he hadn't said anything other than our brief conversation and his promise to George to stay a 'few' days. I didn't feel like I could say anything in front of the kids and instead I busied myself, letting Steve put the kids to bed and excusing myself for an early night.

I threw myself into job hunting over the next few days, spurred on by Jen's success and the news of Luke landing himself a new job. I went into town and signed up with all the agencies. I calculated that I must have applied for about fifty jobs by now and I'd not even had an interview. Even the most positive person would be feeling a little disheartened now, surely. The man at the agency empathised with my plight, agreeing that it was a hard market out there and assuring me he'd be in touch.

I had had to mention Steve's extended stay to Jen and it went down slightly better than I thought as she had the generosity to fake empathy despite how uncomfortable anyone would feel in these circumstances. The weekend came though, and Steve was still sleeping on my sofa. I was now taking all my calls to Jen locked in my bedroom or bathroom. I could sense she was growing anxious about my ex being cosily ensconced back in the marital home and I realised that I needed to have this conversation with him. I waited until the children had gone to bed, Sunday evening, and wandered into the kitchen where he was stacking the dishwasher after clearing up the Sunday roast he'd whipped up. I poured myself a large glass of wine for courage and cleared my throat.

"It's been lovely," Steve started speaking before I could start. "Being back home."

"When are you going home?" I asked, just diving in before the bravery deserted me.

"Home?" Steve looked up at me surprised. "You mean Greg's sofa?"

"Uh, yeah," I nodded. "Or Charlotte's."

He shook his head. "We're kind of taking a break at the moment. She really struggled with me being around here when George was in hospital and, to be honest, I need to start prioritising my kids for once."

I eyed him suspiciously wondering whether this was a trick.

It didn't even sound like something Steve would say. He crossed the short distance across the kitchen to me and put his arms around me. I tensed up in horror.

"I'm so proud of you," He said, oblivious to my discomfort. "I know I've been selfish and I know you've done pretty much everything for these kids. I'm really going to try to be around more."

"Right." I tried to slide out from his embrace without looking rude. All I had wanted for years was for Steve to take a share in the mental and physical workload of raising the children. It was typical of my damned life that my wishes were being fulfilled at the detriment to my new relationship. I reached for my glass and took a large gulp of wine.

"I'm going to condense my hours in work," He said proudly. "I was chatting to one of my colleagues and agile working is massive right now. I'll be able to do a few school runs and everything."

"The kids will love that." I replied. "So, about you going back to Greg's..."

"I was hoping," Steve stepped back and took the wine bottle, pouring himself a glass. "That I could stay here for a few weeks. Greg and Alicia have been having some, uh, problems of their own so it's a bit awkward me being there and it seems silly to shell out money for a hotel."

I shook my head. "You can't just stay on a sofa. It's not

practical."

"Just for a few weeks," Steve almost pleaded, his tone changing. "Unless you can take the bills immediately? I need to rustle up a deposit and the first month's rent. The account is so far in the overdraft and if I max the credit card out God knows how we'll afford Christmas without you wiping out your redundancy or selling a kidney."

My redundancy was almost wiped out as it was. I'd started Christmas shopping in optimism that I'd have a job soon and wouldn't get the chance again to spend all day browsing for online deals. There were Apple products on everyone's Christmas wish list as well as Games consoles and designer clothes. Just under a quarter of that nest egg was now in plastic bags hidden in my attic. Another quarter had been frittered away and the way my job hunting was going, I was too scared to spend any more.

"I could maybe lend you the deposit from my redundancy?" I offered, knowing that this would put me in a risky position if I did.

Steve shook his head slowly. "Seems silly, doesn't it? Wasting that money when I can just stay here for a few weeks and get myself in a position where I can get a place that the kids can stay."

I pursed my lips together. If I had got a bloody job, I wouldn't be in this situation. I cursed myself for being so slow getting my arse into gear job-hunting.

"Lucy," Steve took my hands in his, in another unwelcome show of affection. "I haven't asked you for anything and I've carried on paying the bills despite living out of a bag for the past few months. Can you please just be reasonable?"

I was spineless under pressure. "Just a few weeks?"

He nodded, and I turned my back to him to pour another wine. It would go quickly, I told myself, and Jen would understand.

It wasn't a few weeks though. Steve was still there at the beginning of December. Esther had given up her bedroom for him; suddenly her father's biggest advocate now he had denounced Charlotte and chosen his children over the 'cow'. Esther had moved some of her things into Matilda's room and Matilda was now a permanent fixture in my bed. After years of Steve rolling home after work anytime between 8 and 10pm most nights, he was home by 6pm nearly every day. I utilised my new on-tap childcare by frequent visits to Andy and John's, signing up to some evening classes at the gym and forging a new-found social life with the school mums that I'd avoided for years. Basically, anything that kept me out of the house and away from Steve's subtle flirtation.

I'd had a few job interviews, which was definite progress, thanks to the nice man at the agency. Nothing had come of them though and I was beginning to think I would never find anything. I voiced these concerns to Andy, one evening in early December, as I sat on his sofa demolishing a pizza.

John was away for a few nights filming on location and we were enjoying a cosy night of trash TV and takeaway.

"Something will come up," Andy assured me. "The right job is out there, and the universe is stopping you from making a bad decision."

I smiled at his attempt to placate me. "I hope so. I feel like such a bloody failure. You guys are all so successful and I can't even score an entry level analyst role anymore."

Andy's promise to me came true but the bit about the 'right job' was subject to opinion. Under pressure from the agency, I'd applied for a supervisory job at a High Street Bank. I'd had the interview and the day after my conversation with Andy, I had a phone call from the manager offering me the job. As grateful as I was that someone actually wanted me, my heart sank at the thought of going back to what was basically one step down from my last role. I was sat in my kitchen as I took the call and I eyed Steve's 'Dad' mug on the kitchen counter and knew I would have to take it. I was due to start at the beginning of January, and I calculated that if I budgeted to the very penny, I could afford to take enough bills from Steve to leave him enough to cover a small one-bedroomed place in a slightly less desirable area. I could gift him half my remaining money and keep the other bit back for emergencies. I stared at the largest figure, the mortgage, scribbled on my workings out; at some point it was inevitable that we would have to consider moving areas or down-sizing.

Steve came home that evening in a jovial mood.

"You're happy." I commented, as I set out plates as he stir-fried our dinner.

"Work is going great," He smiled. "There's a potential promotion coming up and I had a good meeting with my boss earlier, who thinks I should go for it."

I offered up a silent prayer of thanks for this second potential financial windfall.

"That's great." I replied before telling him about my new job and my budgeting proposal.

I was expecting Steve to look pleased at this, but he frowned instead. He doled out the stir fry and carried the plates through to the children at the dinner table.

"You don't seem excited." I remarked, trying to keep my voice casual.

"We'll talk about it later," He said, gesturing at the children. "Let's have our dinner and then I'm taking George to football training. We'll sit down and work things out this evening."

I felt the familiar rush of anxiety that I'd lived with daily during my relationship with Steve. I was struck by the memory of how he always twisted everything to get his own way; whether that was keeping his social life when I'd all but abandoned my own for nappies and night feeds or buying a flash apartment when we could barely afford our own monthly outgoings. I felt a surge of anger and I welcomed it, allowing it to override my tightening chest and jittery nerves.

"Fine." I snatched up my plate and took a seat as far away from him as I could. I needed to speak to Jen and tell her all about this, but she wouldn't be home for a few more hours. I finished my dinner, ungratefully wasting the majority of it as Steve's attitude had suddenly left a bad taste in my mouth, and locked myself in the bathroom, lounging for well over an hour in the bath. When I came out, Steve had cleared up and taken George to football. I spent a bit of time doing homework with the children before getting them ready for bed. I felt exhausted by the time Steve and George came home and George was soaking wet from training outside, so I ran him a bath. By the time George had gone to bed, I was too emotionally drained to face having a challenging conversation with Steve and I felt like I needed Jen's help to plan for what would no doubt be a difficult discussion. I cried off and went up to bed wiling away the hour until it was time to take my usual spot in the en-suite to Facetime Jen.

"Hey." Her smiling face made my heart flutter a little despite my day.

"Hey," I smiled back. "Have you had a good day?"

"Yes, thank you." She said but she looked a little distracted.

"Everything ok?" I asked. She had seemed a little distracted when she called yesterday, but I'd been zipping Esther to an orthodontic appointment and we hadn't had chance to talk properly. I hadn't texted her about my job offer, wanting to explain face-to-face so she didn't think I was selling out.

"Kind of," She admitted looking conflicted. "There's been a bit of a change with dates in work and I don't think I'm going to make it home for Christmas."

My heart dropped, and I felt devastated. "Not at all?"

"I'm so sorry." She looked genuinely unhappy. "I've got meetings that I need to be at up until 23rd and I need to be back for 27th. The flights I can find aren't great, and I'd be in town for less than forty-eight hours."

I blinked back tears of disappointment. "I was so looking forward to seeing you."

Jen's big brown eyes filled up with tears. "I know, me too. I'm so sorry."

"It can't be helped," I said, trying to be mature and not burst into self-pitying tears. "I'm glad work is going well for you though."

"Thank you." She smiled gratefully. "I know it's hard being apart."

"It is." I nodded. "Guess what, though? I got a job!"

Jen's face lit up and she clapped her hands together. "Well done! I'm so proud of you. Tell me everything."

I filled her in on my job, trying to sound more enthusiastic than I felt.

"Are you sure you want to take it?" She asked hesitantly. "It sounds like it's going to be like your old job."

"It wouldn't be my first choice," I admitted. "But I just want to be able to pay my bills and for Steve to get his own place."

Jen pursed her lips at the mention of Steve's name but said nothing.

"I know it must be hard for you," I continued. "Steve being here. I just want him gone."

"Has he tried it on?" Jen asked, and I could tell she was holding back anger at the thought.

"No!" I exclaimed. "And you know I wouldn't."

Jen nodded doubtfully. "Don't tell him I'm not coming now. That'll be a good excuse for him to leave. If he knows I'm not coming, he'll string it out to the New Year."

"Good idea," I nodded. "I'll say you're coming back early and then just make an excuse at the last minute when he's already gone."

Jen looked marginally reassured. "I need to get on now. I am so sorry though that I won't be able to see you as soon as we'd hoped."

“Me too.” I sighed. “I’ll let you know how I get on. I love you.”

I had a little cry before I could get off to sleep; mainly over the upset of Jen not being back for Christmas but a little bit over my frustration at having to take the bank job. I tried to focus on the positive though. I had a job and Steve would be gone soon. I just needed to stick to my guns tomorrow and not back down.

I spent all day practising my best counter arguments to anything I pre-empted that Steve would throw my way. I felt hyped up and ready for this conversation, and I waited until the children had gone up to bed before I invited Steve to take a seat at the kitchen table with me.

I raised my request with a serene confidence, gushing over the positives; the children had loved having him so involved in their lives and how grateful I’d been for his support but thankfully I could now take on more financial responsibility allowing him to find a more permanent home. Before he could interject, I explained that my girlfriend was coming home earlier than planned and I needed him to leave before this.

I watched as the easy-going, family-focussed façade disappeared a little more with every argument I was able to counter; leaving behind the bad tempered, irrational person I’d been married to.

“I can’t believe this.” His nostrils flared with temper. “I’m being kicked out of my own home, so your rebound can play happy families."

"She's not my rebound," I said, struggling to keep my cool as the frustration of the last few days bubbled under the surface. "And we're not playing happy families. This is my life."

"You really think Jen is going to want to stay here in this mad house?" He snapped.

"What's that supposed to mean?" I took a deep breath and faced him square on.

"She doesn't want kids. She'll be here five minutes and realise that you're just a fling." He gave a snort of bitter laughter at me and I felt my blood start to boil.

"Don't judge her on your experience with Charlotte," I spat out. "Jen is used to being around my kids and she loves them."

At the mention of Charlotte, I could see him ready to explode.

"We'll soon see when she's around them twenty-four hours a day," He fired back. "She's hardly going to happily play Step-Mummy when she didn't even want her own pregnancy."

I took a step back stunned. I'd been friends with Jen for years before she'd told me about the abortion. "How do you know about that?"

My mind raced back to what Jen had told me and that night we'd first met. I pictured her holding my hair back as I vomited on that terrace. Jen, beautiful, sophisticated and sympathetic to this sweaty pregnant mess whose husband was nowhere to be seen since he'd disappeared at the bar. I felt the blood drain from me as I watched, coiled and waiting for Steve's response.

His face twisted into a smug smile and he finally answered me in a tone as cold as ice, enunciating every word. "How the fuck do you think?"

Chapter 33

I could barely remember the aftermath of Steve's bombshell or possibly, I didn't want to remember. Steve disappeared of his own accord, realising that he had pushed me too far this time. I didn't ask where he went, I didn't care. I never wanted to see him again.

I didn't want to speak to Jen. I had nothing to say. I didn't want to hear her side of the story. Recalling Steve's words were enough to send me racing to the bathroom, retching violently until my stomach muscles felt as raw and painful as my heart. I cried until there were no tears left in my body, until my head ached, and my body felt empty and numb.

I blocked Jen on my iPhone and on all my social media. I asked Andy to pass on the message that I was aware of everything and to make it clear that I didn't want to speak to her.

"Don't get drawn into a conversation with her," I told him coldly. "I'm not interested in excuses."

I saw the surprise on Andy's face at my hard resolve. I had been manipulated too many times into taking both Steve and Luke back. I was done being the forgiving doormat. It hurt too much.

"I mean it," I fixed Andy with a frosty stare. "Just tell her I don't want to be with her anymore."

I felt doubly crushed by the deception. All I had ever wanted was to be happy. I had finally worked up the courage to cut out the two things I thought were weighing me down; my marriage and my job. But lo and behold, the happiest relationship I'd ever known was based on a web of lies and I was back to square one career-wise with nothing more to look forward to than a different colour polyester uniform and a salary that was less than my friends' annual tax deductions. I was done with trying anymore. I spent the next few weeks going through the motions for the children's benefit; going to bed early every night pleading exhaustion and then lying awake all night alternating between overwhelming sadness and furious rage.

At the end of the school term, I packed the children and the dogs into the car and headed to my sister's home to spend Christmas. For once, I was putting myself first. I didn't care if Steve was spending Christmas alone. He had ceased to be of any concern to me when he had shattered my happiness.

Even in the pit of my own despair, I couldn't help but notice that my lovely, hard-working sister wasn't herself. She'd accepted the children and I into her home with open arms when I'd called her in floods of tears, and I had been too consumed with my own heartache to even consider whether I was putting her out.

Emily had been busy in the run-up to Christmas with a spate of festive weddings and, at first, I assumed that it was just the hectic hours of running her own business and being a mother that had her falling asleep on the sofa every evening. As I emerged from my self-absorbed bubble of misery, I started to notice how Shaun refused to let Emily do even the slightest bit of housework. Not in a controlling, or even a best-husband-award, kind of way, but as if he was concerned about her. He tried to hide it from her; rushing to put a wash on, empty the dishwasher or make dinner before she did. The day after Boxing Day, when I should have been thinking about packing up and heading back to London, I walked in on them talking in hushed whispers in the kitchen.

"I can do it!" Emily reached past him to take the washing basket, but Shaun was holding it stubbornly to his chest.

"I know you can." He insisted. "But you need to rest!"

"I am resting." Emily said. "You're worrying about nothing."

"It's not nothing." Shaun replied, wrapping his arms around my little sister.

She rested her head against his chest and said nothing.

I meant to walk away, feeling I was intruding on a private conversation, but I froze in the doorway; the seriousness of Shaun's tone echoing in my head.

"Lucy!" Emily had broken away from Shaun's embrace and caught sight of me before I could react.

"Emily," I stepped forward, suddenly seeing how pale and thin she looked. "Are you ok?"

I waited for Emily to laugh and insist that Shaun was just being over-protective, but I saw the look they exchanged, and my heart sank, fearing the IVF hadn't worked.

Emily reached for my hands, taking them between hers.

"I was going to tell you." She said quietly.

"What's the matter?" I asked, already praying it wasn't anything serious.

Emily looked back at Shaun and I watched as they communicated without the need for words, such was the strength and depth of their relationship. Shaun was at Emily's side in an instant, and they faced me together as she told me.

"Lucy, I'm pregnant."

"Oh! Wow!" I reached out to hug her. "Congratulations!"

She felt tense in my arms, and I pulled back to look at her, feeling my concern return. This was everything that Emily wanted. Why wasn't she happy?

"It's very early days." Emily warned me.

I could tell there was more, and I looked between her and Shaun questioningly.

"I've had a little bit of bleeding," She said finally, breaking the silence. "I feel ok though."

Shaun looked like he wanted to add something but

remained quiet.

"You should have said!" I gave Emily my sternest look, feeling awful that I'd put all this added stress on her. "I would have stayed home! You need to rest!"

"I wanted to see you." Emily insisted. "I'll be fine."

A little later, I assembled the kids and the dogs, and we headed out to the woods behind Emily and Shaun's cottage. Emily had given in to Shaun's nagging and was having a lie down. I heard a voice calling out to me and turned to see Shaun jogging down the field to catch us up.

"Everything ok?" I asked, surprised to see him.

Shaun nodded, but I could see the worry behind his eyes. I knew how much they wanted another baby.

"If this..." He broke off, not wanting to voice his fears aloud. "I don't know if she'll be ok if anything happens."

My eyes prickled with tears of empathy at the desperation in his voice and I slipped my arm through his.

"What has the Doctor said?" I asked.

"Not much," Shaun shrugged. "Just to take it easy."

We fell into silence as we watched the kids and the dogs run ahead of us.

"I want her to stop working," Shaun admitted. "Just until she's feeling better."

"What does she think?" I asked diplomatically.

"She wants to," He replied. "But she's committed to so much work. Joanna's let her down and she can't afford to take someone else on."

I thought about this for a while and turned to Shaun, suddenly feeling a little reckless.

"I'll do it."

"What?" He stopped walking and stared at me.

"I can do it." I repeated. "Just until she's back on her feet."

Even as I said it, the logistics were racing around my mind. I didn't want the job I'd taken. I'd only taken it because I'd felt guilty about Steve sofa-surfing. It was inevitable that we'd have to sell our house and downsize. I had no reason to be in London, apart from the kids, of course. The majority of the work Emily did could be done remotely, and Steve would just have to suck it up and have the kids on the weekends I needed to be in Wales.

"We can't pay you much." Shaun shook his head apologetically. "Joanna was only doing a few hours."

"It's fine." I insisted. "I want to do this."

Shaun looked doubtful, but I could already see a glimmer of hope in his eyes. "I didn't mean to put this on you. It's just, you know what Emily is like. She doesn't want to let any of her clients down."

"I one-hundred-percent want to do this." I promised my brother-in-law. "We just need to figure out how we're going to sell this to Emily."

I took the children back to London the next day. Steve hadn't kicked off about me taking them away for Christmas, and I told him curtly that he could have them until New Year.

"I don't have anywhere to have them." He replied, via message, the only medium I could bear to speak to him on.

I still felt uncontrollable anger towards him, for shattering what I had believed was my happy-ever-after, and he was more than aware of how I was feeling. Not a day went by when I didn't wake up feeling sick to the stomach at the betrayal and the loss, but I had to accept the fact that he was a permanent fixture in my life.

"Stay here with them," I replied. "I'm going to my sister's. The kids can't come. Will be back on 1st."

I waited for his excuses. There was no way he would give up New Year's Eve to look after his own kids, but his guilt was obviously a heavy burden and he agreed.

I went back to Wales to finalise the details, sitting on the end of Emily's bed as we chatted animatedly, and I realised that I was actually looking forward to this. I reassured Emily that money wasn't an issue. It was only an issue for Steve, but I didn't say that to her.

“It’s so nice to spend time with you,” Emily said, as we sat up chatting into the New Year like we had as little girls. “You know you can talk to me about Jen, don’t you?”

“I don’t have anything to say.” I said, meaning it, but my voice wobbled, and I turned away, blinking back tears and trying to regain control. A lone tear escaped and cascaded down my cheek. I wiped it away, and I could see Emily wanted to say something.

“Do you think?” She started tentatively. “That maybe you should talk to her about it?”

I shook my head. “I don’t want to. Sorry, Em, I think I’m going to go to bed.”

I felt awful leaving Emily, but Jen was constantly on my mind and the pain was still fresh and raw. I spent the night, crying as pitifully quietly as I could, unable to sleep as if just hearing her name had broken my heart all over again. I watched despondently as the clock ticked away the first few hours of another new year, wishing I could summon up the optimism of the past few months but unable to feel anything more than aching sadness, when I realised it was exactly midnight in New York. As much as I tried, I had Jen’s local time embedded in my brain and couldn’t stop myself thinking like this. I wondered what she was doing right now and feeling the pain in my chest, chastised myself for even venturing into this territory.

I reflected on the difference a year had made; I’d shed my job and my marriage. I had been deliriously happy and then it had all fallen apart. I tried to focus on the positives; I was going into a new year with (mostly) psychologically-undamaged, healthy, happy children, I was in a position where I could help my little sister and I wasn't being lied to by my significant other. I smiled wryly at the last point. It seemed like the only way I could guarantee that that continued was to stay single for the rest of my life.

Chapter 34

My phone rang, and I balanced the clipboard, handmade mood-board and take-away coffee cup on top precariously, rooting around in my handbag to answer it. I saw Andy's name flashing up on the screen and I dropped the phone back into the depths of my bag.

"Do you need to take that?" Nicole, my client, asked politely.

I shook my head. "No, it's fine. Now, where were we?"

Nicole's wedding was one of the last on Emily's books and was still a full four months away. Emily had warned me that she was a particularly stressed bridezilla, which was why I was wandering around the grounds of her venue early on a Saturday morning in April, trying to reassure her that Willow Gardens was still the perfect destination for her wedding.

"I just..." Nicole chewed on her cosmetically-enhanced lower lip nervously. "I can't see myself getting married here."

She held out her hands, gesturing at the rolling acres of greenery as if to solidify her point.

I bit back the urge to respond that she was right, and it was a hideous dump, feeling the sarcasm would be lost on her. The venue was absolutely stunning, the grounds were impeccable, the hotel was exquisite, and the hefty deposit was one-hundred-percent non-refundable.

If her own eyes, and the shining write-ups in Bridal Magazine, couldn't convince her, I wondered what I could do to change her mind. I regarded the attractive young woman for a moment, trying to remain objective and see beyond the inflated lips and the synthetic hair. Her nerves were genuine. I could tell by the way her feet were moving ever-so-slightly even when we were stood still, and she was unconsciously fidgeting with the strap on her bag, the arm of her oversized sunglasses or pushing the sleeves of her hoodie up and then down. The anxious energy reminded me of myself.

I had an engagement party later that day which I should have been running last-minute checks for, and I had only intended to meet up with Nicole to show willing, but her vulnerability made my heart swell with empathy for her. In that moment, I knew that this wasn't about the venue at all.

"Nicole," I said softly, taking her gently by the arm and leading her over to a bench that looked out at the beautiful landscape. "Tell me about your dream wedding."

"My dream wedding?" Nicole would have frowned if the Botox would have allowed her to.

I nodded. "The one in your head. What does it look like?"

"I don't know," She seemed confused by my question. "Just a really nice wedding. Loads of flowers and candles, a kind-of rustic vibe, dancing under the stars."

Nicole was probably as detached from rustic and outdoorsy as a person could get. This was a far cry from the glamourous, shiny, jewelled wedding she had described to Emily when they had first met almost eighteen months ago.

"Show me your dress." I ordered.

She opened up the gallery on her phone and held out the image for me to see.

"Wow!" I said emphatically, sounding out the word so she could tell that I meant it. "You will look so beautiful in that dress. It wouldn't go with wellies though."

Nicole smiled. "Probably not."

"I know what you mean about the whole rural vibe," I said quietly. "There was a gorgeous photoshoot..."

"In Bridal magazine." Nicole agreed excitedly. "It looked amazing. That's what I want."

I knew then that my instincts had been right. Nicole, despite her perfect exterior, or even because of her perfect exterior, felt an overwhelming pressure to have the perfect day. She was so image-conscious and sensitive to the perceptions of others. If Bridal Magazine thought that dancing under the stars to a live band, while your guests sip gin from mason jars was where it was at then Nicole's fairy-tale white dancefloor, Ibiza-worthy DJ and sophisticated cocktails wouldn't cut it anymore.

I chose my word carefully. "I thought the wedding you've

got planned really suited you and Adam."

"Did you?" She lowered her designer sunglasses slightly to regard me suspiciously over the lenses.

"Sophisticated, chic, classic," I nodded. "I mean, it's so you."

"Do you think it's a bit much though?" She asked, back to fidgeting.

"Not at all," I continued confidently. "A hay bale looks nice- have you ever sat on one?"

"Well, of course." Nicole answered.

"And a band is nice, but have you ever paid 100 euros to get into a little pub on a Friday night?" I said, waiting for the doubt that I knew would come creeping in at any moment. "You've got a DJ that played Ibiza!"

"She's not like a big name or anything though." Nicole said disdainfully.

"She played bars in Ibiza," I shrugged. "That's amazing. And dancing under the stars is nice, but has it ever rained in August in Britain?"

"Well, there is that." Nicole agreed doubtfully. "We could have a marquee. Faith said that..."

"What matters more than what people think?" I hit her with my piece-de-resistance. "You and Adam's day. Nicole, you need to be comfortable at your own wedding day. Not cold or wet, or walking through mud to queue for the Portaloo behind Adam's Nan. If I thought an outdoor wedding would make you happy, I promise I'd do everything to turn that dream into a reality. But I don't think it's your dream, is it?"

I was taking a risk now. Emily was from the school of the-customer-is-always-right. I couldn't help myself though. I genuinely believed that Nicole had worked herself up into such a knot of anxiety that she was doubting her own decisions.

"You think my wedding is classic?" She asked hesitantly as she processed my words.

"It will be beautiful." I told her.

"I don't know what I was thinking," She got to her feet, the glasses firmly back in place and a hand defensively on her hip. "I don't want to change a thing. I'm just a bag of nerves about this day. I didn't realise how much pressure it would be."

I smiled sympathetically, and we completed another lap of the venue. This time, Nicole waxed lyrically about every room, detail and view, and I breathed a sigh of relief as I walked her back to her car.

God, I knew what that pressure felt like. I had strived for a perfect house, to be a perfect mother to perfect kids and regularly berated myself that I'd quit the perfect career-path because I couldn't juggle it all. I'd stayed married to a perfect-arsehole because I'd been too caught up in perception, feeling like the expectations, and the subsequent failures, were all on me. I'd been a bag of nerves, the slightest change to my routine sending my house-of-cards tumbling down. I'd compared myself to the successful people around me; Andy, Jen, Steve, and felt crap my annual income didn't match up. I'd compared my parenting skills to the organic-homemade-cooking, multi-language-speaking families at the school. I'd compared my own physical appearance to the gym-bunnies who had countless hours to work on their physiques. It had made me miserable and stressed-out.

It had taken a cheating husband, a horrible boss and a selfish bit-on-the-side to make me realise that I didn't need a big house, the prestige of a career or the validation of a hottie thinking I was attractive enough to text back. Everything had seemed to happen for a reason; Roger's bullying ways had pushed me from a job I had only taken because Steve had encouraged me to, and Luke had temporarily boosted my confidence to finally kick Steve's cheating ass out of my house. I just needed to work out what the purpose of Jen had been, I thought as I climbed into my own car and headed back to Emily's.

I called Andy back in the car.

"Are you in Wales?" He wailed when he answered. "John's away. I'm bored."

"I'm in Bristol," I replied. "But I'm on my way to Wales now. I'll be back tomorrow. Come over."

"I wanted to go out." He sulked. "I went out for a few last night. I've got a taste for a night out now."

"Sorry." I said, not meaning it. "Who'd you go out with?"

"James."

I felt myself tense up. I knew, from putting various cues and clues together, that James had been out in New York since the start of the year. I had more than a sneaking suspicion that he and Jen had reignited their previous acquaintance. Any mention of James came with a prickle of jealousy and the anxious wait for Andy to tell me that they were back together.

"Guess who else I saw?" Andy continued, and I felt my heart freeze with trepidation.

"Lois." He said when I didn't reply. "Your friend from the bank."

"Oh." I said, relieved. "I was meant to meet up with her last week but didn't get around to it."

"She said," Andy told me. "She's desperate to see you. She was all stressed out because she thinks Steve is going out with one of the girls you used to work with. She didn't know how to bring it up."

"As if I'd care." I replied honestly. My heart was still thumping with relief that he hadn't brought up Jen. Poor Lois though. She was such a sweetheart.

"Don't you want to know who?" Andy asked, sounding disappointed.

"I couldn't give a shit." I responded, meaning it.

"Someone called Leanne." Andy said, sounding hopeful for a reaction.

I laughed at this. "Good luck to them both."

"So, what's that?" Andy baited me. "His third girlfriend since you've been broken up?"

"Something like that," I said, refusing to be drawn in. "I'm not counting."

"Don't you think it's time you met someone?" He said.

"I'm too busy." I said calmly. "Work has been hectic."

"As long as you're not sitting around waiting to hear from..."

I cut him off before he could finish. "I've got to go. I'll phone you later."

I hung up the call and was immediately transported back to my default melancholy state. I was surprised that she hadn't reached out and had accepted Andy's message so easily. Once the initial shock had died down, I'd tried to process how she could have been so deceptive striking up a friendship with me so soon after jumping out of an affair with Steve. The image that I'd had of her just didn't calibrate with the person who had deceived me. Nothing surprised me about Steve, and none of his affairs or new relationships made me feel anything. It was only the thought of him and Jen together that made me feel physically sick.

I couldn't help but feel proud of how well I'd coped after my world had fallen apart. Just a year ago, I'd been living on the constant brink of tears. I was stressed at work, stressed at home and masking my anxiety with a bottle of wine every night to help me sleep. I had lapped up Luke's bullshit; hungry for any affection and any distraction from my unhappy existence. My relationship with Steve had sapped away all my confidence and all the enjoyment I should have felt raising my family. I'd thrown myself into my new job; deriving pride and satisfaction in keeping Emily's reputation for amazing events until she was ready to take back the helm.

And yet I still couldn't bear to hear her name. Four months had passed and, while I had progressed from lying awake crying all night, just the mention of her by Andy had left me feeling bruised and sore. It had been two months before I was able to go even a couple of hours without thinking about her. I would start to smile anytime I saw or heard something that invoked a memory that Jen and I had shared, like a certain song, a little dog at the park or a specific cocktail and then, as if my heart had its own memory, I'd feel the physical ache and sadness. I'd thrown myself into my new job and I loved it. I would never have thought that planning and organisation would be my forte, but even that stung when I realised that the person I most wanted to share my news with was gone. I'd felt a fresh wave of loss again when her return date came and went. Even though I'd been adamant that I didn't want anything more to do with her, I had expected her to at least reach out when she was back in the country. Even if our relationship had been new, our friendship had been built up over eleven years. I might have blocked her number and her profiles on all my apps, but she knew where I lived. After a month of relapsing, secretly expecting a letter or a knock on the door, I had to face up to the reality that she didn't care enough to want to try to explain or to apologise. Andy was right; I needed to move on.

Chapter 35

I was still a little rattled when I finally made it to Emily's but seeing her sat on the sofa, using her growing bump to rest her laptop, soothed the ache in my heart.

"You reassured Nicole." It was a statement, not a question, and Emily's bright smile was infectious.

I nodded, before sinking down next to my sister. "She was just doubting herself. Feeling the pressure of 'perfect'."

"I feel her pain." Emily agreed. "Well done, Lucy. I know Nicole can be a little highly-strung. I half-expected her to change her mind about everything a hundred times before her big day. You've been amazing."

I had taken over the physical side of the business for Emily. The venue visits, the running-around and the hundreds of little jobs that required manual labour. Emily was still firmly at the helm but had happily taken a step back to ensure she was prioritising her health and the baby boy she was growing. Emily insisted that I was paid for the hours that I worked and, while the pay wasn't amazing, it was enough to keep me ticking over until Steve and I finalised our divorce.

"I love it." I admitted honestly. "It's been a breath of fresh air, and I'll be gutted to go back to the corporate world."

"Would you consider coming into business with me?" Emily asked suddenly, surprising me.

"I'd love to," I replied, meaning it. "But I need to stay in

London, for the kids, and when the finances are sorted, I'm going to have to get a better paid job just to keep afloat."

Emily put the laptop down and turned to me, her face serious.

"It's such a shame," She said thoughtfully. "You are so good at this. I know I said I'm not taking any more clients on for a while, but we've got an established business, reviews, contacts. There's nothing to stop you doing this in London. You could charge more, and I bet Andy and John could get you some business with their contacts."

I opened my mouth to protest, but then I thought about what she was suggesting. I felt a little tingle of excitement at the thought of being able to keep doing something that I loved. The ingrained pessimist in me threw up a million worries immediately. Could I take a risk? What if it didn't work? Emily was the one who was doing all the hard work down here. I was just schmoozing and messing around with decorations.

"I couldn't, Em," I said finally. "You're the brains behind this. And I can't risk not being able to pay my bills."

"Just try it." Emily urged me, and I turned to her, surprised by the forcefulness of her tone. "Look how happy it makes you. Last year, Lucy, you were stressed and miserable. Like you'd been for bloody years. Steve used your 9-to-5 as an excuse to live like a single man. You never stood up for yourself. You've only stood up to him because it's to help me! If I hadn't needed your help, you'd be rushing back from your office job to pick them up and there's no way in hell Steve would have taken the kids away on his own for Easter."

"He took them last summer!" I protested. "And he did have them sometimes."

Emily rolled her eyes. "Sometimes. Lucy, you can't deny that you working evenings and weekends has made Steve have to step up."

"I'm not denying it," I knew what she was saying was true, but in the back of my mind I was convinced that this was just temporary. Steve was clearly feeling guilty for almost causing me to have a complete breakdown. The guilt would wear off and his next girlfriend would become his priority, and then it'd be back to his old ways of doing what he wanted. I said as much to Emily. "And then I'm stuck letting clients down."

Emily let out an exasperated sigh. "Lucy, you've changed so much. And for the better. I know you don't want to talk about..."

I knew what she was going to say, and I shot her a stern look of warning.

"No." She said emphatically. "I need to say this. Being with Jen changed you. Yeah, what she did was shitty. She should have told you the truth. But I swear I saw you turn from a stressed-out doormat into the amazing, superwoman you always were. You believed in yourself again, and you can't lose that now!"

I shrugged and turned away from Emily not in the mood to hear how Jen had been my saviour.

"Don't look like that," Emily grabbed my arm and turned me to face her. "I'm not telling you to get back with Jen or Steve. That would be a really stupid thing to do, by the way. I'm telling you to be your own dazzling self and do what makes you happy. Surround yourself with the people who love you and do what you're good at. Which is this!"

"Have you branched out into greeting's cards and motivational speaking?" I smiled, despite myself and Emily enveloped me into a hug.

"Shut up." She responded, but I could see she was grinning. "Will you just give it a chance? It's not like I'm trying to make you start dating."

"I'll think about it," I said. "I need to get over to check on the progress for this party."

"You've got hours," Emily wrinkled her nose at me. "Anyway, I want to come. I need to watch you manhandle the ice statues."

"You're meant to be resting." I warned her. "You can come, but don't touch anything."

Emily got to her feet and forced me into another sisterly hug. "I'm so excited we're going to be going into business together!"

“I haven’t said yes.” I warned her.

“I know,” Emily smiled confidently. “But you will.”

A few days later, I was thinking about Emily’s proposal while I waited in the short stay carpark at arrivals. She had had a proposal put together and had done a fair bit of research into the London events market. I knew I was going to say yes. My nerves were in overdrive, as my anxieties tried to convince me that I’d be a mess if it didn’t work out, but I silenced them. Even after my heartbreak at Jen’s deception, I didn’t regret the time we’d been together. Even if the whole venture into party planning blew up in my face, I’d get over it. It was worth a shot just to delay the inevitable return to office misery. God knows, I deserved to extend my career break.

Eventually, my four beautiful children rolled up, looking tanned and healthy from their break in the sunshine. I could tell by Esther’s face that the holiday had been more successful than their last one and I got out of the car to hug them. I took their cases and hefted them into the boot. Steve loitered awkwardly behind.

We had barely exchanged more than a few words since December, but I was done with the anger now and I managed to smile.

“Would you like a lift home?” I offered.

Steve looked surprised. "Oh, thank you. I've got a friend picking me up though."

"No worries." I got back into the car. "Say bye to Dad."

Steve had been much more hands on since I'd started my new job, and this had benefitted all the children. The time they spent together was quality compared to when he'd just been a passing ship in the family home. I cringed when I thought back to the relationship that I'd put up with.

I couldn't help but compare my relationship with Steve to the one with Jen. Despite our time together being short, I had felt more loved and supported in that time than in all the years I'd been with Steve. I thought back to Andy's words about how I hadn't moved on. There had been times over the past few months when I had come close to asking Andy about Jen's response. At the time of Steve's revelation, I'd been absolutely floored, and I didn't want, or couldn't cope with, having a conversation with the person that I'd truly believed to be my soulmate about how she had omitted to tell me, over years of friendship, that she'd fucked my husband. The first few weeks were torture. I replayed every event that I could remember both Steve and Jen being present. Steve and I rarely mixed socially so there weren't many occasions however I poured over the sketchy memories, searching for clues or signs of previous intimacy between them. Jen had always had a cool demeanour with Steve and I couldn't remember them ever spending any time talking or laughing together. If only she had told me. This thought had circled my mind so many times as I cried and cried over the betrayal but mainly over the loss. I was furious with Steve for being the one to ruin this for me and furious at Jen for not having the guts to tell me the truth. It was only now, now that time had soothed the fury and the raw heartbreak, that I could begin to realise that if Jen had told me it would have changed everything.

She could have told me when she first met me. I pictured the scene playing out like a movie in my head. Jen, dazzling in her gown, gliding towards me as I nursed a soft drink, loitering uncomfortably amongst the glamourous and the sophisticated City slickers enjoying their Christmas festivities. I was wondering where my husband had disappeared to, dying to go home and feeling like an ugly frump in my basic black dress that I'd chosen because it was the only thing that made me look remotely pregnant instead of just dumpy and fat.

"Hi." She'd smiled warmly before engaging me in an easy conversation that made me feel grateful and less self-conscious at the time.

"Hi," She could have said. "I had sex with your husband and got pregnant, just like you! I'm not having mine though but really sorry about that. He spun me a load of crap about how he was separated, and I would never have done it otherwise."

I almost laughed at my imaginary scene. How that would have changed the course of my life. I wondered if I would have split up with Steve for good then and there. The funny thing was, Steve and I had actually split up briefly before I had fallen pregnant with George. He had insisted he wasn't seeing anyone in the interim but even naïve twenty-something me wasn't stupid enough to truly believe he wouldn't have shagged anyone. Maybe I would have just accepted the lady's apology, had a blazing row with Steve but eventually got back with him and gone on to have Leo and Matilda too. The only difference would have been I wouldn't have developed a friendship with Jen. Or would I have ended things with Steve then and there. Maybe we'd have pulled out of the house we were buying, and I'd have settled into a flat with Esther and baby George in an affordable area. Leo and Matilda would never have been. Steve would have gone on to do the bare minimum parenting before eventually snagging himself a slim, blonde wife and starting a new, improved little family. The common denominator, whatever the outcome, would have been the absence of mine and Jen's friendship. I was fascinated by the "what if's" but none of them mattered as that's all they were; if's. She hadn't told me and now I knew. I couldn't un-know it and that was pretty final. I was just tormenting myself by going back over it. I had blocked Jen on every platform I could think of but if she'd really loved me, she would have reached out. If only to apologise. My heart ached. This probably hurt more than the lies; knowing I must have been so replaceable.

Chapter 36

Despite Steve's improved attitude towards parenting over the Easter holidays, it wasn't long before my fears were realised.

Steve had plans on a Saturday night, at the end of April, and I'd had to arrange for a babysitter for Steve to drop the kids back to, as heaven forbid he miss drinks with the boys when I was out attending to the million-and-one-details of the Williams' big day. I arrived back, a little after midnight, exhausted, to relieve the babysitter of her duties.

"Everything ok?" I asked, searching in my bag for the money I owed her.

"All ok," She nodded. "I couldn't make it much earlier, but I got here as soon as I could when Steve text."

I had arranged for the babysitter to meet Steve at the house at 7pm. This was the first I had heard about her coming any earlier.

"What time did you get here?" I asked diplomatically.

"Just after 5," She said. "Esther only had to watch the kids for about half an hour though, so it worked out ok."

"Steve dropped them off here before 5pm and just left them?" I asked, trying hard to hide my growing annoyance.

"Esther said he got here about 4.45pm." She shrugged.

"Has he paid you for that time?" I asked. "Sorry if it was short-notice. I didn't know he was dropping them back early."

"No, he didn't pay me," She looked embarrassed. "Esther was here so it all worked out alright."

"Esther was here?" I repeated, and she nodded dumbly.

The expression on her face screamed "Keep me out of this", so I paid her what she was owed and thanked her again.

I went up to bed, deciding I'd deal with this in the morning. There was no point trying to speak to Steve at this hour.

"What did you get up to yesterday?" I asked Esther the next morning, not wanting to ask outright and put Esther in an uncomfortable position.

Esther shrugged. "Nothing really."

"Did you do anything nice Friday night?" I tried again.

"I slept over Izzy's." Esther said, and then glanced quickly at me for my reaction.

"I thought you were staying at Dad's?" I said.

Steve had finally found himself a place to live, now that I was earning a small amount of money.

Esther shrugged. "I wanted to go to Izzy's. He said it was fine."

“Did he pick you up Saturday?” I probed.

“No, I saw him when he dropped the kids back.” She grabbed the bowl of fruit she had made and headed out of the kitchen quickly before I could continue my interrogation.

For fuck’s sake, I fumed. This was exactly what I’d worried about when I’d tried to turn down Emily’s offer. Steve wasn’t fit to supervise the bloody dogs, let alone the kids. Esther basically had a free house since I’d left at 5am this morning, with the exception of the dog walker popping in and out. She could have had boys here and I would have been none-the-wiser. It wouldn’t be long before he was leaving the lot of them here overnight whenever he got better plans. I could be miles away and, God, if anything happened… I had to speak to him about this. I couldn’t believe that he could be so selfish, especially after George’s accident.

This got me worrying about my job. It was all well and good me being on my high horse about Steve’s lax attitude, but I was just as responsible. If I knew that he couldn’t be trusted, and I left them in his care, surely that made me just as bad as him.

I fought the urge to hurl myself onto my bed and have a tantrum at the unfairness of my life. I couldn’t help but feel that I was cursed. Every single thing that made me happy seemed to be snatched away. I tried to remind myself that I had a lot of things to be thankful for, but I was already on my downward spiral. I was already picturing myself back to an unfulfilling 9-to-5, dying alone with just my dogs for company.

It had only taken one incident for me to forget my mature truce with Steve and be back to raging with fury at him. I knew Emily's heart was set on us working together, and the thought of letting her, and myself, down exacerbated my anger. It was bad enough that he'd ruined my relationship with Jen because he had to sleep with every woman that he had ever set eyes on. I reached for my phone and sent him a short, sharp message, insisting that I needed to speak to him.

I wasn't expecting a response, but he replied immediately.

"I wanted to catch up with you about Esther. Be over in an hour?"

I paced the house, trying to get my emotions under control before Steve appeared. I knew, from experience, that there was no point going in all guns blazing as once he was on the defensive, it would be game over for any hopes of a positive outcome.

"I'm glad you wanted to talk," Steve said, looking remarkably relaxed about our meeting. "I've been at the end of my tether with Esther. She point-blank refused to sleep over mine Friday. She's been a nightmare since we came back from Portugal."

"Have you been finding Esther difficult when she's at

yours?" I asked.

I hadn't noticed any major change in her. She was her usual difficult, snarky teenaged self, as far as I was aware.

"A little bit," He admitted. "She clearly doesn't want to be there, and I assumed it was just because of Leanne..."

"Leanne?" The kids hadn't even mentioned their dad's new girlfriend, so I had assumed he was keeping his love life separate from his family life. "I heard you were seeing her, but the kids haven't mentioned anything."

"She's still got her own place," Steve looked a little sheepish. "I explained how difficult Esther found my relationship with Charlotte so when the kids are over, Leanne stays at hers, but we're pretty serious."

He paused like he had something else to say.

"Does Esther know?" I asked, wondering whether this behaviour was a typical teenage rebellion worsened by Esther's conflicting feelings about her dad replacing her family.

"I don't hide Leanne's stuff," Steve said. "And she might have seen..."

He trailed off guiltily.

"What might she have seen?" I asked calmly, wondering what damage limitation would now be required to rescue my daughter from a life of anti-social behaviour.

"I was going to tell you," He said defensively. "But it's early days and we were waiting until after the first scan."

It took a moment for his words to register and my mouth dropped open in horror.

"Are you fucking joking?"

"Congratulations, most people say." He replied sarcastically.

"And Esther might know?" I asked, fighting the urge to scream and trying to focus on the matter at hand.

"There were some magazines and some of those vitamins." He shrugged.

"You better go and speak to your daughter." I replied coldly. "You impregnating every woman you've ever met has fucked up enough of my life. You can sort this out."

I got up and turned away. Esther was my priority but hearing Steve's baby news had brought back the horrible crushing feelings of that night in December when he'd blown my world apart. I needed to get away and clear my head before I completely lost it.

Steve grabbed my arm as if to pull me back.

"What's that supposed to mean?" He snapped at me.

"You know exactly what it means!" I was struggling to control my temper now and I brushed his hand away.

"I don't! I haven't got anyone pregnant. Except you!" He

exclaimed, before adding sheepishly. "And Leanne."

He gave me a small smile as if what he was saying was funny and I frowned at him.

"You're forgetting Jen." I said, my voice icy-cold.

"What?" Steve looked bewildered. "Is that what you thought? No!"

I shook my head in confusion. "But, you said-"

"Greg!" He exclaimed, looking horrified. "It was Greg! Not me! He cheated on Alicia with Jen. Jen was furious when she found out he was married. I had covered for Greg and she fucking hated me for it. I thought you knew!"

"Greg?" I sunk back into the chair, feeling the fight leave my body. "You didn't?"

Steve shook his head. "No, never! She would have told you if I'd even tried it on."

"Fuck." I got back up and I was trembling now. "I need to go."

"Lucy?" Steve was looking at me like I was crazy.

"Just speak to your daughter," I urged him. "Sort this shit out yourself."

I slid my feet into a pair of shoes at the door and walked out of the house.

I walked and walked; my mind spinning with this revelation. If I hadn't had the tie of four children waiting for me, I don't think I would have stopped walking. I couldn't even begin to process what this meant. Why hadn't Jen defended herself? Why had she let me think the worst? I didn't know where to start unravelling this all in my mind.

Even in my own shock, I'd taken my phone with me. I couldn't trust Steve to resolve things with Esther and I wanted to be on call in case she needed me. No matter what I was going through, I was an adult and could deal with it. Esther, as much as she thought she was grown up, was my daughter and I would be back in an instant if she needed me. The phone rang now but it was Andy. I debated letting it go to voicemail but decided I needed to ask him.

"Everything ok?" I asked.

"Yeah." He sounded happy. "Listen to this..."

"I need to ask you something," I interrupted him. "I know I told you to not tell me, but I need closure. What did you say to Jen?"

"Oh, good for you," He sounded pleased. "I just said what you told me to. It's in my messages somewhere."

"Will you look?" I asked, stopping abruptly and sitting down on a low wall so I could concentrate.

I could hear Andy fumbling around with his phone. "Here it is. Ready?"

"Ready." I confirmed, feeling my heart start to race.

"'Steve has told Lucy everything. She is understandably very upset. Lucy has asked that you don't contact her. Please respect her wishes.'" Andy read.

Oh, God. It was pretty much what I'd told him to say but hearing it now it sounded quite ambiguous.

"What did she reply?" I asked, swallowing nervously.

"Are you fucking joking?" He said.

"What?" I frowned, confused.

"That was her reply," Andy clarified. "I replied 'No, I'm not. She asked me to text you. This is very hard for Lucy'."

"Oh." I felt like I'd been punched in the stomach. Did Jen interpret that as I was back with Steve? What had she thought I meant? And why hadn't she cared enough to try to reach out.

"Then she said, "Tell her I hope she's happy even if it's not with me"." Andy finished.

If it was possible to feel your actual heartbreak, I felt it then and there.

"Thanks," I said quietly. "I just wanted to know."

"Are you ok?" I could hear the concern in Andy's voice. "Why are you asking now?"

"It wasn't Steve," I told him. "I don't remember Steve's exact words, but I got it wrong. It was Greg."

"Oh, Lucy!" Andy exclaimed in dismay. "I'm so sorry. But we can fix this!"

"No." I said resolutely. "She didn't care. Jen didn't care enough to find out. It's fine."

"It's not fine!" Andy said passionately. "I'm coming over."

"You can't," I stood up and started walking back in the direction of my home. "Steve's over. He's dropping a pregnancy clanger to Esther and I need to be on hand to pick up the pieces."

"Oh, bloody hell," Andy replied. "Good luck! Call me if you need me."

The house was eerily silent when I got back. I had been gone for almost two hours and I let myself in, bracing myself for the fall out. I walked through to the living room and was surprised to see Steve and Esther sat side by side on the sofa. Esther was sprawled across the sofa with her long legs draped across Steve's lap. He was showing her something on his phone and they were both laughing. They looked up at me as I came into the room and I could tell Esther had been crying but was surprised to see Steve looked a little red-eyed. I sat down on the opposite sofa.

"Everything ok?" I asked tentatively.

Esther nodded wordlessly, and Steve gave her a little nudge.

"Sorry I was a bit of a nightmare," Esther said in a small voice. "I'm ok now."

Steve looked pleased and I shot a questioning glance at him.

"We've talked about everything," Steve said confidently. "And we've reached some compromises, haven't we?"

Esther nodded again.

"That's good to hear." I decided I wouldn't pry. This was between Steve and his daughter. I would have to trust him to maintain their relationship.

"Are you ok now?" Steve asked, looking concerned. "I'm really sorry about the mix up. I hope I didn't ruin anything?"

It was Esther's turn to look curious now. "What's happened?"

"I'm fine." I told Steve before turning to my daughter. "Just a silly mix up. No harm done. It is what it is."

Esther bit her lip as if she was going to press me for more details but then thought better of it.

"I think I'm going to have a lie down," I told them. Now that Steve and Esther had resolved their dramas, I didn't feel in the mood for company. "No need to rush off, Steve."

They both nodded and went back to whatever they were laughing at.

I slept better than I thought I would. The sadness of

knowing I just hadn't meant that much to Jen was easier to accept than the torment of the alleged betrayal and the constant nagging at the lack of closure. I felt better at knowing she hadn't been lying to me all those years as, even before I'd fallen in love with her, I had so many happy memories based on our friendship. They no longer felt tainted and I reasoned that someone as amazing and as beautiful as Jen would never have settled for someone like me long term. I would try hard to chalk this one up as experience and I would try to move on. I even got as far as downloading a dating app, later that day, and I made a note to tell Andy later as I knew he'd approve.

As if summoned by my thoughts, Andy's name flashed up on my phone.

"How's the drama?" He asked.

"Resolved." I replied dryly. "Sorry that I dropped all that on you earlier."

"But Steve is having another kid?" Andy sounded confused.

"Yeah," I agreed. "But I really couldn't give a shit."

"Really?" Andy asked, doubtfully.

"Really." I confirmed. "Anyway, what's up with you? I'm assuming you wanted something?"

"I did." Andy admitted. "I had some news for you."

The tone of Andy's voice made me sit up, suddenly

intrigued.

"Tell me."

"We're getting married!" Andy burst out

"Congratulations!" I squealed, genuinely beside myself with joy for them both. "Tell me everything!"

Andy recounted the romantic proposal and I oohed and aahed in all the right places.

"Is that why you phoned me?" I asked, feeling selfish that I'd monopolised the conversation earlier.

Andy nodded. "It's fine though. I just hope you're ok."

I couldn't bear to rain on his parade. "I'm better than ok. I'm ready to move on. I've even downloaded a dating app."

Andy gave a cheer. "Well done, Lucy!"

"Go and get back to your fiancé," I grinned. "I'll come and see you in the week."

"We're counting on it!" Andy exclaimed. "You've got your first London-based party to plan!"

Chapter 37

My first real London job! And a celebrity too!

Andy and John wanted quite an informal engagement party, which was a relief for my first solo job. I read my own tribe the riot act as we got into the taxi and made our way to the venue.

"Once more," I demanded in my most authoritative tone. "What are the rules?"

"No swearing." George offered.

"No shouting." Leo chipped in.

"No fighting." Matilda said confidently.

"No having fun." Esther joked and they all fell into a fit of giggles.

I smiled despite myself and surveyed my little family with a burst of pride. The boys were dressed smartly in crisp shirts and chinos. Matilda looked like a little princess in a pretty white dress and sandals. Her hair had been tamed into a cascade of curls at the salon this afternoon and Esther had painted her nails in a pale pink. Esther looked stunningly beautiful in a lacy skater-style dress and strappy heels. She'd opted for an elegant up-do and I had discreetly snapped a photo of her doing her makeup and sent it to her Dad.

"Heartbreaker!" He replied followed by a row of broken

hearts and crying emojis.

Steve and I had been making more of an effort to get on lately. I had even met Leanne a few times while dropping the kids off and she'd actually been lovelier to me than she ever had been when I knew her professionally. According to the kids, she was really fun and nice which was a relief.

I had had also opted for an up-do, although I had had to run it by Esther first to make sure it wasn't too similar to hers. Esther had insisted on doing my make-up and she'd done a pretty good job, creating cheekbones where previously there were none. I'd struggled to find an appropriate outfit, typically hating my dress at the last minute. It didn't go with my hair and made me look mumsy. I searched through my wardrobe and found my floaty knee length skirt and a navy top slung over it. Esther, who'd been loitering in my room, saw me surveying it.

"Oh Mum!" She pointed at the skirt. "That's a good look. Wear that."

I held the top up against me and realised instantly that it was Jen's. I must have tossed it in my suitcase by mistake. I put the outfit on anyway. It did look good and was just right for this evening.

"That one." Esther gave me an approving nod and the decision was made.

My phone had pinged then, and it was Alex, from my dating app. I ignored the message and continued to get ready. I hadn't gone on any dates yet, but I was talking to a few people. Nobody had quite piqued my interest enough for me to give up my spare time, but it was all progress. I might even package up the top and send it back to Jen to reach out. After I'd worn it to the party, obviously.

The taxi pulled up outside the country restaurant that John and Andy had hired out for the occasion. The children and I headed inside and were shown to the suite. The room had been decorated beautifully and there was an adjoining suite with an area set up for any younger guests. I conducted my final checks, breath held that it was a success.

"I need to be on professional greeting duty," I told the kids. "Get drinks and entertain yourselves. Just don't mess up the decorations. And stay out of the sweets until the other guests are here."

"What?" Matilda looked incensed. "First come, first served!"

Esther whispered something to her conspiratorially and Matilda gave her a knowing nod before they all wandered away. I smiled to myself but decided to let it go. I trusted them to not disgrace me. They were good kids.

I took a glass of champagne from the waitress, poised at the entrance, and made polite small talk with her until the guests started arriving in dribs and drabs. I introduced myself to those I didn't know as "the party planner" and apologised that the happy couple were running slightly behind. The suite was filling up now and the waitress had replenished her champagne tray several times. John's brother arrived next.

"Hi James." I had met James a few times since we'd had lunch at John and Andy's. The subject of Jen had never come up again, but I was always on edge, waiting for him to drop into conversation how they'd rekindled their friendship. Even today, in professional mode, I felt a bubble of uneasiness in the pit of my stomach. Please don't bring her up. I need to be on my A-game, not sobbing in the corner.

"Hi Lucy." He flashed me a perfect white smile. "The place looks amazing."

"It does," I smiled my gratitude. "How are you?"

"I'm good," James replied. "A bit tired. Literally just flew in for the party."

"Work or holiday?" I asked politely, knowing that it was the former and already glancing towards the doorway, looking for an excuse to escape.

"Work, unfortunately." He confirmed.

"Still based in New York?" I asked out of politeness.

"I am." He adjusted his glasses as if he was preparing to tell me something.

"Cool." I said lamely.

My awkward response caused him to look curiously at me, but before he could say any more, something caught my eye. A dark-haired woman had entered through the main doors, head bowed and had paused there, as if unsure whether to come inside. My heart skipped a beat and I felt a flutter deep in my stomach. I couldn't hear anything John's brother was saying, and my eyes were fixed on the woman.

Was it her? I wondered. I couldn't be sure but then she started moving; walking towards us with a hesitant but graceful stride that I would have recognised anywhere. I could barely process what was happening before she was there in front of me.

"Hi." She said, and the butterflies erupted, swarming from deep in the pit of my stomach.

"I'm wearing your top." I spoke without thinking and Jen's nervous expression melted into a warm smile of amusement.

"It looks lovely on you." She leaned forward and kissed me gently on the cheek.

"Hi, Jen." James interrupted.

She greeted him with a polite formality, barely glancing in his direction. This wasn't the body language of two people who were shagging. Or were they trying to throw me off the scent? Why was she here? Was she James' plus-one? Had John invited her? Andy? Oh God, I needed to get out of here.

"I just need to…" I tried to form a sentence to excuse myself.

"Can we talk?" Jen directed her question at me and my mouth dropped open in surprise.

I glanced at James dumbly, unable to respond.

"I'll take over the meet-and-greet." James said and winked at me.

Jen took my arm and led me towards the door. If my loss of coherent speech hadn't given away my nerves already, the goose bumps that rose at her touch would have.

"Shall we go outside?" Jen asked, taking charge. "I've got cigarettes."

"I don't really smoke anymore." I admitted.

"Nor me," She confided. "I only used to smoke with you. I bought some especially for tonight. Just in case."

I followed her out to the front of the building and she indicated a smoking terrace around the corner. We stood silently for a moment, side by side, not looking at each other. My heart was racing, and my stomach was a knot of nerves. I stole glances at this beautiful, amazing woman from the corner of my eye. She had been my favourite person for so long. She had picked me up when I was at my lowest and believed in me when I hadn't even believed in myself. I had fallen in love with her so slowly and steadily that I hadn't even noticed until I was head over heels. It was like my wildest dream had come true when she seemed to love me back. I just wanted her back in my life; one way or another.

"Jen," I started quickly before my confidence failed me. "I'm so sorry. I got something really, really wrong."

"And me." She said, fumbling in her bag for the cigerettes and a lighter.

"You did?" I felt my heart sink. Was she going to admit that I'd just been a fling and we were better off as friends.

"I thought Andy's message meant you were back with Steve," She said matter-of-factly. She paused, lighting a cigarette and passing it to me before lighting her own. "I came to yours New Year. I saw Steve."

"What?" I asked shocked. "I wasn't there! I was at Emily's. He was there with the kids."

"I know that now." Jen admitted, tucking a strand of dark hair behind her ear. "I was devastated when you wouldn't speak to me, and I came back. I didn't even make it as far as the door. I watched him with the kids and I couldn't bring myself to disrupt your perfect family."

"I never got back with Steve!" I protested. My mind was racing with the revelation that she had come back. She had tried to speak to me. "Oh, Jen. Steve told me about Greg, but, the way he said it, I thought you'd had an affair with him. I'm so sorry. I should have known."

She smiled sadly. "I can't believe you thought I wouldn't have told you if I'd had a thing with Steve."

"I know! I know!" I closed my eyes in frustration at myself. "I'm so sorry."

"It's fine." She shrugged but I could see the hurt in her eyes.

"No, it's not." I turned to her and put a hand gently on her bare arm.

She froze at my touch and, for a second, I wondered if she was going to push me away. After a moment, I felt her relax and she looked at me regretfully.

"I was heartbroken that you didn't want to speak to me," She said honestly. "It was the main reason why I agreed to extend my secondment."

"You've been there all this time." I stated this more to myself than Jen, feeling ashamed that my whole judgement had been based on foolish assumptions. "I would really love it if you could forgive me and we could be friends again."

The moment was pierced by my phone, and I remembered that I was working. I glanced at it, expecting it to be Andy or John.

"Sorry," I apologised. "I'm on duty."

I saw Shaun's name flash up, and I let it go to voicemail. As the screen cleared, I noticed the notification for 6 missed calls from him. My own emotional make-up scene was forgotten as panic rose in my chest.

"Everything ok?" Jen asked, seeing my face fall as I looked at my phone.

"My brother-in-law." I pressed dial and held the phone up to my face. "Sorry, I think there might be..."

Jen watched with an expression of concern as I called Shaun back. He answered on the first ring.

"Lucy!" He sounded frantic. "Thank God you answered. Emily has been rushed in to hospital. It's pre-eclampsia. They're prepping her for a c-section. I'm going back in."

"Oh my God," I felt floored. "Is she ok? Is the baby ok?"

"She's not great," Shaun said, and I could hear the tears in his voice. "They say they've got no choice but to deliver him."

"Oh, Shaun!" My hand flew to my mouth. She still had 10 weeks to go until her due date.

"I've got to go," He repeated, sounding scared. "I'll phone you when I can."

He hung up the phone and I stared blankly at the screen. As if Emily hadn't already been through enough. She'd been in hospital the previous week, because of her blood pressure, but they'd been happy enough to let her out. Oh, please let her be alright.

"Lucy," Jen took my hands. "What's happened?"

I quickly filled her in on my conversation with Shaun.

"I just want to be there for her." I said earnestly, my eyes filling with tears at the thought of her and her helpless little baby. All kinds of thoughts were racing through my head. What if one of them doesn't make it?

"She's not due yet." Jen said, and I nodded even though it wasn't a question. "Do you think you should go?"

I shook my head. "Steve's in Portugal with his girlfriend. I've got to be here."

"Just go, Lucy," Jen urged me. "I'll stay with the kids."

"I can't." I protested, fighting the urge to do what she said. The need to be with my sister was overwhelming. "It's Andy and John's engagement party."

"And all the details are taken care of." Jen said firmly. "I'll stay with the kids and take them back to yours. I'm here for a few days. I think Emily and Shaun will want you there."

"I can't." I repeated, but Jen already had her phone out.

"Go and see the kids," She said. "I'm calling you a taxi. Are you ok to drive from yours or do you want a car to take you the whole way? I'll pay. Don't argue."

"No!" I shook my head hurriedly. "I'll drive."

She shot me a look and I smiled, despite my fears.

"I'll drive carefully." I promised.

Chapter 38

The next few hours were a blur. Jen took control, so that I didn't alarm the children, and I rushed off barely stopping to get a change of clothes, before I was hightailing it to the hospital. I completed the three-hour drive in a little over two-and-a-half hours, but there was still no word from Shaun.

It was late by the time I raced through never-ending, empty corridors of the hospital, following the signs for 'Maternity'. I pressed on the buzzer to the main ward, hopping from foot to foot with anxious unrest. I knew that they'd send me away, but I just wanted someone to tell me that Emily and the baby were alright.

The corridor in front of me, locked away by security doors, remained empty and there was no response to my buzz.

He'd be born by now, I thought helplessly. I wondered how big he would be. I wished that I could remember any of the things I was told about pre-eclampsia from the times I had been pregnant, but despite how hard I tried to recall the symptoms, nothing came back to me.

I tried to control my impatience, knowing that my own desire for news about my sister wasn't a priority to any of the people working hard behind those doors, but after a few minutes, I pressed the buzzer again.

Why Emily? I couldn't help thinking. It was so unfair. I had fallen pregnant unintentionally 75% of the time, whereas she, who was a much better mother than me, had struggled to conceive and then to carry, and now this. Emily was healthy. She actually looked after her body. She took fucking pregnancy vitamins and read pregnancy books. I felt shaken by how I had taken having my healthy babies for granted. I had had the nerve to feel hard done by the sacrifices I had made. Emily would have given up the world to have it as easy as I had it. Please, please, please let them both be ok.

The door blocking my path made a buzzing sound, and I pushed it, feeling both relief and fear as it yielded to me. I hurried up the corridor to the desk.

"My sister." I said breathlessly. "Emily James?"

The nurse glanced down at her desk. "She's in recovery. I'm afraid you can't see her, but I'll let her know you came by. Visiting..."

"No, it's ok." I said hurriedly. "I know it's too late. I didn't need to see her, but I was waiting for her husband to phone me. I just wanted to know if they were ok?"

"Her husband is still with her." The woman said. "I'll tell him you called. Can I take your name?"

"Lucy." I said. "Can I wait for him?"

She nodded. "He'll have to leave soon. There's a waiting room just outside the doors you came in."

I thanked her and turned to leave when I heard footsteps in

the corridor. I turned to look, and my heart fluttered with nerves when I saw Shaun's familiar shape moving slowly towards me.

"Shaun!" I waited until he was closer, conscious of our surroundings, before I called out to him.

"Lucy!" He looked shocked to see me and hurried over.

"How are they?" My eyes searched his face frantically for any clues.

"They're ok, they're ok." He said quickly.

"They're ok?" I stared at him hopefully.

Worry was etched across his face, but he nodded.

"Emily is fine." He confirmed. "The baby is up in special care. They said I can go and see him."

"He's ok?" I couldn't help but ask again.

"He's tiny." Shaun said, his voice catching a little with emotion. "He's in an incubator and they're helping him breathe, but he's doing alright."

"Oh, Shaun!" I felt the nervous energy that had carried me here leave my body, suddenly feeling exhausted.

"I know." He squeezed me to him in a bear hug. "I don't think they'll let you see him tonight, and I've just left Emily to sleep."

"It's ok," I said hurriedly. "I didn't expect to see them. I just wanted to be here."

I waited in the corridor for Shaun, unable to relax until he'd returned twenty minutes later, looking overwhelmed and stressed but happy.

"How is he?" I asked, as Shaun and I walked back to the car park together.

It was past midnight now, and the hospital grounds were still and deserted.

"Beautiful." Shaun said proudly, and I didn't have to look at him to know there were tears of pride glistening in his eyes. "He's a little fighter. Like his Mum."

I felt my own eyes fill up with tears and I didn't trust my voice to not betray the emotion I felt.

"I can't believe you drove down from London." Shaun said.

"I was worried." I admitted. "I'll come back tomorrow if Em feels up to seeing me."

"You can't go home!" Shaun shook his head. "Come back with me. Emily will definitely want to see you, and you can help me with Fin. Unless you need to get back for the kids."

I wanted, more than anything, to see my sister and the baby. I realised I didn't have Jen's number saved since changing my phone, and I sent Esther a message on the off chance that they were still up. Steve was home tomorrow. I could see if someone could have the kids until he came home if Jen didn't mind staying with them.

My heart skipped a beat at the thought of her there, in my house, and for the first time since hearing about Emily and the baby, I recalled mine and Jen's conversation. Even in my preoccupation with Emily and the baby, I was aware of tiny buds of hope flowering in the pit of my stomach.

I received a reply from Esther and opened the message.

"We're all fine. Back home. Kids asleep. How's Auntie Emily?? Jen says stay as long as you need. She'll speak to you when you're back. Love you x."

I was relieved to hear they were all alright, but I felt a twinge of disappointment that my conversation with Jen had been cut short. I quickly responded to my daughter and headed back to Shaun and Emily's.

The next morning, Shaun picked Finley up and I played with him for a few hours, anxiously waiting for any news on Emily and the baby. Shaun sent me the visiting hours, and I drove up to the hospital with little Fin strapped in the back of my car. We raced up to the ward Emily was now on and I watched my sister's face light up to see her son.

I cautiously helped him to sit next to her, taking care not to disturb the wires and tubes still attaching Emily to various medical bags. She swivelled around into a sitting position, doing a pretty good job of disguising the discomfort she was clearly still in.

"Have you seen him?" Emily asked when, after a while, Shaun took Finley up to have a peek at his new baby brother.

I shook my head.

"He's tiny." Emily said, and I reached for her hands.

There were so many things I wanted to ask Emily. Would she be ok now? Would the baby be ok? I held back, knowing that this wasn't about how I was feeling. I needed to be here for Emily and her family.

"Thanks for coming down," Emily managed a small smile. "Have you spoke to Mum?"

I made an apologetic face. "She's trying to get a flight home in the next few days."

Emily nodded, but didn't add anything or make a joke about our mother like she usually would. I waited, breath bated, for her to say something.

"I was really fucking scared." She said eventually, squeezing my hands for emphasis.

"Oh, Emily!" I hugged her gently close to me. "I was scared for you. I'm so glad you're ok."

I felt my sister's tears on my shoulder as she finally released the emotions she'd been holding in.

"Sorry," She sniffed, pulling away with a grimace of pain. "I can't stop crying. You should have seen me when I saw the baby this morning."

Shaun and Finley appeared back at the doorway, and Emily broke off what she was saying, hurriedly wiping away any signs of her upset.

"They're really pleased with how he's doing." Shaun announced to my sister proudly, and I watched Emily's face light up.

"Is he going to be alright?" I couldn't help but ask.

"It's early days," Emily said cautiously. "But he's looking pretty strong and healthy. The doctor said that he'll be here for some weeks, and we just need to take it day-by-day."

"He's going to need a name." Shaun directed this to Emily, and they shared a happy, loving look that reminded me that I was just a third-party onlooker to this intimate moment. I was so grateful that Emily had someone like Shaun in her life.

Finley started getting restless and I offered to take him home. Shaun and Emily both looked relieved and grateful, and I was glad that my presence meant they could be together.

"Are you staying all day?" Emily asked hopefully, clutching Shaun's hand as I hustled Finley into his jacket.

"Steve's back from Portugal tonight," I explained. "I can stay if you want me to watch Fin, but I'll just have to check

Steve's having them."

"Who's got the kids?" Emily frowned.

"Jen." I admitted.

Emily's eyes widened. "You should probably go home then."

"It's not like that," I waved a hand dismissively. "I'm fine to stay."

Emily shot me a doubtful look, but I insisted. I spent a busy day entertaining my nephew and running around trying to get Emily and Shaun's house in some semblance of order for them. I managed to get hold of Steve, who didn't even sound annoyed to be swinging past mine to get the kids straight from his flight. I stayed until the following afternoon, when my mother and step-father arrived back in the country to relieve me of my nephew-sitting duties. Emily was up and on her feet by now, and she took me to see her baby son, tiny, pink and vulnerable in his plastic incubator.

"You haven't told me any more about Jen." Emily said casually as I helped her back to the main ward, and we'd done drying our tears at the sight of the baby.

"There's nothing to tell," I shrugged. "Hopefully, we can be friends again when she's back in the country permanently."

"Is that what she said?" Emily asked. "Is that what you want?"

I was surprised at Emily's loaded questions, and I tried to laugh it off.

"I'm happy to have Jen back as a friend." I said confidently. "I need a little break from relationships."

Emily tilted her head to the side as she regarded me with a mixture of concern and disbelief.

"I wouldn't usually stick my nose in," Emily said hesitantly. "But I thought Jen was your Shaun."

"My Shaun?" I couldn't help but laugh at Emily's sentiment.

"I wanted to say soulmate," Emily admitted sheepishly. "But I didn't want to be sick in my mouth."

We both laughed, but I could feel her eyes staring holes in me waiting for a response.

"I did to." I admitted. "But, it's done now. I've come to terms with it all."

"It's not done. You'll always regret it if you don't at least try." Emily reached out and took my hand. "Please, just try!"

"Ok." I said, not meaning it.

Emily regarded me sceptically. "You're not going to, are you?"

"I will." I turned away, knowing she could see straight through me. "I want us to be friends again. And I owe her for offering to watch the kids."

Emily stayed quiet until I faced her again. "I think you'll regret it if you don't at least ask her if she wants to try again."

I shrugged.

"If you want to be an old lady on your death bed bitterly regretting spending your life alone or worse, with the wrong person, that's fine," Emily said quietly. "But I would regret it if I didn't push you. I know she made you happy."

I was prepared to brush off anything Emily said to me. I'd already made up my mind that the most I could hope for was for Jen and I to be friends. Even more so now she'd made up her mind to stay in New York. I didn't know whether it was the emotions running high from Emily's traumatic birth, or the poignant tone in her voice, but something resonated with me, and I reflected on Emily's words. I thought about living with the "what if's" and all the hours I'd wasted of my life so far, tormenting myself, wishing I'd done things differently.

"Ok." I said decisively. "I'll go straight to Jen's Gran's."

"You will?" Emily's face lit up.

"I promise."

I hugged my little sister goodbye after helping her back into her hospital bed and dashed back to the carpark to start my return journey home, after a little detour to tell Jen how I felt.

Chapter 39

As soon as the decision was made, I felt electric. I drove on auto-pilot, a million thoughts running through my head, but at the same time thinking of nothing except for my mission. I thought of Jen, I thought of our friendship, all the things we'd done together, and that amazing time in New York. I thought about all the times she had been there for me; through the dramas with Steve, the frustrations in work, my difficulty finding a job, all the stresses of motherhood. I thought about how she looked when she woke up, how she always smelled like cocoa butter, how her lips felt when I kissed them. I thought about how I would feel if she didn't want to be anything more than friends, and then I instantly dismissed this thought. I would get over it. Because that's what I did. I got through stuff and I kept going.

The nerves kicked in on the last leg of the journey. I slowed to a crawl in the painfully slow stop-start traffic of the last few miles, sandwiched in by commuter traffic. I purposely avoided thinking about what I was going to say, knowing that if I over-thought things, I'd end up tying myself up in knots of anxiety. By the time I turned into Jen's Gran's street, I was sweating and beside myself with anticipation. I managed to find a space to park at the end of the road and I hurried towards the house, feeling I could barely catch my breath with excitement.

I knocked on the door, suddenly wishing I'd brought a gift to say thank you. It would have given me a conversation-opener and would have been a nice gesture. I heard someone moving inside the house and my heart started to pound in my chest.

Jen's Gran opened the door, looking surprised to see me.

"Oh, hello, Lucy!" Coco came darting from inside the house and I caught her up in my arms.

"Hi!" I said breathlessly. "Is Jen here? I wanted to say thank you."

Her face fell. "Oh, sorry. You haven't long missed her. She's gone back to New York."

I felt my heart drop into my stomach in bitter disappointment. "Already?"

She nodded, seeing my upset. "I'm sorry, Lucy. She was meant to be going back yesterday, but she changed her flight to today, because of everything. How are they? Your sister and the baby?"

She'd changed her flight to look after my kids. I couldn't believe she'd put herself out for me. I held Coco close to my chest, resting my cheek against her warm, fuzzy face and willed myself not to burst into tears in front of Jen's Gran.

My disappointment must have been evident as she invited me in, and we chatted about my sister, the baby, the kids, Coco and Jen's job over a cup of coffee, before I made my excuses to get back home to my children. I promised to come back and see her soon, and as I gathered myself up to leave, she put a gentle hand on my arm.

"I'm sorry it didn't work out between you," She said tenderly. "It would have been nice to have you in the family."

Her heartfelt words brought tears to my eyes, and she pulled me into a maternal embrace.

"It would have been difficult," I tried to be nonchalant, even though I could feel my heart breaking at her kindness. "Her in New York, me in London. All the kids."

"Still," She said wisely, as she walked me to the door. "You made her happy, and that's all I want for her."

I kept myself together until I got back into my car, and then I let the racking, self-pitying tears flow freely. This would be my one self-indulgence, I promised myself. Once I got back to the house, I'd pack away my misery and pull myself together.

The children were happy to see me, and Steve looked like he'd be happy to have his living space returned to normal. I felt a little bad that he was cramped into a studio flat, while I was living it up in our spacious home, but that would soon change when we sold the house. He'd definitely need a bigger place once the twins arrived before Christmas.

"Did you manage to see Jen before she went back?" He asked as he helped me carry the children's belongings back to my car.

I shook my head.

"That's a shame." Steve said. "I think the kids were hoping you'd get back together."

I looked at him sharply. "Really?"

"Really." He gave me an affectionate squeeze, which caused me to almost jump in surprise. "I hoped you would too. I can't help but feel responsible for you breaking up. You both seemed really happy together, and I can tell Jen still has feelings for you."

"How would you know?" I stared at Steve, shocked at his uncharacteristic display of concern for me.

"She missed her flight to look after your kids," Steve shrugged. "She could have just left them with the babysitter. I just got a vibe that she was waiting for you to get home."

A spark of hope lit up inside me.

"What time is her flight?" Steve asked when I didn't reply. "Maybe you could still catch her?"

I shook my head sadly. "She'll be taking off any minute. It did cross my mind."

"Well," Steve tried to cheer me up. "If you want to head out there, I'll be around this week to do the school runs."

"I wish." I gave him what I hoped was a brave smile.

"I mean it," Steve said seriously. "Leanne is making me stay sober for the duration of her pregnancy, so I've got no life."

Before I realised that I was even doing it, my mind was searching through my calendar. I had a few potential clients to meet with, but I didn't have another wedding until the following week. I could do this. Steve saw the change in my face and he grinned.

"Go and get your girl, Lucy!"

I spent the evening searching for flights and then hurriedly closing the window of my browser each time I reached the payment screen, until Esther snatched my phone from my hands in frustration.

"Enough!" She commanded, holding out her hand expectantly. "Give me your card. You're going."

A little over twelve hours after I'd knocked on the door to Jen's childhood home, I was running through the airport like someone who does exciting, spur-of-the-moment things!

I hadn't been able to fall asleep, and I'd battled the screaming voice that told me, over and over again, that this was a crazy idea. I'd eventually drifted off, sleeping through my extra-early alarm, and had been woken by Steve banging on the door and urging me to hurry. He'd come over to get the kids ready for school, and I'd barely had enough time to grab my passport and my bag before I was making a mad dash to the airport.

I hadn't told her I was coming. I could have tracked down her number. I could have contacted her on social media, but I didn't want to. I needed this to be my 'gesture'. I had believed the worst of her and this was my attempt at making amends.

God, it felt exhilarating. I wasn't even nervous any more. Yeah, I fucking loved Jen. Without a shadow of a doubt, she was my person. What Shaun was to Emily, and John to Andy. I wanted what they had found, or I didn't want anyone at all. As I ran, like a crazy person, I realised I wasn't scared of her saying no. Maybe she would and, yes, I'd be heartbroken. But I'd get over it. I'd already proved to myself that I could be happy on my own.

Even as I ran, red-faced and struggling to breathe (my social smoking habit was clearly catching up with me), I felt like my own self-discovery had unfurled two massive metaphorical wings. I didn't feel plodding, boring and plain any more. I was a fucking butterfly.

I've organised a celebrity engagement party. I ran a business. I birthed four pretty awesome kids. I'd shed the burden of my dickhead husband and I didn't give a shit if I were penniless, I wasn't taking a soul-destroying corporate 9-to-5 for any amount of money.

If Jen didn't want to be with me, that was her choice. But I was going to give it my best shot. Because that's all I could do. And life would go on, no matter the outcome.

Unlike my previous journey, I was too restless to enjoy the

luxury of doing nothing, and I fidgeted for approximately 3500 miles, much to the enjoyment of the man sat next to me. I jumped into a taxi and headed towards the city, wondering whether Jen would be straight back to work or whether she'd have taken the day off to catch up on her emails, as she often did after a break from work. I paid the cab driver and dashed into the entrance of the serviced apartments, grateful that Andy had tracked down the address whatever method he had used.

I spoke to the smartly-dressed concierge, who seemed appreciative that the dishevelled, curly-haired mess that had flown through their doors was willing to leave voluntarily, without the need for security, and told me that I'd just missed Jen.

It was almost midday, she must have taken the day off if she wasn't in work already, I thought to myself as I made my way back onto the sidewalk. So now what to do? Did I just wait? I could be here all day. I phoned Andy to call in another favour. A few minutes later, I was armed with Jen's phone number and I set out in the direction of Central Park, planning on killing time being a tourist if she didn't answer. After a few rings, she picked up. My heart skipped a beat at the sound of her voice.

"Jen," I started nervously. "It's Lucy."

"Oh my God!" She sounded happy to hear from me. "How are you? How's Emily? The baby?"

"Good, good," I said, picking up pace, spurred on by her

voice. "Where are you?"

"I'm back in New York." I thought I could hear regret in her voice.

"Where to?" I pressed.

"I'm just going for a walk in Central Park." She told me.

"I wanted to say thank you..." I started, seeing the sky open up to my right-hand side as the entrance to the park came into view.

"It's ok." Jen replied quickly. "I'm glad I could help."

"And I wanted to apologise." I said. "For everything."

"Where are you?" Jen asked. "It's really noisy in the background."

"I'm walking."

"You sound out of breath." Jen replied. "I can barely hear you."

"Where are you in Central Park?" I asked. "Which bit?"

"What?" Jen sounded confused.

"Which bit?" I repeated. "It's fucking massive. Just give me a clue."

"You are not in New York." She said, her voice a little higher than usual. "Tell me you're not in New York."

"I'm not in New York." I said, but then giggled with nerves. I was into the park now and my first thought was to head towards the lake. "I wanted this to be romantic. Where are you?"

"Oh my God!" She was definitely entering the vocal range of hysteria now. "You're here! You're really here?"

"Oh my God, are you crying, Jen?"

"Nooooo!" She replied, but I couldn't tell whether she was laughing or crying, or both.

"Where are you?" I asked again, suddenly desperate to see her.

"I'm not actually *at* Central Park yet," She admitted. "I'm a couple of blocks away."

I stopped abruptly and turned around.

"Blocks?" I couldn't help but tease. "Are you American now?"

"You are joking, aren't you?" She asked, ignoring my joke. "Please don't be winding me up!"

"No!" I exclaimed. "God, I don't know what I thought I was doing. Which "block"? I'm going to find you."

"I'm at CVS," She admitted. "On 58th and 9th."

"Ok," I said, squinting at the street signs as I made my way back across the busy road. "I'm nowhere near that. I might be a while. Will you play some love songs on your phone while you wait? I wanted this to be romantic."

"Where are you?" Jen asked, the excitement evident in her voice.

Before I could answer, there was a beep in my ear.

"Oh my God, my battery is about to die!" I realised. "Please stay where you are! Jen, I promise I'll be there soon."

"How soon..." But my phone died, and I fought the urge to throw it into the gutter in frustration.

Fuck! I didn't even have Google maps now. It was just me and my awful sense of direction. I took a moment to get my bearings and catch my breath, and then I took off at speed, chanting the coordinates in my head, terrified that I would suddenly develop amnesia and leave my poor, beautiful Jen loitering outside the pharmacy for hours.

I jostled slow-moving tourists, stopping to Instagram every second of their trips, and put to shame the quick-marching native New Yorkers with my urgency. I turned a corner and caught sight of the storefront. My heart expanded before I'd even sought her out in the throng of people.

She stood to the side of the doorway. I could see the uncertainty on her face and she looked vulnerable. Her usual confident demeanour gone. She was dressed simply, in workout leggings and trainers, a hooded jacket slung over her shoulders. She looked up and I saw her posture change as she recognised me across the street. She started moving towards me, slowly and hesitantly, like she wasn't quite sure it was me, but as I propelled myself towards her, side-stepping pedestrians, her face lit up into a joyous smile.

"Lucy!" Her voice filled my whole heart, and I felt weightless with happiness.

Without caring about the people around us, I dashed the last few metres between us and pulled her into my arms.

"Oh my God!" She clung to me as if she couldn't bear to let me go and, in that moment, I knew that she wouldn't say no. I was her person as much as she was mine.

I found her lips and kissed her there on the streets, amongst tourists and shoppers, outside a drugstore chain, in the middle of New York City on a Tuesday afternoon.

"I love you." I said, feeling so happy that I could burst.

"I love you." She replied and kissed me again.

There were a few honks from passing vehicles and a group of teenagers whooped from across the street.

"Shall we take this somewhere a little more private?" I murmured into Jen's hair as we came up for air.

"Wherever you want to go," Jen sighed happily, slipping her hand into mine. "I'm going to be there."

Epilogue

I felt the nerves building up inside me. All my senses were heightened so the overriding sensation was my heart pumping the blood around my body. I knew that I had just seconds to defuse this before I completely panicked and made things a hundred times worse.

"I can't do this," I exhaled several times trying to calm my racing heart. "There are too many people."

Esther hefted the baby up onto one hip.

"Mum," She warned me. "You're being ridiculous."

At almost 17, she towered above me now. She definitely got her height from her dad but the rest of her was a mirror-image of me.

"I know." I bent my head over and tried a few deep, mindful breaths. I hadn't had a panic attack in years. What a day for my anxiety to kick back in.

Matilda came to my side and fiddled with the strap of my dress. She tilted my chin with her hand and peered appraisingly at me.

"Mum," She said, with all the wisdom of an 8-year-old. "You look beautiful. We'll be with you every step of the way."

I managed a laugh at her serious advice and I drained the glass of champagne that Esther handed me.

I had planned this day for months now, I reassured myself. Everything was under the careful control of Lois, my amazing right hand woman, at the London branch of mine and Emily's Event Planning business. We had executed events one hundred times the size and budget of this. I just needed to take some deep breaths and get on with it.

"Are you all decent?" George knocked on the door and Matilda hurried over to let her brothers in. Andy was stood with them, looking dapper in his suit.

"Wow!" I said. "You all look amazing."

"Not as amazing as you!" Andy bent down and kissed my cheek, looking like a proud brother. "Are we ready?"

Esther handed baby Elijah back to his father and Andy kissed his little son's head affectionately.

"Have this first!" Leo passed me the almost-full glass of champagne that I'd been letting Esther sip. I gave my handsome son a grateful smile.

"I nearly forgot!" Esther exclaimed suddenly, rushing back and pulling a small blue box from her bag.

"What's this?" I asked, opening it up to reveal a beautiful white gold bracelet with a tiny charm attached. "Is this from you?"

Esther shook her head. "It's a gift from Jen."

I held the bracelet close to my face and inspected the tiny

charm. I smiled, feeling my heart bursting with happiness, as I read the little card: "You'll give me butterflies forever".

"I want to wear this now." I held the jewellery out to Esther and she fastened it onto my wrist.

Together, we made our way down from my suite before they left me alone and went to join the guests milling around outside. I could see some of the guests through the flower-covered arch and I smiled at the sight of Steve and Leanne struggling to make their rowdy toddler twins sit still. My mother was throwing them irritated glances and I could make out Emily's smirk at our mother's annoyance. Finley and Samuel were sat either side of Emily and Shaun like perfect little angels. Lois hustled over like a true professional and handed Steve's mischievous duo a pair of iPads and over-ear headphones.

Oh, nice touch, Lois. I mentally high-fived her. I'd make a note to add that to one of our packages. There was nothing that woman didn't think of.

I'd had a quick whirlwind tour of the reception suite earlier, but they'd still been setting up the outdoor altar. I was desperate to sneak a peek before everything kicked off and I didn't have time to enjoy the aesthetics. I got as close as I could without attracting any attention and, despite this being very much my day job now, I gasped in awe. The trees that sheltered the private garden from the lakefront were strewn with rows of twinkling fairy-lights. The arbour had been supplemented with armloads of heavenly white flowers. It looked more perfect than I'd dreamed it would. I stepped back and hid myself quickly as Lois started to direct the guests down from the terrace to their seats.

I touched the tiny butterfly charm, as if for luck, and then when I looked up, I saw her. Jen met my eyes from across the room and I felt the butterflies explode, even after all these years together, as she made her way over to me.

We waited silently together for our musical cue, fingers entwined and the widest, happiest smiles across our faces.

"Ready?" She whispered.

"Let's do this." I squeezed her hand and we made the short walk together down the aisle. The children were waiting for me, stood with Jen's Gran, and by the time we had said our vows, there wasn't a dry eye in the room.

After we'd kissed, and the room had erupted in applause, I remembered my bracelet. I held my hand up to Jen.

She laughed and held her hand up to, revealing her identical bracelet. "Great minds!"

She took my hand in hers and I glanced down at the tiny charms dancing together as I walked back up the aisle with my new wife.

ABOUT THE AUTHOR

. Lily worked in Financial Services for fourteen years before quitting her job to write Butterflies, her debut novel.

Lily is passionate about books, travelling, animals and equality. She lives in Wales with her four children, three cats, two dogs and a husband.

Follow Hayden Woods Creative on Facebook, Twitter, Instagram and LinkedIn for up-to-date news and releases.

Praise for The Village Online

"A very modern murder mystery!"

"...Clever, great plot, relatable and hilariously funny..."

21441031R00274

Printed in Great Britain
by Amazon